Joan Jonker was born and bred in Liverpool. She founded the charity-run organisation Victims of Violence and she lives in Southport with her son. She has two sons and two grandsons. Her previous Liverpool sagas have received warm praise:

'A hilarious but touching story of life in Liverpool'
Woman's Realm

'You can rely on Joan to give her readers hilarity and pathos in equal measure and she's achieved it again in this tale'
Liverpool Echo

'Packed with lively, sympathetic characters and a wealth of emotions'
Bolton Evening News

'Mrs Jonker is blessed with the ability to write with a style which is at once readable while crafted with care and precision for her characters'
Skelmersdale Advertiser

'As usual our Joan has come up with an easy-read story full of laughter and smiles – set in the colourful back streets of the 1930s'
Liverpool Echo

'Joan Jonker has written a book worth reading; a book that will reduce you to tears – of sadness, but of happiness too'
Hull Daily Mail

Also by Joan Jonker

When One Door Closes
Man Of The House
Home Is Where The Heart Is
Stay In Your Own Back Yard
Last Tram To Lime Street
Sweet Rosie O'Grady
The Pride Of Polly Perkins
Sadie Was A Lady
Walking My Baby Back Home
Try A Little Tenderness

Stay As Sweet As You Are

Joan Jonker

HEADLINE

First published in 1999
by HEADLINE BOOK PUBLISHING

First published in paperback in 1999
by HEADLINE BOOK PUBLISHING

10 9 8 7 6 5 4 3 2 1

All characters in this publication are fictitious and any resemblance to real persons, living or dead, is purely coincidental.

ISBN 0 7472 6111 3

Typeset by
Letterpart Limited, Reigate, Surrey

Printed and bound in Great Britain by
Caledonian International plc

HEADLINE BOOK PUBLISHING
A division of the Hodder Headline Group
338 Euston Road
London NW1 3BH
www.headline.co.uk
www.hodderheadline.com

I dedicate this book to the many readers who have written to say how much they enjoy my books. I appreciate your letters, and hope my characters find favour with you.

A friendly greeting from Joan

Lucy Mellor is the heroine of this story, and I think you'll love her. But leave room in your heart for the other larger-than-life characters who will have you reaching for your hankies. There is a baddie, and you'll meet her soon enough.

Happy reading!

Chapter One

The flickering flame from the streetlamp cast an eerie glow over the face of the young girl huddled on the step of the two-up two-down terrace house. Her elbows were resting on her drawn-up knees and her two hands cupped her dirty, tear-stained face. Her eyes kept darting up and down the silent street as though anxious for the sight of someone, and occasionally her head would turn to look back through the open front door and into the darkness of the house.

Lucy Mellor let out a long sigh. She was in for a hiding now, no matter what she did. Her mam would say she should have taken herself off to bed while it was still light, instead of staying up until this time. But when she'd gone out at half-past seven, her mam had said she'd only be out for half an hour so Lucy had stayed up waiting for her. Then it had started to get dark and she was afraid to go upstairs with no one in the house. She had thought about striking a match and lighting the gas-light, but her dad had warned her about standing on a chair striking a match. She was small for her eleven years and he said it was too dangerous. And now, with the house in pitch darkness she was too afraid to go inside, never mind climbing the stairs to her bedroom.

She heard a door close nearby and Lucy quickly swivelled her legs around into the hall, hoping whoever it was would pass without seeing her. She was in enough trouble without the neighbours knowing she'd been left alone until this time of night. They wouldn't think twice about having a go at her mam; they were always telling Ruby Mellor that she wasn't fit to be a mother. Then the girl heard the slow slithering footsteps and knew it was old Mrs McBride who lived three doors away. She'd be on her way to the corner pub for her nightly half-pint of stout. That meant it must be nearly ten o'clock because the old woman never went until just on closing-time.

Lucy held her breath, hoping their neighbour would pass without glancing in the doorway, but the old woman had sharp eyesight.

'Is that you, queen? What on earth are yer doing sitting there at this time? Yer should have been in bed hours ago.' There was surprise in Aggie McBride's voice, and her eyes narrowed when she noticed the house was in darkness. 'Are yer all on yer own, queen? Where's that mother of yours got to?'

'She's only gone out for half an hour, Mrs Aggie – I'm waiting for her.' Lucy was used to making excuses for her mother, she was doing it all the time. 'She'll be here any minute now.'

Aggie huffed. This girl had the face of an angel, with thick dark curly hair framing her heart-shaped face, and green eyes as big as saucers. She was a daughter any mother would be proud of, but not Ruby Mellor. She was too fond of herself, out for a good time and to hell with everyone else. All the neighbours had her taped and not one had a good word for her. She treated her daughter like a skivvy, making her do housework, shopping and even sending her scrounging to the neighbours if she ran short of anything. But she'd gone too far tonight, leaving a child in a dark house on her own; she deserved horse-whipping. 'Would yer like me to come in and light the gas for yer, queen? Then yer could get yerself off to bed before she comes in.'

If Lucy had been frightened before, she was now terrified. 'No, I'll be all right, Mrs Aggie, honest. Me mam will be here any minute now, yer'll see.' There was a sob in the girl's throat.

'Yer won't say anything to her, will yer, Mrs Aggie? Please?'

Aggie's temper was rising. How she'd love to give Ruby Mellor a piece of her mind. But if she did, Lucy would be the one to suffer. 'I'll not say a dickie-bird, queen, I promise. Anyway, yer dad will be finishing his two-to-ten shift any minute, so if yer mam knows what's good for her, she'll make sure she's home by then. If he finds you still up, and nothing ready for him to eat, then the sparks will fly.' Wrapping the knitted shawl across her arms, Aggie managed to hide the jug she was taking to the pub for her half-pint of stout. Not that she needed to hide it, everyone in the neighbourhood knew Aggie and her drinking habits. 'I'll be on me way, queen, before Alec puts the towels on and I miss me nightly dose of medicine. And that would be a fate worse than death.' She began to shuffle away. 'I hope ye're not here when I come back, Lucy, 'cos if yer are I'm going to sit with yer and wait for that mother of yours.'

'I won't be, Mrs Aggie,' Lucy said, willing the old lady to move away so she could think of what to do. She had two choices. She could brave the dark and run up to bed, or she could brave her mother's anger. It wasn't often that Lucy rebelled against her life, but right now she was asking herself why *she* should be the one to be afraid. She hadn't done anything wrong. Her mam was in the wrong, she had no right to stay out all this time.

Lucy sighed. She knew she'd get a hiding when her mam came in. Never a day passed without her feeling the force of her mother's hands. And yet she never did anything to deserve it. She never answered back or gave cheek, never even looked sideways. But it didn't take much to send her mother into a temper, and she was always the whipping boy. It wasn't so bad when her dad was in; her mother wouldn't dare hit her in his presence. But he worked three shifts and she didn't see much of him. If he wasn't at work he was in bed. And she'd been well warned what would happen to her if she went running to him telling tales.

★ ★ ★

Ruby Mellor was gasping for breath as she ran up the street. She'd cut it fine tonight, and she'd be lucky if she got home in time to have Bob's bacon sizzling in the frying pan when he came back from work. She should never have listened to the friends she'd been drinking with when they coaxed her to stay a bit longer. But she'd been flattered by the attention of Wally Brown, who kept paying her compliments and keeping her glass filled. He was a handsome man in his thirties, a bachelor who was fond of the ladies. And Ruby lapped it up, telling herself another five minutes wouldn't do any harm. Well, she now understood that five minutes could make all the difference. If Bob got home before her there'd be hell to pay.

She reached into her coat pocket for the door key and her hand was outstretched when she realised the door was open and Lucy was standing on the step. 'What the bleedin' hell are you doing still up? Get in that house, quick.' Pushing past her daughter she ran into the living room and felt on the mantelpiece for a box of matches. She struck one, held it to the gas mantel and the room flooded with light. Then she spun around. 'What the hell d'yer think ye're playing at, yer little faggot? Why aren't yer in bed?'

Lucy dropped her eyes. 'Yer said yer were only going out for half an hour, and I waited for yer. Then it got dark and I was frightened to be in the house on me own.'

Ruby swung her arm out and her open palm caught Lucy on the side of the face, sending the girl reeling back. 'Frightened, were yer? Well, I'll give yer something to be frightened about, yer little faggot.'

Her hand touching her cheek, Lucy could feel the tears well up in her eyes and their warmth as they rolled down her cheeks. It was so unfair, she just had to speak out. 'It's not my fault, it's you what told lies. Half an hour yer said, and now it's gone ten o'clock.'

'Don't you dare answer me back. And what I do has got

nothing to do with you. Ye're big and ugly enough to see yerself to bed, and I'll make yer sorry yer didn't.'

Neither of them had heard the front door open or knew that Bob was standing in the hall listening. It was only when Ruby reached out to give Lucy a hiding that he made his presence known. 'Touch her and yer'll be out in that street on yer backside before yer know what's hit yer.' He put his arm across his daughter's shoulders and bent to kiss her hair. 'Don't cry, pet, you just take yerself off to bed while I have a word with yer mam.'

Lucy shivered. 'I'm cold and thirsty, Dad, could I have a hot drink, please?'

'I'll bring yer one up when yer mam decides a man needs a meal after a day's work. You poppy off and I'll bring yer a cup of tea in a minute.'

After Lucy had fled without a word or a glance, Ruby's face and manner changed as if someone had waved a magic wand. In the place of anger, there was a smile. 'She's making a mountain out of a molehill, the silly thing. I was busy talking in me mate's house and didn't realise the time. But I told Lucy to go to bed before I went out, and she should have done as she was told. Still, there's no harm done.' She made a move towards the kitchen. 'I'll see to yer supper, it won't take five minutes.'

Bob put his cap on the sideboard. 'You stay right where yer are until we get a few things straight.' He didn't speak for a while as he took stock of the woman he'd married fifteen years ago. She'd been nineteen then, and as pretty as a picture. Nice slim figure, mousy-coloured curly hair, laughing hazel eyes and a peaches and cream complexion. The woman he was facing now bore no resemblance to that happy-go-lucky girl. The mousy-coloured hair was bleached to a horrible pale yellow, the hazel eyes were hard and calculating and Ruby's face was caked with make-up. She looked like a brazen, cheap tart, and her actions matched her looks. 'Where have yer been from half-seven until now?'

'I told yer, I was in me mate's and the time just seemed to fly over.'

'Don't you lie to me!' Bob's voice was raised in anger. 'You must take me for a right bloody fool. I can smell the drink on yer from here, and it's not just one glass yer've had – yer've had a bellyful. And while ye're out enjoying yerself, yer leave an eleven-year-old girl on her own in the house. And I'll bet that yer never gave her one thought as yer sat boozing with yer cronies. What sort of a mother are yer? In fact, what sort of a wife are yer?'

Ruby tried to wheedle her way out of it. 'It's the first time it's happened, Bob, so don't get in a temper. I'll see to yer supper now and promise it won't happen again.'

'Ye're not getting away with it that easy, so you just stay right where yer are. I should have put a halt to yer gallop years ago, before yer started going off the rails. I should have done it for Lucy's sake because she deserves a better mother than you. She's a good kid and I'm proud of her. But I can see now that she gets more hidings off you than she does hugs or kisses. And I blame meself for that.' He crossed the room and, putting his hands on his wife's shoulders, he turned her around to face the mirror hanging over the fireplace. 'Take a good look at yerself, Ruby, and see yerself as others see yer. Peroxide blonde, thick cheap make-up, a face as hard as nails and smelling like a brewery.' He dropped his hands and let out a deep sigh. 'You are not the woman I married, but so help me, I'm stuck with yer. And so is our daughter.'

Ruby rounded on him. 'Who the hell d'yer think yer are, talking to me like that? Just because I like to get a bit of enjoyment out of life, instead of being bleedin' miserable, like you. You might be happy with work, bed, the wireless and a pint on a Saturday, but it's not my idea of a good life. I've no intention of being the dutiful wife, who sits knitting or darning every night, so yer can get that out of yer head. Life is short and I intend to get the best out of it while I'm still able.'

He gripped her arm and held it tight. 'Frankly, Ruby, I couldn't care less what yer do. If yer want to drink yerself to death and get a name like a mad dog, then go ahead. But while I am the one working and handing my hard-earned money over to yer, I expect the house to be kept clean and meals on the table on time. I also expect me daughter to be dressed decent and to be treated with kindness and affection. I do not want her to be doing the work which you should be doing, or being ordered around like a skivvy.' His grip tightened. 'And if I ever find yer've raised yer hand to her in anger, then heaven help yer.' He pushed her away as though in disgust. 'Make a pot of tea so I can take a cup up to Lucy before she goes to sleep.'

Ruby glared at him. This was all that little faggot's fault, and by God she'd pay for it tomorrow. There was no fear of Bob finding out, Lucy would be too scared to tell him.

Her husband watched her face and could almost read her mind. 'Don't for one moment think of taking yer spite out on her tomorrow, thinking she'll be too frightened to tell me. 'Cos from now on I'll be taking a very keen interest in me daughter's welfare. Lay a finger on her and I'll know about it.' He waited until his wife was at the kitchen door before adding, 'Oh, yer'll be five bob down in yer money this week. I'm taking Lucy to town on Saturday to buy her something decent to wear. She's the prettiest girl in the street but always looks like an unwanted orphan. But from today there's going to be big changes around here, whether yer like it or not. So yer'd better start getting used to being a housewife and mother again. Yer don't have to worry about being a wife to me, yer stopped being that years ago. And if ye're looking for anyone to lay the blame on for all this, look no further than yerself.'

Aggie McBride was passing the Mellors' house on her way back from the pub, and when she heard raised voices she felt no guilt in standing outside the window and listening. She kept nodding her head when Bob spoke, and muttered, 'It's about time yer came to yer senses, Bob Mellor. That's right, lad, you tell her. Ye're about five years too late, like, but as they say, it's better late than never.'

She ambled on her way, chuckling to herself. She felt happier now she'd heard the queer one get her come-uppance, and when she got home she'd go over every word she heard as she sat in her rocking chair supping her stout.

Ruby was in a foul temper the next morning. Her head was splitting, what with having too much to drink and then the row with Bob. There was malice in her eyes as she dropped the plate of toast in front of her daughter. 'Get that down yer and hurry up or yer'll be late for school.'

Lucy looked down at the burnt bread and knew this was part of her punishment. She picked up a slice and bit into it. Then, in a quiet voice, asked, 'Can't I have some butter on it, please, Mam?'

Ruby mimicked her daughter's voice. ' "Can't I have some butter on it?" ' She closed the living-room door quietly. Bob didn't get up until ten o'clock when he was on the afternoon shift, and for all she knew he could be lying awake listening. So she kept her voice low. 'Yer'll be getting dry toast every morning from now on, seeing as yer dad is docking me money so he can buy yer some fancy clothes.'

Lucy raised her face and stared directly into her mother's eyes. What she saw there caused her to turn away in distress, thinking, she doesn't even like me, never mind love me. 'I never asked me dad to buy me anything, Mam, I wouldn't do that.' She picked up her plate and got to her feet. 'I'll make meself a round of bread and jam because I'll be starving if I don't have anything to eat.'

Ruby watched her daughter go into the kitchen before lighting a cigarette. Inhaling deeply, and with a sneer on her face, she leaned against the door-jamb. 'Yer dad won't always be here, just remember that.'

Instinct told Lucy she would be well advised to get out of the house as quick as possible and away from trouble. She could eat the bread on her way to school. So without a word, she passed her mother, took her coat from the hallstand and let herself out of the front door. She stood for a moment with the bread in her mouth while she slipped her arms into her sleeves, then began to walk up the street.

Aggie McBride was standing on her front step, her shawl around her shoulders. She'd been waiting for Lucy to make sure the child hadn't come to any harm. She was a kindly soul, was Aggie, with steel-grey hair combed back off her face and plaited into a bun at the nape of her neck. She wore false teeth when she was going out, but this morning she'd decided to give her gums a rest.

'Were yer late getting up, queen?' Aggie nodded at the bread. 'No time for a proper breakfast?'

'Just a bit late, Mrs Aggie, but I don't think I'll be late for school.'

'Yer didn't get into trouble last night, did yer? I heard yer mam and dad rowing when I passed on me way back from the pub. I hope she didn't try and lay the blame at your door?'

Lucy shook her head. No matter what her mother did, she would never talk about her to anyone. After all, she was still her mother. 'I went straight to bed and me dad brought me a nice hot cup of tea up.'

'That's good, queen.' Aggie put her hand in the large pocket of her wrap-around pinny and brought out a rosy red apple. 'Here yer are, girl, I kept this specially for you.'

When Lucy's face lit up it was as though the sun had come out. 'Oh, thank you, Mrs Aggie, I'll eat it at playtime.' She rubbed the apple on the sleeve of her coat and held it up to the old lady. 'Look how shiny it is – I can see me face in it.'

Aggie chuckled. 'I bet the apple thinks there's an angel looking at it. Now, run along, queen, or yer'll be getting the cane.'

Lucy took to her heels, shouting over her shoulder, 'Ta-ra, Mrs Aggie.'

Aggie was waving to her when she heard the sound she'd been waiting for. She turned her head to see her next-door-but-one neighbour stepping into the street. Irene Pollard had a part-time cleaning job in the corner pub and she left the house every morning dead on ten minutes to nine. The Pollards lived next door to the Mellors and Aggie was eager to know if Irene had heard the rumpus.

'Good morning, Aggie! What are yer waiting for – better days?'

'Irene, I had me better days fifty years ago, and, by God, I made the most of them. All I've got left now is to stick me nose into other people's business – which brings me to the reason for standing on me step this time of the morning, getting me bleedin' death of cold.' She gave a toothless smile. 'Did yer hear the carry-on at the Mellors' last night?'

'Couldn't help it, Aggie. They were shouting so loud we could hear every word. Yer know how thin the walls are, yer can't sneeze without the whole street knowing.' Irene Pollard was a bonny woman, with plenty of flesh on her bones. She had auburn hair, brown eyes, a pretty round face and a good sense of humour, and her husband, George, was a riot when he'd had a few drinks on a Saturday. They had two sons, Jack fourteen, and Greg, twelve, and were well liked in the street. If anyone needed a helping hand, it was the Pollards' door they knocked at. 'I don't know what started the row, but Bob certainly had a go at Ruby. She must have gone too far this time because Bob puts up with a lot from her. As George said, she's had it coming for years now, the brazen hussy.'

'I'll tell yer what started it.' Aggie quickly recounted what had happened. 'The poor kid was terrified, all alone that time of night in a house in pitch darkness.'

Irene tutted as she shook her head. 'She doesn't deserve that child. I always wanted a girl but it wasn't to be. How is it that someone like Ruby Mellor has a beautiful girl that she treats like dirt, and me, who was longing for a daughter, can't have one? I love me two boys, yer know that, and having a girl wouldn't have made any difference to the love I have for them. It's just that a girl is a mate to her mother when she grows up, someone to share things with. If Lucy was mine, she'd get as much love off me, and George and the boys, as she gets hidings off her mother. Many's the time the boys have been upset when they've heard her being belted. When they were younger they used to say she was like a fairy, with her being so pretty and dainty.'

Aggie sighed. 'Well, let's hope that Bob sticks to his guns and makes that wife of his toe the line. He must rue the day he ever set eyes on her.'

'Only time will tell, Aggie, only time will tell. But I think in future, when Bob's at work, and I hear any shenanigans from her, I'll poke me nose in.' Irene smiled. 'I'm bigger than her and one swipe from me would knock her into the middle of next week.'

'Give me a knock first, girl, 'cos I wouldn't want to miss that for the world.'

'I'll sell tickets, shall I, Aggie?' Irene started to walk away. 'If I don't get a move on I'll be getting me cards. I'll see yer tonight, sunshine, ta-ra for now.'

By dinnertime, the story had gone the rounds of the street. And when Ruby left the house to go to the shops, she could sense the hostility of the women who were standing at their doors talking to their neighbours. With their eyes boring into her, she tossed her head and sauntered past them, her jaunty step saying she didn't give a damn what they thought. And she didn't either. It was a pity the poor buggers had nothing better to do than stand gossiping. The only time they seemed to enjoy themselves was when two women got into an argument over their kids. Then the whole street would be out watching and shouting encouragement as the two women belted hell out of each other. And, of course, there was always a stir when a football was kicked through a window and none of the boys would own up to being the culprit.

There was a sarcastic smile on Ruby's face as she neared the shops. If the truth were known, there wasn't a woman in the street who wouldn't change places with her, given the chance. They just didn't have the guts. Then she had a thought that took the smile from her face. If she was going to be five shillings down in her housekeeping it would mean she'd be skint all the time. She wouldn't be able to keep up with her friends, splashing out on drinks and handing cigarettes around. She'd be like a poor relation and that idea didn't appeal to her one little bit. The truth was, if she had no money, she'd soon lose her friends.

Ruby hit on an idea as she turned into the butcher's shop. She'd make the money up by cutting down on food, that's what she'd do. If she was clever, no one would be any the wiser. And she'd start right now. 'Just half-a-pound of steak, Stan, and a quarter of kidney.' There, she gloated as the butcher cut the steak into small pieces, a quarter of steak less has saved me a few coppers. If I do that in every shop, every day, I'll soon make up the five bob.

The meat was simmering on the stove when Lucy came running in from school. 'I'm going out to play hopscotch with Rhoda, Mam. I'll only be in the street.'

'Just you hang on a minute, buggerlugs.' Ruby threw her cigarette end in the hearth. 'Yer can get in that kitchen and peel the spuds, never mind playing bleedin' hopscotch.'

Lucy's face fell. 'But it'll be dark soon and we won't be able to play.' There was pleading in her large green eyes. 'Go on, Mam, please?'

'Yer haven't got cloth ears, so out in that kitchen before I belt yer one.'

Lucy was close to tears. 'Just for half an hour, Mam?' When she saw Ruby jump from her chair and make for her, the girl pressed back against the wall and lifted her arm to protect her face. 'Don't hit me, Mam, please.'

Ruby grabbed a handful of the dark hair and pulled. 'Yer get those spuds peeled or I'll break yer bleedin' neck. Now—' Her words were cut short by a loud banging on the open front door. Her face livid, she bawled, 'What the hell d'yer want?'

'Ruby, it's Irene Pollard. Is everything all right? Young Rhoda here's waiting for Lucy to come out to play, and she's been knocking hell out of yer door for the last five minutes but can't get anyone to answer. I just wondered if anything was wrong?'

Ruby bit so hard on the inside of her mouth she could taste blood. Any other neighbour she would have told to sod off, but Irene Pollard was a woman to be reckoned with. And her husband was very pally with Bob, too. 'She's coming now.' Ruby took her daughter's hand and squeezed until it hurt. She pulled her out to the front door. 'I was telling her to wash her face before she went out, it's filthy.'

'Oh, I wouldn't worry about that,' Irene said calmly. 'She'd be dirty again in no time, so what's the point? My two lads are playing ollies in the gutter, and they're both as black as the hobs of hell. To say nothing about the state of their kecks. But they'll be well-scrubbed before they go to bed.'

'Will yer let go of me hand, please, Mam?' Lucy asked. 'Rhoda will be getting called in for her dinner before we've had a game.'

Ruby was almost spitting feathers with temper. And the look she gave her daughter as she joined her friend on the pavement, wasn't lost on Irene. She'd bet a pound to a pinch of snuff that the girl would get a hammering for this. Unless Ruby was warned off. It was worth a try.

Watching the two girls marking the paving stones with a piece of chalk, Irene said casually, 'If yer ever want to go out at night, Ruby, when Bob's at work, yer can always leave Lucy with us, yer know. We'd love to have her.'

You bitch, Ruby thought. I bet yer had yer ears to the wall

last night, listening. 'What made yer ask that? Yer've never asked before.'

'It was just a thought. She gets on well with the boys and would probably enjoy playing cards with them.' Irene stretched to her full height and folded her arms under her ample bosom. 'The offer's there, if yer want to take me up on it sometime.'

'No, Lucy usually goes to bed about eight o'clock.' Then begrudgingly, she added, 'But thanks all the same.'

'Well, if yer change yer mind, just knock on the wall.' Irene was determined to get her point across. 'We'd have no trouble hearing yer – these walls are so thin yer can hear *everything* that goes on either side.' She smiled as Lucy hopped from one square to another, her pink tongue peeping out of the side of her mouth. 'She's a beautiful child. I hope yer know how lucky yer are.'

Ruby had no intention of answering that. The nosy bitch had gone far enough. The next thing, she'd be inviting herself in for a cup of tea. 'I'll have to go in, or me stew will be sticking to the bottom of the pan.'

There was a half-smile on Irene's chubby face. She'd gone as far as she could; she only hoped the message had got home. She'd keep her ears open tonight, just in case, but she had a feeling Ruby would be keeping her hands to herself, for a while at least.

Irene waited until Rhoda had completed the course before asking, 'Who's winning?'

'We're even, Mrs Pollard.' Both girls were puffing and red in the face. After all, it was hard going hopping from one number to another. If you couldn't keep your balance, and your other foot touched the ground, you were counted out.

Lucy grinned. 'We always end up even, Mrs Pollard. We let each other win, don't we, Rhoda?'

Rhoda's long, stringy hair had been tied back with a piece of ribbon, but with the exertion, most of it had come loose and was hanging down her cheeks. She was the same age as Lucy, but a much bigger girl in every way. Inches taller than her friend, she was very heavily built. She worried about that, but her mam had told her it was puppy fat and she'd lose it as she grew older. A big smile covered her face now. 'Lucy means we cheat, Mrs Pollard.'

Irene chuckled. 'If yer both know ye're doing it, then it's not cheating, sunshine. It means ye're such good friends yer want to share.'

'Me dad's taking me to town on Saturday, Mrs Pollard, to buy me some new clothes.' Lucy's face was aglow. Never before had she had anything so exciting to brag about. 'Aren't I lucky?'

Irene put on a suitably impressed face. 'I'll say yer are! I hope he buys yer a pretty dress to match yer pretty face.' To say she was surprised would be putting it mildly. It sounded as though Bob had changed with a vengeance. 'Will yer call and let us see yer in yer new clothes, sunshine?'

'If me mam will let me.' Some of the shine had gone from Lucy's face. 'I'll ask her, but she might say I'm showing off.'

'Anyone with new clothes wants to show them off, it's only natural. Anyway, seeing as it's yer dad what's mugging yer, it's him yer should ask.'

Lucy thought that over for a few seconds, then smiled. 'Ye're right, Mrs Pollard, I'll ask me dad.'

Rhoda looked down in the mouth. 'I wish me mam would take me with her when she buys my clothes, then I could pick what I like.'

'Your mam buys yer lovely clothes!' Lucy said. 'Yer always look pretty.'

Irene took a deep breath. Next to her friend, Lucy always looked like a tramp, but she never complained. There was no envy or malice in her, she was a good kid through and through. What a pity her mother didn't appreciate it. They say God makes them and matches them, but He had certainly slipped up when He'd matched this angel with a devil like Ruby Mellor.

Chapter Two

Lucy didn't let her excitement show until she was standing on the pavement watching her dad pull the door closed behind him. All morning she'd been on pins in case something happened to spoil the treat she'd been looking forward to. Her mother's face had been like thunder, and although she didn't lift her hand to Lucy, she gave her a dig in the ribs every time she passed. It would have taken very little for her temper to explode, so the girl did as she was told without a word, while willing the hands on the clock to move faster until it was time for her dad to get up at ten o'clock. Even then she didn't feel safe because although her dad seemed at ease chatting to her, not a word was exchanged between him and her mam. Still, it was over now and they were on their way.

Bob took his daughter's hand and smiled down at her. 'I think we'll hop off the tram at Great Homer Street and try the market there, see if there's anything doing. Yer never know, we might just be lucky and pick up a bargain. If not, we won't have lost anything, and we can carry on into town. What d'yer think?'

'I'm that excited, Dad, I don't care where we go.' Lucy began to swing their joined hands. 'I've never been into town before.'

Bob looked surprised. 'Of course yer have!'

'No, I haven't, Dad, honest!'

'I used to take yer through town, when yer were little, to

get down to the Pier Head. Don't yer remember going on the ferry boats?'

Lucy's brow creased in concentration. 'I remember little bits, but not much. I must have only been a baby, Dad.'

Bob nodded. 'Yeah, I used to carry yer on me shoulders and yer mam was left to lug the sandwiches and towels and things.' Suddenly he was filled with a great sadness. What had he been thinking of all these years, while his daughter's childhood was passing her by? It would be easy to lay the blame at Ruby's door, but he must bear some of the responsibility. He should have put his foot down at the very beginning, when his wife made the excuse of visiting one of her old workmates and came home smelling of drink. He'd been blind and stupid, and the one to suffer most had been his beloved daughter. All he could do now was try to make it up to her. 'I'll take yer on the ferry to New Brighton next time I've got a Saturday off. Would yer like that?'

'I'd like it, Dad, but ye're buying me new clothes and that's what I'd like most. After all,' she grinned up at him, 'ye're not made of money.'

'Ye're right there, pet, but what I've got I'll have to stretch a long way. Like it was a piece of elastic.'

They didn't have long to wait for a tram, and Lucy made for a window seat. Her eyes were wide as Bob told her the names of the streets and pointed out landmarks. When they reached Everton Valley, he said, 'Next stop's ours, pet.'

The market was absolutely packed. Lucy gripped her father's hand tight, frightened by the mass of heaving bodies. 'We'll never get through there, Dad, we'll get separated and I'll lose yer. I wouldn't know how to get home on me own, and I've no money for a tram.'

Bob put an arm across her shoulders. 'You just hang on to me jacket like grim death, pet, and we'll do what everyone else is doing, push our way through.'

Lucy gradually calmed down as she got used to the

pushing and shoving and the noise of the stallholders shouting out their wares. She would have liked to have seen what they were selling, but the crowd standing in front of the stalls was so deep it was impossible to see anything.

'There's a woman selling children's clothes,' Bob said. 'Let's make our way over there.' He elbowed a path through the crowds, pulling Lucy behind him. 'Some of those look nice.' He pointed to a makeshift rail where there was a display of girls' dresses. 'Is there anything there that takes yer fancy?'

'They're all nice, Dad, but it doesn't say how much they are.'

'There's only one way to find out, and that's to ask.' Ignoring the dark looks being cast his way, Bob pushed and manoeuvred until they were in front of the trestle table which was piled high with secondhand children's clothes. 'How much are those dresses, Missus?'

'They're all different prices, lad,' said the stallholder, wearing the uniform long black skirt and black knitted shawl. 'Show me which one and I'll tell yer the price. Dirt cheap, they are – yer won't get anything cheaper if yer travel the length and breadth of Liverpool.'

'Which one, Lucy?' Bob looked down into those wide green eyes which were now shining with excitement. 'What about that one with flowers on, and a lace collar? That would look nice on yer.'

But Lucy knew which one she liked the best as soon as she'd set eyes on it. It was in a deep maroon cotton, very plain with a round neck and long sleeves. If she was going to get a new dress, that was the one her heart would choose. She pointed to it. 'That's the one I like, Dad, but it might be too dear.'

Bob crossed his fingers as he asked, 'How much is that one?'

'Two and six, lad, and that's practically giving it away.'

'Would it fit me daughter?'

The stallholder eyed Lucy. 'How old are yer, girl?'

Lucy had never felt so important in her life. Being able to choose her own clothes was something she'd never known before. She took what was thrown at her and was never asked if she liked it. 'I'm eleven, Missus, but I'll be twelve in four weeks' time.'

When the stallholder smiled, she showed a row of yellow teeth, but her smile was wide and friendly. 'Ye're very dainty for yer age, girl, and very pretty, too. That dress will fit yer like a glove, as though it was made for yer. Yer'll have all the lads whistling after yer when yer walk out in it.'

Bob handed the half-a-crown over, and as he waited for the dress to be hooked down, Lucy was looking through the clothes piled on the table. She tugged on her father's sleeve and when he looked down, she beckoned for him to bend so she could whisper in his ear. 'Dad, there's girls' knickers here. Could I have a pair, please?'

'But they're secondhand ones, pet. Yer wouldn't want to wear someone else's cast-offs, would yer? Not knickers, anyway.'

'They'd be clean if I gave them a good wash, wouldn't they?' Lucy was embarrassed and averted her eyes. 'They're better than the two pair I've got. The elastic's gone on them and I have to pin them up.'

Bob closed his eyes. Dear God, what was that wife of his thinking of? He gave her enough money to keep the child well fed and clothed. Had she no love at all for her daughter, no shame that the child was going around with pins in her knickers? And this was only the start. There was plenty more he didn't know about, of that he was sure. 'Pick three decent pair out, pet, and they'll keep yer going until we can get yer new ones.'

The stallholder didn't appear to be listening, but she heard every word. Working the markets gave you an insight into people, taught you how to sort the wheat from the chaff. So when Bob handed over the three pair of knickers, she knocked a penny off the price of each pair. 'That'll be a tanner, lad. And if yer don't mind me saying so, yer've got a little cracker there, so you take good care of her, mind.'

Bob smiled his thanks then guided Lucy through the crowds and out into the street. 'How would yer like a little treat? What d'yer say about getting a tram down to TJ's and having a cup of tea in the café there?'

Lucy was clutching the paper bag and telling herself this was the best day of her life. She couldn't wait to show Rhoda her new dress. She wouldn't tell her about the knickers though, she'd be too ashamed. 'That would be the gear, Dad, but can yer afford it? Yer've spent a lot of money on me as it is.'

'I've still got a few bob left, pet, so don't be worrying. Come on, let's get down to London Road, me throat's parched.'

The butter ran down Lucy's chin as she bit into the toasted teacake, her eyes wide as she gazed around the tables. Every chair was occupied and the room was buzzing with adults trying to talk above the sound of screaming children. 'All these people, Dad, wouldn't yer wonder where they came from?'

'Liverpool's a big city, pet.' Bob grinned as he passed over a hankie. 'Wipe yer chin before the butter runs on to yer coat.' He groaned as he silently told himself one more stain on the shabby coat wouldn't even be noticed. It was so faded it was difficult to know what its original colour had been, and the sleeves, about three inches too short, were threadbare. 'In a couple of weeks, when I've had time to save up, I'll mug yer to a new coat. Heaven knows, yer could do with one.'

'This one's all right, Dad, I only wear it to go to school.'

Bob shook his head. 'No, it's a complete new rig-out yer need, and that's what yer'll have as soon as I can get the money together. What about yer shoes, are they in good nick?'

Lucy pushed her feet as far back under the chair as she

could. 'They're fine, Dad, they'll last me for ages yet.'

'Then why are yer hiding them under the chair? Come on, pet, there's no need to be frightened, let me see.'

Lucy cast her eyes down as she slid her feet forward. 'See, I told yer, Dad, there's still plenty of wear in them. I gave them a good polish before we came out.'

That's her mother talking, Bob told himself as he bent down to remove one of her shoes. They weren't the words of an eleven-year-old girl. And the anger he felt when he examined the shoe was so strong, he could feel his head throbbing. The heel was worn right down on one side, which must have made it agony to walk on, and there was an inch-round hole in the middle of the sole. He turned the shoe over and felt like crying when he saw how his daughter had tried to hide the scuffmarks with shoe polish.

Bob swallowed hard, trying to shift the lump that had formed in his throat. What sort of a father was he, not to have seen all this? 'Lucy, why didn't yer tell me yer didn't have a decent pair of shoes? I would have done something if I'd known, but the trouble is, pet, yer never complain. Yer don't have to put up with using pins in yer knickers or wearing shoes that are only fit for the back of the fire. Yer've got to start speaking up for yerself.'

'Me mam said she didn't have any money.' Lucy spoke quietly, afraid of saying too much and then being the recipient of her mother's anger.

Bob sighed. 'I give yer mother enough money to manage on, pet, more than most women in the street get.' He was also careful about what he said. It wouldn't do to criticise his wife to his daughter. 'It's just that she's not very good with money, she spends it on the wrong things. There are lots of women like that, they're just not good managers. So in future, you come to me if yer need anything. And don't be frightened of upsetting yer mam by coming to me, 'cos I'll have a word with her. I'll see to yer clothes, and that'll be one less worry off her mind.'

'Yeah, okay, Dad.' Lucy took her shoe and slipped it on. 'Don't look now, but yer toasted teacake has gone cold.'

'Won't stop me eating it, pet.' Bob folded the teacake and took a bite. 'I noticed the shoe department when we came in. We'll have a gander and see if me money will stretch to a pair of cheap shoes for yer.'

He was counting up in his head how much money he had in his pocket as they entered the shoe department. He had to keep enough for his fares to work, the five Woodbines he bought every day and a couple of bob for drinks tonight. Saturday night was the only time he went out with Ruby. They only went to the corner pub because of leaving Lucy on her own and his wife wouldn't be very happy to forego that pleasure, even for the sake of seeing her daughter in a decent pair of shoes.

Lucy tugged on his sleeve. 'Dad, these plimsoles are only elevenpence ha'penny, they'd do for me.'

'They'd be no good if it rained, yer feet would be sopping wet. Let's look around before we decide.' The price of girls' shoes went from half-a-crown up to the seven and six ankle bands that Lucy was gazing at with eyes and mouth wide open. In black shiny patent leather, with the straps fastening at the front with a button, they were the most beautiful shoes she'd ever seen. Bob saw her face and sighed. She was so pretty, she deserved the clothes to match, but they were out of his reach. 'I'm sorry, pet, me pocket doesn't run to that.'

'Oh, I wouldn't want them, Dad, they're too posh. None of me friends have got them and they'd think I was swanking.' She started to giggle. 'Can yer see me playing hopscotch in them? I wouldn't enjoy meself, I'd be terrified of scratching them.'

Bob picked up a pair of the half-a-crown lace ups. They looked what they were, a pair of cheap shoes. But they were sturdy and she'd get good wear out of them. 'Sit on that stool, pet, and I'll get the assistant to find the right size for yer.'

'Are yer sure yer can afford them, Dad? I can wait a few more weeks, yer know.'

'We'll get them now, while we're here.' Bob had gone well over what he intended spending, and wondered what he could forfeit to make it up. He had to keep his tram fare otherwise he wouldn't be able to get to work, and he wasn't going to give up his Woodbines, they were one of the few pleasures he had in life. So they'd have to give the pub a miss, it wouldn't kill them for one night. And the pleasure on Lucy's face made it worthwhile.

Ruby sat with a scowl on her face as Lucy brought her new clothes out of the bags. She showed no enthusiasm, passed no compliments. And her silence angered Bob, who tried to make up for her lack of interest. 'I can't wait to see yer in the dress, pet. Nip upstairs and put it on for us.'

Lucy was so excited, even her mother's attitude couldn't dampen her spirits. She felt as though a good fairy had waved a magic wand and she suddenly had a beautiful dress, new shoes and even knickers. And she'd been in a café and had tea and toasted teacakes. She had never known a day like this, and she was too ecstatic to wonder if there would ever be another. 'I'll go and put them on, Dad, and swank.'

When Bob heard her taking the stairs two at a time, he quietly closed the door before facing his wife. 'Would it have killed you to show some pleasure in yer daughter's new clothes? What sort of a mother are yer?' He shook his head. 'I don't know what brought on the change in yer, but ye're certainly not the woman I married. It's like living with a complete stranger – someone I don't even like.'

'Those clothes were bought with my housekeeping money.' Ruby spat the words out. 'So don't expect me to go in a swoon over them.'

Bob felt like wiping the sneer off her painted face, but he would never lift a hand to a woman. So he got his revenge in words. 'Not only yer housekeeping, Ruby, but also yer

Saturday-night pleasure. I've no money left for the pub tonight, so yer can settle yerself in to listen to the wireless. It won't worry yer, though, will it? Being the good mother yer are, yer'll be quite happy knowing yer daughter won't have to pin her knickers up again, nor wear a shoe with a ruddy big hole in the sole.'

Ruby's eyes were nearly popping out of her head and her nostrils were wide and white. 'Not going to the pub! The one night in the week yer take me out, and yer've gone and spent all yer money on that little faggot?'

'Not on a little faggot, Ruby, on our daughter. And Saturday may be the only night I take yer out, but it certainly isn't the only night you go out. In fact, ye're out more often than ye're in. So I don't think yer have anything to complain about.' He heard footsteps on the landing and spoke quietly, but threateningly. 'You say one word out of place to that child and by God, yer'll be sorry. It won't be five shillings short in yer money, it'll be ten. So think on before yer put yer foot in it.'

Lucy had never had anything to show off before, and she was shy as she stood inside the door. 'How do I look, Dad?'

'Oh pet, yer look as pretty as a picture. The dress looks lovely on yer, fits like it's been made for yer. Go and stand in front of yer mam and see if she likes it.'

Lucy gave him a quick glance before crossing to where her mother sat. 'D'yer like me new dress, Mam?'

The words were so begrudged, Ruby had to force them out. 'Yeah, it's nice.'

Lucy could sense the antagonism in the voice but wouldn't let it prey on her mind. No one was going to spoil today for her. So tossing her hair, she turned back to her father. 'Can I go and show Rhoda? And Mrs Pollard asked me to call and let her see me new dress.'

That was too much for Ruby. 'You keep away from that nosy cow next door. All she's good for is pulling people to pieces. The less she knows about our business, the better.'

Lucy's eyes widened in surprise. How could her mam say that about their neighbour? 'But she's nice, is Mrs Pollard. Everyone likes her 'cos she's always happy and friendly. She never shouts at the kids like some women,' the girl almost stamped her foot at the injustice of her mother's words, 'and she's not a nosy cow, either.'

Ruby was halfway out of her chair when she caught Bob's eye. So the slap she thought her daughter deserved would have to wait for another time. But that time would come. In the meanwhile, she contented herself with saying, 'Don't yer ever dare answer me back like that.'

Bob was thoughtful as he looked down at his clasped hands. He didn't want to set mother and daughter against each other, but Lucy had to learn that when someone said something bad about a person she liked, and she knew it was untrue, she should stick to her guns and say so. 'Lucy wasn't answering yer back, Ruby, she was stating a fact. Irene Pollard is one of the kindest, nicest people ye're ever likely to come across. If you don't like her, that's your misfortune, but don't expect others to agree with yer.'

Lucy thought it would be best if she made herself scarce, then she couldn't cause any more trouble. 'I'm going, Dad, but I won't be long.'

'Yer'll bowl 'em over, pet,' Bob called after her. 'They won't recognise yer.'

Rhoda opened the door and her eyes popped. She turned her head and called, 'Ay, Mam, come and see who's at the door.'

Jessie Fleming came out drying her hands on the corner of her pinny. 'What is it, love, someone on the borrow?' Then she saw Lucy, standing there looking so proud, and her face split into a smile. 'Well, I never! Who is this young girl dressed up to the nines? I don't recall seeing her before.'

Lucy giggled. 'Me dad took me into town and mugged me, Mrs Fleming. D'yer like me dress,' she did a little twirl, 'and me shoes?'

'Yer look a treat, love.' Jessie was thinking it was about time someone took an interest in the girl. 'The dress looks lovely on yer, and the colour suits yer.'

For the first time, since the day they'd started school together, Rhoda had reason to be envious of her friend. 'I bet yer picked it yerself, didn't yer?'

Lucy nodded. 'They were all hanging on a rail, and I liked this one the best.'

'Yer see!' Rhoda flashed her eyes at her mother. 'You won't take me with yer to buy my clothes, so I have to have what *you* like. It's not fair.'

'But yer mam buys yer lovely clothes.' Lucy was feeling sorry she came. Now she'd started a row between her friend and her mother. 'Yer don't know how lucky yer are, 'cos yer gets loads more things than I do.'

Jessie folded her plump arms and leaned back against the door. 'Take no notice of misery guts here, Lucy, she always finds something to moan about. If I bought her a ballgown, she'd complain because I didn't get her a tiara to go with it.'

Lucy grinned. 'She's not always moaning, Mrs Fleming, not to me, anyway. She's me very best friend.'

Rhoda pulled a face at her mother. 'There, yer see, I'm not a misery guts.'

'I know ye're not, sweetheart, ye're all sweetness and light. And for that reason, next time yer need a new dress I'll take yer with me and yer can choose yer own.'

Rhoda flung her arms around her mother's neck and kissed her soundly. 'Ooh, ye're the best mam in the whole world.'

'It'll be a different story if I've left the dinner to burn. I'd better get back in and see to it, otherwise there'll be ructions if I put a burnt offering down to yer dad.' She leaned forward and stroked Lucy's hair. 'Yer look lovely, girl, a real little princess.' She began to chuckle. 'If I ever get down to buying a tiara for our Rhoda, I'll get one for you while I'm at it.'

When her mother disappeared into the house, Rhoda was feeling very kindly towards her friend. 'Yer do look nice,

Lucy, the dress really suits yer. And I'm not half glad yer came down to show us, 'cos now me mam's promised to let me choose me own, and she never goes back on a promise. So yer've done me a good turn, kid.'

'Yeah, yer owe me one. So next time we have a game of rounders, yer can let me win. That'll make us even.' Lucy rubbed her arms briskly. There was a cool breeze blowing and the cotton dress wasn't much protection against it. 'I'll have to go, Rhoda, I promised to call in and see Mrs Pollard, and it's nearly teatime. I'll see yer tomorrow, eh?'

'Okay, Lucy. Ta-ra for now.'

Lucy took to her heels and ran the short distance to her neighbour's house. The door was opened by Jack, who at fourteen was the eldest of Irene's two sons. He gaped at Lucy, then bawled, 'Hey, Mam, come and get a load of this.'

Irene came to the door, followed by twelve-year-old Greg. Her face lit up when she saw Lucy. 'Oh, sunshine, ye're a sight for sore eyes. My, but yer do look bonny. Come in and let George see yer.'

Lucy had never been fussed over so much, and she loved every minute of it. 'Wasn't me dad good, letting me choose me own? There were a lot of dresses, but this was me very favourite.'

'Yer've got good taste, queen,' George said, thinking you'd go a long way to find anyone with a face and nature as beautiful as this child. And wasn't it sad that most of the time she was dressed like a backstreet waif. He turned to his sons. 'Don't yer think she looks pretty, boys?'

Blushing to the roots of their hair, the lads looked down at their feet. They both liked Lucy, thought she was a smashing girl. But at their tender age they'd never been called on to pay compliments before. Jack was the first to find his tongue. 'Yeah,' he said, 'she looks great.'

The only thing Greg could think of that might be considered a compliment, was, 'Yeah, she looks the pig's ear – the gear.'

George dropped his head back and roared with laughter. 'The pig's ear, eh? Now that is flattery indeed.'

'Well, what d'yer expect from a twelve year old?' As always, Irene was quick to defend her son. 'And when I was young, to look the pig's ear meant yer looked fantastic. And that is just what Lucy looks – fantastic.' She put her arm across the thin shoulders and squeezed. 'Tell yer dad from me that he's done yer proud.'

Lucy's smile was a joy to behold. 'Thank you. I'm made up, I really am. I don't think I've ever been so happy in me life.'

Irene exchanged glances with her husband before giving Lucy another squeeze. 'Yer mam and dad go to the pub tonight, don't they?'

'Yeah, every Saturday.' Forever mindful of what she said, Lucy added, 'They see me in bed first, though, and they leave the light on in the living room. And they don't stay out late.'

'Why don't yer ask them if yer can come in here tonight, and have a game of cards or Ludo with us? Jack and Greg are allowed to stay up late on Saturday and I'm sure yer parents won't mind. George usually walks home with them from the pub, don't yer, light of my life?'

George averted his gaze. He couldn't stand Ruby Mellor, thought she was as tough as an old boot. He got on fine with Bob, they were good mates, but he couldn't stomach his wife. So he always walked behind them with a bloke from up the street. But now wasn't the time to air his feelings. 'Yeah, we all get thrown out at closing time.'

'Would yer like me to come with yer to see what they say?' Irene asked, seeing the look of doubt on Lucy's face. 'I'm sure it will be all right. After all, yer can't come to any harm with us, can yer? The worst that can happen is yer lose a game and have to fork out a couple of matches.' Her chubby face beamed. 'Mind you, sometimes we go mad and play for old buttons.'

Remembering her mother's set face, and the atmosphere in

the room when she'd left the house, Lucy shook her head. 'No, I'll go and ask them. Yer see, me mam likes to know I'm settled in bed before she goes out.'

George put his hands on the wooden arms of his fireside chair and pushed himself up. He was a tall, well-made man with a mop of fine, sandy-coloured hair and a ruddy complexion. And like his wife, he had an ever-ready smile. 'I'll go with her. I want to see Bob, anyway.'

Irene looked surprised. 'Yer'll be seeing him tonight in the pub.'

'I want to ask if he's got a paintbrush I can borrow to whitewash the kitchen, and I don't want the whole street knowing.'

So when Bob opened the door it was to see his daughter holding the hand of their neighbour. He smiled a welcome. 'Come in, George, ye've timed it nicely. There's a fresh pot of tea just brewed.'

George pushed Lucy ahead of him. 'I'll come in, Bob, but I won't stay for a cuppa 'cos Irene's got the meal nearly ready.'

Ruby's welcome was a brief nod, and George's was barely noticeable. 'I came on the cadge, Bob, to ask if yer've got a paintbrush to lend. It's to whitewash our kitchen and the brushes I've got are too small. I need a wide one.'

'Yeah, I've got one, and ye're welcome to borrow it. Shall I get it for yer now?'

'No, there's no hurry, I'm not starting it until Monday night. Now I know I can borrow yours, it'll save me coughing up for a new one.' George put a hand on Lucy's shoulder. 'Now another request. Irene wants to know if yer'll let this fashionable little lady come to ours tonight to have a few games with her and the boys? Yer can pick her up on yer way home from the pub.'

'We're not going out tonight, George, we've decided to have a night in.' Bob saw his wife's body stiffen with anger, but ignored it and kept the smile on his face. 'But that's no reason why Lucy can't go and have a few games with the boys. It'll do her good, having youngsters to play with for a change.'

'I'd rather she didn't go,' Ruby said, feeling if she didn't put her foot down now, Bob would take over completely and she'd never have a say in anything. 'I like Lucy to be in bed by eight, that's late enough for a girl of her age.'

'There's no school tomorrow, so she can have a lie-in.' Bob's eyes were like steel as they bored into hers. 'It must be lonely for her, being an only child and no one to play games with. It's about time she began to enjoy her childhood, before it's too late.' He dropped to his haunches in front of his daughter. 'Yer'd like to go, wouldn't yer, pet?'

Her smiling eyes told him the answer before she spoke. 'I would, Dad, if it's all right with you and me mam.'

'Of course it's all right, why wouldn't it be? I mean, next door is hardly the other side of the world, is it?'

Lucy giggled. 'It's fifteen walking steps from our front door to theirs, but if I do long jumps, I can do it in ten.'

George ruffled her hair. 'What about cartwheels, queen? How many of them would it take yer to get from here to there?'

'Ooh, I can't do cartwheels.' Lucy had never even tried. How could yer do cartwheels when yer had a pin in your knickers? 'Anyway, our teacher, Miss Robinson, said it's not ladylike to show all yer underwear off.'

'She has a point, has your Miss Robinson.' George gave her a beaming smile before reaching for the door knob. 'I'd better get going otherwise I'll have me meal thrown at me. Nothing gets Irene's goat more than making a hot dinner and then having to warm it up again. Send Lucy along about seven, we'll have all eaten by then.'

As soon as he'd gone, Ruby turned on her husband. 'I may as well talk to the bleedin' wall, yer don't take a blind bit of notice what I say. That cow next door only wants Lucy there so she can poke and prod into our business. Before the night's over, she'll know how many flamin' blankets we've got on the bed! But you're too thick to see that.'

'When yer talk sense, I might start taking notice of yer. But yer come out with some of the most ridiculous things imaginable, and I'd have to be a fool to agree with yer. It just shows what a warped mind yer've got when yer think Irene Pollard has nothing better to interest her than how many blankets we've got on our bed.' He sensed Lucy moving restlessly from one foot to the other and cursed himself for letting Ruby rub him up the wrong way in front of the girl. There'd be time enough later, when they were alone, for harsh words. 'D'yer want to change into yer old dress, pet, or are yer keeping that one on?'

'I'll get changed, Dad, 'cos I want to keep this one for best.'

'Go on, then, while yer mam gets the tea ready.'

Ruby didn't even wait until her daughter had put her foot on the first stair before saying what was on her mind. And she didn't keep her voice lowered. 'Who the bleedin' hell d'yer think yer are? This is my house too, yer know, I have as much right to have my say as you have. If yer think I'm going to stand here to be bossed around, and walked all over, then yer've got another bleedin' think coming.'

Bob kept a tight rein on his temper. 'That's another thing I won't have in this house, bad language. In future yer'll keep yer filthy tongue until ye're with yer friends. You do not use it in front of Lucy or me. Is that understood?'

'You can just sod off, Mr High and Mighty Mellor. D'yer hear me? Sod off.'

Next door, the Pollards were sitting down to their meal. Irene jerked her head towards the wall. 'Can yer hear them going at it, high ding dong?'

'I can hear Ruby going at it, but I think Bob's taking it all in his stride. He's not messing around this time, he means business. He's put his foot down with a firm hand, all right, it's sticking out a mile. And yer can tell the way they look at each other, there's no love lost there, I'm afraid.' George began to chuckle. 'He might get her to toe the line in some things, but he doesn't stand a snowball's chance in hell of getting her to clean her mouth out. Swearing is second nature to her now, she thinks it's as normal as pulling the chain after yer've been to the lavvy.' He tapped a finger on his chin and looked thoughtful. 'I've got that the wrong way round, haven't I? Yer pull the chain to clean the lavvy, but when Ruby opens that mouth of hers, nothing clean comes out of it.'

'All right, sunshine, that's enough,' Irene tutted. 'We're having a meal and all you can talk about is the lavvy. It's enough to put anyone off their food.'

'It won't put me off me food,' Jack said, spearing a chip and dipping it into the mound of tomato sauce at the side of his plate. 'Nothing puts me off me grub.'

Greg's eyes were serious as he looked across the table. 'Mam, why is Mrs Mellor so cruel to Lucy? She's not a naughty girl, is she?'

'Of course she's not naughty! Lucy is one of the best-mannered kids I know. And I wouldn't say her mother was cruel to her, 'cos we don't really know that, do we?' Irene pointed her fork at him. 'And yer don't discuss things like that with yer mates, d'yer hear?'

'I hear yer. But I'm not half glad Mrs Mellor isn't my mam. I wouldn't like to get shouted at all the time, even when I've done nothing wrong.'

'If she was my mam I'd run away from home.' Jack sounded quite definite. 'I wouldn't stay with her, she's horrible.'

'Oh, aye?' Irene raised her brows. 'And where would yer run to, sunshine?'

Jack's eyes glinted with laughter. 'I'd run to the house next door, where there was a proper mam.'

George saw the funny side and his guffaw was loud. 'It's a

pity they don't have humour as a subject in your school, son. At least yer'd be top of the class in something.'

There was love and pride in Irene's eyes as she gazed at her two sons. 'But we're not going to mention Mrs Mellor's name tonight, in front of Lucy, are we?'

Two heads shook vigorously. 'Nah,' Jack said, 'we're not that daft, Mam.'

Chapter Three

'I thought yer said yer'd never played this game before?' Jack placed his fan of cards face down on the table as he looked across at Lucy. 'How come, if yer've never played before, ye're the only one with three cards down?'

'I don't know, do I?' Lucy was dead excited. They'd explained the rules of the game to her before they started, and she couldn't believe her luck when she was sorting the cards she'd been dealt to find she had three fours. She couldn't wait for her turn so she could put them down and beam all over her face. 'I must be lucky.'

'Beginner's luck, sunshine,' Irene said, 'that's what it is.'

Jack turned sharply when he felt his brother move and found Greg bent down, peeking at his cards. 'Ay, you, stop cheating.'

Greg sat up straight, grinning from ear to ear. He wasn't in the least ashamed of being found out. 'He's got a cob on because he's got two fours himself and he'd have to be dead lucky to pick another one up.' He chuckled. 'I hope me mam won't be throwing one down now she knows what he's after.'

Irene shook her head and clucked. 'That's cheating, Greg, and it's not fair. Besides, we're supposed to be teaching Lucy how to play cards, not cheat.'

'Shall we all throw our cards in, Mrs Pollard, and deal another hand?' Lucy asked. 'That would make it fair, wouldn't it?'

'Not on yer life!' Jack said. He did have two fours, but he also had two other pairs. It wasn't a bad hand by any means. 'Take no notice of me brother, he still thinks he's a baby. He's more to be pitied than laughed at.'

'Let's get on with the game,' Irene said, 'otherwise we'll be here until midnight. You leave those three cards down, Lucy, and throw one away.'

Lucy stared at the cards in her hand. Oh, decisions, decisions. She had two kings, two jacks and a six. The six looked out of place, so she threw that on the upturned cards in the centre of the table.

Irene picked a card from the pack, looked at it and snorted before throwing it down. 'That's not a ha'porth of good to me, I've got a lousy hand.'

Jack shrieked with delight as he snatched up the king his mother had thrown down. 'Ta very much, Mam.' He matched the card with the two in his hand and laid the three down. 'How about that, then? And,' he said with an air of a superior being, 'I can put my two fours on to Lucy's.'

Irene clamped her lips and shook her head. 'Not a very wise move, sunshine. Yer should have kept one back.'

Jack, thinking he'd been very clever, looked puzzled. 'Why?'

'Because yer've got to throw a card in now, which leaves yer with two in yer hands. And yer could sit there all night waiting for somewhere to put them.'

'Well, yer never know.' The lad felt like kicking himself for not hanging on to one of the fours, but he put on a brave face. 'Anything can happen in a game of cards. Come on, Greg, it's your turn.'

His brother picked up a card, checked it against those in his hand before throwing it down in disgust. 'I might as well pack in now, I've got nowt.'

Lucy's green eyes were like saucers as she picked up the card Greg had thrown down. 'Will yer tell me if I'm doing right, Mrs Pollard?' She put three jacks down in front of her and showed the other two cards to Irene. 'I can put these kings on Jack's now, can't I?'

Irene's tummy was rumbling with laughter. 'No, sunshine, yer have to throw one away first. Then yer can put the other one on Jack's run, and yer've won the game.'

As Lucy flipped the card across the table she caught sight of Jack's open mouth, and the look of disbelief on his face. She didn't want to laugh because that would be rude. It wasn't her home, she was only an invited guest. But after another quick glance across the table she had as much chance of keeping the laughter back as she had of stopping the rain which they could hear pelting down outside.

Lucy's laugh started as a tinkle, then gathered momentum until it filled every corner of the room. 'I've won three buttons! Me first game of cards and I won! And because ye're looking at me as though I cheated, Jack Pollard, I want nothing less than a pearl button off you.'

'I'll get it back off yer before the night's over,' Jack threatened. 'Like me mam said, it's just beginner's luck.'

'That's what you think, clever clogs.' Lucy had been shy at first, but now she was really relaxed and happy. There was no tension in her body, no worry in her mind that any minute now she'd get a clip around the ear and not know what she'd done to deserve it. 'I bet I win more games than you.'

'Yer won't if he starts cheating,' Greg said. 'He's very good at cheating, is our Jack. Aren't I right, Mam?'

'It takes one to know one, sunshine, and I'd say that when it comes to cheating, you'd win hands down.'

Lucy had been listening with interest. 'Mrs Pollard, d'yer think yer'd better teach me how to cheat so I'm in with a chance?'

The brothers thought this was hilarious and once again the room rang with laughter. She was good fun, was Lucy Mellor, and they hoped their mam would ask her to come again.

★ ★ ★

Bob Mellor lowered the newspaper and looked across at his wife. 'Can yer hear them next door? They're having the time of their lives, and I've never heard our Lucy laugh like that for years. It's about time she had someone her own age to play with.'

Ruby's scowl deepened. 'I still think Irene is a miserable cow. She should doll herself up and go to the pub with her husband on a Saturday night, instead of sitting in playing stupid games. Some wife she is, letting him go out on his own all the time.'

'She won't go out and leave the boys on their own. Besides, Irene is not a drinker and doesn't enjoy sitting in a pub all night. George doesn't mind, he understands. It isn't as if they never go out together, they often go to the pictures.'

Ruby's lip curled. 'Aye, with the kids in tow.'

'Which is the way they want it. Those boys are their life, and that's the way it should be. They are a very happy family, and George and Irene have a good marriage.' Bob raised the paper but couldn't concentrate, the words kept running into each other. So he went back to his thoughts. He envied George and Irene and their two children. They were what he would call a perfect family. They laughed together, played together and their love for each other was there for all to see. It wasn't only the wall that separated the two families, it was everything. And his daughter would be experiencing the difference tonight.

Bob rustled the paper as he crossed his legs to make himself more comfortable. He tried to think back to a time when things started to go wrong with his marriage. After much soul-searching he realised things hadn't gone wrong, they were never right! Oh, Ruby had kept the house clean and fed them well. She made sure his clothes were washed and ironed ready for work and his socks were always neatly darned. She'd looked after Lucy properly, too, when she was little, buying her pretty clothes and taking her for walks to the park so she could play on the swings. Bob had been very content in his marriage in those early years, thinking they had everything for a long and happy life. It was only now, looking back, he realised there'd always been something missing: the most important ingredient in any marriage – and that was love and affection. It hadn't worried him at first that Ruby never hugged or kissed him, he thought she was shy. And when she spurned his advances in bed he blamed himself for being over-passionate and selfish.

He shifted restlessly in the chair. Surely to God, in all those years, when she never once kissed or hugged him spontaneously, he should have realised she didn't have any love or affection to give. He must have been blind, or was it simply that he didn't want to rock the boat? Anything for an easy life, that was him. But he should have realised his baby daughter wasn't getting the love she deserved, either. When he wasn't at work, the child was always handed over to him to nurse and play with. He was the one who tucked her up in bed after a kiss and cuddle. The signs were there, but he didn't see them. He thought Ruby lavished her love on the child when he was at work. How could he have been so wrong? Lucy was nearly twelve years of age now, and had never known a mother's love.

'It's a quarter to ten,' Ruby said, through gritted teeth. 'Yer'd better go and get her because they wouldn't think of sending her home.'

Bob threw the paper down and left the room without a word. He had nothing to say to this woman who left her child on her own while she was in a pub drinking with her so-called friends. A woman who gave clouts instead of kisses and used foul language instead of words of praise. A woman who had the gall to scoff at a fine person like Irene Pollard for putting her beloved children before herself.

Jack opened the door wide. 'Come in, Mr Mellor, we're just finishing a game.'

Bob's troubled mind eased when he saw the joy on his daughter's face. She was bouncing up and down on the chair looking more relaxed and happy than he'd ever seen her. 'There's no need to ask if yer've enjoyed yerself, pet, it's written all over yer.'

Lucy held out her hand. 'Look, Dad, I've won six buttons. That means I've won two games.'

'Has she behaved herself, Irene?' Bob asked.

'Behaved herself! She hasn't been a ha'porth of trouble. In fact, we've had more of a laugh tonight than we've ever had. She's got quite a sense of humour, has Lucy, she's had us in stitches. My sons are not very good losers, I'm afraid, but tonight they paid up without any argument. In fact, it was worth losing to see her face.'

'Can she come again, Mr Mellor?' Jack asked. 'We haven't half enjoyed ourselves.'

'As long as yer mam doesn't mind. But not when it's school the next day.'

Jack's shoulders went back and his chest came out. 'I won't have to worry about school soon – I leave in four weeks. I'll be getting meself a job, then, and me mam's going to buy me some long trousers.'

'Good for you, son. I can still remember getting me first pair of long trousers, and me first pay packet. And did I think I was somebody that day! Oh boy, me head was so big I couldn't get through the front door. And me mam, God rest her soul, was standing in the hallway with her hand out for me pay packet. She was only joking, like, and we had a good laugh about it. Not that I didn't have to give it to her unopened, mind, 'cos I did. And with me shilling pocket money burning a hole in me pocket, I swaggered down the street like James Cagney. I went to the picturehouse and bought meself a fourpenny ticket for the front stalls.'

'Good old days, eh, Bob?' Irene smiled. 'A shilling in yer pocket and not a care in the world. And a bob went a long way in those days, I can remember.'

'It went up to one and six when I got me first rise, and I thought meself a rich man.' Bob sighed inwardly, thinking how carefree life had been when he was a youngster. 'Come on, pet, it's ten o'clock, Mrs Pollard will be wanting to get the boys to bed.'

'Ah, ay!' Greg cried. 'We're in the middle of a hand. Can't we finish it?'

'No,' Irene said firmly. 'Yer dad will be in any minute. Put the cards back in the boxes and put them in the sideboard, ready for next time.'

Lucy didn't want the night to end and was sad as she pushed her chair back under the table. 'Thank you for having me, Mrs Pollard, I've had a smashing time.'

'It's been a pleasure having yer, sunshine, and ye're welcome to come at any time. And don't forget that, either. Any time, night or day, for whatever reason, just give us a knock.'

Bob was working the night shift the following week, and on the Monday night he was hammering an iron rod into shape when the whistle sounded to down tools for their break. He worked in an iron foundry near the Dock Road, where they made everything from small nuts and bolts to huge girders. He'd worked there since he left school and was skilled in all the jobs, so was able to move from a furnace to one of the machines when needed. He got on well with the blokes he worked with, who were easygoing and always willing to help. If one of them was off-colour and not able to keep up the pace, they'd all muck in to keep his job going so he wouldn't have any pay docked from his wages. They all had families to support and every penny counted.

Bob brought the hammer down one more time, then satisfied the rod was perfect he laid it beside the pile he'd been working on, and reached for his carry-out. He could just go a cup of tea, his mouth was parched. He quickened his steps and caught up with Billy Gleeson, who'd been working nearby. 'Me mouth feels like sandpaper.'

'Aye,' said Billy, 'it's the heat from those bleedin' furnaces what does it. The sweat pours off yer, but yer mouth stays as dry as a ruddy bone.'

They walked past the nut and bolt section to the canteen, and as soon as they walked through the door, Billy groaned. 'Blimey, listen to those cackling women. They put me in mind of a flock of turkeys being chased by a farmer with a ruddy hatchet.'

'I heard that, Billy Gleeson, yer cheeky bugger,' one of the women shouted. 'Yer want to listen to yerself some time.'

'Oh, ye're there, are yer, Peg? If yer've nowt else going for yer, girl, yer've got a good pair of lug-holes on yer. I bet if yer shut up long enough to listen, yer'd hear Big Ben chiming.' Billy was smiling as he made his way to the table where the women were sitting. 'Move up and make room for me and Bob.'

'I've a good mind to tell yer to sod off,' Peg Butterworth said as she shuffled her bottom along the wooden bench. 'Turkeys, indeed.'

Bob waited for his mate to sit down, then slid on to the end of the seat. He winked at the woman facing him. 'Billy knows how to flatter a woman, doesn't he, Kate? He's just oozing with charm.'

There were eight women on the shift and their job was sorting and inspecting the thousands of nuts and bolts turned out every day. They were a happy bunch, even if their language would make your hair curl. They could certainly hold their own, too, and gave the men back as good as they got. But Kate Brown was the odd one out. She was always pleasant but kept herself to herself. She was quietly spoken and never a swearword passed her lips. Bob knew she was a widow with a young daughter to keep, and he often thought it must be hard for her trying to hold down a job and bring up a child. But apparently her mother was good and helped out by minding the daughter when Kate was at work.

'That's why all the women run after him,' she said now, her

shy smile appearing. 'With his looks and personality, he's a real ladykiller.'

'I'll have to keep me eye on him, then, to see if I can pick up a few tips.' Bob was smiling when he took the lid off his carry-out box, but when he saw the contents his jaw dropped and he couldn't keep the words back. 'Bloody hell!'

Kate followed his eyes and gasped. There were two rounds of bread in the box and they were cut as thick as doorsteps. 'Did yer daughter do yer carry-out?'

Bob tried to control his temper as he shook his head. 'No, the missus did it.' He lifted the top slice of bread and it took all his willpower not to shout out in anger. In the centre of the sandwich was a piece of brawn about two inches square. He couldn't believe his eyes. What the hell did his wife take him for? Did she think he was a bloody fool who wouldn't mind being belittled in front of his workmates? She hadn't even bothered to cut the bread in two, and if he lifted the huge sandwich out of the box as it was, he'd be a laughing stock. Thankfully, apart from Kate, the others were too busy yapping to have noticed.

He put the lid back on the box in disgust. He'd throw it at her when he got home, along with a piece of his mind. He'd rather starve than eat it. 'We had a blazing row over the weekend, and this is my dear wife's way of getting her own back.'

Kate's heart went out to him. 'A bit drastic, isn't it?'

'I think the word that suits her best is spiteful. Still, I'll make sure it doesn't happen again.'

Kate's eyes swept around those sitting at the table and, confident that no one was looking, she slipped two of her sandwiches across the table and put them at the side of his box, out of sight. 'It's not much, but it'll keep the hunger pangs at bay. And I've got a cake yer can have, too, thanks to me mam. She does the baking, and even though I shouldn't boast, she's a dab hand at it. My sandwich cakes always sink in the middle, but not hers. And her fairy cakes melt in yer mouth.'

Kate knew she was talking too much, but it was only to stop any embarrassment Bob might feel. And she sighed with relief when he nodded his thanks and picked up one of the butties. 'They're only meat-paste, I'm afraid, me money doesn't run to boiled ham. But they'll fill a hole.'

'Beggars can't be choosers, Kate, and besides, they're very tasty. I'm beholden to yer on two counts.'

Kate raised her brows questioningly. 'How d'yer make that out?'

'Well, for helping to stop my tummy from rumbling for one thing, and for not laughing yer head off like some would have done. I really appreciate that.'

A faint blush came over Kate's face. 'I've not done anything the others wouldn't have done if they'd known.'

'Oh, they'd have helped, I know that. But they'd have made a song and dance about it.' Bob leaned closer. 'I could have said me wife had played a joke on me, and they'd have laughed their heads off. But I'm not lying about it. It was done for spite, and the missus will be sorry she signed when I get home.'

Kate, her hair hidden beneath the turban all the women had to wear on the shop floor, showed a set of strong white teeth when she smiled. 'Having a row won't solve anything, it seldom does. Wouldn't it be better to just kiss and make up?'

Bob gazed at her for a second before lowering his head. He had no right to burden this woman with his problems, she probably had more than enough of her own. So he met her hazel eyes and smiled. 'Yeah, ye're right. I'll probably throw me carry-out at her, then give her a cuddle. It beats a black eye any day, doesn't it?'

Billy Gleeson, who'd suddenly realised Bob hadn't contributed anything to the general conversation going on around the table, turned to him. 'What beats a black eye, mate?'

Kate surprised herself by stepping in. 'A fairy cake. I was just asking Bob if he'd like one. Me mam baked a batch today and put two in with me carry-out. I couldn't eat both of them so I was trying to palm one off on Bob.'

Holding out his hand, Bob said, 'Which I accept with pleasure.'

Billy pursed his lips and tapped the side of his long, thin nose. 'They say the way to a man's heart is through his tummy, Kate, but don't forget this feller's a married man. In other words he's took, spoken for.'

'Men are the last thing on me mind, Billy.' Kate flicked a crumb from her chin. 'I'd rather have a fairy cake any day.'

'That's put me in me place,' Billy chuckled. 'And you, Bob.'

Peg Butterworth stood up when the whistle sounded. 'Back to the grind, folks.' She leaned over the table and grinned in Billy's face. 'Kate's right. All men are nothing but a load of bleedin' trouble. The only time they're happy is when they're in the pub supping beer, or in bed taking advantage of their poor, longsuffering wives.'

There was a surge towards the door, and Bob just had time to smile at Kate, and say, 'Thanks a million.'

Bob let himself in and closed the front door quietly behind him. He felt like flying up the stairs and having it out with Ruby, but the thought of waking Lucy held him back. He'd keep it bottled up until she'd left for school, then he'd have his say. Usually, when he was on nights, he'd make himself a pot of tea and some toast, then slip into bed as Ruby was getting out to see to Lucy. But today he only made himself a pot of tea. This was one morning he'd have his breakfast cooked for him.

Sitting at the table, smoking a Woodbine and supping his tea, Bob was asking himself where it was going to end. They couldn't carry on like this, at loggerheads with each other all the time. It was no way for a married couple to live, and certainly not the right atmosphere to bring up a child in. Something had to be sorted out, and quickly, because he couldn't stand much more. A row between man and wife was one thing, it happened in every household, but in most cases it could be ended with a bit of coaxing and a kiss. But what was happening here was no ordinary row; it had gone too far to be sorted out with coaxing and a kiss.

He heard a sound from the room above and knew Ruby would be down any minute. He didn't move, just stared at the door. And when it opened and she walked through, yawning and scratching her head, he never uttered a sound, just stared.

'What's the matter with you? Why haven't yer gone to bed?'

Bob closed his eyes to shut out the sight of her matted, dyed blonde hair, the hardness in her eyes and her bloated face still caked with yesterday's make-up. Was this really the girl he'd fallen in love with and married? He opened his eyes and sighed. 'I'm waiting for yer to cook me breakfast.'

'Yer what! You cook yer own breakfast!'

Bob picked up his carry-out box and threw it on the floor at her feet. 'Not after the little trick yer pulled on me last night, I don't.'

'What are yer on about? I didn't pull no trick on yer! I did yer carry-out, didn't I? What more d'yer expect?'

'I'm not going to argue with yer, Ruby, I'm not even going to raise me voice. At least not until Lucy has left for school. Then I intend to raise the roof, and I don't care who hears me. So while I'm waiting, yer can cook me breakfast.'

'I don't know what the bleedin' hell ye're on about, and I don't ruddy well care, anyway.' The washed-out cardigan Ruby was wearing was wrapped across her chest as she bustled out to the kitchen. 'Yer've sat there for an hour, like a stuffed dummy, too bloody lazy to toast two pieces of bread! Yer want yer head testing, you do.'

'No, Ruby, that's where ye're wrong. The day I needed me head testing was the day I married you. But we'll discuss all this later, when Lucy doesn't have to listen to her parents pulling each other to pieces. Right now, though, I'll have me two rounds of toast, lightly done, and a fresh pot of tea.'

★ ★ ★

Lucy was surprised and pleased to see her father sitting at the table. 'I thought yer'd be in bed by now, Dad. Yer usually are.'

Bob gave her the brightest smile he could muster before biting into a piece of toast. 'I felt like some company with me breakfast this morning, so I waited for yer.'

'That's nice, I'm glad yer did.' Lucy looked down at the plate her mother put in front of her. There was no burnt offering this morning, the bread was toasted to a nice golden brown. She knew her father's presence accounted for this, and she also knew this would be one morning she wouldn't be subjected to her mother's taunts or clouts. 'How did work go, Dad?'

'Same as usual, pet, I can't complain. It's a job, and I'm lucky to have one with so many men out of work.' He looked across at his wife who was sat on a fireside chair with a plate on her lap and her cup of tea close to hand on the fire hob. 'We wouldn't know what had hit us if I wasn't working. We'd really be in Queer Street.'

'I know it's a long way off,' Lucy said, 'but when I leave school my wages will help out, won't they?'

Ruby snorted. 'Blimey, we might all be dead and buried by then.'

'That's right, Ruby, there's nothing like starting the day on a happy note.' There was sarcasm in Bob's voice. 'Always laughing and joking, that's you. The life and soul of the party.'

'Well, I'm not going to die, I'm too young.' Lucy nodded her head to show she meant it. 'I'm going to live until I'm as old as Mrs Aggie.'

'Don't let Aggie hear yer say that, pet, 'cos she's not that old, yer know. I'd say in her early sixties.'

'Oh, I didn't mean I thought Mrs Aggie should die, Dad!' Lucy said. 'I'd be very sad if anything happened to her, she's lovely and she's me friend.'

'She's a nosy old witch,' Ruby snorted. 'All she needs is a broomstick and she could fly away over the houses. And it would be good riddance to her.'

Lucy looked down at her clasped hands for a second, then twisted in her chair. 'Mrs Aggie's not wicked, she's nice and kind.'

'That's enough now.' Bob pointed to the clock. 'Don't yer think yer'd better be making tracks, pet? Yer don't want to be late for school.'

Lucy's heart was beating fast. She'd rather have had a clout off her mam than have her say those things about Mrs Aggie. Why did she hate everyone so much? There wasn't one neighbour she had a kind word for. 'I'll get me coat, Dad.' She pushed her chair back under the table, and knowing her father's presence would prevent her from getting a hiding, she had the courage to face her mother. 'You don't like no one, you don't.'

Bob stood up. 'Come on, get yer coat on and I'll see yer out. One of the reasons I stayed up was to sneak a kiss off yer. I don't get nearly enough.'

This brought a smile to Lucy's face. 'I'll give yer six, that'll be one for every day.'

Bob gave her a playful smack on the bottom. 'I'll put five in me pocket and take one out every morning.'

After waving his daughter off, Bob closed the door with a heavy heart. He was tired after working all night and would have loved nothing better than to get his head down. But things needed sorting out, and they needed doing now. But where to start, when his wife was making it plain she had no intention of meeting him halfway?

Ruby lit a cigarette and drew deeply on it when Bob came into the room. 'Ye're making a rod for yer own back with that girl, she's getting far too cheeky.'

'Let's leave Lucy out of it, shall we? This is just between you and me.'

She raised her eyebrows. 'Aren't yer going to bed?'

'Later.' Bob looked down at the littered table. 'Will yer clear these things away, please?'

'I'll do it when I've finished me cigarette. There's no bleedin' hurry, I've got all day.'

'You might have, but I haven't.' Bob made no move to sit down. 'I want a bit of comfort in me own home, if it's not too much trouble.'

With the cigarette dangling out of the side of her mouth, Ruby began to stack the plates and cups. She did it almost in slow motion, with that hard look on her face and all the while blowing smoke in Bob's direction. Her actions were deliberate, and her way of telling him she wasn't going to knuckle under to him or anyone else.

Bob's temper snapped as the incident in the canteen came back to remind him why he had to put his foot down. He leaned across the table, snatched the cigarette from her lips and flicked it into the grate. 'I have never been nearer to hitting you than I am this minute. Don't try me patience too far, Ruby, or yer'll be sorry. Now get this mess cleared away and we'll sit down and air our differences.'

The table was cleared within minutes and the chenille cloth put back. Then Bob gestured to a chair facing him. 'I'm tired and ready for bed, but I'll not leave this room until we come to an understanding. We can do it in a civilised manner or we can do it the hard way. It's up to you.'

Ruby narrowed her eyes. 'What d'yer mean, an understanding?'

'If we're to live under the same roof, there's got to be give and take. For Lucy's sake, we've got to try and get on together so she has a decent home life. Show each other a bit of respect and politeness. I'll say what I would like, then you can have your turn. I'd like good food on the table when I'm home, and I'd like carry-out that doesn't shame me in front of me workmates. I don't want yer to use bad language in the house and I don't want yer pulling the neighbours to pieces.

Especially in front of Lucy.' When Ruby opened her mouth, Bob raised a hand to silence her. 'No, let me have my say first. Yer don't leave our daughter alone in the house while ye're out boozing with yer so-called mates, and I don't want to see her treated like a skivvy. Other women in the street do their own housework and shopping, there's no reason why you can't. God knows, yer've got all day to do it in. And last but not least, I don't want yer raising yer hand to her. She's a good kid, not cheeky or forward. I've only heard her answering yer back twice, and that was called for because yer were saying nasty things about people she likes. She doesn't deserve to be bawled at all the time, a kind word now and again wouldn't go amiss. So I'm asking yer to keep yer voice down and yer hands to yerself.' He met his wife's eyes and could see the blazing anger there. 'I've had my say, now it's your turn.'

Ruby couldn't get her words out quick enough. 'You arrogant bastard! There's got to be give and take, yer say, then reel off all the things I can and cannot do in me own flaming home! I'm a grown woman, not a child!'

Bob said quietly, 'Then act like one.'

'Everything yer've said is what *you* want, not a mention of what *I* might want. If you had your way, I'd be stuck in the house like a bleedin' prisoner. I'm allowed to go to the shops because darling Lucy mustn't do any shopping. She mustn't help with the housework, either, 'cos she's not a skivvy. No, *I'm* to be the skivvy!'

'I'm only asking yer to do what every other mother does. Keep the home clean and warm, feed and look after yer family, and be pleasant. Is that too much to ask?'

'And be the dutiful little wife? How soft you are!' Anger made Ruby reach for her cigarette packet. And after she'd lit up, she stared him out. 'And what happens if I don't agree to this understanding, as yer call it?'

'Yer'll find out soon enough.' Bob pointed to the cigarette packet she was holding. 'Yer won't be able to afford them, for a kick-off. And there's a lot more yer won't be able to afford. Like the stuff yer bleach yer hair with, and the muck yer thicken on yer face. Yer've had it easy with money up to now, buying yerself everything yer wanted while yer daughter walked around in rags. But all that will change if yer don't agree to mend yer ways.'

Ruby could tell by his eyes and the tone of his voice that he meant every word. She'd be well advised to agree, or pretend to. 'If I agree to everything yer've asked for, what do I get in return? Can I have a night out with me mates now and again, so I get a bit of pleasure out of life?'

'When I'm on early shift, yer can go out every night if yer want, I'm not that interested. But when I'm working, you stay put.'

Ruby was gloating inwardly. As long as she got her housekeeping, and she had a few bob in her pocket, that's all she was interested in. She'd found ways of getting out before when he was at work; she could do it again. Even if it was only an hour, after Lucy was asleep. He'd never find out, she thought craftily, so she'd go along with him. 'What about me money? Do I go back to what I was getting before?'

Bob shook his head. 'Not for a few weeks, until I've got enough saved to buy Lucy a new coat. She certainly could do with one, and I'm hoping to take her to town on her birthday so she can choose one she likes. After that we can go back to normal, but you'll be responsible for buying her clothes and making sure she always looks decent. If it doesn't work out, I'll dock the money again and see to her meself.' He stretched his arms over his head and yawned. 'Have yer anything else to say? If yer have, get it off yer chest now.'

'No, we'll see how it works out. I'll do my bit.'

'Right! I'm off to bed then, 'cos right now I could sleep on a clothes line. If I'm not awake, give me a call about five o'clock.'

Ruby heard him climbing the stairs and pulled a face. What a miserable man she was married to. He had no life in him at all. All he thought about was work, bed, his tummy and his beloved daughter. Not like the men her mates were married to. They liked nothing better than taking their wives to the pub a few nights a week and having a laugh and a sing-song.

She threw the cigarette stub into the hearth, and after telling herself she didn't have much to do and all day to do it in, she decided another smoke wouldn't do no harm. And as she watched a smoke ring drift towards the ceiling, she asked herself what she'd ever seen in Bob Mellor. Oh, he was tall, dark and handsome, all right, but he wasn't exciting. And that's what she wanted, some excitement in her life.

Chapter Four

'Hey, Aggie!' Irene Pollard saw her neighbour walking up the street ahead of her and hurried to catch up. 'What's the big rush, sunshine? Have yer got a heavy date?'

'Yer could say that, queen.' Aggie's smile was wide, showing that this wasn't a day for her gums to be on display. 'The postman brought a letter from Titch this morning and his ship's docking some time today.'

Irene linked her arm and squeezed. 'That's what yer call good news, eh?' Tommy McBride was Aggie's son, the only family she had. And she idolised him. 'It's been a long trip this time, hasn't it?'

'Four months. I've been expecting a letter every day, 'cos I knew he was due any time. But he's still caught me on the hop, with a pantry as bare as Mother Hubbard's. So I'm off to the shops to stock up, 'cos yer know what an appetite he's got. He eats me out of house and home when he's here, but it's a pleasure to see the way he tucks into anything yer put before him.' Aggie's chuckle was hearty. 'He used to lick his bleedin' plate clean when he was a youngster, but I had to put a stop to that when he was twenty-one 'cos it didn't look right somehow.'

'Yer can tell he likes his food, Aggie, he's a giant of a man. That's why I can't understand how he got the nickname Titch! There's nothing small about him.'

'The kids called him that when he started school because he was very small and skinny. He didn't start growing until he was about twelve, and so help me, Irene, I thought he'd never stop. But everyone knew him as Titch, and the name stuck. The only time I call him Tommy is when I'm telling him off.'

Irene chortled. 'Yer can't tell a forty-year-old man off, Aggie, that's daft.'

'That's what he gets told off for, queen, being daft. He might be forty, but he's never grown up in the head. He's always playing tricks on me, and if he wasn't so big I'd box his ears for him.' When Aggie laughed, her top set of teeth became loose and she stuck her thumb in her mouth to push them back into place. 'Last time he was home he hid me purse on me. I didn't know he'd hidden it, like, and I searched high and low for the bleedin' thing. I didn't let on to him in case he said I was careless, but after looking everywhere, I was getting frantic. It was only when the club woman knocked he took it out of his pocket and handed it to me, looking all innocent, as though butter wouldn't melt in his mouth. "Is this what ye're looking for, Ma?" he asked. I could have brained him, I didn't think it was a bit funny. But when I came back after paying the club woman, he had one of the wooden chairs in the middle of the room. He held his hand out and said, "Here yer are, Ma, I'll help yer stand on it. I deserve me ears boxing for pulling a stunt like that. I'm a fool to meself, that's what I am. After all, yer could have had a heart attack, and who'd have made me dinner for me then, eh?" '

Irene was shaking with laughter as she pictured the scene. 'There's never a dull moment with your Titch around, is there? But I bet yer wouldn't have him any different, though, because I know yer love the bones of him.'

'Ye're right there, queen. He's been going to sea since he was eighteen, and I don't see that much of him. But I treasure every minute he's with me.' Aggie put a hand on Irene's arm and pulled her to a stop outside a butcher's shop. 'I'm going in here, love, to get some shin beef. When Titch gets home there'll be a pan of scouse simmering on the stove, and four light-as-a-feather dumplings ready to pop in. He always looks forward to his favourite meal on his first day home.'

'I'm made up for yer, Aggie, and I hope he gets a decent leave this time. Tell him to give his friends a knock when he can, we'd love to see him.'

'If I know my son, he'll make sure he's home in plenty of time to eat his meal and go down to the pub. He wouldn't miss either on his first night. Nor would he miss asking George and Bob to go for a welcome home drink with him. So tell George to expect a knock, will yer?'

Irene nodded. 'I'll do that, he'll be tickled pink to see Titch again. And as luck would have it, Bob's on early shift this week, so he can join them.'

'I'll have to go, queen, 'cos I've a fair bit of shopping to do to make me larder look a bit healthier. One egg and one rasher of bacon doesn't look out of place when yer live alone, but yer can't feed a hungry man on it. Besides, I can afford to splash out a bit today because Titch put a pound note in with his letter.'

'So, ye're not only happy, but rich as well?' Irene was pleased for her neighbour. Aggie never complained, but she must get lonely at times. Her husband, Les, had died ten years ago, and although Titch had offered to find a shore job at the time, she wouldn't hear of it. The sea was in his blood, and although he argued otherwise, she knew he wouldn't be happy working in a factory and sent him off to join his ship, so great was the love this mother had for her son. 'I might see yer tonight, then, Aggie, if Titch doesn't bring a bottle of the hard stuff home with him, like he did last time. Yer were too drunk to go down to the pub!'

'Nah, I wasn't, queen.' Aggie's teeth fell down again. The trouble was, her gums felt much better without them and kept pushing them out. So there was a constant war between teeth and gums. But the gums were fighting a losing battle today. No way was Aggie having her son come home to a mother with no teeth in. 'I was a bit tipsy, perhaps, but certainly not so legless I couldn't make it down to the pub. I just felt the men would feel more free to talk if they were on their own.'

Irene laughed. 'I'll believe yer, where thousands wouldn't. Anyway, sunshine, I'll be on me way. Ta-ra for now.'

Aggie heard the key turn in the lock and stood up. Her tummy was doing somersaults with excitement and her heart was crying out with hunger for the sight of her beloved son. Then she heard his familiar voice. 'What's that delicious smell? I must be in the wrong house. We never have no smells like that in our house, 'cos me ma's a lousy cook.'

Aggie rounded the table and held her arms wide. 'Ye're a cheeky bugger. But I'll forgive yer, seeing as it's yer first day home.'

'Ma, it's good to see yer.' Titch put his hands on her waist and lifted her until their faces were on a level. 'Ye're still as pretty as ever. I swear yer look younger every time I come home. Give us a kiss.'

They hugged for a while, then Aggie whispered in his ear, 'I'd better put the dumplings in before the stew burns dry.'

'What! Dumplings as well!' Titch gently set her down. 'Anyone would think yer were glad to see me.'

'And they wouldn't be far wrong, son, I'm over the moon.' Aggie pushed the sleeves of her dress up. 'Let's get this dinner on the go, ye're probably starving.' She turned at the kitchen door. 'Where's yer bag?'

'I dropped it in the hall in me haste to feast me eyes on yer.'

'Well, get yer dirty clothes out and I can put them in the tub to steep overnight.'

Titch leaned against the door jamb. 'There's no need, Ma, yer can do that tomorrow.'

For a brief second, Aggie felt a stab of sadness. He had all the mannerisms of Les, right down to the way he walked, held his head, and even his lopsided grin. He had the same mop of brown hair, too, and blue eyes. But he was taller than his father had been, and broader. And his face was weather-beaten with being at sea for so long, out in all weathers. She shook her head to dispel the memories. 'Do it now, son, so I'm not rushing to get them washed and ironed at the last minute.'

There was a smile on her son's face as he watched for her reaction to what he had to say. 'Ma, I'm home for two and a half weeks. So yer've got all the time in the world.'

Aggie's mouth gaped. 'If you're having me on, I'll break yer bleedin' neck for yer.'

'Scout's honour, Ma, I'm home for eighteen days. And with being away such a long time, with nothing to spend me wages on, I've got quite a bit saved up. So I'll take yer into town tomorrow and treat yer to whatever takes yer fancy. Yer can have anything yer like, the sky's the limit.'

'I don't want nothing, son, having yer home is treat enough for me.' Then the mother in her came out. 'And don't yer be carrying a load of money around with yer, either. If I know you, yer'll be treating everyone in the bleedin' pub. Throwing yer money around like a man with no flaming hands.'

'I'm not that soft, Ma, it's got to last me until I sail again. And I want to see you're all right when I leave. So I'll just mug me mates, George and Bob, and that's about it, apart from a few pennies for the kids. Does that meet with your approval?'

'I'm not a miser, son, and I'll help anyone out if they're stuck. But yer should be putting some money aside in case yer ever need it. One of these days yer might meet a girl, fall in love and want to settle down. And yer'll need money to do that.'

There was a smile on her son's face as he watched her lift two plates down from the shelf that ran the length of the kitchen wall. 'Ma, it's true what they say about a sailor having a girl in every port, yer know. It's not that I've never had me chances, 'cos to tell the truth I've been spoilt for choice. I've had plenty of flings, because being a red-blooded man I do like the ladies. But I've never met one who I could fall head over heels in love with. One who I would want to spent the rest of me life with. So ye're stuck with me, Ma, because I've not come across one yet that can hold a candle to yer.'

Aggie tutted. 'Go 'way, yer daft ha'porth. Sit yerself down and stop yapping to me, or I'll be burning the backside out of this pan.'

Half an hour later, Titch pushed his empty plate away and rubbed his tummy. 'The captain would have a very happy crew if the ship's cook could make dumplings like you. The ones he makes are so heavy I'm surprised the blinking ship hasn't sunk by now.'

'Ah, well, there's a knack to it, yer see.' Aggie nodded knowingly. 'He probably puts too much suet in them. Tell him I said to just put half the amount in that he usually does, and see how they turn out.'

Titch smiled as he imagined what the scene would be in the galley if he told the cook his mother had advised him to put less suet in his dumplings. The air would be blue with words his mam wouldn't even know the meaning of. 'I'll do that, Ma.' He leaned back against the chair and reached into his pocket for his pipe. 'Any news for me? How are the Pollards and the Mellors?'

'The Pollards are fine. They're a lovely family, the salt of the earth. Young Jack leaves school in two weeks and he's a scream. He was leaning against the wall last night, watching his mates playing marbles, and I asked him why he wasn't playing. "I'm practising, Mrs Aggie," he said. I asked him what he was practising, because all he was doing was leaning against the wall. "I'm practising not playing marbles. Yer see, Mrs Aggie, I'll be going into long kecks when I leave school, and me mam said if she sees me even looking at the gutter while I've got them on, she'll box me ears for me. And as I'm fond of me ears, and don't want them boxed, I'm practising hard at not playing marbles." '

Her son's hearty guffaw filled the room. 'Oh, that's a good one, that is. I can see he takes after his mam. Irene's always had a quick sense of humour. George has too, but he's not as quick off the mark as his wife.'

Aggie sighed. She didn't like gossiping about the neighbours, but if Titch was going to be home for nearly three weeks, he'd notice things for himself. Better he was forewarned so he didn't say anything out of place. 'As for the Mellors, well, what's happening in their house is anyone's guess.' She told him briefly what she knew, and watched him shake his head. 'I feel sorry for Bob, and for Lucy. Their home is not a very happy one, I'm afraid.'

'Trouble's been brewing in that house for a few years now, Ma. Anyone with half an eye could see that. I'm surprised Bob's put up with it for so long. Whenever we go for a pint, which isn't often with me being away, but when we do he never mentions Ruby's name. And as they say, silence speaks louder than words. George is full of Irene and the boys, but Bob only ever talks about Lucy. And that set the alarm bells ringing for me ages ago.' Titch drew on his pipe and there was a look of contentment on his face. He knew he'd be craving for the sea by the time his leave was over, but right now it was bliss to sit with the mother he adored, in the house he was born in. 'I don't know what the solution is there, Ma, only Bob and Ruby can sort that out. And they have to have the will to do it.'

'It's Lucy I feel sorry for,' Aggie said. 'Poor little mite, always has a smile on her face even though her mother gives her a dog's life. Mind you, Irene has brought about a few changes for her. She heard Ruby having a go at the girl one night and knocked to ask was something wrong because of all the shouting and banging. It seems to have done the trick because Irene said it's gone much quieter. And, thanks to George, Lucy goes in their house now to play cards with the boys.'

'Is Lucy still as pretty as ever?'

'As pretty as a picture, son. She'll break a few hearts when she's older.'

'Then I think I'll wait for her to grow up and marry her.'

'I'll knit yer a wife, if yer like. That way, if yer ever got fed up with her nagging, yer could stick her in a sideboard drawer.' Aggie began to clear the dishes. 'I'll get these out of the way, then yer can have the sink to spruce yerself up. I told Irene yer'd be knocking for George, so he'll be expecting yer.' She put the plates on the draining board, then popped her head back in the room. 'Bob's on early shift, so yer'll have yer two mates to jangle to. Yer can tell them all about these girls yer've got in every port, and the goings-on that yer wouldn't dare tell yer old mother about in case she clocked yer one.'

Titch chuckled. 'If I did that, Ma, they'd both pack their bags and sign up on the next ship out of Liverpool!'

'That's as maybe, son. But a life on the ocean wave doesn't appeal to everyone. Heart and hearth are what most men are satisfied with. Especially if they have a family.'

'Yeah, I know, Ma. And in ten years' time I might envy them. But right now I'm happy being foot-loose and fancy free.'

'I'd better get foot-loose and see to the dishes,' Aggie said, disappearing into the kitchen. 'Otherwise yer won't have time for yer usual quota of the liquid brown stuff. We can't have yer sober on yer first night.'

'Ma, I could drink the pub dry and still be able to put the key in the lock. And I'd never be too drunk to miss yer lips for me goodnight kiss. I couldn't sleep without that.'

Aggie smiled as she poured hot water over the dishes. Oh, it was so good to have him home.

'It's great to see yer, Titch.' George's smile was wide when he opened the door. His words were sincere, his handshake firm. 'And yer look the picture of health, as usual.'

'I wouldn't say you were exactly sickly-looking yerself, mate. Irene must be taking good care of yer.'

'And why wouldn't I? He's the only husband I've got.' Irene was waiting for him, her pretty face lit up and her arms opened wide. 'Come and give us a kiss, Titch McBride. And make it a good one, seeing as yer've stayed away a long time.'

They embraced as two friends who had a deep fondness for each other. And his eyes looking over her shoulder, Titch glimpsed the two boys watching with interest. 'Yer don't mind if I kiss yer mam, do yer, fellers?'

'I've got me eye on yer, Mr Titch,' Jack said, his face deadpan. 'Me dad gets one kiss when he comes in. I was watching to make sure you didn't get two. Otherwise me dad would have had to go out and come back in again.'

'Oh, if I'd known that's how yer worked it, I'd have pinched two kisses. Maybe even three! Then yer dad would really have been grateful to me.'

Greg grinned. 'More likely he would have belted yer one. He's very generous, me dad, but not with me mam's kisses.'

'Oh, aye, I think I'm going to have a hard time in a few years. Yer mam will have three big men to make sure no one gets more than one kiss.' Titch winked at Irene as he went to stand behind the boys' chairs. Putting a hand on the back of each of their necks, he turned their faces towards him. 'Anyway, don't I get a welcome-home kiss off you two?'

The boys looked horrified as they tried to pull away. 'Not blooming likely!' Jack cried. 'Only cissie boys get kissed.'

'Gerroff!' Greg twisted his head in an attempt to break free. 'Ye're not getting no kiss off me.'

It was difficult to know who laughed the loudest, Titch or George. 'Yer'll be singing a different tune in a few years,' their dad said, 'when the girls start giving yer the eye.'

Jack gave a superior smile. That time would come for him two years before his brother. 'Ah, well, that's a different kettle of fish. If Mr Titch was a girl, I'd have given her a kiss.'

'Yer mean yer'd have given *him* a kiss,' his brother corrected him.

'I said if he was a girl, soft lad.'

Greg stuck to his guns. 'If he was a girl, he wouldn't be Mr Titch, would he? It means yer'd be kissing a total stranger, and yer can't go round doing things like that. She'd probably slap yer face for yer.'

George was grinning as he walked into the hall for his coat. 'They'll keep that up all night, Titch, so we'd better leave them to it.'

'Does Bob know we'll be giving him a knock?'

'I haven't seen Bob,' Irene said, 'and I don't have much to say to Ruby. If I'd known for sure yer were coming, I'd have made it me business to let him know, but nothing is definite with a sailor, is it? Anyway, I know he'll be that delighted to see yer, he'll have his coat on in five seconds flat.'

George kissed his wife's cheek. 'I won't be late, love.'

'Yer better hadn't be, sunshine, or I'll be waiting in the hall with the poker in me hand.' Irene turned her laughing eyes on Titch. 'If my husband has one over the eight, I'll hold you personally responsible.'

Titch clicked his heels and gave a mock salute. 'Aye, aye, sir.' He put a hand to the side of his mouth and in a loud whisper, said to the boys, 'Blimey, she's worse than our captain.'

The two men walked into the hall with Irene at their heels. Then Titch suddenly turned around. 'I won't be a tick.' He marched back into the living room and grinned at the boys. 'How would yer like to come to first-house pictures with me one night? And we could take Lucy with us.'

'Oh yeah, that would be the gear.' Jack's face was aglow. 'Thanks, Mr Titch.'

'Blinking fantastic!' Greg said, leaning his elbows on the table. Then he narrowed his eyes. 'What night?'

'Unless yer've got heavy dates, we'll make it tomorrow night, eh?' Titch left the room with shrieks of delight ringing in his ears.

Ruby's face was sullen when she opened the door, but it changed miraculously when she saw the two men. 'Well, this is a surprise,' she said, patting her hair into place and hoping her lipstick wasn't smudged. 'Come on in.'

Bob threw the paper down and jumped from his chair. Grabbing Titch's hand he pumped it up and down vigorously. 'Ye're a sight for sore eyes. I didn't even know yer were due home.'

'Me ma didn't know until today, and even then she didn't know what time I'd get home.' Titch's eyes were fastened on the girl sitting at the table, a book opened in front of her. 'Hello, Lucy.'

There was a smile on the heart-shaped face and a twinkle in the green eyes. 'I bet Mrs Aggie's like a cat with two tails. She often talks to me about yer, Mr Titch.'

'Oh, aye? What does she say?'

Lucy's infectious giggle rang out. 'I can't tell yer that, she'd have me life. But she never says nothing bad.'

Titch put on a stern look and folded his arms. 'Now what could she say about me that was bad? I've got a heart as pure as the driven snow and I'm as handsome as a Greek god. Now what more could she want?'

Again Lucy's giggle filled the room. 'Not all gods are handsome, Mr Titch. Have yer seen the state of the God of Thunder? His face is enough to frighten the living daylights out of anyone.'

Ruby was fuming inside. She was being ignored while a chit of a girl was getting all the attention. And she was all dressed up, too, because it was one of her nights out. 'That's enough, Lucy,' she said, pushing her way to stand in front of the fireplace. 'I'm sure Mr McBride came to talk to yer dad, not you.'

'Oh, I don't know,' Titch laughed, 'her dad's not as pretty as her.' He winked before turning to Bob. 'Besides, I've got plenty of time to talk to me mates while we're downing a few pints in the pub.'

Bob glanced at Ruby hoping she would offer to stay in, but one look at her face told him he'd be wasting his time asking. 'I'm afraid I can't go with yer tonight, much as I'd like to. Ruby's promised to go and see a friend of hers and I'll have to stay in with Lucy.'

George raised his bushy eyebrows. 'Can't yer go another night, Ruby?'

If they'd asked her to go to the pub with them, Ruby would have agreed like a shot. But she wasn't prepared to be stuck in the house when she could be out enjoying herself. 'I've promised, and she'll be expecting me.'

The miserable bitch, George thought, before saying, 'Not to worry, there's another way around it. Lucy can go in our house for a couple of hours. It won't hurt her to be late going to bed for one night. Irene and the boys would be delighted to have her.'

Refusing to meet the dark look on her mother's face, Lucy clapped her hands together in glee. 'Oh yes, I'd like that.'

'That's settled then.' George held out his hand. 'Come on, sweetheart, I'll take you to ours while yer dad gets himself ready.'

When Bob was in the kitchen swilling his face, Ruby eyed Titch up and down. God, he wasn't half handsome in a rugged sort of way. Life with him wouldn't be dull, he was a real live wire. 'How long are yer home for?'

Titch shrugged his shoulders. 'Seventeen, eighteen days, it depends when they send for me.'

'If ye're ever stuck for somewhere to go, I'm in every day and yer'd be more than welcome to a cuppa.' Ruby's bold eyes bored into his and she didn't even try to mask the attraction she felt for him. 'As I said, yer'd be more than welcome.'

Titch knew he was getting the 'come on', and was disgusted. If Bob hadn't been in the kitchen, likely to enter the room any second, he would have told her the truth. That he wouldn't touch her with a barge pole. As it was, he said, 'I won't be stuck for somewhere to go. Yer see, I'll be with the only woman in the world for me. That's me ma.'

Bob bustled in, fastening the buttons on his shirt-cuffs. 'I'll just run a comb through me hair, then I'm ready.'

Ruby turned her back on them to stand the fireguard in front of the hearth. 'Don't forget to take a key with yer.'

Bob didn't answer. He was too angry even to look at her. Once again she'd made him look a fool. What would his neighbours think when she wouldn't even forego a night with her so-called friends so he could go for a pint with a mate he hadn't seen for months? The answer to that was easy. They'd think he was crazy.

He jerked his head at Titch and the two men left the room without a word.

'Before we go in, let's get one thing straight. The drinks are on me tonight, so I don't want any argument. Next time, we'll all buy our own, but tonight is my treat.' Titch pushed the door of the saloon open and was greeted by voices from all sides. He was popular with everyone because he was so easygoing and friendly. His weatherbeaten face creased in a huge smile, he punched the air. 'Eighteen days I've got! Eighteen bloody days!' He leaned across the bar and grinned into the manager's face. 'Alec, by the time I go back yer'll be a rich man. I'll be skint, like, but you'll be laughing sacks.'

'Is that a solemn promise, Titch?' Alec kept his face straight. 'Can I give me notice in and look for a cottage in the country to buy for me and Betty?'

There was silence in the bar as men, some still wearing their cloth caps and overalls, listened in anticipation of a good belly laugh. 'Ay, hang about there, Alec,' Titch said, scratching his head and pretending to be deep in thought, 'if I had enough money to spend to make yer rich enough to buy a cottage in the country for you and your Betty, I might as well buy the bloody cottage meself! Mind you, I'd help yer out as much as I could. I'm quite prepared to take your Betty along with me.'

When the laughter had died down, Titch said, 'I'd be good to her, Alec, yer know that. I'm an old softie at heart. And think of the money yer'd save with one less mouth to feed. Yer'd be quids in, able to retire in no time. And then yer could come and lodge with us, in the cottage. I'd let yer have the spare bedroom, what's next to the one me and Betty will be sleeping in.'

The loud laughter and cheers brought Betty down from the living quarters over the pub. She saw Titch and nodded knowingly. 'I might have known it was the wanderer returned to the fold. It's good to see yer, me darling.'

'And it does me heart good to see you, sweetheart. But before I make the most important decision of me life, can I ask yer something?'

'Fire away, Titch.'

'When you make dumplings, are they as light as a feather?'

'Huh! Some hope! I wouldn't even know how to make the bleedin' things.'

Titch shook his head sadly at the man behind the bar. 'I'm sorry, mate, but the deal's off. What good is a cottage in the country, with roses around the door, cows in the field, buttercups in the meadow and Betty in the kitchen not making dumplings?' He sighed. 'Alec, give us three pints of bitter and I'll sit in the corner with me mates and we can cry in our beer. Yer see, I could tell by George and Bob's faces that they were all set to come to the cottage for their holidays. We've all been dealt a bitter blow, all because your wife can't cook.'

'Ay, yer cheeky bugger, I'll have yer know I'm a good cook.' Betty wagged a stiffened finger while giving her husband a sly kick on his shin. 'Alec will tell yer, he gets food fit for the King himself, don't yer, my heart's delight?'

Alec put the third pint on the counter. 'Anything yer say, dearest heart.' He held his hand out for the ten-bob note Titch was passing over the bar. Through gritted teeth, he growled, 'That bloody brainwave of yours about the cottage just cost me a bruised shinbone.'

Titch chuckled as he picked up the three glasses in his huge hands. 'Look on the bright side, Alec, it's always raining in the country. Yer wouldn't have liked it one little bit.' He spotted an empty corner. 'Come on, lads, let's get supping.'

Bob and George slipped behind the table and sat on the long wooden bench that ran along the wall, while Titch perched himself on a round stool. 'I don't half look forward to me first day home, yer know. Seeing me ma and finding her still as fit as a fiddle, and then meeting me mates for a few bevvies.' He lifted his glass, drank a third of the contents in one go, then wiped his mouth with the back of his hand. 'By, but I enjoyed that. This is the only country where yer can get a decent pint of beer.'

'Where did yer get to on yer travels this time, Titch?' George asked. 'Yer were away long enough to sail around the world.'

'We should have been home a month ago, but we ran into the worst weather I've ever known. There were times I thought I'd never set foot on dry land again. I've sailed through storms before and it's never really bothered me. But this was something else, I can tell yer. For four days and nights the ship was tossed around like a cork. She was built in 1893, the same year I was born, so she's been sailing for forty years. I honestly didn't think she'd stand up to the battering she got, I kept expecting her to break up. And to make things worse, we had a full cargo and the ropes keeping it in place broke, leaving the bloody lot to slide all over the place. We couldn't do a thing about it either, because it would have been suicidal for anyone to venture on deck to get to the hold. They'd have been washed away by waves that were higher than the ship. It was a ruddy nightmare, and one which I wouldn't like to repeat.' Titch saw the rapt expression on his friends' faces and grinned as he picked up his glass. 'Still, I've lived to tell the tale, haven't I?'

Bob shook his head, 'Rather you than me, mate. I feel seasick just thinking about it.'

'Nah, I've never been seasick. Green in the face, maybe, but never sick. Anyway, the old ship was badly damaged, and when we got to India it had to go in dry dock for repairs. That's why I've been away so long, but for God's sake don't tell me ma or she'll worry herself silly every minute I'm away.' Titch finished his pint off and nodded to his two mates to drink up. 'By the way, me ma wouldn't come with me tonight because she thinks I tell yer all about the girls I've got in every port. And the things I get up to that I wouldn't dare tell her about because she'd clock me one.'

George chuckled. 'Yer never say anything, but I bet yer don't go short.'

'I have me moments, George, but I'm choosey. In every port there's young girls and women hanging around outside the docks, hoping to make a few bob. But yer never know what yer could pick up off them. Some of the crew can't wait to get ashore and they'll go with anyone wearing a pair of knickers. But that's too risky for me, I'd rather do without.' Titch picked up the empty glasses. 'I'll get these filled up. I'm hoarse now with all the talking.'

Bob watched him walking to the bar, laughing and chatting to neighbours as he went. 'I can't make up me mind whether I envy him or not.'

George shook his head. 'It wouldn't suit me. I'm more than happy with me life as it is. I've got a job, which is more than can be said for some of the poor buggers around here. And I've got a loving wife and two fine children. I consider meself a rich man.'

And a lucky man, Bob thought. A very lucky man.

'Who's a rich man?' Titch asked, setting the glasses down carefully. 'Has someone come up on the pools?'

'I'd have a job, seeing as I don't do them,' George said. 'No, I was telling Bob I'm very content with me life. There's more ways of being rich than having money.'

'I should bloody well think yer would be content with a wife like Irene! She's got everything it takes to make a man happy, and she's a good mother. I'd even give up the sea if I could find someone like her.' Titch drank deeply, smacked his lips and wagged his head from side to side. 'There's nothing to beat the taste of draught bitter.' He looked across the table as he reached in his pocket for his pipe. 'How about you, Bob? Unless I'm very much mistaken, relations between you and Ruby seemed a bit strained tonight.'

Bob took a deep breath, then blew it out slowly. 'She'd try the patience of a saint, Titch, and that's putting it mild. Look at tonight, for instance. Wouldn't yer think she'd have offered to stay in and mind Lucy? But no, she's too selfish to put herself out. She's only going to see a mate, for God's sake, it's not as though she had something important on.'

Titch puffed until the tobacco caught, then threw the match in an ashtray. His eyes on his pipe, and his voice low, he asked, 'Have yer ever tried putting yer foot down with her?'

Bob was fed up pretending, there was no point in it. Besides, these two were his best mates. If he couldn't talk to them, who could he talk to? 'Apart from giving her the hiding that most husbands would have given her by now, I've tried everything. She's changed so much over the last few years I hardly know her any more. If I said she was as hard as nails, that would be being kind to her. I've tried coaxing, threats, even docking her housekeeping, but none of it has any effect. I just don't know what to do any more.

I'm at my wits' end. If it was only meself that suffered I wouldn't mind so much. But it's Lucy I'm concerned about. She's at an age now where she needs a motherly figure, someone she can confide in. She deserves that at least, 'cos she's a lovely kid.'

George had been listening with head bent. He was glad Titch had brought the subject up, it was something he'd wanted to do for ages. It was only because he was afraid of embarrassing Bob that he'd held back. 'I don't like to interfere between man and wife, but for Lucy's sake I will. She does need someone she can talk to. Someone who will explain how yer body changes when yer get in yer teens, and other facts of life. And with the best will in the world, Bob, I can't see Ruby being that someone. I think yer best bet is Irene. She's very fond of the lass, and they're getting to know each other now. She'd be the ideal person to answer questions and confide in. So if I were you I'd have a word with Lucy and encourage her to call into ours more often. Tell her she doesn't have to wait to be invited, like she is when she plays cards with the boys, but any time. Even if it's only a case of popping her head around the door, or staying for ten minutes. That way she'd get to know Irene better, and in time, come to trust her.'

Bob lowered his eyes. Once again Ruby had made him look like a weak fool – a man who couldn't even control the woman he married. Well, he might be weak, but he wasn't going to let his beloved daughter suffer for it. 'I appreciate all yer've said, George, and I'll do me best to see Lucy spends more time in your house. I do worry about her when I'm at work, yer know, she's never out of me thoughts.'

'By the way,' Titch said, 'I'm taking George's boys to first-house pictures tomorrow night and I said I'd ask Lucy to come, too. Is that all right with you?'

Bob's troubled face broke into a smile. 'I'll say it is! She'll be over the moon. And thanks. I might be unlucky in love, but I'm certainly not unlucky with me two mates. Ye're the best, bar none.'

Titch pushed his stool back and reached for the glasses. 'I'll get them in again. The rate we're going, we'll never get drunk tonight. And if I go home sober, me ma will think I'm sick and send for the doctor.'

Chapter Five

'Yer should never go out boozing when ye're on early shift.' Bob sat in the canteen with his elbows on the table and his head in his hand. 'It's nice when it's happening but yer don't half pay for it the next morning.'

'I don't know how yer can afford to go drinking through the week,' Billy Gleeson said, chewing on a sandwich. He was tall and thin, was Billy, with a long thin nose, pale blue eyes, and a mop of ginger hair. He had a sprinkling of freckles on his face right now, but come the summer he'd be covered in them. 'I know I couldn't. Saturday night, and that's me lot. I'm skint the rest of the week. The odd half-pint, maybe, if the wife's got any coppers to spare. But that doesn't happen very often and it's only enough to whet me whistle, certainly not enough to give me a hangover.'

'I wasn't spending me own money, Billy. Well, I mean, yer can't spend what yer haven't got, can yer? No, one of me mates, a neighbour, is a seafarer and he came home yesterday. It's been a ritual for years now, that the day he comes home he takes me and another mate out to celebrate. That's if I'm not on afternoons, of course. The trouble is, he can drink like a fish and thinks everyone's the same.'

'Is this bloke married?' Peg Butterworth asked. 'I could do with meeting a feller with a few bob to his name.'

'Peg, yer've already got a husband,' Billy reminded her, 'and three kids.'

'Yeah, a husband who never has a bean, and three kids

what are little buggers.' Peg could call her family fit to burn, which she often did in very colourful language. But let anyone else try and she'd marmalise them. 'Anyway, Billy Gleeson, mind yer own ruddy business, no one asked you to stick yer oar in. There's no harm in me asking Bob a question, even if it does look as though I'm not going to get a bleedin' answer.'

'No, he's not married, Peg,' Bob told her. 'And all the questions I know ye're going to ask, I'll answer in one go. He's tall, built like an ox, and I guess women would say he's very attractive. He's a nice bloke, and very generous.'

'Lead me to him. I've been looking for someone like him all me life.' When Peg smiled, it changed her face from being ordinary, to being easy on the eye. 'Tell him yer've got a mate in work who'd like to meet him.'

'D'yer want Bob to ask if he'd like to meet yer husband, as well?' Billy asked. 'And yer three children?'

'Oh, ye're there again, are yer, nose fever? I'd never get a bit on the side with you around, you old misery guts.' Peg turned to the woman sitting next to her. 'He's a right pain in the arse, isn't he, Elsie? A girl gets the chance of living it up for a change, and he has to go and put the blocks on it.'

Bob felt something brush over his foot, and after checking under the table, he looked across to where Kate was sitting. 'Eat up,' she said, 'it's nearly time to go back to work.'

He pulled a face. 'Me tummy's upset, I've no appetite.'

'Yer can't work on an empty stomach.' Kate had kept a friendly eye on him since the episode of the doorstep sandwich. He and Billy had sat at the women's table every day since, and the two seats on the bench were always left free for them. 'Yer'll feel better if yer get some food down yer.'

Bob smiled and took a sandwich from the box in front of him. 'If you say so.'

'I do say so,' Kate said, returning his smile. 'Anyway, how's yer daughter?'

Interest flared in Bob's eyes. 'She's fine. In fact, I bet at this moment she's got a big smile on her face. The bloke I've just been telling yer about, he's taking her to the pictures tonight, with the two lads from next door. She'll be like a cat on hot bricks all day, full of excitement. And it's her birthday next week, that's something else for her to look forward to.'

'Will she be having a party?'

Bob lowered his eyes. He was too ashamed to tell Kate his daughter had never had a birthday party in her life. 'No. Instead of a party I've promised to take her into town for a new coat. If I've any cash left, I'll treat her to tea in the Kardomah.'

'Oh, that's nice, she'll like that.' Kate looked puzzled. 'Will yer wife be going with yer?'

Bob raised his head and faced her. 'No, my wife will not be coming, Kate.'

'Don't tell me you two haven't made it up yet?'

Bob glanced at the others sat at the table, but they were too busy listening to Elsie Burgess telling them about a woman in her street who was getting her milk for nothing because she was having it off with the milkman. He sighed and turned his gaze back to Kate. 'Me and the wife are having a hard time, I'm afraid. We don't see eye to eye at all.'

'Oh dear, I'm sorry to hear that. It's not still over yer carry-out, is it?'

'No, nothing as trivial as that.' Bob met her eyes. 'It's a long story, Kate, and this isn't the place to tell it. Anyway, yer've probably got enough troubles of yer own without listening to mine.'

'Sometimes it helps to get things off yer chest. And I'm a good listener.'

'Another day, perhaps.'

There was a burst of loud laughter and both turned towards Elsie, who was still holding forth. 'I'm telling yer, it's the truth! Her feller comes out at half-seven, and the milkman goes in at eight. Yer can set yer alarm by them.'

'Come off it,' Peg Butterworth said. 'He probably goes to

every house in the bleedin' street! Yer can't tell me he's having it off with everyone, unless he's got the strength of a ruddy lion.'

'Yes, he does go to nearly every house in the street, I'll grant yer that. But he doesn't go inside every house and stay for half an hour, leaving his pony and trap outside. It's a dead give-away, that is. The stupid cow must think we were all born yesterday.'

'D'yer not think,' Billy said, his face straight, 'that ye're all being bad-minded? The poor bloke probably gets a cup of tea off her.'

That got Elsie on her high horse. The arms were folded and the bosom hitched. 'Well, you tell me how come the woman who lives opposite saw the milkman at the bedroom window? He wouldn't be going upstairs for a cup of tea, now, would he, smart arse?'

Peg's eyes were glinting wickedly. There was nothing she liked more than to get Elsie's dander up. 'Perhaps she'd asked him to fix the bedroom curtains or something. Or, she could have had a bad back and asked him to make the bed for her. And being an obliging man, he didn't like to refuse.'

'Oh, he's obliging all right.' Elsie's lips were a thin straight line. Here she was with a bit of juicy gossip, and they didn't believe her. 'And I suppose yer'll say the coalman is obliging as well?'

'What the hell has the coalman got to do with it?' Peg asked. 'Yer can't tell me he comes around at half-eight after the milkman's left?'

'Because she's bleedin' well having it off with him, too!' Elsie was getting to the state where she felt like clocking every one of them. 'Hers is the only house he goes in, and he's there for half an hour. Every Tuesday, like clockwork, he goes in with hands as black as the hobs of hell, and comes out with them snow white.'

'The simple answer to that, Elsie, is that the woman asks him to wash his hands before he makes the bed.' Billy was really enjoying himself, he thought it was hilarious. 'That's what anyone would think if they didn't have a bad mind.'

'What would yer say if I told yer that the milkman doesn't get no money, nor the coalman?' Elsie was red in the face by this time. 'I suppose yer'll say that apart from being very obliging and making her bed for her, the two bleedin' men are also very generous?'

Peg slapped her on the back. 'No, queen, we think it's the woman what's generous. I mean, everyone in your street can't be wrong, can they? But just out of curiosity, what film star does this generous woman look like? She must have plenty going for her, snaffling two men from under yer noses.'

'She's nothing to write home about, that's what we can't understand.' The bell rang to signal it was time to get back to their workbenches, and as she stood up, Elsie got her own back. But she made sure she wasn't standing too close to Peg when she added, 'She looks a lot like you, actually, now as I come to think about it.' Before her mate had time to digest her words, she took to her heels and legged it, with Peg in hot pursuit.

As they walked through the canteen door, Bob said, 'It's amazing what a good laugh can do, isn't it, Kate? I feel a helluva lot better than I did an hour ago.'

Kate grinned. 'I thought Elsie was going to burst a blood vessel when they were pulling her leg. She wanted to be dead serious and they wouldn't let her.'

'We still don't know whether the woman's a harlot or just a pleasant, friendly soul who likes giving out cups of tea.'

'I think that's the trouble. The whole street doesn't know what to make of it either.' Kate veered to the left when they came to the nut and bolt section. 'I'll see yer tomorrow, then, Bob.'

'Yeah, see yer tomorrow, Kate. Take care.'

Lucy sat at the table, her head bent as she chewed on the

over-toasted bread. She didn't look at her mother who was sitting in her favourite chair, smoking as usual. It was seldom you saw her without a cigarette these days, she was always puffing away like a chimney. But Lucy wasn't going to do or say anything that would bring on her temper. Today she wanted to go out to school without having to listen to a load of abuse. She was so excited about going to the pictures with Mr Titch and the boys, she wanted nothing to happen that would mar her happiness.

Ruby watched her daughter through a cloud of smoke. She's keeping her nose clean today, she thought. And well she might, with all the attention she was getting. New clothes, bought with money that should have come into the housekeeping purse, going in next door to play cards and be fussed over, even though she knew it was against her mother's wishes that she got matey with that crowd. And now, to top it all, Titch McBride was taking her to the pictures tonight. He'd spurned Ruby's offer of a cup of tea and a friendly chat and was rubbing salt in the wound by taking her daughter out. And all these things had been sanctioned by her dear husband. Well, there was little she could do to pay Bob back, but she could certainly make life unpleasant for his daughter.

Lucy lifted her head when she heard a chair on the opposite side of the table being pulled out, and her heart dropped when she found herself looking into her mother's face. Another five minutes and she'd have been away. Oh, why hadn't she put a move on and been out of the house by now?

'So ye're away gallivanting tonight, eh? Off to the pictures with the great Mr Titch. It's a fine life ye're having these days.'

'He's not only taking me, Jack and Greg are coming, too!' As Lucy picked up her plate, she told herself not to be drawn into an argument. That was what her mother wanted, she could tell by the glint in her eyes. But she couldn't not stick up for someone who was a friend and always good to her. 'I think it's nice of him to take us, so there!' With that, Lucy marched out to the kitchen and put her plate down. The sooner she was out of the house the better. Her mother wouldn't be able to pick on her tonight because her dad would be in.

But Lucy hadn't reckoned on Ruby's burning desire to take her spite out on someone. And the only person available was her daughter. So she waited until the girl was putting her coat on in the hall, with her back to her. Then, silently creeping up behind her, she put her hand up Lucy's dress, and with thumb and forefinger, pinched the flesh at the top of the girl's leg as hard as she could.

Tears welled up in Lucy's eyes. 'Stop it, ye're hurting me!'

'That, you little faggot, is the general idea.' With an evil look in her eyes, Ruby spun the frightened girl around and pressed her face close. 'And that's one place yer won't be showing yer dad, isn't it?'

Lucy made a dash for the front door. When it was open, and freedom at hand, she dared to looked back. The pain, the injustice and the sadness in her heart, gave her the courage to cry out, 'Mothers are supposed to love their children, but you don't love me, you hate me!'

'Are yer putting yer best dress on, pet?'

'Yeah, we can't let the side down, can we?' Although she didn't feel like smiling, Lucy managed one for her dad. He looked so happy for her she didn't want to spoil it. How different it would be if he could see the inside of the top of her leg. There was a big ugly bruise there, and the skin had been broken where her mother's nails had dug in. It hurt like anything when she walked and her two legs rubbed together. And she'd been in pain all day, sitting on a hard bench at school and wishing there was someone she could ask for help without fear of them getting in touch with her dad. 'I'll go and get changed now so I'll be ready in time.'

'It would be nice if yer had a new coat, but it can't be helped. Tell Mr Titch ye're getting one next week for yer birthday, and yer'll be a proper swank then.'

'Now if I told him that, I would be swanking, wouldn't I? The boys would think I was showing off and they'd skit me.' Lucy blew him a kiss before leaving the room to go upstairs. She was on the third stair when she heard her dad speak.

'You could take a brush to her old coat while she's upstairs and try and make it look a bit respectable,' Bob said. 'The lads from next door will be well turned out, Irene will make sure of that. I wouldn't have to ask if yer showed some interest in yer daughter's appearance.'

'She's big enough to brush her own flamin' coat,' Ruby said. 'She'll be wanting a maid next, the way she's getting spoilt.'

Lucy jumped down the stairs and went back into the living room. 'I'll brush me own coat, Dad.'

'Yer mam will do it, it'll only take five minutes.'

'Dad, I'd rather do it meself, honest. I don't want me mam doing it for me.'

Bob looked puzzled at Lucy's tone. 'Are you all right, pet? Yer mam hasn't been shouting at yer, has she?'

'No, it's just that I'd rather do it meself. I've got plenty of time, so I'll have a good go at it when I come down.'

'Oh well, if that's what yer want.' But Bob wasn't completely satisfied, and as soon as Lucy was out of earshot, he glared at his wife. 'Have you been upsetting her? It wouldn't surprise me in the least, it's just the sort of thing yer would do.'

'In the name of God, I only saw the girl for half an hour this morning!' Ruby was so good at telling lies, she didn't even blush. 'You've been home since she got in from school, mollycoddling her, as usual.'

With that, Bob had to be content. But if he could have seen his daughter at that moment he would have gone berserk. The cuts on the top of Lucy's leg were bleeding with the constant rubbing, and she didn't know what to do. Even if she had a bandage it would be no good because the wound was in an awkward place and a bandage wouldn't stay up. She sat on the side of her bed wondering what to do. There was no one she could talk to, so she'd have to think of something herself. How crafty her mother had been, knowing her daughter was far too shy to show anyone what she'd done.

Lucy rested her elbows on her knees and cupped her face in her hands. If the bleeding got worse, it would run down her leg and everyone would see it. And she'd die of shame if that happened. Besides, it would ruin her new dress, and that would be terrible. She racked her brains but couldn't think of anything she could do without help. Then, just when she was about to give up, thinking there was no answer to her plight, she suddenly had a brainwave. She jumped from the bed and crossed to the small chest of drawers. Her old knickers were in there and unless she was much mistaken, the pins would still be in them. Her prayers were answered and she clutched the washed-out knickers to her chest. If she could make a pad out of one of the pairs, she could use the two pins to pin them to the knickers she was wearing and the elastic in the leg would help keep the pad in place. Then came disillusionment when she realised the knickers were far too big to make a pad. But the feeling of hopelessness didn't last long, because she was determined not to be beaten. That would mean her mother had won, and she couldn't let that happen. So she began pulling at the seams of the material and found it ripped easily, being so old and well worn. And five minutes later, with the pad in place and easing the pain, Lucy was smiling as she pulled her best dress over her head.

'Who's a clever girl, then?' she asked herself in a low voice, feeling very proud of her achievement. 'Yer can do anything if yer try hard enough.'

But as she skipped lightly down the stairs, Lucy knew that no matter how hard she tried, she would never forgive her mother for what she had done today.

* * *

Bob stood outside the Pollards' house with Irene and George, waiting to wave Titch and his young friends off. 'There's about fifteen pubs between here and the picturehouse,' George reminded him. 'D'yer think yer can resist the temptation?'

'I've got a blindfold in me pocket.' A huge grin covered the weatherbeaten face. Titch wouldn't admit it, but he was as excited as the children. They were doing him a favour, not the other way around. 'When we get to the top of the street I'm going to put it on and the kids can lead me.'

'I'll lead yer, Mr Titch,' Lucy said, her hand held tight in his. 'I won't let yer walk into no lamp-post.'

'And me and Greg will make sure yer don't walk into a pub by accident,' Jack said with his usual deadpan face. 'We'll put a hand over yer nose when we pass one so yer won't be tempted.'

Titch shook his head at Irene and the two fathers. 'Yer had no need to train them, yer know. I got all the instructions off me ma, this afternoon. I'm not allowed to smoke, drink or use bad language. But she gave me permission to breathe, I'm happy to say.' He squeezed Lucy's hand. 'Come on, let's go, or we'll miss the shorts. I hope Laurel and Hardy are on, they're me favourites.'

When they reached the top of the street they all turned around for one last wave. 'They'll worry themselves sick until ye're home again,' Titch said. 'I don't think they trust me, having no family of me own.'

'Even when ye're grown up, do parents still tell yer what to do?' Jack asked, walking on Lucy's other side. 'If they do, there's not much point in growing up, is there?'

'A mother stays a mother all of her life. You might grow up and change, but she never will. She'll always love yer and worry about yer. But yer've got one consolation when ye're grown up, son – yer don't get a clip around the ear if yer don't do what she says.'

'I can't wait to be grown up.' The words were out before Lucy could stop them. 'And my mam doesn't have to worry about me, 'cos I'll be able to look after meself.'

Titch kept his voice casual. 'I'm sure you don't get many clips around the ear off your mam, do yer?'

It was Greg who answered. 'Yeah, she does. Her mam's always clouting her and bawling at her. We can hear it in our house.' He saw the warning glance his brother gave him, but ignored it. 'I'm glad she's not my mam.'

Lucy could feel the colour rise from her neck to cover her face. 'She doesn't hit me no more, me dad told her she hadn't got to.'

'I should jolly well hope she doesn't.' Titch bit on his bottom lip. Out of the mouths of babes comes the truth, he thought. 'If she ever tries to hit yer again, sweetheart, run like blazes out of the house and wait for yer dad to come home.'

'She can always run to ours,' Jack said. 'Me mam would look after her.' He leaned forward and looked past Lucy to catch Titch's eye. 'Me mam always wanted a daughter, yer know. She told us that before each of us was born, everything she knitted was in pink. And of course she couldn't throw it away, so we had to wear the stuff. I've been told I was dressed like a girl until I was two years of age.'

'Ye're not the only one,' Greg told him. 'I was, too! Me mam said she was sure the second baby would be a girl, she didn't think she could be unlucky twice. Me dad used to pull our leg soft about it, didn't he, Jack? He said people used to pop their head around the pram hood and say, "Oh, isn't she lovely, what have yer called her?" '

Titch roared with laughter. 'Your mam wouldn't swap you two for a dozen girls. She loves every hair on yer heads and every bone in yer bodies.'

'Yea, we know that.' Jack stroked his chin thoughtfully. 'Mind you, a dozen girls would be quite a temptation. Six I'd feel safe with, but twelve would have me worried. I believe she'd give the matter careful consideration.'

'Go 'way, soft lad,' Lucy said, not quite used to Jack's dry sense of humour. 'Your mam wouldn't swap you for all the rice in China.' Her brow furrowed. 'Or should it be all the tea in China? I forget.'

'Both commodities are plentiful in China, sweetheart, so either will do.' Titch looked down into a pair of bright green eyes set in a heart-shaped face framed by a mass of dark curly hair. How, he asked himself, could any mother not love this girl? Ruby obviously didn't or she wouldn't hurt her. 'I believe there's two special treats coming up next week, eh? One of yer is having a birthday and the other leaving school. Now which is which?'

Lucy giggled, bringing a smile to all three faces. 'It's me having a birthday, I'll be twelve years of age. I'll change over with Jack if he likes, 'cos I wish it was me leaving school.'

'Fat chance of that!' Jack said, stretching to his full height. 'I've been waiting fourteen years for this.'

'I'm included in these treats, Mr Titch.' Greg gave him a broad wink. 'I've got a brother what's leaving school, going into long kecks, getting himself a job and giving me thruppence a week pocket money.'

'Some hope you've got, soft lad,' Jack said. 'If yer behave yerself I might give yer a penny, and then yer'll have to clean me shoes to get it.'

They reached the cinema entrance and Titch let go of Lucy's hand to delve in his pocket for the ticket money. 'What's it to be? Front stalls, back stalls, the circle or up in the gods?'

'Can we go in the front stalls, please?' Greg asked. 'If we sit at the back, it would be just my luck to sit behind a big fat woman with a hat on.'

'And don't forget the ostrich feather,' Jack said. 'If she's got a hat on, it's bound to have a flipping big ostrich feather sticking up on it.'

'The front stalls it is.' Titch was chuckling to himself as he paid for the tickets. It was a long time since he'd enjoyed himself so much. Then he crossed the foyer to the kiosk where there was a lady selling sweets. 'What would yer like? How about fruit pastilles?' Three eager faces nodded, and Titch gave the order to the assistant. 'Three packets of pastilles and one packet of jelly babies, please.' As he waited for his change, he spied the three children giving each other looks. 'The jelly babies are for me, they're me favourites.'

'Ooh, I like jelly babies,' Lucy said. 'They're my favourites too.'

'And mine!' Greg gave his brother a dig in the ribs. 'And they're yours, as well, so why don't yer open yer mouth?'

'I know,' Jack said, looking sheepish. 'But I thought jelly babies were like marbles. You parted company with them when yer left school.'

'Not on your life! If yer like something, yer don't stop liking it just because ye're getting older.' Titch remembered what his mother had told him, and added, 'Except for playing marbles, of course. I mean, can yer imagine me kneeling in the gutter? I'd look a right nit.' He turned back to the kiosk where the woman was standing with a smile on her face and three packets of jelly babies in her hand. 'I'm sorry to be a nuisance,' he said as they did a swap, 'but they might as well have what they want.'

'Don't worry about it, just enjoy the picture.'

'I'm going next door to wait for Lucy.'

Ruby looked up from the paper she was reading. 'My God, d'yer think the wind might have blown on her?'

Bob walked out without answering. He was weary of all the slanging matches and the arguing. The only way to cope with it, and stay sane, was to ignore it. It didn't seem to worry Ruby, she thrived on it.

Irene opened the door and the welcoming smile on her face had Bob comparing her to the woman he'd just left. He shouldn't compare them, he knew, but the whole atmosphere was so different it was hard not to. This house was in a different world to the one next door.

'I was just going to put the kettle on, so yer've timed it nicely.' She held the door wide. 'The gang should be home any time now.'

'It's to be hoped Titch hasn't taken on more than he can chew.' Bob raised a hand in salute to George. 'Taking three children to the pictures could turn out to be a headache.'

'Don't you kid yerself,' George laughed. 'He'll have a whale of a time with them. He's so good with children, it's a pity he hasn't any of his own.'

They heard the laughter and chattering before the knock came. 'What did I tell yer?' George said, as Irene went to open the door. 'I bet they've had the time of their lives.'

The three children ran in, all trying to get through the door at the same time. Their faces were alive with excitement and eagerness to tell what a marvellous time they'd had. Lucy made straight for her father and sat on his knee. 'I've never enjoyed meself so much, Dad. It's been wonderful.'

He hugged her close. 'I'm glad, pet. In fact, I'm jealous because Titch didn't take me along with yer. I could have put a pair of short kecks on and pretended I was only twelve.'

'Yer'd never have got away with it, Dad. Anyone can see ye're at least fourteen. But yer didn't half miss a treat.'

Titch stood inside the door and viewed the scene with warmth in his heart. Lucy's pretty face was animated as her words poured out. And Irene was standing with an arm around each of the boys' shoulders, listening as they vied with each other to be first to tell all they'd seen and done. There was so much talking going on, George couldn't keep track of it all, so he clapped his hands and called a halt.

'Can we have a bit of hush, please? Now, seeing as yer've had such a good time, don't yer think the least yer can do is show a few manners to the man who made it possible, by asking him to sit down?'

The children were immediately contrite, and three pairs of

willing hands led Titch to the couch. 'I'm sorry, Mr Titch,' Lucy said, 'but yer gave us such a good time I couldn't wait to tell me dad about it.'

'Yeah,' said Jack. 'If me head hadn't been up in the air I wouldn't have forgot me manners and yer'd have had a cup of tea in yer hand by now. So yer see, Mr Titch, what it boils down to is, ye're a victim of yer own generosity.'

Greg looked at his brother with narrowed eyes. 'Ye're showing off, you are, with yer fancy words. There'll be no living with yer when yer start work. We'll have to get a dictionary out every time yer open yer gob.' He gave Titch a broad smile. 'I'm not as clever as him, so I'll just say it was the gear, and thank you very much.' He started to walk away, then changed his mind. 'I'll pay yer back when I'm older. I'll take yer to the pub on the corner for a pint.'

'I'll hold her to that, son.' Titch laughed heartily. 'I'll be walking with a stick by then, like, but, please God, I'll still be able to lift a pint glass.'

'Aye, look at the time,' Irene said. 'It's nine o'clock and time yer were in bed.'

There were groans from the two boys. 'Ah, ay, Mam, we've got loads to tell yer.'

'Do as yer mam says,' George told them. 'Don't argue with her.'

Irene saw the three young faces drop. 'Yer can tell us everything, from beginning to end, tomorrow night. But right now, I'll let each of yer say what one thing sticks in yer mind the most. Lucy, you can go first.'

'Oh, that's an easy one. Laurel and Hardy were on, and Mr Titch laughed so much he had to hold his tummy. And he had tears rolling down his cheeks.'

George roared. 'Still a kid at heart, eh, Titch?'

'Yer don't have to be a kid to enjoy Laurel and Hardy,' Titch said. 'I think they're the best, bar none.'

'Your turn now, Greg,' Irene said, her eyes on the clock. 'And don't make a meal of it, either.'

'I'll talk fifteen to the dozen, eh, Mam?' Greg moved to the other side of his mother. 'I'm getting out of Lucy's way in case she belts me one. Yer see, the big picture was a sad one. And every time Janet Gaynor cried, Lucy cried. And when she wasn't crying, she had her eyes shut tight. Yet when we came out of the picturehouse, she said it was a lovely film.' He shook his head as though it was a mystery to him. 'How is it, that girls are never happy unless they've got something to cry about.'

'Nobody answer that,' Irene warned. 'Now, Jack, it's your turn.'

'I'm telling tales out of school now,' Jack said, 'but yer could have knocked me over with a feather when Mr Titch bought himself a packet of jelly babies.'

The laughter that piece of information brought was loud and long. And it would have continued if Irene hadn't taken the boys by the scruff of their necks and pointed them to the door. 'Up those stairs, now!'

Jack's eyes slid sideways, 'Mam, if yer strangle me, yer won't only be losing yer lovely son, yer know. Yer'll be losing the wages I'd have been earning if yer hadn't strangled me.'

'And if yer strangle me,' squeaked Greg, 'I'd be losing the pocket money he'd have given me if yer hadn't strangled both of us.'

Her eyes showing her love for them, Irene hugged them close and kissed them. 'If I ever kill yer, it'll be with love. Now, behave yerselves and get up to bed.'

The boys stood in front of Titch and thanked him again. 'If yer were a girl,' Jack said, 'then I would most definitely give yer a kiss.'

'Oh, don't start that again, our kid,' Greg pulled on his arm, 'or we'll have our dad after us.'

As the boys clattered noisily up the stairs, Bob moved Lucy from his knee and stood up. 'Those two boys of yours are real cases,' he said. 'Sharp as a razor, both of them.'

'I know someone who's a match for them, eh, Lucy?' Titch chucked her under the chin. 'She had them fair flummoxed at times, I can tell yer. With her looking so shy, and speaking in such a matter-of-fact voice, they don't know whether she knows she's being funny, or not. But between the three of them, they made tonight very special for me. They were a treat to take out.'

Lucy bent down and kissed his cheek. 'Thank you, Mr Titch.'

'Come on, pet,' Bob took her hand, 'yer'll never get up in the morning.'

'Come back when Lucy's in bed,' George said. 'We can have a good natter.'

'That's a good idea, it'll round the day off for me.' Titch started to push himself up from the couch. 'I'll nip down to the corner and get a few bottles.'

He was thrown back on the couch before he knew what was happening, and Irene was standing over him. 'Oh, no yer don't, Titch McBride. For one night in yer life yer can do without knocking the brown stuff back. Yer can make do with a cup of tea like the rest of us, and one of me home-made scones. So put that in yer pipe and smoke it.'

'What! I wouldn't dream of putting one of yer home-made scones in me pipe and smoking it. Not when it was made by those fair hands of yours.'

George was watching Lucy and could see her eyes becoming heavy. 'Take the lass home, Bob, before she falls asleep on her feet. She's had enough excitement for one day. Titch will still be here when yer get back, Irene will see to that. If he makes one move, she'll sit on him.'

His grin reaching from ear to ear, Titch held his arms wide. 'Oh, yes, please.'

[illegible]

Lucy sat down [illegible] the table. [illegible]

[illegible]

[illegible] a good [illegible]

[illegible]

[illegible]

[illegible]

Oh, yes, please.

Chapter Six

'What sort of time is this for her to be coming in?' Ruby had been listening to the noise coming through the wall, and with each burst of laughter her temper had grown. 'She'll get used to all this fussing and yer'll never do anything with her – she'll expect it all the time.'

Bob didn't answer, but his eyes spoke volumes. He took Lucy's coat from her and said, 'I'll hang this up, pet, you'd better run down the yard before yer go to bed.'

'Yeah, I think I better had.' Lucy was glad to get away from the room and her mother's spiteful tongue. There were no hugs for me from a loving mother, she thought. Mine couldn't even ask me if I'd had a nice time. Still, she can't take my memories of tonight away from me, that's one thing. I can lie in bed and go over it all again, relishing every second.

Inside the house, Ruby wasn't to be silenced. 'Did yer hear what I said? It's too late for her to be out. She should have been in bed an hour ago.'

'Yer didn't think of that the night yer left her on her own until nearly half-past ten, did yer? But I don't suppose that counts, seeing as you were out enjoying yerself.' Bob shook his head in disgust. 'It's hard to believe that a grown woman could be jealous of her own daughter. You never take her out because, apart from the fact yer can't be bothered, it might cost yer a few pennies, and yer need them to keep up with yer boozing friends. Yet yer don't like it when someone else gives her what you should be giving her. And that's a little love and attention.' He heard Lucy running up the yard and pointed a warning finger. 'One word out of place to her, and by God, yer'll be sorry.'

'I'll go straight up, Dad, I'm dead tired.' Lucy gave her father a kiss and left the room without a glance at the woman who had given birth to her. She didn't act like a mother, Lucy's sore leg reminded her of that, so she wasn't going to treat her like one. But no matter how brave the words were that were running through her mind, in her heart she was hurt and sad. Why didn't her mother love her like Mrs Pollard loved her boys? She wasn't a bad girl, she'd done her best to make her mother love her. If she did, this house would be as happy as next door, and that would be wonderful. And her dad wouldn't have that sad look she sometimes glimpsed in his eyes when he thought she wasn't looking.

Lucy climbed into bed and pulled the clothes up to her chin. She was very tired and it wasn't long before she could feel herself drifting into slumber. And as she did, there was a smile on her face as a picture flashed through her mind of Mr Titch biting the head off a green jelly baby.

Bob stood aside while Billy Gleeson slithered along the bench in the canteen, then he sat on his usual end seat. 'It doesn't seem like twenty-four hours, does it, Kate? I've never known the time to go so fast. It's just flown over.'

'I remember when I was about fifteen, me mam heard me saying I wished I was seventeen and able to go to dances. She gave me a lecture, saying I should make the most of my teenage years, because when I got to twenty-one the years would fly over.' Kate smiled. 'She was right, too, although I didn't believe her at the time. But twenty-two years have gone by since then and I've hardly noticed them passing. It's frightening when yer think about it.'

'Go 'way, ye're still a young woman,' Bob said. 'A mere slip of a girl.'

Billy had had his ear cocked. 'He's flattering yer, Kate, yer want to keep yer eye on him. I knew yer never should have given him that fairy cake.'

'It's not very often anyone flatters me, Billy, so I'm going to make the most of it. Just think what would have happened if I'd given him *two* cakes! Me head would be twice the size. I think when I go home I'll tear me birth certificate up, then when I'm feeling weary I can tell meself I'm only twenty-one. There'll be nothing to prove otherwise.'

'Only that yer'll still feel weary,' Billy said, tapping the side of his long nose. 'Yer body's the one thing yer can't fool. I should know because I feel every day of me thirty years.'

Bob chuckled. 'Yer've lost fifteen years somewhere along the way, Billy.'

'That's only first thing in the morning, mate. I wake up as spritely as a spring chicken, ready to take on the world. But by the time I've bent down to put me shoes on, then try to straighten up again, those fifteen years let me know they're still there.' He cocked an ear. 'Ay out, let's listen to this.'

'Hey, Elsie,' Peg Butterworth spoke through a mouthful of corned beef sandwich. 'Any more news from that house of ill-repute? The one where the woman's having it off with the milkman and the coalman? At least, according to everyone in your street she is.'

Elsie's eyes slewed sideways to see if Peg was making fun of her. But her mate's face was dead straight. 'Not everyone, Peg, there's one silly cow who won't hear of it. Mind you, the tight-fisted bitch is making a few coppers out of it, so she's bound to believe what she wants to believe. It's in her best interest, isn't it?'

Peg put her buttie down and swivelled her bottom round. 'Ye're not going to tell me she stands at the door and charges the men? And then afterwards the two women split the dosh between them? Well, that takes the biscuit, that does. What sort of a street d'yer live in, girl?'

'Don't be so bleedin' stupid, Peg Butterworth, of course

she doesn't stand at the door taking money. There'd be a lynch mob out if she did that. Besides, she's a sneaky thing, she doesn't do anything in the open, it's all underhanded.'

'I know I'm a fool for asking,' Peg said, 'but I wouldn't get a wink of sleep if I didn't. How does this sneaky, under-handed woman make money out of the carryings-on of one of her neighbours?' Then Peg banged a closed fist on the table. 'I've got it! The men pay her money to keep her mouth shut. I'm right, aren't I?'

'Are yer hell,' Elsie said. 'Ye're miles out! She doesn't get no money off the men, she gets it from the horse.'

Disbelief showed on all faces for a few seconds, then laughter broke out. 'Elsie, ye're a real case,' Billy chuckled. 'Yer had us going for a minute.'

'I'm not pulling yer legs, it's the truth,' Elsie said, a smug smile on her face. She'd teach them not to make fun of her. 'She makes money out of the horse.'

'I've got it!' Once again Peg banged the table. 'While the milkman's in the house, doing you know what, this sneaky woman gives people rides in the trap and charges them. That's it, isn't it?'

'Ye're not even warm.' Oh, how Elsie was enjoying being the centre of attention. 'I know,' said another workmate, Ada Smithson, 'she lets the kids stroke the horse and charges them a ha'penny.'

'Ye're not even close.' Elsie's face was now wearing a haughty expression. She was going to milk this situation for all it was worth. 'Try again.'

'Not on yer life,' Peg said. 'Ye're taking us for suckers. There's no way she can make money out of the horse.'

'Yes, there is, so there,' Elsie snapped.

Peg was equally determined. 'And I say there isn't.'

'There is, and don't you call me a bleedin' liar, either, or I'll clock yer one.'

'Yer'll have to prove it, 'cos I don't believe yer.'

Those sitting at the table looked as though they were

watching a tennis match, as their heads moved from Peg to Elsie. And when it looked as though Elsie wasn't going to deliver the goods, Billy chipped in, 'Go on, Elsie, put us out of our misery. We're all on edge, waiting for yer to solve the mystery. How can she make money out of the horse?'

'Manure.' Elsie was still wearing her haughty face. 'That's what.'

Nine voices spoke in unison. '*Manure?*'

Elsie folded her arms and looked down her nose. 'Are yez so ignorant yer don't know what manure is?'

'We know what it is, Elsie, but I don't think we quite understand the connection.' Billy decided to see if a bit of soft soap would work. 'Ye're very good at telling a tale, girl, yer have a way with words. Why don't yer fill the picture in for us? You know, every little detail, so we can see it all in our minds.'

Elsie smiled. That was more like it. Not before time they were beginning to appreciate her. 'Well, this money-grabbing little cow's name is Flo Durning. She's small, as thin as a rake and as miserable as bloody sin. Yer never see her without a mobcap on and a pinny with a big pocket in. She's got beady little eyes, and believe me she doesn't miss a trick. If she's not standing at the door, taking all in, then she's peeping behind her curtains. There's not a thing goes on in our street that she doesn't know about. In fact, she knows about it before it bleedin' happens.' Elsie glanced around the faces. 'Are yer with me so far?'

Peg Butterworth tapped her on the arm. 'Yer did that beautiful, girl. I can see the little squirt as if she was standing in front of me. Now, carry on.'

Elsie beamed. That was praise indeed from her mate. 'Well, now we'll go to the horse. It's a dark brown one, with a patch of white on its face. The milkman, Taffy, he's got it well trained, I'll say that for him. When he says "Wait", then wait it does. And after about ten minutes, out comes droopy drawers, Flo, with a bucket and shovel. And sure enough, the flaming horse obliges and she shovels the manure up as soon as it hits the ground. In the bucket it goes, then the queer one makes a dash for her house with it. Honest to God, can yer imagine what her house smells like? Anyway, down the back entry she scarpers, and sells it to a bloke in the next street what's got an allotment. Tuppence a bucket she charges him, the crafty cow.'

'Well, I'll be blowed.' In repose, Peg's mouth was far too big, it stretched the full width of her face. But when she was animated and smiling, it did wonders for her appearance and drew eyes like a magnet. 'They're an enterprising lot in your street, I must say. Not only do they give the neighbours plenty to talk about, they make a few bob into the bargain.'

'Ay, yer can cut that out for a start,' said Elsie, looking as suitably outraged as she thought the occasion warranted. 'We're not all tarred with the same brush.'

'Only because the milkman wouldn't have the energy to cover the whole street, and the horse will only oblige once a morning.'

'Are you insulting what I think yer are, Peg Butterworth?'

'All I'm saying is, chance is a fine thing. And before yer get on yer high horse and tell me ye're going to knock me block off, just remember I'm bigger than you. You might have the weight, but that can be a disadvantage in a fight. So think on before yer take yer false teeth out and put yer boxing gloves on.'

Elsie's eyes and mouth opened wide. 'Ay, you, ye're asking for it, you are. Yer know bleedin' well I don't wear no false teeth!'

Bob was grinning as he turned to face Kate. 'Are they always like this, at each other's throat?'

Kate nodded. 'All the time. But they've never come to blows yet. In fact, they're the best of mates. If one of them is in trouble, the other is always there to help out.'

'Thank God for that! For one horrible moment I thought either me or Billy would have to be referee and stand between them. I wouldn't fancy that, not with the weight Elsie's carrying. One blow from her and I'd be knocked into the middle of next week.'

'No fear of that, she's as soft as a brush, is Elsie. If yer told her yer neighbour's cat had been run over, she'd cry her eyes out.' Kate gave a quick glance to make sure no one was listening. 'As yer know, Peg can tell a good story. And last time we were on the early shift she went to the pictures. The film was a real weepy by all accounts and she had Elsie in floods of tears, telling her all the sad parts and really piling the agony on. Then when she'd finished, she handed over a piece of cloth for Elsie to dry her eyes on. "Seeing as yer won't need to go and see it now, girl, I think yer should pay me what it would have cost yer. I won't charge yer the tram fare, though, seeing as ye're me mate." That soon put a stop to Elsie's tears. "Yer know what you can do, Peg Butterworth," she said, "yer can just sod off." '

Bob chuckled. 'It sounds something like the picture Lucy went to see last night. By all accounts she cried all the way through it, and then at the end said it was a lovely film. The two boys from next door pulled her leg soft.'

'I was going to ask yer how she got on. Did she enjoy herself?'

'They all had the time of their lives. Especially Titch, the bloke who took them. He said it was a real eye-opener, just listening to them. The boys have inherited their mother's sense of humour and he said the wisecracks out of them had him in stitches. And he surprised me over Lucy. He said she was as quick off the mark as they were and had an answer for them every time.' There was a trace of sadness in Bob's smile. 'Who she inherited that from I don't know, because no one could say I'm the life and soul of the party. And her mother certainly isn't.'

'Oh, come off it, Bob! Listening to you anyone would think yer were a real misery guts. Yer've got as much sense of humour as the next man, so don't be running yerself down.'

If Bob had spoken his thoughts, he would have said his life over the last few years had robbed him of any humour he might have had. Instead, he said, 'Oh, I can laugh at other people's jokes, but I'm no good at telling them meself.'

'You're as bad as me, then. My husband used to laugh when I tried telling jokes, because I always told the end bit first. So I gave it up as a bad job.'

'He must have been very young when he died?' Bob asked the question before giving it any thought. When he saw Kate's hazel eyes cloud over, he cursed himself for being so insensitive. 'I'm sorry, I shouldn't have said that. I've upset yer now.'

'The people who say time is a great healer don't know what they're talking about. It's five years now since Vic died, but it still hurts like hell. There isn't a day goes by that I don't miss him because there's so much to remind me of him. Oh, I've gone past expecting him to walk through the door, and I've got used to his favourite chair being empty. But our daughter, Charlotte, is the spitting image of him and a constant reminder.'

'And then yer've got thoughtless people like yours truly. I really could kick meself, Kate, for being so stupid.'

They hadn't heard the bell, and Bob was startled when Billy clamped a hand on his shoulder. 'It's time to move, mate, but before we do, let us in on the secret. What have yer done that's so stupid yer could kick yerself?'

Once again Kate came to the rescue. 'Don't tell him, Bob, or he'll want one.'

Billy was intrigued. 'Want one what?'

'Ye're a nosy bugger, Billy.' By now, Bob had sorted his head out. 'But since I know yer'll keep at me until I tell yer, it's a fairy cake. I've been promising to bring one in for Kate, and blow me if I don't keep forgetting.'

'A likely tale,' Billy snorted. 'Come on, shift yerself.'

'If I forget again tomorrow, Kate, yer have my permission to kick me.' Bob winked. 'See yer.'

'Yeah, see yer, Bob.' Kate picked up her carry-out box and put it under her arm. Then she smiled and called after him, 'I'm not very good at kicking, so I'll get Elsie to do it for me.'

'Come on, Ma, let's go into town and I'll buy yer something.' Titch faced his mother across the table. 'We can go to Blackler's and have a look around – yer like it there.'

'There's nothing I need, son,' Aggie said. 'And there's no use buying something just for the sake of it. That would be a waste of good money.'

'Ma, if I'm going to waste me money, there's no one else in the world I would rather waste it on. I haven't even bought yer a drink yet.'

'Buying me drinks would be money down the bleedin' drain. I'm quite happy with me half-pint of stout every night, suits me down to the ground. It's nice and smooth and puts me in the mood for a good night's sleep.' Aggie had a thought. 'Ay, Irene's going into town to buy some long trousers for Jack – why don't yer go with her? It would save yer hanging around the house twiddling yer thumbs.'

'Oh, aye,' Titch laughed. 'George would love me taking his wife out. And we'd be the talk of every wash-house in the neighbourhood.'

'Not if I was with yer.'

'Yer've just said yer didn't want to go into town!'

'What I said was, I didn't want yer spending money on me just for the sake of it. But I wouldn't mind going around the shops with Irene, in fact I'd be made up. Me and her get on like a house on fire, and she's always good for a laugh.'

'Well, that's settled then.'

Aggie tutted. 'It's not settled, son. Not until we've asked Irene if she minds us going with her. I'm sure she won't mind, but it's manners to ask.'

'You'll have to do the asking, Ma, I wouldn't have the nerve.'

'Oh, my God!' Aggie threw her hands in the air. 'A girl in

every port he tells me, but he's shy with a woman's he known for nigh on twenty years.'

Titch grinned. 'I steer clear of married women, Ma, they're not on me list. Yer see, I'm not a good runner.'

Aggie pushed herself up from the chair and studied her reflection in the mirror over the mantelpiece. 'I'll nip up and have a word with her. If it's all right, I'll have to do something to titivate meself up. I can't go out with me son looking like an old hag.'

'Ye're still a fine-looking woman, Ma, and I'd be proud to have yer on me arm even if yer were dressed in a sack. And people would still think yer were me wife, not me mother.'

'Ye're full of flattery, Titch McBride. It's no wonder yer've got a list of girlfriends as long as me arm. But I'm a bit too long in the tooth to fall for such blarney.' Aggie cupped his face and planted a noisy kiss on his lips. 'While I'm out, be a good lad and wash these few dishes for me.'

Irene was drying her hands on a towel when she opened the door. Her face lit up, as it always did when she set eyes on one of her favourite people. 'I've just finished doing the spuds ready for tonight. Save me worrying meself to death while I'm out. Come on in, sunshine, yer don't have to wait to be asked.'

Aggie brushed past and walked into the living room which, as usual, was shining like a new pin. 'I came to see if yer felt like some company on yer shopping trip?'

Irene reached into the kitchen to hang the towel on a nail behind the door. 'I'd be highly honoured to have yer, Aggie. It would be company for me and yer can help me choose Jack's trousers. Then if he doesn't like them, I can put the blame on you.'

'How d'yer fancy Titch's company, as well?'

Irene's eyes widened. 'Your Titch, coming round the shops? I don't believe it, he'd be bored out of his mind.'

'That's for him to find out, girl,' Aggie chuckled. 'He wanted to take me, anyway, to buy me something. Yer know what he's like when he's got money, it burns a hole in his pocket. So I thought it would be nice if we all went together.'

'It's fine by me, Aggie – as I said, I'd be glad of company. But I can't for the life of me see Titch enjoying himself. George only ever came to the shops with me once, and he said blow that for a lark, he'd rather do a hard day's graft.' Her pretty face smiled at a memory almost forgotten. 'He was buying me a dress for me birthday, and the first one the assistant in TJ's brought out, he said, "That's nice, we'll take it." I hated it – it was a dark muddy-brown colour and dead old-fashioned. There was no way I was going to settle for that! And half an hour later, after I'd tried six on, George was nearly spitting feathers. But I was determined. It wasn't often I got new clothes, and I wasn't going to settle for something I didn't like. So I dragged him from TJ's to Blackler's. The third one I tried on there was a smasher, I really loved it. My dear husband was so impatient when the woman was wrapping it, I swore it was the last time I'd take him shopping with me. I didn't have time to tell him that, mind, because once outside the shop he told me straight: "Don't ever ask me again, love, it's a mug's game." '

'Shopping is a mug's game, girl, same as washing and housework. And women are the mugs what have to bleedin' do it. If it was left to the men the houses would stink and no one would eat. And I've said all along, if it was men what had to have babies, the human race would have died out thousands of years ago. Still, we can call our men fit to burn, but we wouldn't be without them, and that's a fact.'

Irene glanced at the clock and pulled a face. 'We'll have to hurry 'cos I've got to be back for the boys. Go and tell Titch he's very welcome to join us, but on his own head be it. If he starts getting restless and grumbles, I'll put him over me knee and smack his backside good and proper.'

'That's not a threat, girl, it's a bleedin' promise. And I'll not be passing the message on 'cos I know what a devil me son can be at times. Anyway, can yer give me fifteen minutes to doll meself up a bit? Give us a knock and we'll be ready.'

'They're a good strong pair, girl, he'd get plenty of wear out of them,' Aggie said as she fingered the dark grey material. 'A sensible colour, too.'

The assistant at Blackler's hovered behind the counter. 'Are you sure you have the right inside leg measurement, Madam?'

Irene nodded. 'Twenty-nine inside leg, thirty-two waist. He's only fourteen, but he's tall for his age.' She cast a critical eye over the trousers again. 'How much did yer say these were, sunshine?'

'Five and elevenpence, Madam, and they're a good buy. He'll get years of wear out of them.'

'Not if he keeps on growing at the rate he is.' Far from being bored, Titch was enjoying himself. 'He's going to be a six-footer, without a doubt.'

The assistant gave him one of her best smiles. 'He will if he takes after his dad. If you don't mind me saying so, you're well above average height.' She had them down as man and wife, with a mother in tow, and looked surprised when they all burst out laughing. 'Have I said something wrong?'

'Yer've only married me off to me best friend's wife.' Titch was tickled pink. 'Look, yer've got her blushing.'

'Take no notice of him, sunshine,' Irene said, 'I've always got rosy cheeks. It would take more than that to make me blush.' She took three two-bob pieces from her purse. 'Do I pay you?'

'I'll have to call the supervisor over. I'm new here, so I'm not allowed to make receipts out on my own. I'll call her over.'

But Miss Simpson, the supervisor, had been keeping an eagle eye on her new recruit and raised a hand to say she was on her way over. 'Can I help you, Miss Marsh?'

'The lady wishes to purchase these trousers, Miss Simpson, and I need to make out a receipt.'

Vera Simpson was weighing Titch up and down as she walked to stand behind the counter. She liked what she saw, and directed her smile at him. 'I'm sorry to keep you waiting, sir, but Miss Marsh is new and has to be supervised.'

'That's all right, my dear.' Titch could feel his tummy rumbling with laughter. 'My wife and I are not in too much of a hurry.'

Aggie chuckled, Irene turned her head away and the new assistant bit on her bottom lip. As for Miss Simpson, she was telling herself it was just her luck. The only men worth having were already married. Still, she'd keep on trying, otherwise she'd be left on the shelf. And the prospect of being a spinster, living on her own with only a cat for company, was one that didn't appeal to her at all.

The trio waited until they were outside before letting the laughter free. 'Oh dear, oh dear, oh dear!' Aggie wiped her eyes with the back of her hand. 'Yer could have had yerself a click there, son, if yer hadn't been married.'

'She was too stuck-up for my liking, Ma. I'd have to be on me best behaviour all the time and watch me language. Did yer see the way she looked down her nose at poor Miss Marsh? Blimey, she doesn't half think she's the whole cheese.'

Irene's shoulders were shaking as she dropped the change in her purse. 'Do they send yer to prison in this country for bigamy? I don't think my feller would be too happy, he certainly wouldn't come and see me on visiting day.'

'Well, we've had a good laugh, haven't we?' Titch said. 'And Jack's got a nice pair of kecks, so everyone's happy.'

'He needs another pair for a change, but I couldn't afford two pair in one go. So if yer've got a day free next week, yer can both come with me. It doesn't hurt so much parting with money when ye're enjoying yerself.'

Titch looked at his watch. 'Yer've got bags of time, it's only two o'clock. Let's go to Reece's for a cuppa and a cake. Eh, what say yer?'

Irene shook her head. 'No, I can't afford it, Titch, and I'm not sponging off you. Yer paid me tram fare, and that's enough.'

'In the name of God, Irene, can't yer let a friend mug yer?' Aggie said. 'I could do with a cuppa and a sitdown, me legs are not as young as they used to be.'

Irene tutted. 'Aggie McBride, I've seen yer scarpering up our street like a two-year-old. Yer can run faster than me, so don't be making that an excuse.'

Titch wagged a finger. 'My ma always taught me never to argue with someone older than meself, it's not good manners. So if she says she's got old legs, then we've got no option but to agree with her.' He put an open hand to the side of his mouth and in a loud whisper, said, 'Even though she climbs our stairs three at a time.'

Irene gave in. 'Okay, if you insist. I'll have a cup of tea, but no cake.'

At the time, Irene meant it. But when Titch ordered a selection of cream cakes, her mouth started to water. 'That's not fair, that. Definitely hitting below the belt. Aggie knows I can't resist cream cakes, that's why I'm so fat.'

'Not fat, Irene, bonny.' Titch handed her the plate. 'The chocolate eclair looks very inviting. And you can have the cream horn, Ma, I know yer've got a weakness for them.'

'Ye're right there, son. What I say is, sod me bleedin' figure.'

'My sentiments exactly.' There was a look of pure bliss on Irene's face when she bit into the eclair and the cream oozed out of the sides. This was a rare treat and she intended to savour it. 'Ye're spoiling me, Titch McBride. My feller won't be able to do a thing with me after this high living.'

Aggie was thoughtful as she nibbled the end of the horn. 'Is it next Friday your Jack leaves school?'

'Yeah. He's already told me he'll wear his short trousers until he goes to bed, then Saturday morning he wants to wear his new ones. So expect a knock on yer door 'cos he'll be doing the rounds, showing off.'

'And it's Lucy's birthday on the Saturday, isn't it?'

Irene licked her fingers before answering. 'Yeah, I'll have to get her a card and a little present of some kind. If me money runs to it, I'd like to get her a nice underskirt. I don't think she's got one, 'cos when she wears her new dress yer can see right through it.'

'You get one, and I'll go half with yer.' Aggie turned to her son who was exchanging smiles with a girl at the next table. 'Ay, you, buggerlugs, behave yerself. There's only two things ever on yer mind . . . beer and women. That's all yer think about.'

Not in the least put out, Titch grinned. 'Ah, be fair now, Ma. Yer know very well that you come before the beer and women.'

'In that case, put yer eyes back in yer head and listen to me. Yer said yer wanted to buy me something, and I've just thought of the very thing.'

'Just name it, Ma, your wish is my command.'

'To celebrate Lucy's birthday, and Jack leaving school, I'd like to have a little tea-party for the youngsters. Just Jack and Greg, and Lucy can invite her friend, Rhoda. That's if you'll fork out for the food.'

'Ma, that's the best idea yer've had since I came home.' Titch looked chuffed. 'That wouldn't be money down the drain, would it? But why can't the grown-ups come, as well? I'm not going to be left out, that's for sure, and yer can't leave the others out.'

'Can I butt in?' Irene asked. 'I think yer should have a word with Bob first. I'm sure they won't be having a party for Lucy, and I know she'd be delighted if you had one for her. But yer couldn't invite Bob without Ruby, not if me and George are there.'

'That's no problem – we'll ask Ruby!' Titch looked to his mother. 'That's all right with you, isn't it, Ma?'

'My idea was a children's party, son, but you seem to have

taken over. I don't mind, though, the more the merrier. And while I don't like Ruby Mellor, I agree that yer couldn't ask Bob and not her. So you go ahead and make the arrangements, seeing as ye're forking out for it. But I don't want the children to know, I want it to be a surprise. And I'm determined about that, so woe betide anyone who lets the bleedin' cat out of the bag.'

'My lips are sealed,' Irene said.

Titch squeezed his mother's hand. 'My lips are not sealed, Ma, but I'll be very careful what comes out of them. Especially after I've had a few jars.'

'Which is only every bleedin' night.' The tenderness in Aggie's eyes belied her words. 'Yer'll end up with a big red conk and a beer belly, mark my words.'

'Nah, there's no chance of that. And when I pack the sea in, I'll change me ways. It'll be you and me, Ma, down to the pub every night, just before closing-time, for a pint of stout. And I'll carry the jug – save yer hiding it under that shawl of yours.'

'Who's been telling tales out of school?'

'Don't look at me, Aggie,' Irene said. 'I've never said a word.'

'Nobody's been telling tales. It was Alec what mentioned it, and it was a compliment. He said yer might not be his biggest-spending customer, but ye're definitely his most regular.'

'He won't get rich on what I spend, son, but you make up the shortfall when ye're home. He must rub his hands in glee when he knows yer ship's docked.'

'Ye're right there, Ma. He really gave me down the banks for being away so long this time. He said our captain had no consideration for folk like him what are trying to make an honest living.'

Aggie gasped. 'He never did!'

Titch grinned. 'No, Ma, he never did.'

★ ★ ★

Bob stood outside the confectioner's window and gazed at the cakes on display. He spied what he was looking for and smiled when he saw the sign which said they were three for twopence. He could just about manage that.

The bell behind the door tinkled when he pushed it open, and the sound brought a young assistant through from a back room. Her grin told of a sunny disposition and her voice was friendly. 'What can I get for yer that takes yer fancy?'

'There's a lot of things I fancy, love, but me pocket tells me I can only afford three fairy cakes.'

'Well, that's better than a kick in the teeth.' The girl tugged a white bag from a hook and reached into the window. 'Beats a drippin' buttie, any day.'

'You sound on top of the world,' Bob said. 'Are yer always so cheerful?'

'I try to be. People don't want to be served by someone with a face as long as a fiddle, it only makes them miserable. Mind you, I have a hard time on a Monday. Me face refuses to smile and I can't get a joke past me lips. I've tried giving them a good talking to, but they're not having any. So Monday is misery day.' She folded the top of the bag over and placed it on the glass-topped counter. 'I make up for it on the other days, though, and try to spread a little happiness. I make sure that not one person goes out of this shop without a smile on their face.'

She took Bob's sixpence and opened a drawer for his change. 'There yer go, a thruppenny joey and a penny.' Then, as though she could no longer hold it in, she said, 'I'm very happy today because I've got a date tonight.'

'Ah, yer've got a boyfriend?'

'He's not me boyfriend yet, but I'm hoping he will be after tonight. Yer see, I've had me eye on him for months. I couldn't believe me luck when he asked me for a date 'cos all the girls in our street are after him. He's not half handsome.'

Bob smiled at her openness. 'Keep that smile on yer face,

love, and yer'll bowl him over. The other girls won't be in the meg specks.'

'Ooh, I hope ye're right. Next time yer come in, I'll let yer know how I got on.'

Bob waved as he passed the window. She seemed a nice kid and he wished her luck. But it was doubtful she'd ever see him again. That was the first time in his adult life that he'd been in a cakeshop, and it would probably be his last. Now he could repay Kate, there would be no need to.

Chapter Seven

'You go on ahead, Billy, I'll catch yer up,' Bob said. 'I've got to get something out of me coat pocket.' With his carry-out box under his arm, he made haste to the cloakroom. They only got three-quarters of an hour dinner break, so every minute was precious. And he was concerned about the fairy cakes that had been left in the bag in his pocket since he'd bought them the day before. They'd probably be a mass of crumbs by now with his luck. But he couldn't let Ruby see them or there'd have been ructions. He could almost hear her shrill voice shouting that she couldn't afford the luxury of cakes on the money he gave her, but he could find it for his mates all right. He'd never have heard the last of it.

Bob breathed a sigh of relief when he opened the bag and found that the sponge cakes, in their crinkly white paper cases, appeared to be in one piece. Thank goodness for that, he thought, hurrying to the canteen where, even from this distance, he could hear Peg giving forth on the joys of motherhood. 'What a night I had with those blinking kids of mine. They just wouldn't go to sleep even though I promised them a ha'penny each to buy bull's eyes on their way to school. Three times I was up to them, but even a clip round the ear wouldn't shut them up. Mind you, I couldn't hit them hard because I was too tired and didn't have the bleedin' strength to knock them out.'

Elsie, her dimpled elbows leaning on the table, glanced sideways. 'What did yer do in the end, girl?'

'Threatened to send them to the bleedin' Cottage Homes, that's what. It shut them up all right, but the trouble was I was wide awake by then, and in a right temper, I can tell yer. Not with the kids, but with my feller. Here was me, in and out of bed like a bleedin' yo-yo, and he was away to the world. Sleeping like a baby, he was, without a care in the world. That's until I kicked him out of bed, like.'

Ada Smithson gasped. 'Yer never did, did yer?'

'With both feet, Ada.' Peg nodded slowly. 'And on his way to the floor he banged his head on the tallboy and didn't know what the bloody hell had hit him 'cos he was seeing stars. When he came to, he said, "What the hell did yer do that for, yer stupid cow?" I told him it was for making something and not looking after it. He scrambled to his feet and stood at the side of the bed. "What the hell are yer on about, woman? It's nearly one o'clock in the morning, a fine time to be kicking me out of bed and telling me I've made something and not looked after it." '

'Well, he had a point there, girl,' Elsie said. 'My feller would have marmalised me if I'd done that. Whatever it is he made and doesn't look after, it would have waited for another time, surely? It can't be that important.'

'Ah well, yer see, Elsie, the timing was perfect. As I told him, he'd made the kids, so it was his job to look after them. And in future, he could take a turn in getting out of bed to shut them up.' Peg put her buttie down and pinched the bridge of her nose. 'But d'yer know what? He looked so comical standing there in his long johns and short shirt, with this surprised look on his clock, I couldn't help but laugh.'

'Ooh, ay, he wouldn't like that, I bet.' Ada was small, thin, and downtrodden. Her husband was built like an ox and a bully to boot. She was completely dominated by him; he only had to open his mouth and she jumped. She was afraid to look sideways, never mind laughing at him. 'Was he as mad as hell?'

Peg chuckled. 'He was at first. Called me for everything

and his language was choice. But when he climbed into bed, he said, "Well, yer've woke me up now, so I may as well make something else for yer to look after." '

Billy joined in the laughter before saying, 'All in all, Peg, there was a lot going on in your house last night. Yer were busier than Lime Street Station.'

'Yeah, it was all go, Billy. But isn't it surprising how yer can be tired one minute, and full of energy the next? My feller's no oil painting, but he can be very passionate when he's in the mood. And in the dark I can make believe he's me heart throb, Tyrone Power. So, all-in-all, the night had a happy ending and I went to sleep with a smile on me face.'

'Yer must have a bleedin' good imagination,' Elsie snorted, ''cos your feller doesn't look a bit like Tyrone Power. Even if yer met the pair of them together, down an entry on a dark night, yer couldn't make that mistake.'

'I wouldn't want to, smart arse.' Peg's hackles rose. 'I'm quite content with my feller the way he is. At least he's not cross-eyed, like some poor buggers.'

Elsie hitched her bosom until it was nearly touching her chin. 'I hope ye're not insinuating that my feller's cross-eyed?'

'I'm not saying anything, not a dickie-bird. Except,' Peg waved a hand casually, 'if the cap fits, wear it.'

Bob raised his brows at Kate. 'Elsie's husband doesn't squint, does he?'

Kate smiled as she shook her head. 'When will yer learn not to believe a word Peg or Elsie say? They make these things up for something to talk about. I'll bet any money that Peg was in bed sound asleep at half ten last night, and it wasn't the kids that woke her, it was the alarm clock. Elsie goes along with her for a laugh, and yer've got to admit they do brighten things up.'

Billy closed the hinged lid of his carry-out box and moved it so he could rest his elbows on the table. 'The truth is, Peg's husband is nicer-looking than Tyrone Power. He's a good bloke, too, and a ruddy good husband. As for Elsie's feller, he's as quiet as a mouse. The most easygoing man yer'll ever meet. He never gets in a temper or raises his voice. She calls him Tiger, but he's a tiger that never roars.'

'How d'yer know all this, Billy?' Bob asked.

'Well, I don't live far from them, do I? And I meet them in the pub now and again on a Saturday night, when I take my one out for a drink. And yer can take it from me, after a few jars, Peg and Elsie have the pub up. I think the landlord should give them their drinks free, because they're more entertaining than going to the flicks.'

'I'm afraid I can't think of anything to make yer laugh, Billy, but will a fairy cake do instead?' Bob tore the bag open and pushed it across to Kate. 'Ladies first.'

'Ooh, lovely!' Kate picked one with pink icing on the top. 'Yer shouldn't have bothered, but thanks all the same.'

Billy licked his lips. 'I'll have the lemon one.'

Elsie's eyes never missed a trick, and they didn't miss this. 'Ay, Bob Mellor, yer lousy nit! What have they got that we haven't?'

Bob shrugged his shoulders and held out his open palms. 'Sorry, Elsie, but I'm not made of money. If I was I'd have mugged all of yer to cream cakes.'

'Aye, and pigs might fly.' Elsie reached down into her bag and brought out a small parcel wrapped in newspaper. With a jerk of her head, and a quivering of her bosom, she placed it on the table. 'Well, smarty pants, ye're not the only one with a surprise. I've brought one as well.'

Peg was intrigued. 'I love surprises, girl. What is it?'

'Guess.'

'Give us a clue, then. Can yer eat it?'

Elsie's whole body shook with laughter. 'Aye, I suppose yer could. But yer'd have to be bleedin' hungry, though.'

'Oh, I've lost interest now,' Peg said. 'If yer can't eat it, it's not much good to us.' Then her mouth widened. 'I know, yer've brought yer false teeth.'

Now Elsie, who was the proud possessor of healthy white teeth, got on her high horse. 'Ye're too clever for yer own bleedin' good, you are, Mrs Know-it-all. Well, for your information, that,' she pointed to the parcel, 'is me proof.'

Interest flared in Peg's eyes. 'Proof of what?'

'What I've been telling yer about the goings-on in our street. None of yer would believe me, so I've brought yer proof.'

'Yer milkman must be very small if he fits in that,' Billy laughed. 'Mind you, he might have worn himself down to that size.'

'Ho, ho, ho, very funny.' Elsie rolled her eyes upwards. 'None of yer have got an ounce of bleedin' sense in yer heads.'

'Well, it certainly ain't the horse,' Peg said. 'Unless yer've brought a piece of his tail.'

'Near enough.' Elsie's expression was haughty. 'It's a piece of his manure.'

Faces showed their horror as mouths stopped chewing and sandwiches were whipped from the table. 'You filthy cow!' Peg moved as far away from her friend as she could. 'What the hell d'yer think ye're messing at? Yer've put us all off our food now.' She pointed to the offending parcel. 'Get that filth out to the toilet and flush it down the pan.'

Her face as innocent as a baby's, Elsie said, 'Oh, yer can't flush coal down the lavvy, girl, it'll block it up. Yer own common sense should tell yer that.'

Silence reigned as Peg held her head in her hands. 'And to think I bleedin' well fell for it. Me what's known yer all these years, and I fell for a trick like that. I want me head testing.'

Kate grinned across at Bob. 'See what I mean?'

'I certainly do. From now on I'll take everything they say with a pinch of salt.'

Billy was chuckling. 'It was dead funny, though, wasn't it? Mind you, I'm glad I'd eaten that cake. Somehow manure and cake just don't go together.'

★ ★ ★

Titch was standing at the front door when Bob came down the street. 'Just the man I've been waiting for. Can yer come in for a few minutes, Bob?'

'Yeah, sure,' Bob said, following him into the house. 'I've no heavy date on, me diary is empty.'

Aggie grinned when she saw him. 'Are yer bragging or complaining, Bob?'

'Neither, Aggie. I've got no social life to brag about and complaining doesn't get yer anywhere.'

'Well, sit down, son, and make yerself at home. I want to ask yer something, and I hope ye're agreeable. As yer know, young Jack leaves school a week today, and the day after it's Lucy's birthday. I was wondering if yer'd let me have a little party for them? Just the two Pollard boys and Lucy and her friend, Rhoda. I'd be tickled pink to do it, so I hope yer'll agree and make an old lady happy.'

Bob looked at Titch and winked. 'Who's the old lady she's on about?'

'Whenever me ma wants anything, she piles the years on to get sympathy. Yer'd better humour her or she'll bawl her eyes out.'

'I think it's a cracking idea and I know Lucy would be thrilled to bits. But wouldn't yer be putting yerself to a lot of trouble and expense?'

Aggie's eyes were twinkling. 'It wouldn't be any trouble, it would be a pleasure. And my beloved son is footing the bill. He wanted to buy me something, and I said the thing I'd like best would be to see the kids enjoying themselves. Irene knows, but I've asked her not to tell the boys yet. I want it to be a surprise. So, can Lucy come?'

'Of course she can. I think it's very kind of yer and yer have my thanks.'

'Good.' Aggie sat back in her rocking chair and rested her clasped hands on her lap. 'Now Titch has got something to say.'

Bob feigned surprise. 'Let me guess. He's getting married.'

'If the day ever comes when I tell yer I'm getting wed, that's the day yer'll know I've lost me marbles. And I want yer to promise yer'll send for the men in white coats and have me certified insane,' Titch said, crossing his long legs. 'Anyway, back to business. I don't see why the kids should have all the fun. So I've suggested asking Irene and George, and you and Ruby. How does that strike yer?'

'It's fine by me, I'd be delighted to come. But I can't speak for Ruby, I'm afraid.'

'Will you ask her? Or d'yer think it would be better coming from me or me ma? A secondhand invitation isn't very polite, is it? She might be put out if she thought we couldn't be bothered asking her.'

'It's up to you, but yer know what Ruby's like. I'll mention it to her when I go in, then by the time you ask her, she'll have had time to think about it.'

'You do that, son,' Aggie said. 'Then I'll make a point of giving her a knock tomorrow. But don't forget, I don't want Lucy to know.'

'I won't breathe a word.' Bob stood up. 'Yer've been very kind to Lucy over the years, and don't think I haven't noticed or appreciated it.'

'It would be hard not to like or be kind to her, Bob,' Aggie told him. 'She's a little angel, is Lucy, and yer should be proud of her.'

'Oh, I am, Aggie, make no mistake about that. She makes my life worth living.' Bob headed for the door. 'I'll get home now and have a word with Ruby before Lucy gets in from school. Will we see yer in the pub tomorrow night?'

'Not me,' Titch said. 'I'm going into town for a night out with some of me mates off the ship. We usually do a round of the pubs, so I'll probably roll home in the early hours of the morning.'

'Well, enjoy yerself. I'll see yer, Aggie.'

'Ta-ra, Bob, see yer tomorrow.'

* * *

As Bob let himself in, he wondered what his wife's reception would be to the invitation. She couldn't stand the neighbours, but that was nothing new. Ruby hadn't a good word to say about anyone. Except her mates, of course. Invisible mates Bob had heard plenty about, but never seen.

'Ye're late today. I had a pot of tea made for yer and it'll be cold by now.' Ruby planned to be pleasant from now on. The week after next she should start getting the extra five bob back in her housekeeping, so it was in her interest to keep her nose clean. 'I'll make yer a fresh brew.'

There was a surprised look on Bob's face as he watched her walk through to the kitchen. She seemed to be in a happy frame of mind today. Usually he didn't even get an acknowledgement, never mind the offer of a fresh pot of tea. Perhaps she'd come round to thinking he was right, and life would be much easier if they could at least be polite with each other. He hoped so, for everyone's sake.

Ruby came through from the kitchen with two cups and saucers. As she set them on the table, she said, 'It won't be long, I'll just let it mash for a few minutes.'

'There's no hurry.' Bob flopped into his chair and stretched his legs. He was never going to get her in a better mood, so perhaps now was a good time to say what he had to. 'I've been talking to Titch and Aggie, and they've invited us up there next Saturday.' He saw her face change and went on quickly before she had time to say anything: 'Aggie's having a little celebration tea-party for Jack's leaving school, and as it's Lucy's birthday, she asked if we'd let her go. And her friend, Rhoda. I said yes, of course, because I know Lucy would be over the moon.'

Ruby huffed. 'I'm not going to no kids' tea-party, so yer can forget it.'

'We haven't been invited to the tea-party.' Bob was determined not to lose his patience. 'Titch wants us to go along later, with Irene and George.'

'Oh, I might have known the queer one would be in on it. It wouldn't be a bleedin' show without Punch.'

Bob's sigh was deep. 'Ruby, you are my wife and we've been invited as a married couple. Can we not, for once, act like one? I'm asking you to come for my sake, and for Lucy's. Remember, it's our daughter's birthday. Let's not spoil it for her.'

'Oh no, we mustn't do anything to spoil Lucy's day. It doesn't matter about what *I* want as long as she's happy. Well, I'll not set foot over the door of any of them to please her or anyone else. I don't want to go, and I'm not going. That's all there is to it.'

'Then we'll have the birthday party here and invite our friends and neighbours. If you don't want to go to them, I'll bring them to you.' Bob knew there was no possibility of this, but he wanted to shake his wife into some sort of action.

Ruby looked at him as though he'd gone mad. 'Some hope you've got. If yer think I'm going to run around after that lot, yer've got another think coming.' Then that hard-boiled look came to her face. 'And where d'yer think the money's coming from for yer grand idea?'

'I wouldn't be able to get Lucy's coat for her birthday, she'd have to wait a few more weeks.' Bob saw the flash of anger in her eyes and knew his words had hit the mark. 'She wouldn't be upset – she'd rather have a party.'

You sly bugger, Ruby was thinking. That's my five bob a week you're talking about. My extra ciggie and beer money. But she wasn't going to give in so easily, she'd give him a run for his money. 'Anyway, they wouldn't miss me if I didn't go because they don't really want me. If they did they'd have asked me themselves, instead of making you the messenger boy. You go on yer own and they won't even know I'm not there.'

'Not true! Aggie's coming down tomorrow to ask yer. Oh, and don't forget, Lucy's not to be told.'

Ruby was blazing inside. If she made a big deal out of it

and refused point blank to go, she'd be cutting off her nose to spite her face. It would take Bob at least six weeks to save up the money for Lucy's coat, and that meant being the poor relation amongst her friends for all that time. Having one drink to their two, and waiting for them to offer her a cigarette because she didn't have enough to go round. So even though she couldn't stand the thought of spending a couple of hours in the company of the Pollards and the McBrides, the alternative was even worse. There was five bob a week at stake here, and for that money she'd sup with the devil himself if need be. But she had one more try to turn things in her favour. 'Why can't we all go to the pub? It would be a damn sight more lively than sitting in the McBrides' twiddling our fingers.'

'Because Irene won't go to the pub and Aggie wouldn't dream of leaving her out. Besides, they've been good enough to ask us and it would be an insult to refuse. So it's up to you. We accept their invitation or we ask them here.' Bob could read her like a book and knew he was on safe ground. Otherwise he'd never have mentioned it because he wouldn't let Lucy down for the world. She'd been looking forward so much to getting a new coat. 'I could tell them you would like to have your daughter's party in her own house, and they are welcome to come.'

'Oh, I'll go with yer, then, because I'm not having them here, that's a dead cert. But I'm going under duress, and if there's any snide remarks or dirty looks, I'll be out of that house like a shot. I won't stay around to be insulted.'

'Ruby, yer ask for everything yer get. If you're not pleasant with people, yer can't expect them to fawn over yer. Give a smile and yer'll get one back. Crack a joke and yer'll get one back. Give a sneer or a dirty look, and that's what yer'll get back. Life is what yer make it, but your trouble is, yer can't be bothered. If there's nothing in it for you, then yer don't want to know.'

'I've said I'll go, so there's no need for a lecture. And I'd better see to that tea, it'll be stiff by now. I'll add more boiling water to it 'cos I can't afford to throw another pot away.'

Bob cocked an ear. 'Here's Lucy. Remember, not a word.'

There was a half-smile on Ruby's face as she struck a match under the kettle. The silly bugger thinks he's got one over on me, and I'm going to be the dutiful little wife. If that makes him happy, then let him get on with it. When next Saturday comes I might just be feeling sick with a bad headache or an upset tummy. And if that doesn't work – well, what the hell. A couple of hours of misery won't kill me. I'll just think of the weeks ahead when I'm in the money and can doll meself up and go out and really enjoy meself.

She could hear Bob talking to Lucy, and her smile turned into a full one as an idea came into her head. This is where I put on me act as the dutiful wife and mother, she thought, and I can't wait to see their faces. Popping her head around the kitchen door, and her smile still intact, she said, 'There's a pot of tea made, Lucy, would yer like a cup?'

Lucy's surprised expression turned to one of suspicion. She never ever got a smile off her mother, and the offer of a cup of tea was unheard of. There had to be a catch in it somewhere. 'I'll have one if me dad's having one,' she said cautiously.

'Of course he's having one, I made it for him.'

'I was just saying she looks pale today,' Bob said. 'She's got no colour in her cheeks and her eyes look dull.'

Ruby threw a brief glance at her daughter. 'She looks all right to me.'

'I am all right, Dad, honest! I don't know why me face is pale, 'cos I feel the same as I always do.'

But Bob wasn't convinced. He'd got a hug and a smile off his daughter when she came in, but he'd noticed the smile didn't reach her eyes. 'I think yer might be sickening for something, so to be on the safe side yer can take a Beecham's Powder before yer go to bed.'

'Ah, ay, Dad! I promised Rhoda I'd play out with her until dinner was ready. Just for half an hour, please?'

When those large green eyes looked so appealing, he didn't have the heart to refuse. 'Okay, after yer've had a cup of tea. But remember, it's a Beecham's before yer go to bed.'

Lucy looked to make sure her mother was in the kitchen before throwing her arms around his neck. 'I love you, Dad.'

'And I love you, pet, more than yer'll ever know.'

Lucy stretched her arms wide. 'As much as this?'

'Oh, much more than that.' Bob smiled. 'Run around the world twice, and that's how much I love yer.'

A sparkle appeared briefly in Lucy's eyes. 'If I ran around the world twice, Dad, there'd be nothing left of me for yer to love.'

Ruby carried two cups of tea through and set them on the table. 'Come and sit here and drink it, it's too hot to hold in yer hands.'

Lucy blew on the piping hot tea, wishing she dared ask for more milk to cool it down. 'I can't drink any more, Dad, I've had enough. Can I go out now?'

'Yeah, okay, we'll give yer a shout when dinner's ready.'

She was near the front door when Lucy heard her mother's voice. 'I've told yer, ye're making a rod for yer own back, spoiling her like that.'

And she heard her dad answer, 'It's my back, Ruby, not yours.'

Lucy sighed as she jumped down the step, right into the path of Jack and Greg.

'Hey, watch where ye're going, yer nearly sent us flying,' Jack said, securing the football under his arm. 'Where are yer going in such a hurry?'

'I'm not in a hurry, I just jumped off the step, that's all. I can't see around corners, clever clogs.' Lucy nodded to the ball. 'I see ye're off for a game of footie.'

'He's making the most of it,' Greg said, chuckling. 'Me mam said that this time next week, footie will be a thing of the past. And marbles and kick-the-can. It'll be long kecks, hair combed and flattened down with sugar and water, a tie when he's going out, and mind yer manners if yer please.'

Lucy grinned. 'It'll be worth it when he's got money jingling in his pocket.'

'Yeah, too true.' Jack gave his brother a dig. 'And before yer start making cracks when I put me long kecks on, just remember yer penny pocket money is at stake.'

'Blimey, what I've got to do to get this penny is nobody's business. I've got to polish his shoes and run any messages he wants. I haven't got to laugh when he's got his long kecks on in case he thinks I'm laughing at him, which means on top of everything else I've got to lose me sense of humour, as well.' Greg appealed to Lucy. 'Be fair, now, don't yer think all that is worth more than a miserly penny?'

'Oh, I'm not taking sides, Greg, that wouldn't be right. But when Jack sees how well yer polish his shoes, I'm sure he'll think it's worth tuppence.' Lucy wanted to be on her way, there was something she had to do. 'I'll have to go, or Rhoda will think I'm not coming. Enjoy yer game of footie, but don't break any windows.'

She waited until the boys reached the end of the street, then went to stand in front of their house. She was nervous, and biting her fingernails. But Mrs Pollard had told her to knock if she ever needed help, and right now Lucy was desperate to talk to someone. And she'd never get another chance like this. The boys were out and Mr Pollard wouldn't be home from work until six o'clock. Plucking up courage, she knocked on the door.

'Hello, sunshine.' Irene's smile was welcoming to the frightened girl. 'Come in.'

Lucy stood by the table in the living room, wondering how to start. 'Yer said I could come to yer if I needed anything, Mrs Pollard, so yer don't mind, do yer?'

'Of course not, sunshine, sit down.' Irene's heart went out to the girl who had a look of fear in her eyes. Her voice gentle, she coaxed, 'Come on, out with it. Whatever it is will remain a secret between the two of us, I promise.'

'I've got a sore at the top of me leg and it's getting worse. I don't want to tell me mam, and I can't show it to me dad because of where it is. So I wondered if yer'd look at it for me and tell me what to do to make it better.'

'Is that all! Come on, don't be shy, show it to me.'

When Lucy lifted her dress and took away the dirty pad, Irene gasped. There were large bruise marks which had now faded to a pale blue and yellow, but there were two slits in the skin which were oozing a yellow pus. And in the pus were bits of navy-blue fleece from the piece of knickers. 'In the name of God, sunshine, how did yer do that?'

Lucy dropped her head. 'One of the girls in school did it in the playground.'

'Good God! Did yer tell the teacher? Yer should have done and she'd have cleaned it up for yer and put a dressing on.'

'I didn't want to get the girl into trouble.'

Irene closed her eyes and tried to calm her rising temper. Lucy was telling lies, and she wasn't very good at it. 'Come into the kitchen and I'll bathe it in warm water. I've got some antiseptic ointment we can put on, and I've got lint and plasters. We'll have yer cleaned up and comfortable in no time.' Gently, Irene cleaned the wound and dressed it. 'Ye're lucky, sunshine, it was about to turn septic. Yer should have told me before, instead of going round with a dirty old piece of cloth on it. And how have yer managed to walk? Yer must have been in agony.'

Not used to tenderness and sympathy, Lucy was near to tears. 'It has been sore. But I couldn't come to yer before because yer were never on yer own.'

Irene used two strips of plaster to keep the lint in place. 'There yer go, all done and dusted. I'll have a look at it tomorrow and put a clean dressing on. In a few days yer'll be as right as rain, please God. Now come and sit down.' She led the girl to the couch and sat down beside her. Taking her hand, she said softly, 'I promised this would be our little secret, and I meant it. But we've got to be honest with each other. And I'm afraid yer haven't told me the truth, have yer, sunshine?'

Lucy hung her head in shame. Shame for having lied to this warm, kind-hearted woman, and ashamed to have to admit that her own mother would deliberately hurt her. 'No, I told yer a lie, and I'm very sorry.'

'It's not a sin to tell a lie to protect someone, Lucy, and that's what ye're doing, isn't it? But yer don't have to tell me who did it if you don't want to.'

The tears came then, and rolled down Lucy's face to fall on Irene's hand. 'Me mam did it, but she didn't mean to hurt me, she was acting daft. She does love me, yer know.'

Irene took her in her arms and held her tight. 'I'm sure she does, sunshine. She couldn't help but love yer.' She rocked her like a baby. No mother who loved her child could be so cruel to her, it wasn't natural. But they were the words Lucy wanted to hear. 'She wasn't to know she'd hurt yer that much. She'd never forgive herself if she knew.'

'Ooh, yer won't tell her, will yer?' Two large frightened eyes begged. 'Yer won't tell anyone, will yer, 'cos yer promised.'

'I won't tell a living soul, cross my heart and hope to die.' Irene held her away so they could face each other. 'Anytime ye're worried about anything, even if it's only a little worry, yer can come to me knowing it won't go no further. And if ever I need a shoulder to cry on, or I'm feeling down in the dumps, I'll come to you, eh?'

'You're never down in the dumps, Mrs Pollard, ye're always happy and laughing.'

'Everybody has times when they're down, sunshine, and I'm no different. Sometimes I feel dead miserable without even knowing why. I don't tell George or the boys because men don't understand how temperamental a woman can be when she's having an off day. So I'd be glad to have someone to talk to and get all me moans off me chest. It's surprising how much it helps.' Lucy's tears had stopped now and Irene kept on talking in a matter-of-fact way. 'If yer could see me on a Monday morning standing in front of the pile of dirty clothes I've got to wash, yer'd soon find out I'm not always happy and laughing. Monday is one day I could do without.'

'Yer could talk to me, Mrs Pollard, but I couldn't help yer 'cos I'm only young. I would if I could, though.'

'There's lots of ways yer could help. For instance, if I change me hairstyle and ask the boys or George if they like it, they always say they do without even looking at it. Now if I asked you, it would be different. You could tell me which style suited me best.'

Lucy's eyes brightened with interest. 'Ooh, I could do that! That would be easy, 'cos I could comb yer hair in different ways and see which suited yer best.'

Irene's heart lifted. 'Right, that's settled then. I'll be your confidante and you can be mine.'

'What does that word mean, Mrs Pollard?'

'A confidante is someone yer tell yer secrets to. And that's what we're going to be from now on. But right now, I think yer'd better get down to Rhoda's before she decides to call for yer. We don't want yer dad having the police out looking for yer, do we?'

Lucy, a much happier girl now, grinned and jumped to her feet. 'We're going to have a game of skipping, to see who can do the most cross-overs. And it's Rhoda's turn to cheat. So before we start, she's the winner.'

Irene followed her to the door. 'She's a good friend, isn't she?'

'Yeah, she's the best.' Lucy turned before stepping into the street. 'Thanks for doing me leg for me, Mrs Pollard, it feels a lot better now. I've been really worried about it.'

'Call in tomorrow and I'll get rid of the boys for five minutes while I change the dressing. It's thanks to them I had all the stuff to dress it with. They're always coming in with cuts and scrapes.' Irene waved a hand. 'Poppy off now and enjoy yer game of skipping.'

'Ta-ra, Mrs Pollard.' Now her worries were over, Lucy ran up the street with wings on her heels. She felt so relieved and happy, she didn't mind that it was her friend's turn to cheat.

Chapter Eight

'Ah, ay, Rhoda, I know it's your turn to win, but ye're not half cheating.' Lucy was leaning against the wall outside her friend's house, her arms folded and a look of impatience on her face. 'Ye're not even doing proper cross-overs! Little Milly Simpson could do what ye're doing and she's only five.'

'I am doing proper cross-overs, so there!' Rhoda was red in the face with jumping up and down. 'This is the way you do them, so if I'm wrong, then you are as well.'

'I do not do them like that!' Lucy dropped her arms and stood to attention. Cheating proper was one thing, but this was double cheating. 'All ye're doing is crossing yer wrists and ye're supposed to cross yer arms.'

'Here, you have a go.' Rhoda was happy to pass the piece of clothes line over. She had more weight to heave up and down and she was out of breath. It was all right for Lucy, she was a real skinny links and never got puffed. And as for her mother telling her it was only puppy fat she was carrying and she'd soon lose it – well, she was getting fed up hearing about it and it never happening. 'Let's see how you do it, clever clogs.'

Lucy took in her friend's red face and the beads of sweat on her forehead, and was immediately contrite. 'Let's not do any more cross-overs, yer've won anyway. So how about tying one end to the lamp-post and take turns swinging the rope?'

Rhoda looked relieved. 'Yeah, that's more like it.'

Lucy was tying the rope when a boy came up behind her. 'If yer want any help, Lucy, just sing out.'

'Hello, Steve.' Lucy gave him a bright smile. 'I've done it now, so I don't need no help. But thanks for asking.'

Rhoda's face was set. She glared at the boy who was so poorly dressed he looked like a tramp. His pullover was full of holes, his short trousers torn and frayed, and both his shoes and socks looked as though they were going to fall to pieces any minute. 'Even if we did need help, Steve Fletcher, we wouldn't want it off you, 'cos ye're all dirty.'

'Rhoda!' Lucy looked horrified. 'That wasn't a nice thing to say.'

Her friend was unrepentant. 'Well, he is dirty, just look at him. And he's got scabs on his legs, as well.'

The boy's face flushed a bright red. He was thirteen, and tall and well-built for his age. And anyone bothering to ignore the clothes and look at the lad himself, would see he had the makings of a fine-looking young man. His untidy hair was fair, his eyes a bright blue and he had a cleft in his chin. He stared at Rhoda and half opened his mouth as though he was going to answer her. Then he shook his head and began to walk away. 'I'll see yer, Lucy.'

'Yeah, okay, Steve, I'll see yer.' Lucy waited until he was out of earshot before turning to her friend. 'I'm surprised at you, Rhoda Fleming. That was really mean and cruel of yer.'

'It's true, what I said. Everyone in the street knows the Fletcher house is filthy. He's probably got fleas as well, and I don't want to catch them off him.'

'He can't help being poor! He's got no dad and his mam's too sick to go out to work. They barely have enough money coming in to pay the rent, never mind clothes and food. His mam's a lovely woman, and he thinks the world of her. He goes around asking people if they want any jobs doing so he can earn a few coppers. He helps the coalman after school, lugging heavy bags of coal, and he chops firewood for the corner shop. I admire him for that, and I think he's a nice boy.' Lucy was sick at heart for the way her friend had belittled someone who, through no fault of their own, wasn't as well off as they were. 'I'm surprised at yer, Rhoda, I really am. I just wish I hadn't been here when yer said it, 'cos I'm ashamed for yer.'

'Yer've no need to be ashamed for me, Lucy Mellor, nobody asked yer to. Steve is dirty and I said so. And if he ever comes near me, I'll tell him again.'

Lucy sighed as she untied the knot in the rope. This was the first time she and Rhoda had ever argued, but she wasn't going to let it pass. Her friend was wrong to make a fool of Steve the way she did. He was a friendly boy, always had a smile when he saw you. He didn't deserve to be insulted and he must be feeling terrible now. 'Here's the rope, Rhoda, I don't feel like playing any more.'

'I don't know why ye're getting a cob on over him for.' Rhoda snatched the rope from her friend's hand. 'He's not worth it.'

'That's what you think, I think different. Yer don't judge people by what they've got, but what they're like inside.' Lucy was so upset she could feel the tears welling up behind her eyes. 'I'm going in now.'

Rhoda was feeling sorry inside, she didn't want to fall out with Lucy. But she wasn't going to give in. 'Suit yerself.'

As Lucy crossed the cobbled road, tears blurred her sight. She was wiping them away when she walked headlong into Titch, who was standing outside his front door.

'Hey, young lady, watch where ye're going.' He looked closer. 'Have yer got something in yer eye?'

Lucy shook her head, and in a muffled voice, said, 'No, I'm all right.'

'Are they tears I can see in yer eyes?'

So full up she couldn't speak, Lucy nodded and made to walk past him. But Titch barred her way. 'I don't think I've seen yer cry before, Lucy, so something bad must have happened to upset yer. Come inside and tell me all about it.' He cupped her elbow and propelled her into the house. 'Things don't seem so bad when yer talk them over with someone.'

Aggie was sitting in her rocking chair and at first sight of Lucy, her face lit up. Then she saw the red eyes. 'What is it, queen? Has someone hit yer?'

'No, I'm all right, Mrs Aggie, honest.' But Lucy's trembling voice said otherwise.

Titch pulled a chair from the table. 'Sit down, love, and tell me and me ma what's happened to make yer unhappy.'

Lucy sat down and wiped a hand across her eyes. 'It's nothing, really, I've got meself all upset over nothing.'

'Tell us what the nothing is, queen,' Aggie coaxed, 'and we'll tell yer whether ye're making a mountain out of a molehill.'

'Yer'll think I'm a big baby when I tell yer, but it didn't half upset me at the time.' Lucy sniffed up. 'Yer know Steve Fletcher from the top of the street?'

Aggie looked puzzled. 'Of course we know Steve! He hasn't done anything to upset yer, has he? I'll be surprised if he has 'cos he's a lovely boy, wouldn't hurt a fly.'

'Me and Rhoda were playing skipping, and I was tying the rope to the lamp-post when Steve came up and asked if I needed any help. And for no reason at all, Rhoda told him we didn't need his help because he was dirty and had scabs on his legs.' Lucy closed her eyes as she relived those few awful seconds. 'I didn't know where to put meself, Mrs Aggie, I felt so sorry for him. It was a horrible thing for Rhoda to say and he must have felt terrible.'

Aggie leaned forward in her chair. 'It was a terrible thing for her to say, and she needs her bottom smacking for it. If she was my daughter, I'd drag her by the hand and make her apologise to Steve. Him and his mam have a hard time, and everyone in the street feels sorry for them. And God knows the lad does all he can to bring a few coppers into the house.'

'I told Rhoda all that, Mrs Aggie! But she said she didn't care. He was dirty, their house was filthy, and everyone in the street said so. And if he comes near her again, she'll still tell him he's dirty.' Lucy swallowed the lump in her throat. 'We had a row about it and I gave her the skipping rope back and said I didn't want to play no more. And that's the first row we've ever had in all the years she's been me friend.'

'It'll blow over, queen, don't fret. She's probably feeling worse than you do, 'cos after all it was her what caused the row. But I'm glad yer told her off because she was very naughty to say what she did, she had no right. She must have upset the poor lad something terrible.'

'I won't sleep tonight for thinking about him,' Lucy said. 'I hope he doesn't tell his mam because it would upset her, and with her being sick, she shouldn't be disturbed.'

Titch, who had been listening intently, now said, 'When his dad was alive, things were different in that house. They were the most loving family yer could meet. He was a fine man, was Jim Fletcher. A good husband and a good father. It was a tragedy that he died so young, and losing him nearly killed Olive, his wife. She's been ailing ever since. And hearing all this has put me to shame. I used to call there often when Jim was alive, but it's years since I knocked on their door. Some friend I've turned out to be.'

'It's never too late to put a wrong right, son. I'm sure Olive would love to see yer. And it would do the boy good, 'cos they don't seem to get many visitors.'

'Oh, yes, Mr Titch, please call and see them,' Lucy said eagerly. 'Steve hasn't got many friends because he's always busy doing jobs for people. He'll do anything to earn some money, turn his hand to anything. He'd be made up to have a man to talk to.'

'I'll go tomorrow, I promise.'

'Never put off till tomorrow what yer can do today,' Aggie told him. 'Ye're only sitting on yer backside twiddling yer thumbs, so make the effort now. The lad must be at home if

Lucy's just seen him, and if yer leave it until tomorrow he might be out.'

'He will be out tomorrow, Mr Titch. He helps the milkman on a Saturday morning, then takes orders out for the corner shop.' Lucy held out her palms as though pleading. 'If yer go now, it will help him feel better after what Rhoda said. Cheer him up a bit.'

Titch lifted his own hands in surrender. 'Okay, okay! I'm not going to argue with two women because I know I wouldn't stand an earthly. So I'll go out of the door with you, Lucy, and yer can watch me walk up to the Fletchers' house. Then yer can sleep contented in yer bed tonight.'

It was on impulse that Lucy threw her arms around his neck and planted a kiss on his cheek. 'Oh, thank you, Mr Titch, it's no wonder Mrs Aggie loves the bones of yer. But yer won't let on about Rhoda, will yer? Otherwise he'll think that's the only reason yer called to see them.'

Titch grinned, and with a stiffened finger made a cross on his chest. 'Cross my heart and hope to die, sweetheart. Yer can count on me, I'll be the soul of discretion.'

Across the street, Mrs Fleming was eyeing her daughter. 'What's up with you, coming in before ye're shouted? And why have yer got a face on yer like a wet week?'

'I've had a row with Lucy, that's what, and we've fallen out.' Rhoda was feeling angry with herself. Deep down she knew she was at fault; she should never have said that to Steve. She didn't even know why she had done so, except that it was always Lucy he spoke to, never her. Not that she was jealous. I mean, why would she be jealous of *him*?

'It's not like you two to row. What have yer fallen out over?'

'It was over that Steve Fletcher. He was hanging around and I told him we didn't want him because he was dirty and he's got scabs on his legs. Lucy didn't like what I said, and when he'd gone yer should have heard the way she took off on me! Called me for everything, she did. Then she gave me the rope back and said she wasn't playing out no more.'

Jessie Fleming folded her arms and hitched up her ample bosom. 'Are you telling me that yer told Steve to his face that he was dirty?' She didn't wait for an answer because guilt was written all over her daughter's face. 'You little flamer! Just wait till yer dad gets in and hears that. He'll tan your backside so hard yer won't be able to sit for a week.'

'I don't know what all the fuss is about,' Rhoda said defiantly. 'He is dirty and their house is filthy. Everybody knows it and I was only speaking the truth.'

'Oh, aye, and who is everybody, pray? Yer've never heard me speak ill of the Fletchers because I've had no cause to. They're down on their luck, there's no two ways about that, but we were in the same boat ourselves a couple of years back, when yer dad was out of work. You won't remember because yer were too young, but we were living from hand to mouth then, just like the Fletchers are now. Only it's worse for them because they've no man in the house. So don't you go looking down yer nose at anyone, Lady Muck, 'cos that person could very easily have been you.'

'Mrs Bentley thinks they're dirty,' Rhoda said, feeling sorrier with every second the clock ticked away. 'She won't let her Andrew even talk to Steve, never mind play with him. And she said they've got fleas and bugs.'

'That stuck-up cow! Listen to me, young lady, that Sheila Bentley thinks we're all dirt beneath her feet. She reckons she's a cut above the rest of us, but it's all show. Her husband is only a labourer, like yer dad, but to hear her talk yer'd think he was a bleedin' director or something. She gives the impression they're rolling in money, but yer should stand behind her in the shops and yer'd soon realise very little money goes on food. Outward appearances are more important to her than putting food in their bellies. Her husband's not a bad man, but he's under her thumb and jumps when she tells him to. And as for Andrew – well, he's a proper little snob. Any other kid around here would be called Andy, but that's too common for him. He has to have his full title.'

Rhoda hung her head. 'I'm sorry I said what I did, Mam. Me and my big mouth have got me into trouble. I've lost me best friend, and now me dad will start on me when he comes in from work.'

Jessie tilted her head. 'Are yer truly sorry, or just saying it to get out of being given a hiding off yer dad?'

'I was sorry as soon as I'd said it. I could have bitten me tongue out.' The girl looked the picture of misery. 'And when Lucy took off on me, I felt really ashamed.'

'She's got a head on her shoulders, that girl. She's kind and wouldn't intentionally hurt anyone for the world. It's a pity ye're not more like her.' Jessie saw her daughter's face crumble and held out her arms. 'Come here, yer daft nit. What am I going to do with yer, eh?' She patted Rhoda's back as sobs shook her body. 'Come on now, be a big girl. I won't tell yer dad if yer promise me two things. One, that yer'll say sorry to Lucy and make up with her. And two, that when yer see Steve yer'll give him a nice, big, friendly smile.' She held her daughter away and looked into her red-rimmed eyes. 'Is that a deal?'

Rhoda wasn't so sure about the whole deal. 'I'll see Lucy 'cos I don't want to fall out with her for ever. We've always said we'll be friends all our lives. But I don't think Steve will want to have anything to do with me after what I said.'

'You're the one who started all the trouble, so it's up to you to sort it out. And don't forget, ye're twelve years of age now, and it's time to grow up. Steve's had to grow up quick, he had it thrust upon him. The day his dad died, he became the man of the house. And God only knows, he's done his level best to be just that.'

With every word her mother spoke, Rhoda became more ashamed. Her voice choked, she said, 'I'll do what yer said, Mam. I'll see Lucy and Steve, and I'll tell them both how sorry I am. And in future, when I hear that Andrew Bentley calling Steve names, I'll clock him one.'

Jessie smiled and gave her a hug. 'That's my girl. But I wouldn't go as far as clocking him one, I don't think yer dad would like that. Just call him Andy – that should get his goat.'

Steve opened the door and gaped when he saw who was standing there. He vaguely remembered, when he was a toddler, this man used to come to their house when he was home on leave. But that was all he could remember, and it was years ago. He knew who he was, though, 'cos everybody in the street knew Titch, he was such a colourful character. 'Did yer want something, Mr McBride?'

'I want to offer an apology to yer mam for not coming to see her for so long. If it's possible, Steve, I'd like to have a word with her.'

Steve hesitated. He knew his mam didn't like visitors because of the state of the house. 'I'll have to ask her. She's not been well and she's lying down on the couch.'

'I understand that, son, but a visit from an old friend might just cheer her up. Don't you agree? She used to be full of spirit, your mam, so she'll probably tear a strip off me for staying away so long.'

Steve was torn. He knew if he asked his mother, she'd tell him to make an excuse to this man and send him away. But she never went over the door to meet people to talk to. She said he was all the company she needed, but he worried about her. She was too young to shut herself away from the outside world, and he was too young to know how to change things. If he let this chance slip, he might never get another. 'Step inside, Mr McBride, and I'll give her a shout.'

Titch stepped into the hall and waited for Steve to close the door. Then the boy called out, 'Yer've got a visitor, Mam.'

'Oh, don't let anyone in, son, I'm not fit to be seen.'

Titch took over. 'Then cover yerself up, Olive Fletcher, 'cos I'm coming in whether ye're respectable or not.'

'Oh, my God!' Olive covered her mouth with a hand as she

pulled a knitted shawl across her chest. Her eyes darted around the room, seeing it as she knew Titch would and wishing the floor would open and swallow her up. 'What possessed you to come after all this time? As yer can see, we're not exactly ready for visitors.'

'I haven't come as a visitor, Olive, I've come as an old friend. I'm expecting yer to throw the book at me, so go ahead. Whatever names yer call me, I deserve for not keeping in touch with yer to see how yer were getting on.'

Olive waved a hand around the room. 'Yer can see how I've fared, I don't need to tell yer. I've come as low as it's possible to come. And I've brought me son down with me.'

Titch pulled a rickety chair from the table. 'I never used to wait to be asked to sit down, and I'm not waiting now. Yer might think I've got a bloody cheek to land meself on yer after all these years, and yer'd be right. But we used to be good friends, Olive, and that should stand for something. I'm away a lot, as yer know, but I've watched Steve grow up, and he's a credit to yer.'

Olive's face softened as she looked to where Steve was leaning on a sideboard that was minus a drawer and had a door hanging loosely on its broken hinges. 'My son is one in a million. I don't think I'd have survived without him.'

'Yer've had it hard, have yer?' Titch asked softly, afraid of overstepping the mark and being told it was none of his business.

'It's been a nightmare, a living nightmare. I managed to cope for a couple of years after Jim died, by pawning things. But I never had the money to redeem them, so you can see for yerself how we've ended up. Ornaments, pictures, everything we had went to the pawnshop. And I've never been able to replace them. The furniture, bedding and curtains, they're all on their last legs and there's not a snowball's chance in hell of me being able to renew them.'

'I leave school in nine months,' Steve said, 'and my wages will help.'

Olive smiled at him, and all the love she felt for her son showed in that smile. 'Yeah, we'll be in clover, then, love. And yer never know, I might start to feel better and I'll be able to look for a little job.'

'Have yer been poorly for long?' Titch asked. 'When I used to come, yer were always the picture of health.'

'I've never been the same since Jim died. I just don't seem to have the energy or the willpower. And I've got to say that we don't get the right food to keep us strong and healthy. We can only afford the cheapest of everything.'

Titch was thoughtful. She's not really sick, he thought, she's still grieving for Jim. And until she accepts that, she'll spend her life on that couch. And that's not fair to her son. It was clear that she needed an incentive to bring her to life again. 'That's like asking which comes first, Olive, the chicken or the egg. Yer can't get a job until yer build yerself up, and yer can't build yerself up until yer get a job! Couldn't yer get an hour here and there, doing light work?'

'Me mam can't go to work,' Steve said, quickly defending his mother. 'She's not strong enough to take a job on.'

'It was only a thought, son. I had it in mind that if she got out a bit and mixed with people, she might start to feel better.' Titch smiled at the boy who was left to carry a burden of work and worry that was too great for his young shoulders. He sent a message with his eyes, hoping Steve would understand he wasn't trying to run their lives for them, he was only trying to help. 'Your mam used to be a real goer when she was younger. She could dance the feet off anyone. And she was so pretty she could charm the ruddy birds off the trees. The fellers at the Grafton used to queue up to dance with her.'

Steve seemed to grow in stature and his face filled with pride. 'Me mam's still pretty. I bet she's the prettiest woman in the street.'

This gave Titch the opening he was waiting for. 'She's pretty all right, but there's someone else who would be joining her on the stage if there was a beauty contest. I wouldn't know which one to choose.'

Olive was now getting embarrassed. 'Hey, knock it off, you two. Any man who fell for me charms now would have to have very bad eyesight.'

Titch leaned forward, elbows on knees and fingers laced. 'The other woman I'm talking about is Irene Pollard. D'yer remember her?'

'Of course I remember Irene! I haven't spoken to her for years because I never go over the door. But I see her passing the window on her way to the shops.' Olive's voice was stronger now and there was interest in her eyes. 'A smashing woman, she is. One of the best yer'll find.' A faraway look came over her face as memories flooded back. 'God, when I think of the laughs we used to have. Her and George, and me and Jim, used to go out together until the children came along. They were good times, and I remember it was always Irene who was the one who made people laugh.'

'She hasn't changed,' Titch said, fully aware that Steve was drinking in every word. 'She's put weight on, but it suits her and she's still as pretty as ever.'

Olive looked down at her flat chest and skinny arms. 'Tell her I'll have some of her fat – I could do with it, God knows.'

'Why don't yer tell her yerself? Good grief, if she passes yer door, why can't yer just invite her in?'

'Invite her in to this?' Olive flung an arm wide. 'No thanks, Titch. Leave me with what little pride I've got left.'

Titch raised an eyebrow. 'I thought yer said yer knew Irene well?'

'I do! Well, at least I did. We were the best of pals for years.'

'Olive, if yer think Irene would worry about the state of yer house, then yer really don't know her at all. At least not the Irene I know. She wouldn't care if yer lived in a pigsty.'

'She mightn't, but I would, Titch. I don't want anyone to see what I've come down to.' Olive hung her head. 'Irene did knock here a couple of times, but I pretended I wasn't in. That was years ago, mind.'

'I didn't know that, Mam!' Steve's voice was high with surprise. 'Why did yer never mention it to me?'

Olive sighed. 'Because I didn't want yer to know that yer mother was such a coward she hid behind the door when one of her friends knocked. I wasn't very proud of meself, I can tell yer.'

'Would yer still hide behind the door if she knocked?' Titch asked.

'I couldn't face her, Titch, I'd be too ashamed. It's not only the state of the house, it's me as well. Just look at me! I haven't got a decent stitch to put on me back. And me son, who I love more than words could ever say, has to walk around like a tramp. He gets his clothes from a secondhand stall at the market, and they're worn out when he gets them.'

'I don't mind that, Mam! I don't care what people think, I've told yer. If I had a wish, it wouldn't be for new clothes or a nice house, it would be that you get better.'

Titch sensed the emotion in the air and changed the subject. 'Talking about Irene, did yer know she has a little job?'

'Go 'way!' This was news to Olive. 'No, I didn't know that.'

'Yeah, she does two hours a morning at the corner pub. It's a cleaning job and she's made up with it. Apart from bringing in a few extra bob, she said it gets her out of the house.'

'Well, I never! I didn't think she'd need to go out to work with George's wages coming in every week. That is a surprise.'

'She's got two growing lads to feed and clothe, so the money comes in useful.' There was a reason behind Titch's words. 'Mind you, her eldest, Jack, leaves school next Friday so she may decide to pack the job in then.'

Olive narrowed her eyes in thought. Many of the things Titch said had hit home. But Irene taking a job to give her boys a better life had struck home the hardest. 'Is it a heavy job she's got?'

'That I couldn't tell yer. All I know is that she cleans at the pub. Why?'

'D'yer think I could do it?'

Steve was about to say it would be too hard for her, but thought better of it. Mr McBride had got his mother talking more than she had done for years and he seemed to know what he was doing. So the boy leaned his elbows on the sideboard again and listened.

'I don't know about that, Olive.' Titch was overjoyed and thanked God that Lucy had spurred him into this visit. 'Besides, she hasn't said yet that she's leaving. I could ask her for yer, if yer like.'

'She'll think I've got a bloody cheek after not opening the door to her. I'm certain she knew I was in, and hiding.'

'I wouldn't know, she never mentioned it to me. But when I see her I'll ask and let yer know.' Titch turned his attention to Steve. 'I believe you do odd jobs, son?'

'Yeah, when I get the chance.'

'Have yer ever painted anything? I don't mean a picture, or a house. I'm thinking of whitewashing a wall.'

'Yeah, I've done a couple of walls, and an outhouse. It's easy work, that.'

'Me ma wants her yard wall doing, and she asked a bloke how much he'd charge. He said it would be four bob, including the whitewash. If yer feel like having a go, the money would be better in your pocket than his.'

'I'll say it would!' Steve was beaming. Four bob would keep him and his mam in food for nearly a week. 'When does Mrs Aggie want it doing?'

'Hadn't yer better look at the job first, see what ye're letting yerself in for?' Titch dropped his head back and roared with laughter. 'Me ma's terrible fussy to work for. Spill a drop of paint on her yard and she'll have yer guts for garters.'

It was so long since the house had heard the voice and

laughter of a man, Olive and her son savoured the sound before allowing their faces to break into a smile. 'Will yer ma stand over me with a broom in her hand?' Steve asked. 'Or will it be the poker?'

'That all depends, son, on the mood she's in. If her corns are giving her gyp, she'll likely as not have both broom and poker. And every twinge she gets, she'll lash out at yer. But ye're lucky, 'cos her eyesight's not what it used to be and I guarantee she'll miss yer more often than she hits yer.'

'I'm good at ducking and running, Mr McBride, so unless Mrs Aggie's nifty on her feet I should be safe.' Steve was thinking that for four bob he'd work for a maniac, never mind Mrs Aggie, who was liked by everyone. 'But what about the bloke she's asked? Won't he be expecting to get the job?'

Titch was safe in saying what he was going to say because there was no such bloke. And he'd have a lot of explaining to do to his ma, as well. 'No, there was nothing definite arranged so he won't know the difference. Anyway, come up and see the yard for yerself. I've got another week at home, so if yer decide yer want to do the job, I can get the whitewash for yer on Monday. I need to make a call on someone now, so will yer give me fifteen minutes and then follow up?'

The pleasure on Steve's face was a joy to behold, and wasn't lost on his mother. 'Thanks, Titch, yer've made him a happy lad. And d'yer know why he's happy? Because he'll have a few bob to give me. He won't keep a ha'penny for himself no matter what I say. There's not many mothers can say that about their sons.'

Titch chuckled. 'Me ma would argue with yer on that, Olive. She's always saying that I'm a gift from God.'

'Your ma always doted on yer. Spoilt yer soft, she did.'

'Well, yer must admit, I'm a very lovable bloke. Yer don't get many like me in a pound.' Titch got to his feet. 'I'll see Irene tonight and have a word with her. I think the pub job might be too much for you, but we'll see. I'll give yer a knock tomorrow and let yer know. And I want to see yer off that couch, Olive, even if yer've got to wear a curtain to hide yer modesty. I've got a kink in me flippin' neck looking down at yer.'

There was a trace of colour in Olive's thin face now, as she said, 'Still the same old Titch. Yer haven't changed a bit, have yer?'

'Now who would want to change perfection, Olive?' Titch grinned as he picked up one of her hands and held it in his. All he could feel was skin and bones, and this saddened him. But not for the world would he let this once proud woman see how her appearance had affected him. 'I'm glad I came, it's been great seeing yer. There's no friends like old friends, eh?'

Olive's eyes were shining with unshed tears. 'I'm glad yer came, Titch, yer've bucked me up. And I'm glad yer were cheeky enough to barge in after being told I didn't want to see no one.' She gave his hand a squeeze. 'Yer didn't give me time to hide behind the door.'

'Now I'm up to yer little tricks, I'll come the back way in future.' He laid her hand down on her lap. 'I'd better skedaddle, but I'll see yer tomorrow. And you, Steve, I'll see in fifteen minutes.'

The boy followed him to the front door. 'Thanks, Mr McBride. Not just for the job, which I'm grateful for, but for cheering me mam up. She looks better than she has for ages.'

'Don't thank me, Steve, because I feel like a heel for not coming to see her before now. But we'll talk about yer mam, later, eh? Right now I've got to be on me way. Ta-ra for now.'

Chapter Nine

Titch covered the ground quickly. He could do with more than fifteen minutes to talk his mother round. She'd lay a duck egg when she knew what he'd done. Still, it was all in a good cause so he'd just have to try and out-talk her. A grin covered his face as he told himself it would take some doing to out-talk his mother. She said herself she'd been born with the gift of the gab. To which she'd added, with a smile, that she'd passed the gift on to him.

He let himself in and, as he was taking the key out of the lock, he called, 'It's only me, Ma! Yer don't need to put yer false teeth in or take yer knickers off the fireguard.'

'Well, I know it's not the bleedin' coalman, yer silly bugger.' Aggie was sitting watching the door when he came in. 'Well, how did yer get on? Was Olive pleased to see yer, or did she die of shock?'

'I'll tell yer that in a minute, Ma, but tell me this first. Didn't yer once say that yer'd like the backyard wall white-washing?'

'Yer what? I've never said I wanted no backyard wall whitewashing!'

'Yes yer did, Ma, I distinctly remember. Some time last year it was.'

'Ye're imagining things, son, 'cos it's never entered me head. I don't want me wall whitewashed, and as it's my wall, I should know.'

'Yer only THINK yer don't want it doing, Ma. But deep

down yer one ambition in life is to see yer wall white-washed.'

'D'yer know, son, I often wonder about you. An hour ago yer went out of here to go and visit Olive, who yer haven't seen for years. But yer come back, not with news of her, but with some notion about the state of me backyard! Am I missing something, or have yer lost the run of yer senses?'

'There's nowt wrong with me mind, Mam, yer can rest assured. I just thought it would be nice to look out of the window and see it all nice and white. Those brown bricks are enough to give anyone the willies.'

'Okay, son, spit it out. What have yer been up to?'

Titch grinned. 'I'll tell yer, Ma, if yer promise me yer'll stay in that chair and not reach for the poker.'

Aggie was having trouble keeping a smile off her face. 'Okay, I'll hear yer out. But I'm not making no promises about the bleedin' poker until I know what yer've let me in for. I can't be up to you, I don't know what ye're going to do next.'

Titch glanced at the clock. Time was running out and he'd better make it snappy. So with the words tumbling from his mouth, he told the whole story in as few words as possible. But they were enough to have Aggie hanging on to every one of them. When he'd finished, he asked, 'Shall I pass yer the poker, Ma?'

Aggie looked shocked and was shaking her head. 'Is it as bad as that, son?'

'It's worse. There's not a pick on Olive, she's as thin as a rake. If she doesn't get off that couch soon, and get some decent food down her, she'll just fade away. Some fresh air would do her good, too. And the house is bare, not a bit like the bright home it used to be. It's my belief that Olive has got herself in a rut and hasn't got the energy or the inclination to pull herself out of it. But it's not fair on the boy, he worries himself to death about her. Something needs to be done there, and quick.'

Aggie's sigh was deep. 'Are yer going to see Irene? If anyone can do anything, it's her. And I'll do me bit, too. That's if Olive will let us help, of course. I wouldn't want to stick me nose in where it wasn't wanted.'

'I'll go and see Irene when we've had our tea. But Steve will be here any minute, so it's make-yer-mind-up time, Ma. D'yer want yer yard wall whitewashed or not?'

'It's like yer said, son, I didn't think I did, but yer've shown me the error of me ways. As long as you're forking out, 'cos I couldn't afford it.'

There was a loud ran-tan on the knocker and Titch jumped to his feet. 'This will be Steve. Don't mention anything I've told yer, Ma, just let's play it by ear.'

'I'm not thick, Titch McBride,' Aggie said as he left the room. 'You go and teach yer grandmother how to milk ducks.'

There was a smile on Titch's face when he opened the door. 'Come in, lad, me ma's waiting to see yer.' In a loud whisper, he added, 'Just humour her. She's getting on in years so yer have to make excuses for her.'

'Ay, I heard that, buggerlugs,' Aggie said. 'I may be getting on, but I can still run bleedin' circles around you.' The smile she bestowed on Steve was warm and friendly. 'It's nice to see yer, lad. Take a pew and make yerself at home.'

'Is it true yer want yer yard walls whitewashing, Mrs Aggie?' Steve couldn't bear the suspense any longer. The last fifteen minutes had seemed like an eternity. Getting this job meant so much to him and he was afraid of having his hopes dashed. 'Mr McBride said that yer did.'

'Don't be so formal, lad,' Aggie said with a smile. 'All the youngsters call him Mr Titch, so why don't yer do the same? Sounds more friendly, like.' She sat back, set her rocking chair in motion and tried to keep her eyes on the lad's face, not on the rags that were almost falling off his back. 'I've always wanted me yard doing, but never seemed to get down to it.' She gave a broad wink. 'That's because I'm getting on in years, yer see, lad.'

'I'll do it good for yer, Mrs Aggie. I won't spill no paint or anything, and I'll clean up after meself.' The flicker that Steve had felt the minute he stepped in the room and saw Aggie's smile had grown into a warm glow coursing through his whole body. These two people weren't put off by his appearance – in fact, they seemed not to have noticed. I bet they wouldn't treat me any different if I was dressed like a toff, he thought. And this made him daring enough to say, 'So yer won't need to stand over me with the broom and poker when yer corns are giving yer gyp, will yer?'

Aggie forgot it was wise to alert her false teeth before she laughed, and she just caught them before they parted company from her gums. Beating the chair-arm with a curled fist, she shook with laughter. 'I can see me son's been telling yer tales, eh? Well, lad, you and me are going to get along just fine. And don't you worry none about me corns, they only bother me every blue moon.'

Steve's face was eager. 'When can I start?'

'As soon as yer like, lad. But don't you come knocking on the door at six o'clock in the morning 'cos then I might take the broom to yer.'

'Would nine o'clock be all right?'

'Ay, hang on a minute.' Titch knew these two were going to get along like a house on fire and was delighted. 'We haven't got the blinkin' whitewash yet.'

'The shops open at nine, son,' Aggie told him, knowing it would spoil his lie-in. But the lad was really eager to start. The poor bugger was probably thinking about the money. He could do with spending it on himself, but from what Titch had said, he would turn every penny over to his mam. 'Yer could be waiting outside when they open up.'

'I would go for yer, Mr Titch, save yer getting up early, but I don't have any money.'

'We'll go together,' Titch said. 'I'll do without me lie-in for once.' He explained that they had a brush and a tin for mixing the whitewash in. 'So give me a knock before nine and we'll have yer hard at work by half-past.'

Now everything was arranged, Steve thought he should leave. He was rising from the chair when Aggie said, 'I believe yer mam's not too well, lad?'

'No, she's been sick for a long time. But she seemed better when I left the house and I think it was Mr Titch calling that bucked her up.'

'Yeah, he's good at bucking people up, is my son. He's good at a lot of things, like springing surprises on yer when ye're least expecting them. And he's a bugger for playing tricks that no one thinks are funny but himself.' Aggie could see the lad was far more relaxed than he had been and she was pleased. So she told him the tale about Titch hiding her purse on her. 'He watched me searching high and low and didn't say a dickie-bird. The club woman was banging hell out of the door and I was nearly having a heart attack. Then the bold laddo passes it over as cool as yer like. He thought it was hilarious and couldn't understand why I was hitting him over the head with the poker.'

Steve roared with laughter. 'Ooh, I'd love to have seen it.'

'Yer wouldn't have liked it,' Titch told him, his face deadpan. 'There was blood everywhere. I had to be carted to hospital and they put a hundred stitches in me head. The doctor said I was lucky to be alive.'

Aggie's whole body was shaking. 'That's why he's not quite with us in the head. So while ye're keeping an eye on me, lad, to make sure I haven't got a weapon in me hand, keep the other one on the queer feller here. Yer never can tell when he's going to have a funny turn.'

Not to be outdone, Titch said, 'She's right, yer know. Our captain was sick once, and he asked me to steer the ship. We only ended up in China when we were supposed to be going to India. And d'yer know what? The miserable so-and-so has never let me steer the ship since. The trouble is, he's got no sense of humour.'

'Wait until I tell me mam all these things,' Steve said. 'She won't half have a good laugh.'

'Yeah, you tell her, lad.' Aggie was wiping her eyes on the corner of her pinny. 'And while ye're at it, ask her if I can call one day to have a natter with her.'

The smile dropped from Steve's face. 'Me mam doesn't like visitors, Mrs Aggie, 'cos our house is like a dump and she doesn't like anyone to see it.'

'Listen to me, lad, and tell yer mam what I said. People see what they want to see, and in my case I want to see an old friend. If she was living in the workhouse, I'd still like to visit her. Tell her she should know better than to think her old mates are snobs. We've all hit rock bottom some time in our lives, but we've managed to claw our way up. And you and yer mam will, too, lad, take my word for it.'

'We'll be a bit better off when I leave school.' Steve felt some of the weight being lifted from his shoulders. It was good to have someone to talk to. 'I know I won't earn much, but I'll still help out at the corner shop, and do any odd jobs I can to bring in a few coppers. I'm not frightened of work, Mrs Aggie.'

'I know ye're not, sweetheart,' Aggie gave him a smile, 'even when there's an old biddy standing behind yer with a poker in her hand.'

'I can't wait.' Steve was eager to be away, to tell his mam the good news. And to brighten her up with the tales he'd heard. 'I'll see yer in the morning, then.'

Aggie eyed him up and down. 'Ye're a big lad for yer age, aren't yer? I'd say yer were only a few inches shorter than Titch.'

Steve drew himself up to his full height. 'Me mam said me dad was very tall and I take after him.'

'Yeah, yer dad was tall all right, and good-looking. If yer take after him yer won't go far wrong.' Titch made a move towards the door. 'I'll see yer at nine in the morning, Steve. And tell yer mam I'll be calling, but not that early.'

When he came back after seeing the lad out, Aggie was in

the kitchen. 'I'm putting the spuds on, then I'm going upstairs to sort yer clothes out.'

Titch leaned against the door jamb. 'What d'yer mean, sort me clothes out? Everything in the drawers and wardrobe are all neat and tidy.'

'There's clothes there yer haven't had on yer back for years, and probably never will. Rather than let the moths get at them, they may as well go where they'll do some good. And that's on the back of the boy who's just walked out of this house. The poor bugger, me heart went out to him.'

'Be careful Ma, 'cos yer could embarrass him. And Olive might not take too kindly to it, either. If she thinks ye're doing it out of pity, she could shut the door on us for good. And I wouldn't want that.'

'Me neither, son.' Aggie put the pan of potatoes on the stove and struck a match under them. Then talking to herself, she asked, 'Now have I salted them or not? Better put a bit more in, just in case.' The salt in the water, the lid on the pan, she turned to Titch. 'So ye're going to have to be very diplomatic, aren't yer, son?'

'What d'yer mean?'

'When yer ask Olive if she would mind yer giving Steve some of yer clothes. If yer use the right words, I'm sure she won't take umbrage.' Aggie bit on her bottom lip to keep a smile back. 'And if anyone knows the right bleedin' words, it's you. Look what yer've achieved today! The last thing on me mind was having me yard wall whitewashed, but tomorrow morning there'll be a lad out there whistling his head off as he slaps the stuff on in good style. All because I couldn't resist yer smooth tongue and yer charm.'

Titch chuckled as he held his arms wide. 'Come here and give us a kiss.' He held her close and whispered in her ear, 'I love the bones of yer, Ma, and it's not me smooth tongue or me charm talking, either.'

'Away with yer,' Aggie said, loving every minute of it. 'Keep yer eye on the spuds, and lower the light when they come to the boil. Then come up and make sure I'm not giving something away that yer want to keep.'

Titch looked at the lone pan on the stove. 'What are we having with them?'

'I was going to say fresh air, but we haven't got time for jokes. We're having bacon, sausage and egg. And I'm going to mash the potatoes with butter. How does that sound?'

'Music to my ears, Ma, music to my ears.'

'I knew she was in when I knocked,' Irene said, 'but I couldn't understand why she didn't want to see me. After the third or fourth attempt, I gave up.'

'Yer'd understand if yer saw the state of her house.' Titch looked from Irene to George. 'And yer wouldn't know Olive, she's like a bag of bones. Anyway, I'll fill yer in on what's gone on today. It all started with Lucy falling out with her mate.' He went on from there, right through to his mother and his clothes. 'She's got them all stacked up nicely, even to socks. And she said she'll ask Steve tomorrow what size shoes he takes.'

'I feel terrible now,' Irene said. 'I should have made more of an effort.'

'You weren't to know, love.' George reached for his wife's hand. 'I should have given some thought to how Olive and the son were managing. I owed it to Jim to do that. But the years go by and the longer yer leave it, the harder it is to make it up. I've seen how badly dressed the boy's been, and I could kick meself now for not getting off me backside to offer some sort of help. For old times' sake, if nothing else. Jim would have expected that of me because we were good mates.'

'I haven't thought of packing me job in,' Irene said. 'I want to stay on a while to renew some of me furniture and bedding. But if I thought Olive wanted the job, I would pack in. Although, if she's as weak as yer say she is, she'd never manage it. It's hard graft, cleaning the pub in two hours.

Yer've got to get on yer hands and knees and scrub hell out of the floor. Then there's all the woodwork and tables to polish.'

'I wouldn't expect yer to pack yer job in, Irene,' Titch said. 'I only mentioned it to try and liven Olive up. I think it worked, too, because in her heart she knows it's not fair on Steve to have to carry all the worry. He's a smashing lad, he really is. I'm just hoping that between us we can do something to get her back on her feet. Give her an interest in life. Are yer game to give it a try?'

'Of course we are!' Irene was blaming herself for not trying hard enough. She often talked to Steve, but never once had she asked about his mother. Not because she wasn't interested, but because she thought that for some reason Olive didn't want to be friends any more. 'D'yer think she'd mind if I came with yer tomorrow, to see her?'

'I think she'd mind, but only for a few minutes. She spoke very highly of you and George and what good times yer had together. And Steve said my calling had bucked her up, she was better than she'd been for a long time. So we can but try, Irene.'

'Well, I'm game. If she throws me out, at least I'll know I've tried. But I'm at the pub from nine until eleven, so it'll have to be after that.'

'That's fine. And leave yer working clothes on, girl, so Olive doesn't get embarrassed.'

'I want to help too, yer know,' George said. 'If there's anything in her house that wants doing, I'm more than willing to get stuck in.'

'Let's see how me and Titch get on first, love. We can't make up for all those years in one day. If we try too hard, we'll put her off. So we'll do things slowly.' They heard the front door being slammed against the hall wall and Irene put a finger over her mouth and said softly, 'Little pigs have big ears.' Then her face lit up when the two boys barged in, elbowing each other out of the way to be first in the room. They looked so happy it brought a lump to her throat. Thank

God she'd been able to give her children a good home. 'Here's my two angels back from playing footie. There'll be no more peace now until they're in bed.'

'I'm going for a pint, are yer coming, George?'

George grinned at his wife. 'How's the money situation, love? Will it stretch to a pint?'

'Oh, I think I can spare a few coppers. And just think, in a couple of weeks yer'll be able to borrow off yer son.'

'I'll want interest on it, Dad,' Jack said, his face straight. 'I can't go lending money without getting interest. It'll have to be on a business footing.'

George slipped his arm into his coat-sleeves. 'What interest rate did yer have in mind, son? If it's too high, I'll stick to yer mam.'

'I'll make enquiries and see what the going rate is. I can't be fairer than that.'

Titch ruffled Jack's hair as he passed. 'Yer'll end up a rich man, you will.'

Jack grinned from ear to ear. 'That's the general idea, Mr Titch.'

George's chuckle was deep and hearty. 'If I borrowed money off yer and had to pay yer back with interest, it would mean that in a few weeks yer'd be lending me me own money. So I think I'll stick with yer mam. Otherwise I'd have a rich son, but I'd be a pauper.'

There was a look of fear on Olive's face when she opened the door and found Irene standing beside Titch. 'I told yer I wasn't ready for visitors, Titch.'

'Don't blame him, it wasn't his fault.' Irene mounted the step, her usual smile beaming. 'When he told me he'd seen yer, nothing would keep me away.' She was shocked to the core at the sight of her old friend, but not by a flicker did she let it show as she bent to kiss a pale cheek. 'It's good to see yer. I really thought I'd done something to offend yer and yer'd fallen out with me.'

Olive had no option but to stand aside and let them pass. 'I'd never have any reason to fall out with you, Irene, but when yer see the state of the place yer'll know why I shut meself away from everyone.'

Irene stood at the door of the living room, and it took every ounce of self-control to keep the smile pasted on her face. 'Good God, Olive, anyone would think the place was a pigsty to hear yer talk. Yer've got it spotless.'

'There's not much to keep clean, is there? No ornaments or pictures to dust, no grate to clean out because we never have a fire.' The initial shock had worn off now and Olive pointed to the chairs. 'Now ye're in, why don't yer sit down.'

Irene took one of the wooden chairs, but Titch remained standing. 'Where are you going to sit, Olive?'

For a brief second, they saw a glimpse of the old Olive. With a half-smile, she said, 'It's all right, Titch, I'm not getting on the couch.'

'Thank God for that! I had to get me ma to rub me neck with liniment last night because it had a kink in it. That's with bending down to yer for so long.'

'Me heart bleeds for yer,' Olive said.

'Yeah, mine too,' Irene chuckled. 'Men can be proper babies sometimes. The least little thing and they're moaning.'

'Thanks for the sympathy, I feel better already.' Titch waited until Olive had seated herself on a wooden chair next to Irene, then he dropped onto the couch. 'Before I forget, Olive, me ma said to ask yer if she could adopt Steve? The two of them have really hit it off. And I've got to say he's a crackin' worker. He'd have the job done today if me ma would stop making him cups of tea every five minutes.'

'Tell yer ma I wouldn't part with him for the world. He's a good son and I'm so proud of him. It grieves me to see him walking around in clothes only fit for the dustbin, because he's really good-looking. But I've made up me mind that somehow or other I'm going to make life better for him. You woke me up, Titch, and I'm determined to start pulling me weight.'

Irene put a hand over Olive's. 'Titch mentioned the job I've got in the pub. I haven't made up me mind whether I'm packing it in yet, but it would be too heavy for you, sunshine. Yer need something a bit lighter, just until ye're feeling a hundred per cent. I'll scout around and see if there's anything going for yer.'

'Thanks, Irene, I would be grateful.'

'You two probably have lots to talk about,' Titch said, 'and I'll only be in the way. But before I go, I've got something to ask yer, Olive, and I don't want yer to fly off the handle about it.' He gave one of his cheeky grins. 'Before I tell me ma something I think she might not like, I always make her promise not to go for the poker. And I'm going to ask you for the same promise.'

'I'll sit on her, if yer like,' Irene said with a laugh. 'Would that help?'

'There's no need, Irene, I won't take off on him. So go ahead, Titch, out with it.'

'Well, it's like this. I've got stacks of clothes I'll never wear. I'm a bugger for hoarding things, and some of them are years old. But they'd do Steve a turn and I'd be made up to see them put to good use. That's if yer wouldn't mind me offering them to him.'

'I wouldn't mind in the least, as long as you're not going to need them. God knows he could do with something decent to wear. Have yer asked him?'

Titch shook his head. 'I wouldn't do that without asking you first in case yer didn't take kindly to the idea.'

'I wouldn't let me pride stand in the way of me son being able to walk around with his head held high. I love him, yer see, and if I could, I'd give him the world. That's not possible right now, so I'm more than willing to accept help from an old friend. And I thank yer from the bottom of my heart, Titch.'

Titch rubbed his hands. 'Thank you for that! Yer can never tell with you women, which way ye're going to turn.'

'Well, I like that!' Irene said. 'We women are an open book compared to you men.'

'And I don't think! It would take a good man to get to the bottom of a woman, believe you me.' Titch pressed his hands on the couch and pushed himself up. 'I'll leave you two to have a good gab, yer've got a lot of years to make up. Me, I'm going to see how the working man is getting on with me ma's yard walls. I'll see meself out, Olive, so stay where yer are.'

'Remember me to yer mother, and say I was asking after her. I often see her passing the window and she still gets around like a two-year-old.'

Titch turned at the door. 'Olive, a word of warning in yer lily-white ears. Me ma's not going to stay away from here now she's taken a shine to yer son. So be a good girl and keep off that ruddy couch, eh?'

As he walked down the hall he could hear both women laughing, and the sound was like music to his ears.

Titch let himself in and walked through to the living room. He could hear gales of laughter coming from the yard, and when he looked through the window it was to see Steve, paintbrush in mid-air, looking down at his mother. Both of them were in pleats. It would seem that the boy had the same sense of the ridiculous as his mother, he thought, making his way out to the yard. 'Well, you two seem to be enjoying yerselves.'

Aggie had her back to him and his voice startled her. 'Yer silly sod, why didn't yer whistle or something to let me know yer were there? I nearly jumped out of me skin.'

'Ma, yer were that busy gabbing, yer wouldn't have heard me if I'd come in playing "I Belong To Glasgow" on a set of bagpipes.'

'Yer haven't got no bagpipes.'

'There wouldn't have been much point, would there, seeing as yer wouldn't have heard them anyway.'

'Oh, I'd have heard them if yer'd been playing "I Belong To Glasgow". That's one of me specialities, that is. Particularly when I've had a few drinks. Me feet won't keep still when they hear that tune, and I can dance in time to the music, too.'

'I know that, Ma, I've seen yer. And I've seen the way yer show yer bloomers off while ye're doing it.' Titch looked at Steve. 'It's not a pretty sight, lad, for a son to see his mother showing her bloomers off. Particularly when the elastic in one of the legs has snapped.'

Aggie gave him a playful push in the chest. 'Away with yer, yer'll have the lad believing yer. He'll probably go home and learn to whistle "I Belong To Glasgow", just so he can see me bloomers.'

'I can whistle it, Mrs Aggie.' Steve had never heard anyone as funny as these two, nor had he ever laughed so much. He shouldn't be getting paid for this job, he should be paying them. If his mam wasn't so desperate for the money, he'd have done it as a favour. 'D'yer want to hear me?'

'No, lad, I'll sit this one out. Yer see, I haven't got me dance shoes with me.'

Titch put an arm across her shoulders and held her close. 'Shall we stop blabbering and see how the worker's doing?'

'He's doing fine, son, really fine.'

'He certainly is.' Titch nodded his head in appreciation. A grown man couldn't have done better. 'Ye're doing a good job, Steve, it looks really professional.'

Steve blushed with pride. 'Thanks, Mr Titch. But I think it'll need two coats. As yer can see, one coat isn't covering the brown bricks properly. I'll try and get it all done today, then come back tomorrow and give it another coat. We didn't mix all the whitewash, so there'll be enough to finish the job.'

'You're the expert, Steve, so I'll leave it to you.'

'And we'll leave yer alone now to get on with it.' Aggie

linked her son's arm and drew him away. 'I'll give yer a shout when I've got a bite to eat ready.' She pushed Titch ahead of her then closed the kitchen door after them, so her words wouldn't carry. 'Did yer ask Olive about the clothes?'

'Yes, Ma. I used me charm, and all the right words, and she said she'd be delighted. It really got to me when she said she wouldn't let her pride stand in the way of her son being able to walk around with his head held high. We don't know how lucky we are, do we?'

'No, son, we don't. And it's because God's been good to us, we should try and help someone who isn't so fortunate.' Aggie hugged herself. 'I can't wait to see his face. I just hope yer clothes fit him, but it's not the end of the world if they don't. It's years since I did any sewing, but I used to be a dab hand with the needle and thread.'

'Ma, I think ye're in yer element with—' Titch broke off as a knock came on the front door. 'I'll see who it is, you start getting something ready to eat.'

He was whistling as he opened the door. 'Irene, I didn't expect yer so soon. I thought you and Olive would have plenty to say to each other.'

'I'll come in for a minute, Titch, but it'll only be for a minute 'cos I've got all me shopping to do and a dinner to get ready.'

Aggie heard the familiar voice and came through. 'Hello, queen.'

'Good morning, Aggie.' Irene leaned sideways to glance in the kitchen. 'Where's Steve?'

'He's in the yard,' the older woman told her with a smile, 'going like the clappers.'

'He won't come in, will he? I don't want him to hear what I've got to say.'

'No, he won't come in.' Titch looked puzzled. 'Why?'

'Olive's a sick woman, Titch. After yer'd gone we were nattering about old times and she seemed fine. But after a while I could see the effort was too much for her and she was getting tired. She did her best to put up a front, God knows, but she just hasn't got the energy or strength. As for her getting a job – well, there's no chance of that. In fact, unless something drastic is done, and soon, I don't think Olive will ever come out of that house alive.'

Aggie gasped, her face white. 'Don't say that, queen.'

'It's true, Aggie. And I feel heartbroken because I blame meself for it. I should never have let her put me off getting into the house years ago. Me own common sense should have told me what was going on, just by looking at Steve. The old Olive would never have let her son walk around the way he does. I feel terrible, racked with guilt.'

'It's not your fault, Irene, we must all shoulder some of the blame,' Titch said. 'But surely it's not too late for all of us to get stuck in and help?'

'There's one drawback to that, Titch, and that's Olive herself. I doubt if she'd accept help, she's too proud. And anyway, to get her back to what she was would take a miracle. She needs plenty of good food down her, and a tonic from the doctor. That part would be easy, if we can talk her round. But we can't do much about her mental state. With the best food and tonics in the world, she's not going to get better while she's living in a house where all the furniture is only fit for a bonfire, and the decoration is enough to send yer round the bend. And on top of all that she hasn't got two ha'pennies to rub together.' Irene sighed, her pretty face showing her sadness. 'I just don't know what the answer is, I feel absolutely helpless.'

'Don't be getting yerself upset, queen,' Aggie said. 'If we put our heads together and all rally round, we'll find a way.'

'Me ma's right, Irene,' Titch said. 'We can't just sit on our backsides and do nowt. I know I'll be away at sea in eight or nine days, and you lot will be left with the worry. But I can muck in with some money.'

'There's plenty we can do, Titch, like me and Aggie making sure she gets wholesome food every day. And George has offered to decorate her house. But it would all come to nothing if we can't find a way to get through to Olive. She has to have the will to live.'

Aggie pinched on her bottom lip, her brow furrowed in concentration. 'I know of a way to get through to her.'

'What's that, Ma?'

'The way to Olive's heart and conscience is through her son. And if it's all the same with you two, I'll go down tomorrow, while Steve's here, and have a good talk to her.'

'It wouldn't do no harm, Ma.'

Irene nodded. 'If she'd listen to anyone, it would be you, Aggie. But tell Steve to warn her that ye're going, otherwise she won't open the door.'

'I've got it all worked out in me head, Irene. I know a good way of making sure she opens the door. And I'll let yer know how I get on.'

'Yeah, don't forget, Aggie, 'cos I'll be on pins.' Irene looked down at her working clothes and grimaced. 'I'll have to go to the shops in these, I haven't got time to change. I've usually done me shopping by now and got the dinner on the go.' She put her arms around Aggie and kissed her cheek. 'Lots of luck tomorrow, sunshine. I hope Olive listens to yer words of wisdom.'

'We'll see, girl, we'll see.'

When Titch came back after seeing Irene out, his mother was busy in the kitchen. 'What have yer got going on in that head of yours, Ma?'

Aggie tapped the side of her nose. 'That's for me to know, son, and you to find out.'

'How can I find out if yer won't tell me? I don't know what's going on in that head of yours.'

'Neither do I, son, so that makes two of us. So we'll both have to wait until tomorrow to find out, won't we? And while yer've got nothing else to do but wait until tomorrow, go and see how Steve's getting on. Tell him it won't be long now before I've got that bite to eat I promised him.'

[illegible]

[illegible]

[illegible]

[illegible]

[illegible]

[illegible]

[illegible]

[illegible]

[illegible]

[illegible]

[illegible]

[illegible]

Chapter Ten

Steve pushed his plate away and licked his lips before sighing with appreciation. Aggie had made him three thick slices of toast and had grilled it with cheese on top. A feast to a boy who was lucky to get a dripping butty. 'I really enjoyed that, Mrs Aggie. It was very tasty, and very welcome.'

'If it wasn't for me son and his queer habits, yer'd have been having a proper dinner,' Aggie told him. 'But he's so used to having his hot dinner at teatime, he doesn't enjoy it in the middle of the day.' Then she added, by way of an explanation, 'That's because he's away at sea more than he's home, yer see.'

'That's right, Ma, put the blame on me,' Titch said. 'Me shoulders are wide enough to take it.'

'And yer legs are strong enough to walk to the kitchen and pour the lad another cup of tea. It's thirsty work, is painting.'

Titch refilled Steve's cup, then sat down to wait for his mother to broach the subject of the clothes. He didn't have long to wait.

'I was cleaning Titch's room out the other day, lad, and he's got more clothes up there than they've got in Blackler's. There's some he'll never wear again, but they're too good to throw out. So I was wondering if yer'd be embarrassed if I asked yer if yer'd like to take a look at them? There's no harm done if they don't fit yer, or yer don't like them. What d'yer think?'

Steve's face was agog. 'Oh yeah, Mrs Aggie, I'd be made

up. As yer can see, I'm not well off for clothes.' Then a thought hit him and the brightness in his eyes dimmed. 'But I don't know whether me mam would like me taking clothes off yer. I'd have to ask her first, in case she got upset.'

'I've already asked yer mam, Steve,' Titch said. 'I mentioned it to her when I was up there earlier and she wasn't in the least bit upset. In fact, she seemed highly delighted.'

'That's the gear, that, Mr Titch, thanks very much.' Steve became fidgety. He didn't want to seem forward, or cheeky, not after they'd been so good to him. But the thought of going to school in decent clothes and not having the two school bullies make fun of him, was one he couldn't cast aside. And to be able to walk up this street and feel as good as anyone else, that would be like a dream come true. So he took a deep breath and asked, 'When can I see them?'

Aggie could sense the lad's nerves were as taut as a violin string, and thought, God love the poor beggar. 'Yer can see them now, Steve. Titch will take yer upstairs and yer can try some of them on for size. The trousers might be too long in the leg for yer, but that's easily remedied.' Then she hit her forehead with an open palm. 'I forgot, yer can't wear long trousers for school!'

'Yes, I can. There's a couple of boys in my class who wear them. They were hand-me-downs from their dads 'cos they couldn't afford to buy the short ones the school say we've got to wear. The first boy who came in long trousers was sent home by the headmistress and told not to come back until he was wearing short grey trousers like the rest of the class. But the boy's father dragged him back an hour later and played merry hell with the headmistress. He told her if she wanted his son in short trousers she'd have to buy them herself because he couldn't afford to. And he said if she sent his son home again, he'd keep him at home because he'd learned all he was going to learn. But wouldn't yer think the school would understand that people can't help being poor?' Steve's face took on a look of defiance. 'I'm fourteen in just under six months, but I've got to stay on an extra three months until the end of term. I don't think that's fair, not when me mam needs me working and bringing in a few bob.'

'I've got news for yer, Steve,' Titch said. 'Once ye're fourteen, the school authorities have got to let yer leave as long as yer have a good reason. And being hard-pressed for money is one of the reasons. Yer have to apply, of course, and prove that ye're a deserving case. But that shouldn't cause yer a problem. They'll send someone out to the house to see what yer circumstances are, but that's only a formality.'

Steve looked as though he'd lost a ha'penny and found a ten-bob note. 'One of the lads in our class said he was leaving on his birthday, but I didn't believe him, I thought he was pulling me leg.' He shook his head. 'Wouldn't yer think the teachers would tell yer these things? They know how hard-up some of the families are, they've only got to look at us to see that. I mean, would I walk around like this if I had a choice?'

'Ah well, lad, teachers don't come from poor families,' Aggie said. 'They don't know what it's like to have yer tummy rumbling with hunger and no food to eat. Nor have they ever gone bare-arsed or barefoot, like some poor kids. Not that I'm blaming them for not knowing what it is to be poor, they can't help the families they were born into. But they could be a bit more understanding of those less fortunate. I know they're there to teach yer the catechism, yer five times table, and the date of the Battle of Hastings, but they could show some sympathy while they're doing it.'

Titch was wide-eyed. 'That was a long speech, Ma! Yer had me back in the classroom there, getting me knuckles rapped for not knowing the date of the Battle of Hastings. I had it drummed into me so much, I'll never forget it. And a fat lot of good it's done me because no one has ever asked me.'

Steve was rapping his fingers on the table, a contented look on his face. 'Yer know, I'll remember this day as one of the best in me life. Yer've given me a job so I can give me mam some money, yer've offered me clothes which I badly need, and I've learned I can leave school three months earlier than I thought. And as if that wasn't enough, on top of it all, I've really enjoyed meself.'

'I'm glad about that, lad, 'cos yer deserve a bit of luck.' Aggie leaned across the table and smiled into his face. 'Now yer can make *me* happy by going upstairs and seeing if those clothes are any good to yer. If they're not, I'll let yer look through mine and see if there's anything takes yer fancy. All except me fleecy-lined bloomers, 'cos I'm partial to them and wouldn't part with 'em even for King Tut himself.'

Steve was laughing as he followed Titch out of the room. 'Our teacher must be slipping up, 'cos I've never heard of King Tut.'

'Ye're not missing much, Steve, so don't worry,' Titch said, throwing open his bedroom door. 'Even King Tut's never heard of himself.'

Aggie's heart was singing as she collected the dirty dishes. She'd taken a real liking to the lad and was glad to have been able to put a little happiness into his life. She couldn't always be so generous, not when Titch was away, 'cos she had to live on the allowance he left her each week and the tiny widow's pension she got. But it didn't cost anything to be a friend, and that's what she hoped she could be to Steve.

The few dishes washed, Aggie went to stand at the bottom of the stairs. She couldn't hear the words that were spoken because the bedroom door was closed, but she could tell by the high pitch of Steve's laughter, and her son's deep chuckle, that things were going well in that room. And as she made her way to her rocking chair, she thanked God. He was the one Who made it all possible, and when she was saying her prayers tonight, she'd have a word with Him about Olive. It wouldn't hurt to have a word in the right ear.

There came a clattering of footsteps on the stairs and Aggie leaned forward in anticipation. Titch was the first to enter the room and his beaming smile was a sign of things to come. Waving a hand towards the door and bowing from the waist, he announced, 'Let me introduce you to Mr Steven Fletcher.'

Aggie's jaw dropped. The lad standing before her, grinning like a Cheshire cat, would pass for sixteen in the long navy-blue trousers, and a grey pullover over a white shirt. 'Well, I never would have believed it. Yer look like a real toff! And a handsome one, at that! By heck, lad, when yer mam sees yer all dolled up to the nines she'll be that proud of yer, she'll soon get herself better so she can go out holding on to yer arm.'

'I couldn't believe it meself, Mrs Aggie, when I saw the clothes all neatly piled up. There's everything there, from underclothes, hankies, socks, shirts, pullovers and trousers. I'm going to have to pinch meself in a minute to make sure I'm not dreaming.'

'The trousers are a couple of inches too long for him,' Titch said, 'but everything else fits fine. And he takes a size six and a half in shoes, only half a size smaller than me. So he can have the brown pair I don't wear very much.'

Steve's head was somewhere in the clouds, he just couldn't believe all this was happening to him. 'Tell me I'm not dreaming, Mrs Aggie.'

'Yer'll soon know ye're not dreaming when yer get that paintbrush in yer hand, lad, and I'm standing behind yer with me poker.' Aggie was feeling very emotional and had to force herself to speak as though nothing out of the ordinary was taking place. 'Before yer take those trousers off, let me see how much wants turning up on them. Hang on till I get me box of pins.'

'Leave a big hem on them, Ma,' Titch said, 'because at the rate he's growing they'll need to be let down in a month or so.'

'I know what I'm doing, son, I don't need no help. And I'll sit and sew them tonight, while you're off boozing with yer shipmates. If I can, I'll shorten the grey pair, as well.'

'I can't wait for me mam to see them,' Steve said, his tummy beginning to settle down. 'I know she'll be over the moon.'

'I've been thinking about that,' Aggie said, as she got down on her knees and put the pin box on the floor beside her. 'Yer'd better not let the whole street see yer carrying them, yer know what a nosy lot some of them are. So I thought it would be best if I nip down with them tomorrow while you're busy painting. I'd use the back entries so no one would see me.' She put half-a-dozen pins in her mouth, then lowered her head so she wouldn't see the doubt on Steve's face. 'Tell yer mam to leave the yard door open, there's a good lad.'

Busy pinning the hem up to the required length, Aggie reminded herself of the old saying that sometimes yer have to be cruel to be kind. Well, that's what she was doing, and she hoped Steve and his mam would come to realise that in the near future.

'Ye're a crafty one, you are, Ma,' Titch said, as he watched Steve through the net curtains. 'Yer didn't ask the lad, yer told him.'

'And what d'yer think he'd have said if I'd asked him, eh? He'd have put me off, that's what. And I'm not going to be put off. Come hell or high water, I'm going to see Olive tomorrow. If she throws me out on me backside, then so be it. But at least I would have tried.'

'It wasn't a criticism, Ma, I'm proud to have a mother who's a better actress than Norma Shearer. And better-looking than Jean Harlow.'

'If yer hadn't noticed, son, Jean Harlow has blonde hair. And her waist is about the size of the top of my arm.'

'Ah, well, there's an explanation for that. Yer see, she wears a wig. Her real hair is the same colour as yours. And she's laced tightly into a pair of stays, that's how come she looks so slim in the films.'

Aggie was busy unpicking the hem on the trousers and she stopped for a moment to look up at her son with a smile on her face. 'Oh, yer know the lady well, do yer? A friend of yours, is she?'

'We're like that, Ma.' Titch crossed two fingers. 'As thick as thieves.'

'In that case, why don't yer ask her if she wants her yard whitewashing? Steve could get away with charging her ten bob, 'cos she must be rolling in money. Stands to reason if she can afford wigs and stays. Neither of them come cheap.'

'Alas, Ma, she hasn't got a yard. All the film stars have great big houses and they stand in acres of land.' Titch managed to keep his face straight. 'Mind you, if she had a yard she'd definitely let Steve whitewash it for her, if I asked her.'

'Well, if she hasn't got a yard, where does she keep her lavvy?' That's got you, thought Aggie as the chair rocked with her laughter. 'Caught yer out there, haven't I, clever clogs?'

'D'yer know, I've never thought to ask her. I will next time I see her, though, and I'll let yer know. Interesting point, that, Ma.'

'Write it down so yer won't forget. And underneath it write "a reel of navy-blue cotton". The corner shop will have one, so yer'll be there and back in five minutes if yer don't stop to gossip to the neighbours.'

'I'm on me way, Ma, but one good turn deserves another. I know yer want to get the trousers done, but don't let that make yer late with the dinner. I'm meeting me mates at seven so I'll have to leave here, all spruced up, by half-six.'

'Your wish is my command, oh Great One. I am only on this earth to serve you.' Aggie jerked a thumb towards the door. 'Now get yer bleedin' skates on.' She heard Titch laugh as he opened the front door, and called, 'Don't come back with the wrong message or I'll make yer take it back. That's after I've tanned yer backside for yer.'

When Titch stepped into the street, it was to see Lucy standing with her arms folded listening to Rhoda, whose mouth was going fifteen to the dozen. 'Everything all right, Lucy?'

'Hello, Mr Titch.' Lucy put a hand on her friend's arm. 'Hang on a minute, Rhoda, I want to tell him something.' Lucy skipped over the cobbles. 'Rhoda came to say she was sorry, Mr Titch, and she's going to apologise to Steve when she sees him.'

'That's good. Didn't I tell yer it would all blow over? I'm on me way to the corner shop for me ma, but when I come back I want yer to come in our house for a minute. I've got something to show yer.'

Lucy rolled her big eyes and grinned. 'Ooh, er, it sounds all mysterious.'

'It's nothing to get excited about, sweetheart, just something I think yer'd like to see. By the way, did yer sleep all right last night?'

'Yeah, I slept like a log. I told me dad about what Rhoda had said, and he said not to worry it would sort itself out. So when I went to bed, instead of letting meself worry, I thought of something nice. When I finally dropped off, I was just stepping on the tram with me dad and we were on our way to town to buy a new coat for me birthday.'

'Looking forward to yer birthday, are yer?'

'Oh, yeah! As me dad says, it's not every day a girl gets to be twelve. I'm dead excited, I can't wait.'

'That's the spirit.' Titch grinned, thinking about the surprise birthday party. 'Anyway, I'll see yer when I get back from the shop. Okay?'

'I'll talk to Rhoda till yer come, then I'll go in with yer.'

'What did yer want to tell him?' Rhoda asked, when Lucy came across. 'It took yer long enough.'

'Mrs Aggie asked me to go a message for her, and I was just telling him I'd go and see her when I've finished talking to you.' It's only a white lie, Lucy consoled herself. God won't punish me for that. 'Anyway, I'm glad we're friends again, Rhoda, I didn't want to fall out with yer.' Her green eyes danced mischievously. 'After all, who could I cheat with if I didn't have you? If I cheated with anyone else there'd be more rows than enough.'

Rhoda's smile was one of relief. She'd been so miserable last night, her mam said her face had turned the milk sour. But it was over now; she'd finally plucked up the courage to apologise and Lucy had been smashing about it. 'When I see Steve I'll tell him how sorry I am. That's if I can face him after what I said.'

'Yer'll face him all right, Rhoda, and Steve isn't the type to bear grudges. Then we can all be friends again, like we should be.' Lucy saw the familiar figure walking down on the opposite side of the road, and said, 'Here's Mr Titch, I'll go and see Mrs Aggie while he's got the door open. Shall I call for yer tomorrow and we can go for a walk?'

'Make it about two. After we've had our dinner and before me mam collars me to help her wash the dishes.'

'I'll try.' Lucy stepped off the pavement waving a hand. 'If I'm late it'll be because I'm helping with our dishes.'

Titch waited for her. With a sweep of his arm, and a bow from the waist, he said, 'After you. Ladies first.'

'I'm not a lady,' Lucy giggled, 'I'm only a girl.' She was still giggling when she entered the living room to a warm welcome from Aggie.

'It's good to see yer, queen – and with a smile on yer pretty face. Not like yesterday when yer were so upset.'

'I'm all right now. Rhoda came down to say she was sorry, so we're friends again. And when she sees Steve, she's going to say sorry to him.'

'That's all water under the bridge now,' Titch got in quickly, before his mother could say something that would spoil his surprise. He cupped Lucy's elbow and drew her to the window. Lifting the net curtain, he said, 'That's what I wanted to show yer.'

'Ooh, er!' Lucy blinked to make sure she wasn't seeing things. 'Ay, Steve's making a good job of it, isn't he?'

'He sure is.' Titch left her to gaze while he tapped his mother on the shoulder and pointed to the trousers on her knee. 'Put them away,' he mouthed the words. 'Don't let her see them.'

'Can I go out and say hello to him?' Lucy asked. 'I won't stay long or put him off doing his work.'

'Of course yer can, queen.' Aggie pushed the trousers down to the side of the chair. 'He'll be made up to see yer.'

Steve wasn't made up at first, he was embarrassed. But with Lucy's pretty face wearing a huge grin, and her big green eyes dancing, he soon felt at ease. 'Have yer come to give us a hand? I'll get another brush if yer like.'

'I would if I could. But you're miles taller than me, I couldn't reach that far. I mean, look how long yer arms are to mine.'

'I could always ask Mrs Aggie for a chair for yer to stand on.'

'Oh, yeah, and I don't think!' The picture that came into Lucy's mind brought forth a fit of the giggles. 'I'd spill that much paint, she'd have a chair to match her yard walls.' She gave a closer look to Steve's work and thought he was very clever. There weren't many boys of thirteen who could do the variety of jobs he did. 'Have yer only got that one wall to do now?'

'Yeah, I'll be finished in an hour or so. But it needs another coat to cover it properly so I'm coming back tomorrow.'

Lucy was in two minds whether to tell him about Rhoda, and how sorry she was. But if she did he'd think they'd been talking about him. Anyway, it was up to her friend to tell him herself. 'I better go and let yer get on with it, or Mrs Aggie will be calling me for everything for stopping the work.'

If Steve was asked who his favourite person was, after his mam, he would say Lucy. The girl always had a smile and a word for him, no matter how scruffy he looked. She always looked him in the face when she was talking to him, never at the rags he had on his back. And he would never forget that. 'Perhaps I'll see yer tomorrow?'

'Could be. If not I'll see yer in the street on Monday, after school.' Lucy got as far as the kitchen door and turned. 'Ye're doing a real good job, Steve. It'll look lovely when it's finished. Ta-ra for now.'

Aggie was standing by the kitchen sink peeling potatoes, and there was a delicious smell coming from a pan on the stove. Lucy wrinkled her nose and sniffed up. 'Ooh, that smells lovely, Mrs Aggie. It's started me tummy rumbling.'

'It's mincemeat, queen, with onions in. Titch said he felt like cottage pie, and his word is my command.'

Lucy looked closer. 'Have yer been crying, Mrs Aggie?'

'No, queen, it's the bleedin' onions, they always make me eyes water. Titch has just told me that that's how they make film stars cry in the films. They stick a bleedin' onion under their nose and the tears flow.' Aggie picked an eye out of the potato she was peeling, then threw it in a pan of water before resting her hand on the draining board. 'He's a mine of information, is Titch. If it wasn't for him I'd be as thick as two short planks. Here was me, thinking what a marvellous actress Greta Garbo was because she could cry when there was a sad bit in the picture. While all the time, she'd just had an onion stuck under her bleedin' nose. Yer see, queen, ye're never too old to learn.'

Titch came to lean against the wall. 'What's me ma saying about me now, Lucy?'

'How clever yer are, Mr Titch. That if it wasn't for you being a mine of information, she'd be as thick as two short planks.'

'Don't you believe it, sweetheart. When the day comes that I can outsmart me ma, then I'll put the flags out. She might act daft, but believe you me, she's all there on top.'

'It's just as well I'm one step ahead of yer, son, or yer'd

have me out of me mind, the things yer come out with.' Aggie swished the potatoes around in the pan, then emptied the dirty water off and replaced it with clean. 'Now make yerselves scarce, the pair of yer, and let me get this dinner ready in time for me one and only to go out and get plastered with his seafaring mates.'

'I better get home meself,' Lucy said. 'Me dad will wonder where I've got to. I'll see yer, Mrs Aggie, and you, Mr Titch.'

Lucy was humming as she walked through the front door she'd left open when Rhoda had beckoned her through the window. Life felt much happier than it had yesterday. Her and her mate were speaking again, Steve had a little job which would bring him a few bob to give his mam, and she had her birthday to look forward to. This time next week she'd be the proud possessor of a new coat.

'Where did you get to, pet?' Bob asked. 'Yer mam made a pot of tea and I went out looking for yer to see if yer wanted a cup.'

'I was talking to Rhoda, then I went in Mrs Aggie's.' Lucy plonked herself on the arm of his chair. 'Guess what, Dad? Steve Fletcher's painting their backyard wall, and he's making a smashing job of it.'

'Oh aye, whitewashing it, is he?'

'That's the same as paint, isn't it? Yer put it on with a brush, just the same.'

Ruby came through from the kitchen, drying her hands on the corner of her pinny. 'That's one feller I wouldn't have near me house. Apart from being filthy and probably walking alive with fleas, I wouldn't trust him as far as I could throw him. It's to be hoped Mrs McBride keeps her eye on her purse.'

Bob could feel his daughter's body stiffen, and looked up to see her face set. He pulled her down on his knee and put his arms around her comfortingly before saying, 'Ye're bang out of order saying that, Ruby. Steve Fletcher's as nice a lad as yer'll find. Because him and his mam are having a rough time, that doesn't make him a thief.'

'Go 'way, it sticks out a mile. He looks an absolute disgrace, no better than a tramp. And I think he'd nick anything he could get his hands on. He wouldn't get over my door, that's a dead cert, I'd chase him.'

Bob patted Lucy's hand to tell her not to interfere, he'd sort this matter out. 'Has anyone ever said that Steve has pinched something from them? Have yer any proof that he's a thief? Of course yer haven't. D'yer think Joe from the corner shop would let him take orders out if he wasn't honest? Or the milkman he helps? No, that boy's as honest as the day is long, and if I were you I'd be very careful what I said. Yer could find yerself in a load of trouble.'

Ruby threw her head back, a look of contempt on her petulant face. 'Yer can talk till ye're blue in the face, yer won't change what I think. He'll never set foot over my door and that's the end of it.'

'Over your door? What am I, Ruby, a flippin' lodger? No, this is still my house, it's my name on the rent book. So watch what yer say.' Bob pushed Lucy gently from his knee. He wasn't going to get involved in an argument in front of her. But he'd have plenty to say to his wife later. He'd never been as friendly with the Fletchers as Irene and George were, because of working shifts. But he remembered Jim being a fine, honest man, and Olive kind and friendly. Jim would turn in his grave if he'd heard what Ruby had said about his son. And apparently Olive was now a sick woman and couldn't help the dire straits they were in. 'Come on, pet, we'll walk to the shop and see if the *Echo*'s in yet.'

Lucy was glad to get out of the house, she felt as though she was suffocating. Holding on to her dad's hand as they walked up the street, she said, 'I don't care what she says, I like Steve and he's me friend.' Her voice choked, she went on, 'And Mrs Aggie and Mr Titch like him, they think he's a lovely lad, and a good worker. I don't know how me mam can say such terrible things about someone she's never even spoken to.'

Bob tried to appear calm, but he was anything but calm inside. His daughter had come in happy and smiling, and in a few minutes her happiness had disappeared, along with her smile. 'The trouble is, yer mam speaks before she thinks. A bit like your friend, Rhoda. So I wouldn't take much heed to what she says, pet, or get upset about it, it's not worth it. You and I know that Steve's a good lad, as do the McBrides and the Pollards. And that's all that counts in the end, isn't it? He's not without friends.'

When Lucy's answer was a deep sigh, Bob tried to cheer her up. 'Just think, pet, this time next week we'll be back from town and yer'll have yer new coat.'

This went some way towards brightening Lucy up. 'Yeah, I'm looking forward to it. I wonder what colour it'll be?'

Lucy had gone next door for a game of cards with Irene and her sons, and Bob and Ruby were getting ready for their Saturday-night drink at the corner pub. Bob was struggling with the stud at the back of his collar as he looked in the mirror, and he was telling himself that next time he bought a shirt he'd get one of the new-style ones, with the collar attached. He finally succeeded in getting the fiddling stud through the hole and gave a sigh of relief. Most of the men in the pub wouldn't have bothered with a collar and tie, they'd be wearing their silk scarves knotted over their Adam's apple. But Bob didn't go out very much so when he did he liked to make the effort.

When he turned around it was to see Ruby putting more lipstick on a mouth that already looked as though it had been slashed with a knife and was pouring with blood. 'D'yer have to put so much of that muck on? It must be an inch thick. And the bright rouge on yer cheeks makes yer look like a clown.'

Ruby pressed her lips together and looked in the hand-mirror she was holding. She twisted her head from side to side to see the effect from all angles. 'You dress as you want, and leave me to dress as I want.'

'Yer won't give an inch, will yer, Ruby? Yer'll have yer own way and it's to hell with what anybody else thinks. At least I try to be reasonable and meet yer halfway, but I'm fighting a losing battle. If it was only meself I had to think about, I'd throw me hands in the air and say to hell with everything, and let yer get on with it. But yer go out of yer way to upset Lucy, and yer do it deliberately. She can't mention any of her friends, the people she likes, without you having to say something nasty about them. And the sad thing is, I think yer get a kick out of it.'

'Sing us another one, will yer, Bob? It's the same old tune over and over again. You and yer precious Lucy. Because she likes someone, it doesn't mean I've got to. And I'm not bleedin' well going to pretend, just to please her. Yer give in to her too much, she's so soft-hearted she cries at the least thing. It's about time she toughened up.'

'Toughen up? Yer mean like you, Ruby? God forbid that she ends up as hard-boiled as you are. She's kind and caring, and I hope she stays that way. I don't want her to change in any way, I love her just as she is. And I feel sorry for you that yer can't find it in yer heart to love yer own daughter.' Bob's eyes locked with his wife's. 'You don't love her, do yer?'

Ruby turned her head. 'She's all right, but I've never had much time for kids. Not like her next door, she devotes her whole life to her two boys. She doesn't have a life of her own. Well, that wouldn't suit me one little bit. I have a life to live, too, and I intend getting the best I can out of it while the going's good. Lucy can do what she likes with hers when she's grown up.'

'A real mother helps her child to grow up. Is there when she's needed, to give advice or comfort.' Bob stared at his wife long and hard. Then he turned slowly and sat down in his chair. Crossing his legs, he said, 'I have no appetite for a drink tonight. It would be hypocritical of me to sit with you in a pub and pretend there's nothing wrong with our marriage. Not when yer've told me yer have no love for our daughter and don't have one motherly instinct in yer whole body. At the moment I can't even bear to look at yer.'

'You can please yerself what yer do, but I'm not staying in on a Saturday night for you nor no one else.'

'Then go on yer own.'

'I'm not sitting on me own in that dive on the corner. It's as miserable as sin there. And yer can't expect me to sit in and look at your miserable gob all night. The least yer can do is give us a couple of bob so I can go for a drink with me mate.'

Bob leaned sideways and took some money out of his trouser pocket. He picked out a two-bob piece and flipped it towards her with his thumb.

Ruby slipped the coin in her pocket and left the room without a word. But when she'd banged the door behind her, a smile came to her face. She had two bob of her own, money she'd saved by scrimping on food. With four bob she could have a really good night out with people who knew how to enjoy themselves. For once in his life her husband had done her a favour.

Bob was in a sombre mood as he lit a cigarette and inhaled the smoke like a dying man would gasp for breath. His brown eyes were troubled as he contemplated what life held in store for him. He was only thirty-six but felt like an old man. If he lived the three score years and ten which were reckoned to be the average lifespan, it meant he had another thirty-four years to go. Could he endure those years without a woman's loving arms to find comfort in? Without a warm, happy home waiting for him after a day's work? Once Lucy grew up and married, this place would hold nothing for him – only misery.

He could hear the squeals of young laughter coming through the wall from the Pollards', and occasionally George's deep throaty roar could be heard above the others.

He was a lucky man, was George, with a loving wife like Irene. It might be the men who brought the money in each week to run the house, but it was the woman who made the house into a home.

The sound of the Pollards' door banging told Bob his neighbour was on his way to the pub. And without even knowing he was going to do it, Bob leapt from his chair and rapped on the window as George came abreast. 'Hang on a minute, wait for me.'

There was surprise on George's face when Bob came out of the house alone. 'On yer own tonight, mate?'

As the men fell into step, Bob said, 'Yeah, but it's a long story. I need a pint first, then I'll bend yer ear back.'

The pub was crowded and noisy. It was pay day, the one night of the week the families could afford a few bob for a night out. 'Grab those two seats, Bob,' George said, nodding his head in the direction of two spare chairs at one of the circular tables. 'I'll get this round in.'

Bob waved and shouted greetings to the regulars he knew, but the din made it impossible for more. And it wasn't the men creating the noise, it was the women. Saturday was the only time they met socially, and there was a week's gossip to be told and savoured. As he watched the faces, Bob thought how much more expressive a woman's face was, compared to a man's. If a bloke was told that So-and-so did this or that, he would probably just raise a brow and promptly forget it. But not so the fairer sex. Their faces went through the whole range of expressions. While their heads were either nodding or shaking, their eyes would be popping out of their head, their lips would purse, their nostrils twitch and arms would be folded to hitch up their bosoms.

'Get that down yer and yer'll soon feel better.' George put Bob's pint down in front of him. 'Alec could do with help, it's murder trying to get served. I'm surprised Betty isn't down to give him a hand.'

'It's filled up early tonight, she probably doesn't know he's got a rush on.'

George picked up his glass, gazed at it with anticipation in his eyes, then took a long swig. 'I needed that,' he said, wiping the froth from his mouth. 'Me throat was parched.'

'That's with all the laughing yer've been doing, I could hear yer through the wall.'

George chuckled. 'Those kids could leave us standing, yer know, Bob. They're so quick off the mark, an answer for everything.' He studied his neighbour's face for a while, then asked, 'You and Ruby fallen out, have yer?'

'We never do anything else, George. Ruby's not easy to live with, I can tell yer. I try to keep the peace, but as I told her tonight, I'm fighting a losing battle. She went too far today though, and I just didn't want to be in her company.' He explained briefly what his wife had said about Steve. 'They were terrible things to say about the lad, and it didn't half upset Lucy. In fact, Ruby goes out of her way to upset her. The girl just has to mention one of her friends and that friend is pulled to pieces. It really worries me.'

'If she'd said that about Steve in front of me, I wouldn't half have given her a piece of my mind. They were wicked things to say and totally without foundation. The lad is no more a thief than you or me.' George would have said more, but Bob was feeling bad enough without him adding to it. 'Anyway, yer've no need to worry about Lucy. She's a sensible girl, got her head screwed on the right way. Of course she gets upset when a friend is called bad names, because she cares for them. And I'm sure yer wouldn't have her any different. She's loyal, too, and no one on God's earth will turn her against someone she's fond of. So stop worrying about her and just be proud that she's yer daughter. I know I would be.' This time, George emptied his glass in one go and set it down. 'As for Ruby, well that's between the two of yer, Bob. I know yer've had problems for a while, even a blind man could see that. And I know it's through no fault of yours.

But no one can help yer there, it's something yer've got to sort out for yerself. In the meantime, have yer noticed me glass is empty?'

This brought a smile to Bob's face. 'I don't need a house to fall on me to take a hint.' He picked up the glasses and looked towards the bar. 'I see Betty's down, everyone at the bar's got a full glass in front of him. I'll be back in sixty seconds flat, with two of the same.'

'Tell Betty I said if she's feeling generous, she can put a tot of whisky in mine and I'll love her for ever more.'

Bob laughed. 'Some hope you've got.'

'Hope is what life's all about, mate. If yer lose that, what's left?'

As he watched Betty pulling a pint, Bob told himself George was right. Hope was all he had left and he'd better cling to it.

Chapter Eleven

It was eleven o'clock on the Sunday morning when Aggie carefully negotiated the step down into her yard. Over her arm was her shopping basket, the contents of which were covered over with an old cushion cover. She stopped by Steve, who had arrived an hour before and was busy applying a second coat of whitewash to the walls.

'That's a big basket for you to be carrying, Mrs Aggie.' There was a look of concern on the boy's face. 'It looks heavy, too. Shall I come and give yer a hand with it?'

'No, I'll manage fine. Look, I can carry it in front of me using both hands. I'll go down this entry, cross over at the main road, then go up your entry. There's never many people around on a Sunday morning, so I can't see meself bumping into anyone I know.' She glanced up at the back bedroom window where the curtains were still drawn over. 'Yer'll get a cup of tea when Titch decides to get out of bed. It was all hours when he came in and he's probably got a hangover.'

Steve grinned. 'Had a drop to drink, did he?'

'A drop, did yer say? I bet every pub in Liverpool has been drunk dry. Once he gets out with his mates he forgets to stop. His excuse, and he always has an excuse, will be that each one has to buy a round and his turn didn't come up till last, as per usual. And there was no way he could leave without paying his way, 'cos he'd never hear the end of it.'

'How many mates was he out with?'

'From the state he was in, I'd say about fifteen.' Aggie's

face softened into a smile. 'He couldn't get the key in the door and I could hear him fumbling and cursing. Then when he finally got in, he walked into the bottom stair and fell face forwards. I did think of lighting the candle at the side of me bed and going out on the landing with it, so he could see where he was going. Then I thought, To hell with it, he's a big boy now. He got himself in that state, let him get himself out of it.'

'How did he get up the stairs in the end?'

Aggie gave another quick glance at the bedroom window. 'A secret?'

'Yeah, a secret. I promise.'

'On his bleedin' hands and knees, the silly bugger. And when I looked in on him this morning, he was lying on top of the bed in the clothes he'd gone out in. But don't yer say I told yer or he'll be embarrassed. And I don't mind, really, 'cos he spends more of his life on the sea than he does on dry land. So the way I look at it, he's entitled to go off the rails once in a while.'

'I agree with yer, Mrs Aggie. I know he's a good son, and I know he thinks the world of yer because he told me.'

'The feeling is mutual, lad. I love the bones of him.' Aggie patted Steve's cheek. 'I'd better get moving 'cos even with a hangover, me dear son will expect his Sunday roast dinner on the table. So I'll see yer later.'

Aggie hurried down the entry, her eyes looking straight ahead. If she did meet someone she'd have to make some sort of excuse. She couldn't say she was going to the corner shop, not when her basket was already full. She was lucky, though. She made it to the Fletchers' yard door without bumping into a soul. But she didn't open the door straight away, she stood for a while to compose herself. It wasn't often she got the collywobbles, but she had them now. What sort of reception was she going to get? 'There's only one way to find out, yer silly cow,' she muttered under her breath, 'and that's get in there.'

Olive had been watching through the back window, and when Aggie walked up the yard it was to find the kitchen door open and Olive waiting for her. 'Hello, Aggie.'

'Hello, girl.' Aggie put the basket down and held out her arms. 'Come and give an old woman a kiss.'

Safe in the warmth and comfort of Aggie's arms, Olive said, 'Titch told me about this old woman yer keep talking about. Is it anyone I know?'

Aggie chuckled. 'I only bring her into play when I'm looking for sympathy. Otherwise, I'm like a spring chicken.'

Olive bent and picked up the basket. 'Come on through, but be warned, it's no palace.'

'Oh, I thought it was, that's why I put me false teeth in.' Aggie gazed around the bare room and nodded. 'Ye're right, girl, it's no palace. But then, who the bleedin' hell wants to live in a palace? With all those servants around, yer'd never be able to soak yer feet in a bucket of nice warm water or have the tin bath out in front of the fire.'

Olive's smile turned into a full laugh. 'Oh Aggie, yer haven't changed a bit.'

'Only got older, girl, and perhaps a little wiser. But you've changed. Look at yer, there's not a pick on yer.'

'Life hasn't been kind to me, Aggie. It made me older, but not wiser.'

'Aye, well, ye're back in the fold now, one of us again. And I'm not having anyone in my gang who's as thin as a lath.' Aggie told herself she'd gone far enough for now. One step at a time was the right way in this situation. 'Anyway, I've brought the clothes for Steve. There's another pair of trousers to come, I didn't have time to turn them up last night.'

'That's all I could get out of him last night, he was full of it. He described everything in detail, the trousers, shirts, pullovers, socks, and even a pair of shoes.'

'Have a look at them for yerself, girl. They're not new, mind, but they're in good nick. Steve should get plenty of wear out of them.'

Olive put the basket on the couch and sat down beside it. When she took the cover off and saw everything all neatly ironed and folded, she shook her head as though she didn't believe what she was seeing. 'No wonder he was excited. These clothes look as though they've just been bought.'

'Some of them are years old,' Aggie said. 'Titch isn't home very often, as yer know, so he didn't get to wear them all that much and it seemed a shame to leave them lying there when they could be put to good use. And I don't know anybody better to get them to than your son. He's a fine lad, Olive, and I bet ye're proud of him.'

'I have a son in a million, Aggie, and I'm more than proud of him. Nobody will ever know the life that lad's had since his dad died.' She put her hand on top of the clothes. 'He deserves to wear clothes like this, and I'll never be able to thank yer enough. One day, please God, I'll be able to pay yer back in some way.'

'Yer've nothing to pay me back for – that clobber belongs to Titch.' Aggie gave her cheeky grin. 'Still, seeing as he's away all the time, yer can pay me back by letting me be a friend to Steve. I've really taken to the lad, and I'd be over the moon if he called in now and again for a natter. Yer see, it gets lonely when Titch is away.'

'Yer've no worries on that score, Aggie, because I think ye're stuck with Steve whether yer like it or not. He thinks you and Titch are the funniest things on two legs. I must have heard every word yer've spoken in his presence. The tricks Titch plays on yer, and the jokes and wisecracks that fly between yer. I was a bit jealous that I wasn't a fly on yer wall and could have heard it all first hand. Olive stood up and placed the folded clothes carefully on the broken-down sideboard. Then she put the basket on the floor and sat on the couch with her legs curled under her. 'I'm glad he's making friends, Aggie, he needs them. It's not healthy for a young lad to have no other company than a sick mother.'

Aggie was beginning to see what Irene had seen. Olive

could only keep up the pretence of normality for so long, then she flagged. 'What sickness have yer got, Olive? What does the doctor say it is?'

'Oh, I haven't seen no doctor, we can't afford it. Anyway, he'd only tell me what I already know. Years of money worries have worn me down and the lack of good food hasn't helped. And living in this hovel would break anyone's spirit. I just haven't the strength or the will to do anything about it.'

Aggie's sympathy was mixed with impatience. 'Olive, years ago, before yer got in this mess, all yer had to do was walk down the road and knock on my door, the Pollards' or the Mellors'. We could have helped yer out. I would have minded Steve for yer while yer got yerself a job – yer should have thought of that. But all that's by the wayside now. It's the future yer should be looking to.'

'Get off me backside, yer mean, Aggie? I can't, I haven't got the strength. An hour after I get out of bed, I'm lying on this couch, drained.'

Aggie closed her eyes and sighed as she tried to think of the right words. 'Olive, would yer listen to the thoughts of an old woman?'

Olive smiled. 'Yer told me before yer were only an old woman when yer were after sympathy. So what's on yer mind?'

'There's a few things on me mind, but the main two are you and Steve. At his age he deserves some pleasure and happiness. But he can't have either because he's always worrying about you. So for his sake, if not yer own, yer should make a valiant effort to change things. Also on me mind, are the friends who want to help yer. None of them are well-off, so they can't wave a magic wand and change yer life overnight. But they can help in little ways and they'd get a kick out of doing it. And before yer tell me ye're too proud to accept our help, I'll ask yer to think of that lovely son of yours.'

Olive's eyes were guarded. 'What sort of help are yer

talking about? I'll accept the clothes and be more than grateful. But I'd never accept money.'

Aggie huffed. 'Yer'd not be getting offered money, girl! What the bleedin' hell d'yer think I am? A ruddy money-lender?'

In spite of herself, Olive laughed. And memories of the old days came flooding back. Life had been good then, with so many friends and lots of good times. And she remembered in particular how Irene and Aggie had always made her laugh. You could never be downhearted when they were around, they wouldn't let you. 'I'll accept anything within reason, Aggie, except money or blows.'

Aggie rolled her eyes to the ceiling. 'At last, a glimmer of light at the end of the tunnel. I've never suffered with nerves in me life, girl, but right now yer've got me a bleedin' nervous wreck. Anyway, see what yer think of me first offer of help. And keep yer gob shut until I've had me say.' She laced her fingers across her tummy and licked her lips before starting. 'I'm making a roast dinner when I get home, and 'cos Steve's there, I was going to make enough for him. That's if Titch ever gets out of bed, like, 'cos he came in at two this morning, blind drunk. If he doesn't get up, that's his look-out. Me and Steve will share his dinner between us.' A lock of hair fell down to cover her eyes and she brushed it aside, only for it to fall again. 'Blasted nuisance. I've gone off the bleedin' track now. The way I'm going on, no one will be getting anything to eat. So I'll just rush things along, Olive, and ask would yer like some of me roast dinner? And I'll have yer know I'm noted far and wide for me crispy roast potatoes. A proper treat, they are.'

Olive asked, tongue in cheek, 'Oh, how far and wide are they known, Aggie?'

'From me front door to me back door, girl.'

'In that case, I can't refuse, can I? Not when they come with a recommendation like that. So, yes, please, Aggie. And thank you.'

Aggie jerked her head backwards. 'Blimey, anyone would think I was offering yer a dose of arsenic! If it wasn't for me false teeth falling out I'd shout for joy.'

'Aggie, you do me more good than any dinner.'

'That's as maybe, girl, but ye're still getting a dinner.' Aggie got to her feet and reached for the basket. 'I'll take this and Steve can bring it back with enough to eat for both of yer. Seeing as it's a celebration, like, I'll let him have an hour off so he can eat with yer. And I'll tell him to watch yer like a hawk, and report back to me if yer don't eat every scrap.'

'I'll do me best, I promise. And it's been lovely to see yer again, Aggie, I'm really glad yer came.' Olive lowered her eyes. 'I've been stupid, haven't I? Like yer said, I should have knocked on yer door years ago, before all the things I held dear went to the pawnshop.'

'It's no good fretting about what might have been, queen, 'cos yer can't turn the clock back. But that clock is still ticking away, taking yer into the future. And yer can do something about that. For you and Steve.'

'How was me mam?' Steve asked before Aggie had time to get through the entry door. 'Was she all right with yer?'

Aggie tilted her head. 'Yer don't see any black eyes, do yer? She was fine, lad, and as happy to see me as I was her. But she'll tell yer all about it when ye're having yer dinner. Me meat should be done by now, so I'll get the carrots and turnips on the go, and the potatoes. It'll be about an hour, then I'll fill two plates and yer can take them home and eat with yer mam, eh? How does that sound?'

Steve was already thinking of Aggie as his guardian angel, now he could almost see a halo hovering over her head. 'I don't know what to say, Mrs Aggie, except ye're a little love and a really good woman. I know me mam's going to get better now, with you and Mrs Pollard helping her. Oh, and I mustn't forget Mr Titch, he's been brilliant.'

Aggie's face did contortions. 'Has that son of mine seen light of day yet?'

Steve tried to keep a straight face but wasn't successful. 'Yeah, he came down about half an hour ago and made me a cup of tea.' He gave a throaty chuckle. 'I think he was putting it on for my benefit, but he was staggering all over the place. I would have believed he was still drunk except he didn't spill a drop of tea.'

'Never take my son at face value, lad, or yer'll come a cropper. He's the best bleedin' actor I've ever seen. The number of times I've fallen for his tricks, I must want me brains testing. I get me own back now and again, like, but I've got a sneaking suspicion it's because he lets me.' She winked broadly before making her way up the yard. 'I bet he's got a good yarn to tell me about last night, and I bet there won't be a word of truth in it. Still, I wouldn't have him any different.' She stepped into the kitchen then popped her head back out. 'Give me an hour, lad, that's all.'

Titch heard her open the kitchen door and quickly folded the *News of the World* and threw it on the couch. Then he slid forward in his chair, his legs spread out and his head in his hands. He peeped through his fingers, and it was with great difficulty he kept his face straight when his mother appeared in the doorway, shaking her head and tutting. Oh, how he loved to pull her leg, particularly as he knew she enjoyed it as much as him.

'In the name of God, will yer look at the state of him?' Aggie could see the quick rise and fall of his stomach, telling her he was laughing inside. 'If yer picked him up in the dark yer'd bloody soon drop him as soon as it was daylight.'

His voice halfway between a moan and a groan, Titch said, 'Me head is splitting and I feel sick. I won't be able to eat no dinner Ma, I'd only bring it all back.'

'That's all right, son, not to worry. It'll save me doing any extra.' She deliberately turned around slowly and made her way to the sink. Her hand went to the tap, but before she turned it on, she said, 'Olive can have your dinner.' The running water covered any reply her son might have made, but as she knew it would, her remark brought him to the door.

'Yer did it then, Ma?' Looking as sober as a judge, Titch came to lean against the sink. 'Yer got in to see Olive?'

'Did yer ever have any doubts that I wouldn't?' Aggie looked down her nose as her eyebrows were raised in a haughty expression. 'Yer haven't got much faith in yer old mother, have yer?'

'I've got so much faith in yer, Ma, I've already parboiled enough potatoes for four people. And if yer eyesight wasn't failing because of yer age, like, yer'd see there's a pan of carrots and turnips boiling away happily on the stove.'

Mother and son gazed at each other, and the love that flowed between them needed no words. Aggie felt like throwing her arms around him, but knew that when she got sentimental it brought on the tears. And the last thing she wanted was for him to see her crying. He'd be legging it back to his ship before his leave was over if she bawled every time she looked at him. 'Ye're too quick for yer own good, you are. One of these days yer'll meet yerself coming back.' She placed a stiffened finger on her chin and put on a thoughtful expression. 'Mind you, if yer did meet yerself coming back, yer could ask yerself if yer'd had a good time. And if yer hadn't, then yer needn't bother going.'

Titch chuckled. 'Ay, Ma, I had quite a few pints last night. I'd need a clear head to sort that one out. But it sounds good, so it's one up to you today. That's until I'm sober, then I'll see if I can beat it. Anyway, how did yer get on with Olive?'

'Just hang on until I get me meat out of the oven, then I can put the potatoes in while the fat's hot.' Aggie took a towel from the kitchen door and was about to open the oven when her son took the towel from her.

'Stand back, Ma, let me do it.' He bent down and took out the roasting tin, sniffing up as he did so. 'That smells delicious. I see we're doing ourselves proud today with a leg of lamb.'

'That's because you're home, son. If I was on me own it would be a mutton chop.' Aggie pointed to the stack of plates on the shelf. 'Pass one down for us, there's a good lad.' While Titch held the plate, she speared the leg of lamb with a fork and transferred it over. 'Done to a turn, that is. Just the way I like it. A slice of that with a spot of mint sauce and I'll think I'm in heaven. Now you go and sit down while I set everything in motion. Then I'll make us a cuppa and tell yer how I got on.'

Ten minutes later they were sat facing each other either side of the hearth. Titch with his big cup, which Aggie always said was big enough to have a bath in, and her with a dainty china one. In her opinion, tea tasted better out of a china cup. And it was the one luxury she wouldn't do without. She only ever possessed one, and if it got broken she'd hot-foot it down to TJ's to root through their basket of seconds until she found one which was perfect except for a flaw in the pattern. 'I'm glad I've seen Olive for meself. Now I can understand what Irene was saying. It'll take more than a few hot dinners to get her back on her feet again. She made me very welcome, and was fine at first, but it didn't last long. She admitted that after she'd been out of bed an hour, she was whacked.' Aggie shook her head sadly. 'It's no wonder she's lost all her spirit – it would bring anyone down. To think of all those lovely ornaments and pictures she had, all gone to the pawnshop. And she wouldn't get much off them, yer know what pawnbrokers are like. They know the poor buggers wouldn't be there unless they were desperate, and they give yer next to bleedin' nothing for things. They probably paid Olive out in coppers for all those possessions that held her memories. And what gets me mad is, the sods know there's not much chance of people redeeming the things they put in, so yer'd think they'd give a fair price.'

'It's business, Ma. Yer can't afford to have a heart when ye're in business.'

'Aye, well, bad cess to them, I say. If I was them I wouldn't be able to rest me head on me pillow at night. I know they've got to make a living, but they don't have to fleece people who are on their uppers.'

Titch's eyes were looking over his mother's shoulder to the back window. He could see Steve busy at work and veered the conversation back to the lad's mother. 'Any ideas over Olive, Ma? I was talking to Steve when I took him his tea out, and he seems very confident you and Irene are going to work miracles with her. He's got in his head she'll soon be up and about.'

'I'm not making any promises, son, 'cos that wouldn't be fair. If Olive can be helped at all, then there's a few of us will be there for her. But I'm no doctor – I don't know whether she's let herself go down so much there's no turning back.' Aggie stopped the rocking motion of the chair and stood up. 'I'm nipping to Irene's after dinner, and we'll see what the two of us can come up with between us. But right now me potatoes must be browning nicely and I don't want them too crisp.' She bent to smile into her son's face. 'After all, me reputation is at stake here. I've been blowing me trumpet to Olive about me roasties being the best she'll ever taste, so I'd never hear the last of it if she ends up with a plate of burnt offerings.'

'It would be the price of yer, though, Ma, for bragging. Ye're always telling me yer can't stand bigheaded people who never stop bragging.'

'Yeah, but I didn't mean meself, son, I meant everybody else. I'm not daft enough to call meself bigheaded when I know I'm not. Shame on yer, son, for thinking that of yer poor old mother. I'm hurt to the quick, I really am.' With that, Aggie flounced out to the kitchen before allowing a smile to crease her face.

★ ★ ★

Steve placed the basket carefully on the table. 'I've carried it straight all the way, Mam, and Mrs Aggie packed some newspapers down the side, so I don't think any of the gravy will have spilled out.' His pleasure and excitement was such, Olive felt she could stretch her hand out and touch it. 'I've had this wonderful smell wafting up me nose all the way home and me mouth is watering.'

Olive slipped her legs over the side of the couch. She didn't have any appetite, never did these days because usually there was nothing to eat. And after a while your tummy got accustomed to not eating and didn't send out the hunger pangs. But for her son's sake she would eat the meal Aggie had sent down, even if she had to struggle. 'You get the knives and forks, son, and I'll take the plates from the basket.'

'I'll do it, Mam, you stay where yer are.'

'This is one day I'm sitting at the table to eat, Steve. If I don't do the thing proper, Aggie will have me guts for garters. And I don't want it to get cold, not after her going to all the trouble. So hurry up, sweetheart.'

When Steve came back from the kitchen it was in time to see his mother taking the covering plates off. And they stood together and gazed down at the slices of lamb, mounds of carrots and turnips, and the crispy potatoes. 'That looks and smells really good,' Olive said. 'I just hope I can do it justice.'

'Yer will, Mam, once yer get started. Even if yer don't eat it all, do yer best.' He gave a start as he remembered something and pushed a hand into his pocket. 'I almost forgot! Mrs Aggie gave me this little bottle with mint sauce in. She said to tell yer the bottle had been well washed and that she wasn't trying to poison yer.'

Olive pulled out a chair. 'Come on, son, let's get stuck in.' As she sat down she gave a half-smile. 'It's a wonder the table doesn't collapse with shock. It's the first time in years there's been a proper dinner on it.'

'Things are going to get better, though, Mam, I know they are.'

'I'm sure they are, love, I'm sure they are.'

Watching anxiously as his mother picked at her food, Steve asked, 'Yer will let them help yer, won't yer, Mam? Yer won't send them away?'

'Of course I won't send them away, that would be unkind and ungrateful. And I'll let them help us until we get on our feet. That's as long as I know they're not going without themselves, just to give to us.'

Steve suddenly burst out laughing. 'What yer've just said reminded me of Mrs Aggie, and I know what her answer would be if she heard yer saying that. Mr Titch asked her for something yesterday, and what she said didn't half tickle me.' He pushed his chair back and jumped to his feet. 'Pretend I'm her and I'll show yer how she said what she did.' Steve's hands folded over his tummy and his head tilted. ' "I haven't got none, son. And if I haven't got none, I can't give yer none. I mean, it stands to sense doesn't it? If I held me hand out, palm upwards, and there was nothing on it, then I couldn't give yer nothing off it, could I?" ' He was delighted when he heard his mother chuckle. He took his seat and picked up his knife and fork. 'Honest, Mam, they're both a treat to listen to.'

'What did Titch say to that?'

Steve was laughing so much it took a while to compose himself. 'Mr Titch said, "If I had nothing, Ma, I'd still give yer half of it." Then Mrs Aggie said, "That's bleedin' generous of yer, I must say. But if it's all the same to you, son, I'll wait until yer've got something and then I'll have half of it." '

Olive was shaking with laughter. 'They haven't changed a bit – they could always make a joke out of nothing.' She looked down at her plate. 'I know yer've been told to watch me like a hawk and report back, so we'll stop talking for a while and eat this delicious dinner.'

'That's right, Mam, get it down yer. It'll do yer the world of good.'

Aggie took the plates out of the basket and asked, 'Did yer wash these, lad, or lick them clean?'

'Both, Mrs Aggie. I licked and me mam washed. She ate every bit as well, and she told me not to forget to tell yer that. It was lovely and we didn't half enjoy it.'

'It does me heart good to hear that, lad, it really does. There's enough lamb over for tomorrow, so give us a knock when yer've finished yer little job at the corner shop and see what I've got ready for yer. I might go down and see yer mam during the day, but although Titch will have his Sunday roast at midday, he flatly refuses through the week. So you'll have to come up for it.'

'It suits me, Mrs Aggie, I like coming here.' Steve was hopping from one foot to the other, unable to contain his excitement. 'I'll be wearing me long trousers tomorrow, and one of the shirts and pullovers. Yer won't know me when yer see me.'

'In that case, yer'd better introduce yerself in case I mistake yer for the landlord.' Aggie smiled and patted his cheek. 'You get on with what yer've got to do, lad, 'cos I'm going up to the Pollards' for a natter. Titch is having forty winks, so if he wakes up, tell him where I've gone. He's like a fish out of water on a Sunday, with the pubs being shut.'

'Think of the money he's saving, Mrs Aggie.'

'He doesn't see it like that. As he says, money is round to go round. And God knows he tries to spread as much of it around as he can. He can't get rid of it quick enough.' Aggie peeped through the side of the living-room door. 'He's well away, so I'll go out the back to save banging the front door. I'll be back before yer've finished, to pay yer.'

Steve hung his head. 'I wish I could say I don't want nothing for doing it, 'cos yer've been so good to me. But we need the money, Mrs Aggie.'

'Ay, lad, yer've done a job and yer want paying for it, same as any man would. So don't be going all soft-hearted, yer can't afford it. And I'm on me way now, before the queer feller wakes up. I'll see yer later.'

Irene was at the sink washing the dinner dishes when Aggie walked up the yard. 'Yer pick yer time, don't yer, sunshine? Ten minutes earlier and yer could have helped me with the dishes. I think yer've got second sight.'

'I'll dry them for yer, save yer moaning.' Aggie reached for the tea towel. 'I sent a roast dinner down to Olive, and she ate the lot.'

'Go 'way!' Irene rested her dripping hands on the sink. 'Ay, that's a good sign, isn't it? Apart from getting some goodness down her, it means she's willing to let us help.'

'I think there's a few ways we can help that won't cost anything and will brighten the place up. God knows, it needs something doing to it, it's like a bleedin' morgue. A couple of days stuck in there and I'd be ga-ga.'

Irene grinned at her neighbour's way of putting things. 'The boys are out so we can sit and talk in peace when we've finished these. George has already read the paper from front to back so he'll be glad of someone to talk to.'

'Oh, he won't be talking to me, girl, it'll be the other way round. He's going to sit and listen to what I've got to say first, then he can put his twopennyworth in.'

They heard the rustling of paper, then George's voice boomed. 'I heard that, Aggie McBride. Don't yer be coming here throwing yer weight around. On the Sabbath, too!'

Aggie put the last plate on the shelf before hanging up the towel. 'Ye're going to listen to me whether yer like it or not, George Pollard. I'm pulling rank here, being the oldest, like, and the one with the most sense.'

Irene finished drying her hands and pushed Aggie through the living-room door. 'If you two are going to argue, at least do it in the same room.'

'Argue? Me, argue!' Aggie looked hurt to the quick. 'Me,

what's as quiet as a mouse and as timid as a rabbit? Well, that's a new one on me.'

Irene pulled a chair out and motioned for her neighbour to sit down. 'Would yer like to take yer wings off first, sunshine, so they won't stick in yer back?'

'I left them at home, queen, 'cos I didn't want yer to feel inferior.' Aggie chuckled before sitting down and becoming businesslike. 'Olive said she'll accept any help except money. Now there's a few little jobs that want doing that will only need a couple of nails. One is the sideboard cupboard that's hanging on one hinge. The other hinge is still on, but the screws are missing. It wouldn't take a man two minutes to fix that. And the drawer that's missing, I noticed it standing up under the stairs, with the handle beside it. That would be another two-minute job.' She looked at George. 'Those two things alone would improve the appearance of the room. Yer can't expect Steve to know what to do, he's only a lad. And when he's not at school he spends most of his time trying to earn a few coppers. So are yer still prepared to help, George?'

'Of course I am. And I know someone else who'd pitch in, and that's Bob from next door. Yer'd be doing him a favour by asking, 'cos sometimes I think he'd like to get out of the house for a while.' George pushed himself out of the chair. 'Just hang on, Aggie, and I'll give him a knock. More hands make light work, and he knows Olive and Steve.'

Bob was indeed glad to get away from the house. Lucy was out with Rhoda and the place was like a graveyard with never a word passing between him and his wife. He'd been in bed last night when Ruby came in after midnight, reeking of drink. The pubs closed at ten o'clock so she must have gone back to someone's house. He'd been so disgusted he intended to have it out with her this morning, but changed his mind in the light of day. What was the use, it wouldn't achieve anything.

Aggie gave him a smile of welcome. 'How's the world treating yer, Bob?'

'So-so, Aggie, I can't complain.' Bob had only been in the room a matter of seconds but already he felt a different man. What a change it was to see smiling faces and know those smiles were genuine. 'And yerself and Titch? Are yer both okay?'

'I'm fine, but I can't speak for me son. He was out on a bender last night and I've left him sleeping it off on the couch. He never tells me anything about where he goes, and I don't ask. But I've no doubt you and George will hear all about it.' Aggie laced her fingers and rested them on her knee. 'We're having a conflab about Olive, and George said you wouldn't want to be left out.' She quickly brought him up to date on the situation. 'So, d'yer want to join our gang, Bob?' Before he could answer, she held up her hand. 'There's something yer should know before yer decide. I'm the gaffer, and I'm a hard taskmaster. If yer step out of line, yer get punished. Yer'll have to write out a hundred lines saying, "Aggie is the boss". So speak now or forever hold yer peace.'

'Yer can be my boss any day, Aggie.'

'Right, let's get down to business then.'

Chapter Twelve

'Will you stop running in and out every minute?' Ruby grabbed hold of Lucy's wrist and held it in a vice-like grip. 'Ye're getting on me nerves and yer'll know it if I lose me temper.'

'I only want to know the time.' Lucy didn't meet her mother's eyes. It was her birthday but it had never been mentioned. There'd been a card for her this morning with both her parents' names on, but the girl knew it was her dad who bought the card and wrote the greeting. He'd left it propped up on the mantelpiece before he went to bed after finishing his night shift. Lucy had thanked her mother because her name was on it, but all she got in reply was a grunt. 'Me dad said he'd get up about one o'clock to take me into town and I thought I'd start to get meself ready about twelve. I want to look clean and tidy for him.'

'Listen to me, yer selfish little faggot. The world doesn't stop because it's your birthday, even though yer seem to think it should.' Ruby was giving vent to a temper that had been building up all morning. Every time she thought of the money that was going to be spent on her daughter today, she could scream. 'I don't want to see yer in here again until yer dad's up, d'yer hear?' Her grip tightened and Lucy winced with the pain. 'I said, did yer hear me?'

'I heard yer, Mam. Will yer let go of me hand now, please, 'cos ye're hurting me.'

'It's nothing to what I'd like to do to yer. Ye're nothing but a spoilt little brat.' Ruby gave one last squeeze before releasing her grip. 'Now, get out of me sight.'

Lucy stood by the front door, squared her shoulders and put a smile on her face before running to join Rhoda. 'Me dad's not up yet, so we can have another game.'

Rhoda was bursting with excitement. She'd been invited over to the McBrides' to a tea-party, but had been sworn to secrecy. She hadn't got to say a word to Lucy or the Pollard boys. And she was finding it very hard to keep the secret. 'What time are yer going into town?'

'About half-one to two o'clock. Whenever me dad's ready. Don't forget he's been on night shift, so he needs some sleep.'

'But yer'll have to be back for four o'clock.' Rhoda nearly bit her tongue off. She shouldn't have said that, she nearly gave the game away. 'What I mean is, yer'll be back about four, won't yer? I don't want to have to wait until tomorrow to see yer new coat.'

'Oh, don't worry about that.' Lucy managed to put her hurt and sadness aside. 'I'll be swanking up and down the street in it, yer won't be able to miss me.'

'Ye're lucky, you are. I wanted a coat for me birthday but me mam said the two I've got will last me a while, 'cos there's not a break in them.'

'She's right, too! Yer've got a lovely mam, Rhoda, and it's not often she says no to yer. Yer've got more clothes than any other girl in the street.'

Something caught Rhoda's eye. 'Yer dad's outside your door, Lucy, and he's waving like mad.'

Lucy's face lit up. 'He got up early! I've got a lovely dad, Rhoda, I'm very lucky.' She gave her friend a grin before turning to cross the cobbled street. 'I'll see yer later. Ta-ra.'

Bob swept her up in his arms. 'How's my birthday girl?'

'I'm very happy, Dad.' Lucy grinned down into his face, thinking how lost she'd be without him and his love. 'Ye're up early.'

'Yeah, well, by the time we get ready it'll be one o'clock. And we don't want to be rushed into buying a coat, do we?' He set her down and they walked into the house arm-in-arm. 'We have to be sure yer get one yer really like.'

'We will, Dad, I know we will.' Lucy put a hand over her heart. 'I've got a feeling in here that I'm going to see a coat and fall head over heels in love with it.'

'I hope so, pet. Anyway, yer mam's made a pot of tea, we'll have a drink and then get ourselves ready.'

'I'll use the sink first to get washed, Dad, so yer won't have to wait. Then I'll have me drink before I get changed into me best dress.'

The tea had cooled down by the time Lucy had washed, and she was able to drink it quickly. She didn't want to be alone in her mother's company because she knew there'd be sarcastic comments passed, and she didn't want anything to mar her birthday. It should be a day of happiness and she was determined it would be. To prove her intention, she hummed as she changed into her maroon dress and combed her dark curly hair until it shone.

'Yer look as pretty as a picture, pet,' Bob said, bending his arm for her to link. 'Let's go and search the town for a coat that looks as good as you do.'

Ruby didn't even come out of the kitchen to see them off. She didn't trust herself to keep her thoughts to herself. And a few wrong words now could jeopardise the increase in her housekeeping she was relying on to start next week.

When they were passing the Pollards' house, Lucy said, 'I thought Mrs Pollard would have come out to wish me a happy birthday. She said last night she hadn't forgotten it and she'd see me today.'

'The day's not over yet, pet, so give her time. Yer know she works for a couple of hours in the mornings, then she's got the shopping and dinner to get ready.' Bob thought of the surprise in store for his daughter and it gladdened his heart. It wasn't often anything nice came her way.

'Yeah, ye're right, Dad.' Lucy mentally scolded herself for being selfish. Mrs Pollard had been really good to her. Every other day she'd changed the dressing on her leg, and last night when she was taking the pad off, she'd said it was better now and didn't need covering any more. 'I'll give her a knock and show her me new coat. And Mrs Aggie and Mr Titch.'

'Then we'd better make sure yer get a posh one, eh?'

Lucy giggled. 'It doesn't have to be posh, Dad, just nice.'

The assistant in Blackler's couldn't have been more helpful if Bob had said price was no object. But he hadn't. He told her the truth, that four pounds was the limit.

The assistant held out her hand. 'Come with me, Miss, and we'll look along the rails and see if anything takes your eye. Your father can sit down while he's waiting.'

The first and second rails held nothing that Lucy liked. It was while the assistant was taking one from the third rail, that a colour caught her eye. 'Could I have a look at that one, please?'

The coat, in deep cherry red, was brought out for her inspection. It had a pointed collar, slanted pockets, revers that could be turned up to fasten at the neck for warmth, and there were five cherry-red buttons fastened down the middle. 'I like that one, I think it's lovely.'

The assistant looked at the price tag. 'I'm afraid this one is four shillings more than your father said he could go up to. Shall I go and ask him?'

'No, don't do that, please. I'm very lucky to be getting a coat and I shouldn't be greedy. Shall I try that navy blue one on? That looks nice.'

When Lucy came out of the fitting room wearing the navy-blue coat, Bob tried to be enthusiastic but he didn't think it suited her. It was serviceable all right, and wouldn't show the dirt, but it was dull and made Lucy look dull. 'Are yer sure that's the one yer want, pet?'

'Yes, I like it, Dad.'

But the assistant thought the same as Bob. The coat was too dowdy for such a pretty girl. So forgetting the rule that the customer was always right, she made a try. 'There was another coat your daughter really liked, but unfortunately it was four guineas.'

'I like this one just as much, Dad,' Lucy cried, not wanting her father to feel she was getting second-best. 'Honest, I do!'

Bob knew his daughter too well to believe her. He had intended treating her to tea and cakes at Reece's, and then a trip on the ferry. If they did without the cakes and the ferry, he could just about manage the extra four shillings. 'Let me see yer in the other coat, pet.'

The assistant was away like a shot, tugging Lucy after her. And the girl who came out of the fitting room was a different girl altogether. The colour suited her down to the ground, bringing out the rosy blush of her cheeks and highlighting her shining hair. And her stance and bright green eyes told how much she enjoyed the fit and feel of the coat.

'That's the one, pet,' Bob said, swallowing the lump in his throat. 'That's the one yer knew yer were going to fall head over heels in love with. It's a beauty, like yerself.'

The assistant breathed a sigh of relief. She wouldn't have slept tonight if the girl hadn't got the coat she wanted. And it really looked as though it had been made for her. 'Is she having this one, sir?'

Bob nodded, waving Lucy's objections aside. 'I'd like you to wrap her old one up and let her keep that one on. It's her birthday, yer see.'

'And it's a lovely birthday present. But I'll have to take it off her to take to the counter. Once it's paid for, and you have a receipt, she can change into it.'

'Here yer are, pet.' Bob took hold of Lucy's hand and counted out four pound notes and a ten-shilling note. 'Ye're a big girl now, you go with the lady and pay. And don't forget I want me change.'

Lucy felt as though she was floating on a cloud. 'I know,

Dad, yer want six shillings change.' She bent and whispered in his ear, 'This will open a few eyes, eh, Dad? I'll be the talk of the street.'

Bob grinned. 'And the washhouse, no doubt. In fact, I'll be disappointed if ye're not the talk of the whole flippin' neighbourhood.'

When Lucy came back to where he was sitting, dressed in her finery and carrying a bag with her old coat in, Bob thought he had never seen her look so pretty or happy. 'I'm very proud of yer, pet, and the luckiest man alive to be yer father.'

'It's me what's the lucky one.' Lucy linked his arm, then dropped it to wave a thank you to the assistant who was watching them leave with a huge smile on her face. 'She was awful nice, Dad.'

'Yes, she was. Very kind and helpful.'

When they stepped from Blackler's into Elliot Street, Bob pulled her to a halt. 'Now comes the bad news, pet. I intended to take yer for tea and cakes, then a trip on the ferry, as a treat. But I can't afford that now or I won't have the tram fare home. So how about a walk down to the Pier Head, just to watch the ferries coming and going? It's very interesting, lots of hustle and bustle, and it'll pass an hour away.' He'd had strict instructions to stay out until four o'clock. Then on the dot of the hour, he was to knock on Aggie's door. 'It'll blow the cobwebs away, too, 'cos it's always nice and fresh by the river.'

'I'd like that, Dad. I'll be able to swank in me new coat.'

'Come on, then, let's go. Give me that bag to carry, it's too heavy for you.'

When they stepped off the tram, Bob glanced in the pawnshop window at the big round clock on the wall. Five minutes to four – he couldn't have timed it better. Walking at a steady gait, they'd be knocking at Aggie's dead on the hour.

‘Shall we call at the McBrides’ and let them see yer birthday present?’

‘Oh, yeah! Mrs Aggie won’t half get a surprise when she sees me. She won’t be expecting me to be wearing the most beautiful coat in the whole world.’

But it was Titch who opened the door. And being Titch, he was able to hide his surprise and keep a straight face. ‘Hello, young lady. I think yer’ve come to the wrong address, ’cos I’ve never seen yer in this street before. Have yer lost yer way, dear?’

This brought forth peals of laughter from Lucy. ‘Don’t be daft, Mr Titch. I know I look different in me new posh coat, but not that different.’

Titch slapped an open palm on his forehead. ‘Well, blow me down, if it isn’t little Lucy Mellor! And in the poshest coat I’ve ever seen. Yer’d better come in and let me ma see yer. She’ll have to put her glasses on to make sure she’s not seeing things.’ He stepped back and bowed her in, winking broadly at Bob as he followed.

‘It’s only me, Mrs Aggie,’ Lucy called as she walked to the living room. ‘I’ve come to show off me new coat.’ She stopped on the threshold, her eyes and mouth wide. The room seemed to be full of people. Apart from Mrs Aggie, there was Mr and Mrs Pollard with Jack and Greg, Rhoda and Steve. And as she wondered why they were all there, it flashed through her mind that Steve looked more posh than she did.

Titch pushed his way past her and raised his two hands as though he was conducting an orchestra. ‘Right, everyone in tune, now.’ And suddenly the rafters were ringing with voices wishing Lucy a happy birthday. She was dumbstruck at first, until her father put his arm around her waist and hugged her as he sang his head off. Then joy and excitement replaced the shock and her face beamed with sheer delight and pleasure. What a wonderful day it was turning out to be!

When the singing finished, Lucy found herself being kissed and hugged while birthday cards were pressed into her hand. And she got a parcel off Mrs Pollard, who said it was a present from her and Mrs Aggie, one off Rhoda, and another from Steve. The lad looked so embarrassed as he explained it wasn't much, but the thought was there.

Lucy grinned at him. 'Yer've stolen me thunder, you have, Steve Fletcher. Yer look posher than I do in yer long trousers.'

Aggie saw the lad blushing to the roots of his hair and was quick to stand beside him. No one, except her and Titch, knew where the clothes had come from. 'He's been working hard and saving hard, queen. And doesn't he look the young gentleman?'

'He certainly does.' Lucy eyed him up and down. 'He looks very smart.'

Rhoda pushed her way to her friend's side. 'I told Steve he looked nice, Lucy.' She had her eyes on her friend's coat and was green with envy. She might have two coats, but neither of them was a patch on Lucy's.

Lucy was bewildered. She gazed around the smiling faces and was lightheaded with happiness. All her best friends were here. But how did it come about? 'Mrs Aggie, how come they're all in your house?'

'It's all Titch's doing, queen, not mine. Not only is it your birthday, but for Jack, here, it's a big day in his life. He's no longer a schoolboy, but a young gentleman setting out in life. So my son decided we couldn't let the day go by without a celebration. So a small tea-party is his present to both of yer.'

Lucy ran to put her arms around Titch. 'Oh, thank you, Mr Titch. Ye're not a little love, ye're a big one.'

'It's my pleasure, sweetheart. And might I say how elegant yer look in yer new coat? It really is a knock-out.'

There were shouts of approval and praise, causing Lucy to blush with shyness. 'I feel daft, now. A real show-off.'

'Seeing as we're sharing this day,' Jack said, feigning disgust at the fuss over Lucy, 'what about me? I'm standing here in me new long kecks, and not a peep out of yer.'

'How was I to know, soft lad, when ye're hiding behind the

table? Come and stand next to me and we can both look posh and swank together.' When he was beside her, her eyes travelled the length of him. 'Jack Pollard, you are a very, very handsome lad.'

'Yeah, I know. I was told that before I left the house.'

'Oh, aye,' Irene said, her eyebrows raised. 'Who told yer that?'

'The mirror in your bedroom wardrobe.' Jack stuck his two hands in his pockets, feeling very grown up. 'I was standing in front of it, weighing meself up in me long kecks, and the mirror spoke to me. It said, "Jack Pollard, ye're a very, very handsome lad." And as yer know, Mam, mirrors don't lie.'

George chuckled before saying, 'Self-praise is no recommendation, son.'

'But I told him he was handsome, Mr Pollard,' Lucy said. 'And that's not self-praise.'

'So yer did, sweetheart, so yer did. And seeing as he's me son, I can't contradict yer, can I?' Me dear wife would give me the rounds of the kitchen if I did.'

Aggie squared her shoulders and became businesslike. 'I'm going to throw you out now, George, and you, Bob, so I can start setting the table. And as Lucy is the only one who doesn't know what's going on, I'll tell her. The tea-party is only for the youngsters. Then at seven o'clock they're all being packed off to the Pollards' to play cards, so the grown ups can have a knees-up, jars out, booze-up.'

Bob put a finger under Lucy's chin and raised her face. 'Enjoy yerself, pet, and I'll see yer at seven o'clock.'

'Is me mam coming to the party with yer?'

'As far as I know, she is.'

Lucy laid her cards and presents on the couch. 'Will yer take me coat home with yer, Dad? And will yer put it on a hanger so it doesn't get creased?'

Bob took the coat from her and jerked his head at George. 'Come on, mate, before Aggie throws us out.' He was halfway down the hall, with George behind him, when Steve caught up with them.

'Mr Mellor, I want to thank yer for doing those jobs for me mam. I really am grateful.'

'Think nothing of it, Steve, it was only half an hour's work. I was glad to be able to help, and as I'm on the early shift next week, I'll nip up one day and fix that loose shelf in the kitchen for her. They're only little jobs, but every little helps, as they say.'

George waited until he and Bob were on the pavement so their voices wouldn't carry. 'There's a lot we could do for yer mam, but we don't want to rush things. Ye're a sensible lad, and I know yer'll understand that if we try to do too much, yer mam won't like it and we'll be back to square one. So we'll take things slow and easy.'

'I do understand, Mr Pollard. But she seems to be brighter now that people are calling to see her. And she eats the dinner that the ladies take down to her every day. Yer've all been so kind, I really don't know how to thank yer. Mr Mellor says the jobs he did were nothing, but they've made a difference to the house.' Steve grinned. 'The sideboard looks like a sideboard now, not a heap of scrap. And I'm not banging me leg against the broken door like I used to. Anyway, I just wanted to say thanks.'

'We're here any time yer want us,' Bob said. 'Just remember that.'

'Can I open me presents now, Mrs Aggie?' Lucy shouted through to the kitchen where there was a lot of activity going on. 'And me cards?'

'Of course yer can, queen.' Aggie put the last jelly cream on a plate and rubbed her hands down the side of her pinny. ''Cos I'm a nosy bugger, we'll take a five-minute break to see what yer've got.'

Lucy's face was a joy to behold as she read out the verses in each card and the name of the sender. 'Six birthday cards, aren't I lucky?' Each card was put back in its envelope so she could take them home and treasure them. Then she opened the present from Aggie and Irene and let out a squeal of delight at the sight of the pale pink underskirt. 'Oh, it's lovely, thank you so much.' She'd never owned an underskirt before, not since she was a toddler, anyway. 'I'll take really good care of it and only wear it for best.'

Rhoda's present was a perfumed tablet of Lux soap and a cream-coloured flannel. Lucy closed her eyes as she held the soap to her nose. 'Thank you, Rhoda, I'll smell lovely when I get washed with this.'

Steve was dreading her opening his present. It was a tuppenny slab of Cadbury's chocolate, all he could afford. It seemed so cheap compared to the other two presents. But to Lucy it meant just as much. 'Ooh, me favourite chocolate! Thank you very much, Steve. And don't be put out if I don't offer to share it 'cos I'm going to be real tight with it. One square every night in bed and it'll last me nearly all week.'

The knots in Steve's tummy began to relax. He'd been expecting to see a look of disappointment on Lucy's face, but she'd welcomed his cheap gift with the same enthusiasm as the others. And he vowed that next year he'd buy her an extra nice present. He'd be working then, and money wouldn't be as tight. With a bit of luck his mam might be well enough to take on a light job and they'd be quids in.

Lucy's eyes grew wider as Aggie and Irene carried plate after plate through. There were sausage rolls, boiled ham and corned beef sandwiches, colourful jelly creams, iced fairy cakes, crackers with cheese on top and a sponge sandwich cake on a glass stand with a fancy doily underneath. 'Doesn't everything look lovely?'

'It sure does,' Jack said, rubbing his tummy. 'Can yer hear it rumbling? And me mouth's watering that much I'm dribbling.'

Steve was feeling the same symptoms. He couldn't

remember seeing a table so heavily laden with such fare. 'Mrs Aggie doesn't do things by half.'

Greg was sitting facing the back window and he suddenly burst out laughing. 'Neither does Mr Titch. He's just coming up the yard lugging a crate of ale. If there isn't high jinks here tonight, I'll eat my hat.'

His brother shook his head. 'Greg, yer haven't got a hat.'

'I know that, soft lad. Yer don't think I'd be daft enough to say I'd eat it if I had one, do yer? I'd have to be barmy.'

Rhoda thought it was about time she got a word in. They'd think she didn't have a tongue in her head. 'I've always said yer were barmy, Greg Pollard.'

'Well, you should know, Rhoda Fleming, seeing as ye're barmy yerself. They say it takes one to know one.'

Aggie came through from the kitchen, minus her pinny. 'Right, kids, take yer seats at the table and get stuck in. The barmy ones on this side, Lucy and Jack on the other, and me and Steve at either end. So help yerselves to whatever takes yer fancy. Titch will be bringing yer some lemonade in, unless yer'd prefer tea.'

The vote for lemonade was unanimous. After all, they could get tea any time. And when Titch carried a tray of glasses through, he brought coloured paper hats with him. 'Get them on yer heads and let's do the thing in style.'

'Isn't Mrs Pollard coming in to join us?' Lucy asked.

'No, queen, she's slipped home the back way. She's going to put her feet up for an hour because she's been on the go all day. But she'll be back later to give me a hand with the washing-up.'

'I'll wash up for yer, Mrs Aggie,' Steve said, putting the brown paper hat on his head. 'There's no need for Mrs Pollard to come back. She may as well have a rest and be ready for the party tonight.'

'I'll help with the dishes,' Lucy said. 'It won't take long.'

Rhoda thought it would look bad if she didn't offer. 'I'll help, too.'

Jack gave his brother a dig in the ribs. 'Go on, say something.'

Greg grinned. 'What would yer like me to say?'

'That yer'll give a hand to clear up.'

The grin was replaced by a bulldog expression. 'Why don't you offer to give a hand? I don't see anyone holding yer back.'

'I've got me long kecks on, haven't I? And if I get a mark on them me mam will have a duck egg. That's after she's kicked me into the middle of next week.'

Greg considered this piece of information. 'I've a good mind to drop this jelly cream on yer lap. It would be worth it to see me mam lay a duck egg. And the thought of you being kicked into the middle of next week is very tempting.'

'I'll tell yer what,' Jack said, a twinkle in his eye. 'You help Mrs Aggie and I'll leave yer these long kecks in me will. And I'll even leave yer the braces to keep them up. Now I can't be fairer than that, and ye're not likely to get a better offer.'

Greg looked at Aggie while jerking his head at his brother. 'How long d'yer think he's good for, Mrs Aggie?'

'Ooh, let's see now.' She rubbed her chin thoughtfully. 'I'd say, at a guess, he's got at least sixty, seventy years.'

'I'm not hanging around that long for a pair of kecks that will have been eaten by the moths.' Greg patted Jack on his shoulder. 'Sorry, pal, but the only way ye're getting out of helping with the dishes is by breaking a leg. I could arrange that for yer if ye're desperate.'

Lucy's giggling attracted their attention. 'You two don't half look daft with yer paper hats hanging down over yer eyes. And while ye're arguing the toss, we're eating all the goodies.'

Jack glared at his brother. 'See what yer've done? Why d'yer have to talk so much?' He reached out and took a jelly cream in one hand and a fairy cake in the other. 'Honest, ye're like a flippin' parrot what's been living with that Mrs Gibson for a few years.'

This brought forth howls of laughter. Mrs Gibson lived at the very top of the street. She was a thin wiry woman who waved her arms about when she was speaking and her mouth was in constant motion. She lived on her own and because she had no one in the house to talk to, she made up for it by standing at her front door and gossiping to everyone who passed. And once she had you in her clutches she hung on tight. No one knew where she got her information from, but everything that happened in the surrounding streets was known by Mrs Gibson. And she was always willing to pass it on to anyone who would stand and listen to her. The trouble was, she went all around the world to tell you something and people didn't always have the time.

Aggie wiped the laughter tears away. 'We shouldn't be mocking the poor soul, she's harmless enough. Just a lonely old woman, that's all.'

'Yes, she's all right, really,' said Steve, who only lived a few doors from Mrs Gibson. 'She's always got a smile for yer.' Then he couldn't keep the grin back. 'Mrs Aggie, I'm not making fun of her, honest. But have yer ever noticed that people stop just before they get to her house, take a deep breath and then make a run for it?'

Titch, who'd been leaning his elbows on the sideboard, straightened up. 'I've done that meself, son, I've got to admit. She's a nice woman, but by God can she talk! I was coming home on leave one day, with me rucksack over me shoulder, when she stopped me. And I couldn't get a word in edgeways. D'yer know, me leave was up before I could shut her up? I had to turn right around and go back to the ship without even seeing me ma.'

Oh, how Jack was enjoying this. He thrived on laughter. 'Were they only giving yer a few hours' leave, that trip, Mr Titch?'

Titch shook his head solemnly. 'No, son, I had ten days' leave due to me.'

Rhoda gaped. She wasn't used to the McBride and Pollard

humour and had taken Titch seriously. 'That's terrible, that is. Yer should have told her. I know I would have done.' She couldn't make out why this brought forth more laughter. But so she wouldn't look daft, she laughed along with them. What she had succeeded in doing though, was to convince Greg that she was indeed barmy.

By seven o'clock every dish had been washed and the place tidied. All done by the youngsters, who made Aggie sit with her feet up. They'd had the time of their lives and it was their way of saying thank you to her and Titch. And the day wasn't over for them, they'd enjoy themselves playing games in the Pollards'. But Steve was worried about leaving his mother for so long.

'Mrs Aggie, I'll have to nip home and see how me mam is. I wouldn't enjoy meself if I didn't know she was all right.'

'I'm on me way down there right now, lad, so yer've no need to worry. I'm taking her a plate of sandwiches and cakes, seeing as she couldn't come to the party. But if I think there's the least thing wrong, I'll let yer know. Yer have me promise on that.'

Chapter Thirteen

'I can't stay long, girl, 'cos as yer know, our Titch has invited a few friends in for a drink.' Aggie placed the plate on the table and was heartened to see Olive's eyes showing appreciation. 'The kids have had a whale of a time, really enjoyed themselves. And of course, seeing them happy made me happy. Some youngsters are hard-faced and pushy, but not the Pollard boys, or Lucy or Steve. The world won't go far wrong if everyone grows up like them.'

'Thanks for inviting Steve, Aggie, I really do appreciate it. He went out of here with his head held high, his chest sticking out a mile and a real swagger to his walk. All courtesy of the McBride family.'

'He's worrying about leaving yer for so long, but yer don't mind, do yer, Olive? Let him get as much enjoyment out of life as he can, eh?'

'Tell him not to worry, I'm fine. As soon as yer've gone, I'll be tucking into those sausage rolls, sandwiches and jelly creams. God, it's years since I had a jelly cream, and I used to make loads of them.'

'I'll be on me way then, queen, to welcome the guests.' Aggie got to the door before putting into play the plan she'd concocted in her head. Tutting loudly, she turned. 'I've got a head like a sieve. I was going without giving yer this.' She pulled a folded piece of beige linen from her pocket and opened it up. It was a sideboard runner, and it had small coloured flowers embroidered on it. 'I came across this yesterday, when I was cleaning me cupboard out. It's that long since I've seen it, I'd forgotten I had it. I've got no use for it, and it would be a shame to throw it in the bin. Would yer be insulted if I asked if yer wanted it for yer sideboard?'

'Are you sure yer don't want it?' Olive looked suspicious. 'It looks too good to throw in the bin.'

'That's what I thought, girl.' As quick as a flash the runner was on the sideboard and Aggie was standing back admiring it. 'There yer are, it looks a treat.'

Olive thought the runner looked lovely, but she wasn't convinced. 'I've got a feeling ye're telling me fibs, Aggie McBride.'

'What would I gain from telling lies, girl? Not a bleedin' thing. I've got loads of stuff at home that'll never see daylight. Our Titch used to bring me all sorts home after every trip, until in the end I had to put a stop to it 'cos I had nowhere to put the things. A lot of stuff was stored in me loft and I haven't seen it for years. There's vases, ornaments and pictures, everything yer could mention.' Here goes, thought Aggie. In for a penny, in for a pound. 'I'll get Titch on the ladder tomorrow and ask him to hand some of the stuff down. Yer may think it's rubbish, and I wouldn't be offended if yer said so. But yer may as well have a root through it and see if there's anything yer like, instead of it rotting up there. This place could do with a few things to brighten it up, God knows. So how about it? D'yer want to have a dekko, or are yer going to go all stubborn and get yer knickers in a twist?'

'I'm not a stubborn person, Aggie, and I never get me knickers in a twist because they're that old they wouldn't stand the strain.' Olive smiled. 'How can I refuse such kindness?'

'That's settled then. I'll see yer tomorrow, please God. And now I'd better be on me way, queen. Ta-ra.'

Aggie was nearing her house when she saw Bob closing his front door. And even at this distance she could see Ruby wasn't in a very happy mood. If she spoils my son's night, I'll marmalise her, the miserable bleeding cow, Aggie thought, but for Bob's sake she raised a smile. 'I hope yer singing voice is in tune, Bob.' She inserted the key in the lock and looked over her shoulder. 'And you, Ruby – we'll expect a song from you as well.'

'Some hope you've got.' Ruby managed to inject a sneer into her voice. 'I've no intention of making a fool of meself.'

Bob looked sideways and shook his head. With her hair dyed a horrible yellowy blonde, and thick bright make-up plastered on her face, his wife didn't need anyone else to make a fool of her, she did that herself.

As Aggie stood aside to let them enter the house before her, she groaned inwardly. Ye gods and little fishes, this was a fine start to a party. If Ruby kept that face on her all night, Titch wouldn't think twice about telling her. And that would put the cat among the pigeons. Still, one way or another, the evening promised to be a lively one.

Irene and George greeted Ruby warmly, but all they got in reply was a curt nod. Titch was the only one favoured with a smile. 'What's yer poison, Ruby?' He pointed to the array of bottles on the sideboard. 'I've got beer if yer want it, or there's port, whisky or gin.'

'I'll have gin, please, Titch.' Ruby sat in a chair on the opposite side of the room to her husband. A move not lost on the rest of the company. And each one asked themselves why this woman always had to belittle Bob. She didn't know she was born with a husband like him, he was far too nice a person for her.

Irene broke the silence. 'Do yer like Lucy's new coat, Ruby?'

'Yeah.' Ruby smiled up at Titch and took the glass from him. Then, sensing all eyes on her, she added, 'It's very nice.'

George stared down into his glass of bitter. Why should they all put themselves out to be nice to a woman who couldn't be bothered to be pleasant in return? 'Nice, did yer say, Ruby? I thought it was more than nice. I thought it was a real beauty, like the girl herself.'

Titch glanced at his mother as she rocked in her chair, a glass of stout in her hand. He could read her mind and knew that right now she would willingly wring someone's neck. He wasn't surprised at Ruby's behaviour, he hadn't expected anything else. She was an unhappy woman who thought she deserved more out of life than she was getting. A loving husband and daughter weren't enough for her, she didn't want the ties that bound her down.

His elbow leaning on the sideboard, and a grin on his face, Titch said, 'George is right about Lucy being a real beauty, Ruby. A few years from now there'll be broken hearts lying all over the place.'

'So they say.' Ruby lifted the glass to her lips and downed the gin as though it was water. 'Can I have the same again, Titch?'

'Ay, yer'd better watch it, Ruby, this is strong stuff.' Titch had given her a generous measure to begin with, and she'd drunk it in about ten minutes. At this rate she'd be flat out in no time. 'I don't want to see yer rolling home.'

Ruby's lips curled. 'Don't worry, Titch, I can hold me drink. Yer'll never see me rolling home, no matter how many I have.'

Her bragging inflamed Bob. Self, self, self, that's all she ever thought about. 'You get drunk and yer can crawl home on yer hands and knees,' he interjected. 'I won't be carrying yer.'

Ruby lit a cigarette before taking her refilled glass. Then she inhaled deeply and blew the smoke in her husband's direction. 'Yer'd be the last one I'd want to carry me home.'

The rocking chair was brought to a halt and Aggie sat forward. 'That's enough of that. Any families differences yer can air at home, not here. This is supposed to be a friendly gathering, so let's keep it that way. And I don't want to hear no more talk of drunken women, 'cos there's no worse sight than to see a woman the worse for drink.'

George had had enough. At this rate they'd be coming to blows. 'When are yer due back at yer ship, Titch?'

'I'll go down to the docks on Tuesday, see how things are. We'll likely be sailing on Wednesday or Thursday. But it'll be a short trip this time, probably only two or three weeks.'

'Will yer be glad to get yer sea legs back again?' Irene asked, glad the conversation had been steered to safer ground. 'Have yer missed it?'

'I won't be sorry to get back, but I can honestly say I haven't missed it this time. There seems to have been a lot going on to keep me occupied. And of course I've enjoyed me ma's company and good food.'

'I suppose yer've been helping that Olive Fletcher, like soft lad here.' Ruby drained her glass. 'I don't know why yer bother, the house will be filthy again in no time.'

Titch had no intention of going down that road. And he could see his mother's set face and knew she was ready to explode. 'Drink up, fellers, there's a crateful to get through.'

'I'll have a whisky this time, mate,' George said, 'if it's all the same to you.'

'And me.' Bob was on tenterhooks, afraid of what his wife would come out with next. She didn't care who she insulted or offended. Never again would he inflict her on his friends.

'Fill mine up while ye're at it, Titch.' Oblivious to the tension in the room, Ruby held her glass out. 'It's a nice drop of gin, that.'

'Yer'll have to wait until I see to the men. And me ma and Irene.' Titch's even temper was beginning to fray. 'You're last in the queue.'

Ruby put her glass down at the side of her chair and lit another cigarette. 'Like I was saying about the Fletchers, ye're all wasting yer time.'

Irene got to her feet to take her drink off Titch, then she looked down into her neighbour's face. 'Listen, Ruby, we're all friends of the Fletchers in this room, so we'd be grateful if yer would just keep yer mouth shut. Yer don't know the first thing about them, so ye're in no position to discuss their private affairs. So do yerself, and all of us, a favour by keeping yer trap buttoned up tight.'

Ruby was about to let fly with a tirade of abuse, when Titch intervened. 'A gin again, is it, Ruby?'

By a quarter to nine you could cut the atmosphere with a knife. Ruby never stopped talking, and it was always to pull people down. She'd had too much to drink, her eyes were glazed and her words slurred. Bob was so ashamed he couldn't take any more.

'I'll go and get Lucy – it's time she was in bed.' He handed his glass to Titch, his eyes telling of his torment. 'Come on, Ruby, time to go home.'

'I'm all right here, you go for her.'

'I'm not asking yer, I'm telling yer.' Bob snatched the cigarette from her mouth and threw it in the grate. Then he grasped the top of her arms and jerked her to her feet. 'Get yer bag and let's go.'

Ruby struggled as a stream of obscenities left her lips. But too much drink had made her unsteady on her feet and she was no match for her husband. 'I'll be back when I've seen Lucy to bed, Titch,' Bob said, 'if that's all right with you?'

Aggie got her words out before her son had a chance. 'Of course it is. Ye're always welcome in this house, Bob, yer know that.'

'Thanks.' Bob literally dragged Ruby into the hall. 'Needless to say, my wife will not be with me.'

Titch went to the door to make sure Bob could manage the woman who was struggling to get free, even though she would have fallen without her husband's hands holding her up. And her language was the language of the gutter.

'Well, did you ever!' Aggie said when her son came back into the room. 'Fancy having to live with the likes of that! I don't know how Bob puts up with it, he must be a saint.'

'He deserves a medal,' Irene said, her heart filled with

sympathy for the man who had been humiliated in front of them all. 'He's a smashing bloke, far too good for her. What she needs is a man who'll give her a go-along now and again when she steps out of line.'

'I'll tell yer what,' Titch said, 'if I wasn't off marriage before, I certainly am now.'

'Ay, all women are not like Ruby, yer know.' George reached for his wife's hand. 'Take Irene here, she's a perfect wife and mother. Bob just picked the wrong one.'

'Yer can't say that, George.' Aggie pushed her feet down on the floor to set her chair in motion. 'If yer think back to the early years of their marriage, Ruby was a different person. She was friendly and easy to get along with.'

'She wasn't bad looking, either.' Titch crossed the room and held his hand out for George's empty glass. 'But I believe she let us see what she wanted us to see. People don't change that much, and the Ruby we saw tonight was the real Ruby.' He poured a generous measure of whisky and handed it over. 'If we cast our minds back, we can practically put a date on the time she decided life was too dull and she let her true self come to the fore.'

'Titch is right,' Irene said, thinking back. 'It was just after Lucy started school that she started to bleach her hair. Then gradually the make-up became thicker, as though she'd put it on with a trowel, and her nails were painted a bright red. I know Bob's had rows with her over it, yer can hear them through the wall. But she takes no notice of him. She's only interested in herself and couldn't care less for him or Lucy.'

'She doesn't still hit the girl, does she?' Aggie asked. ''Cos if I thought she'd laid a hand on her I wouldn't be responsible for me actions.'

Irene dropped her eyes for a brief second. Bob had suffered enough, she wasn't going to add to his suffering. 'Not as far as I know, Aggie.'

'Let's forget about Ruby for now, eh?' Titch said. 'She managed to spoil a couple of hours for us, but don't let her spoil the whole night. Yer've all got full glasses, so drink up and be merry. And for God's sake, will someone tell a joke to put a smile on our faces?'

'I know,' Aggie chuckled, 'tell them about the parrot and Mrs Gibson.'

'Oh, aye, that was dead funny, that was.' Titch related the whole story and it brought not only smiles, but roars of laughter. 'The funniest part, the one that tickled me most, was that Lucy's friend believed me when I said Mrs Gibson had kept me talking all through me ten days' leave. She said, all serious like, "That's terrible, that is. Yer should have told her. I know I would have done." And the poor girl had no idea why everyone went in a pleat.'

They were still wiping their eyes when Bob came through the door Titch had left ajar for him. He was smiling, but they could see the strain on his face and in his eyes. 'I'm glad you lot can still laugh. I thought me wife had blighted the night for yer. I can't tell yer how sorry I am, but it's me own fault. I should have known better than to bring her.'

'Did yer manage to get her home all right?' Titch asked. 'I would have given yer a hand but thought I'd better not interfere.'

'I had to half carry her up the stairs, and she was a dead weight. Then I took her coat off and lifted her onto the bed. I left her there and went for Lucy. And when she was settled in bed, I looked in on the wife. She was just as I'd left her, out like a light and snoring her head off.'

'She certainly likes her drink,' George said. 'She must have gone through half a bottle of gin in that short time.'

'Perhaps it's my fault,' Titch said. 'I should have refused to give her so much.'

'Don't blame yerself,' Bob told him. 'Ruby sober is no nicer than Ruby drunk. She's got a chip on her shoulder as big as a ruddy tree, and nothing yer do or say will please her. I should know, I've tried everything under the sun but it doesn't have the slightest effect.'

'Forget about it for now,' Irene said, 'and sit down and relax. Get a glass in yer hand and drown yer sorrows.'

Titch raised his brows. 'How about a good stiff whisky, pal?'

'Just the job, mate.' Bob sat down and stretched his legs. He was physically and mentally exhausted. 'Then yer can tell me what yer were laughing about when I came in. I could do with cheering up.'

'Before that, Bob, will yer tell us how the kids got on in Irene's?' Aggie leaned forward in expectation. 'Did Lucy enjoy herself?'

The mention of his daughter's name brought a genuine smile to Bob's face. 'Enjoy herself! She was full of it – they all were. I couldn't get a word in edgeways with them all talking at once, saying they'd had the time of their lives. I felt like an ogre breaking the party up. Lucy said it was the best birthday she'd ever had, and young Jack said he'd never forget the day he wore his first pair of long kecks.' Bob held the glass to his lips and closed his eyes as the liquid warmed and soothed him. 'I'll tell yer what – that Steve's a good 'un. He said he'd stay and help the lads clear up so their mother didn't have to come back to dirty dishes and crumbs all over the floor. Yer'd not get many boys his age being so thoughtful.'

Aggie sat back feeling contented. As long as the children enjoyed themselves, that was the main thing. At least Ruby hadn't been able to spoil their party. 'They're all good kids. I don't know Lucy's friend, Rhoda, as well as I know the others, but she seems a nice enough girl.'

Titch chuckled. 'She's an exceptional girl is Rhoda, with a very unusual sense of humour. Which brings me to what we were laughing at when yer came in, Bob.' Leaning back against the sideboard with a glass in his hand and a twinkle in his eye, he started with Jack telling his brother he talked like a parrot that had lived with Mrs Gibson for years. And he ended with Rhoda's serious reaction to a story that had been made up for a laugh.

If Titch had told the tale once again in the hope of cheering his neighbour up, then he'd been very successful. For Bob, with a warm glow inside him, and feeling relaxed, roared with laughter as he pictured the scene in his mind. 'I wish I'd been here to see it. I bet our Lucy saw the funny side.' He shook his head. 'Rhoda didn't really believe Mrs Gibson kept yer talking for ten days, did she? No, she couldn't have. She was having yer on.'

'If I never move from this spot, she fell for it, hook, line and sinker.' Titch looked to his mother for confirmation. 'Isn't that the truth, Ma?'

Aggie chuckled. 'It is, son. And I bet she'll lie in bed tonight wondering how yer could stand on yer feet for ten days without going to the lavvy.'

'She either believed it, or is a ruddy good actress,' Irene said. 'But either way she's done us a favour. Especially you, Bob. Yer look heaps better than yer did half an hour ago.'

'That's the whisky, sweetheart,' George said. 'It's amazing what a drop of the hard stuff will do.'

'No, George, it's not the whisky,' Bob said. 'It's being with me friends. I was all wound up before, me nerves shattered. But now I feel nice and relaxed. In fact, I feel so full of goodwill to all men, I wouldn't mind if Mrs Gibson walked through that door right now and talked the head off me all through the night.'

George let out a loud guffaw. 'I told yer it was amazing what a drop of the hard stuff will do. But even I didn't think it was powerful enough for anyone to brave Mrs Gibson's company for a whole night. Give him another one, Titch.'

'All in good time, mate,' Titch said. 'The last thing I want is for him to get legless and me have to carry him up the stairs and throw him down next to Ruby.'

Mellowed by the drink and good company, Bob chuckled. 'Yer need have no fears on that score, 'cos I'm kipping down on the couch. I'm at ease with meself now, as happy as a pig in you-know-what. And I'm not about to let the sight and sound of me drunken wife spoil things for me. Time enough tomorrow for rows and recriminations.'

'Take the advice of an old woman, Bob,' Aggie said, 'and forget about it. It's over and done with now and yer can't change things. What's the good of getting all het-up when nothing will come of it? 'Cos I'll tell yer now, lad, no matter how hard yer shout, yer'll never change Ruby.'

'Aggie's right, Bob, yer'd get yerself all worked up for nothing,' Irene said. 'Put it out of yer head and pretend it never happened.'

Bob was thoughtful as he swirled the whisky around in his glass. And when he looked up, he nodded. 'The ladies are right, as usual. I won't forget about it, I can't. But kicking up a stink won't get me anywhere, so to all intents and purposes, it never happened.'

'It's very sensible of yer to take me ma's advice when she becomes an old woman,' Titch said, trying to control his laughter. 'I took her advice, that's why I never married. She told me there wasn't a girl in the world good enough for her son, so I never bothered looking.'

Aggie gaped. 'That is a bleedin' lie, Titch McBride. I never said no such thing.'

'Yes, yer did. I was about twenty-two at the time.'

'Yer must have been hearing things, 'cos if I never move from this chair I never said no such thing.'

Titch slapped a hand on his forehead. 'Well, blow me down! Here I am, forty years of age and unmarried. All because I've gone through life thinking there wasn't a girl good enough for me. And now I find out I must have dreamt yer said it.'

Irene looked at the smiling faces and thought, this was more like it. Mother and son were just getting into their stride and there was a lot of laughter on the way. It was a bit late for it, thanks to Ruby, but better late than never. The disastrous start to the evening had been pushed to the back of their minds and merriment was taking its place. Which was as it should be when friends got together.

★ ★ ★

Aggie stood on the small landing and watched her son heaving the wooden ladder up the stairs. 'I dunno,' Titch grumbled, 'fancy getting me up at this ungodly hour on a Sunday morning.'

'Ah, yer poor thing. The bleedin' streets were aired off hours ago.'

Titch stood the ladder against the wall. 'Where d'yer want me to put it? And I don't want a rude answer, 'cos it wouldn't fit, anyway.'

Aggie chuckled. 'Ye're wide enough awake to give me yer old buck.' She nodded her head towards the front bedroom. 'By me wardrobe.'

Titch opened the ladder in front of the large wardrobe. 'Now what?'

'I want yer to get up there and pass some of the parcels down to me. I want to see what's in them.'

'Ah, ay, Ma! Did yer get me out of bed just so yer could do some spring-cleaning?'

'No, I didn't, so stop yer moaning. I think there's some things up there that would brighten Olive's house up. They're not doing me any good sitting up there, so she may as well have the use of them. So get cracking, son, 'cos I've got a dinner to get ready.'

Titch climbed on to the third rung. 'Is there anything in particular ye're looking for?'

'I don't know until I see it, do I? Just give me the first thing yer put yer hand on.' Aggie reached up to take the small, newspaper-wrapped parcel. While her son looked on, she opened it up to find a pretty, blue glass vase. 'That's nice, she'll like that. Another one now, son.'

The next parcel revealed a statue of a Japanese lady in a bright kimono with a fan hiding the bottom half of her face. Then came another statue. This time it was an old man with a walking stick, bent over with the weight of the pack on his back. The fourth parcel contained a framed picture, and

Aggie studied it with a smile on her face. It was a pretty scene, with children playing in a field of buttercups and daisies. 'That's enough for now, son, otherwise Olive will send yer packing with them.'

Titch nearly fell off the ladder. 'Send *me* packing! I'm not taking them up to her, yer can do it yerself.'

Aggie looked all innocent. 'I'd be happy to do that, son, if you'll see to the dinner. I'll put the meat in the oven for yer, so all yer'd have to do is peel the carrots and turnip, and the spuds. Then when the meat's nearly done, yer can put the potatoes around it to roast. Oh, and yer'd have to make the gravy, as well.'

'Ye're a crafty so-and-so, Ma. Why can't yer put the meat in the oven now? Then yer'd have time to go to Olive's and be back in time to see to the rest of the meal.'

'That sounds all very well, son, but yer see, I can't knock a nail in the wall. If you go, yer can take a hammer and a nail with yer and put the picture up for her.'

Titch shook his head. 'Yer've got it all figured out, haven't yer, Ma? When did yer plan this little manoeuvre?'

'In bed last night. Yer can blame Ruby for it if yer must blame someone. I couldn't sleep thinking about the brazen hussy, so to take me mind off her, I got thinking of Olive. And I came up with this idea. Mind you, it never entered me head that you'd be so bleedin' contrary.'

'I'm not being contrary, Ma, it's just that yer don't tell a person what's on yer mind. And when they refuse, yer blackmail them. Yer know darn well I'd rather go to Olive's for half an hour than eat a dinner I'd made meself.' Titch put his arms around the ladder and lifted it from the floor. 'Are yer sure that's all, before I lug this thing downstairs?'

'Yes, light of my life, that's all. Except I've just remembered I told Olive all this stuff was in the loft, so don't you go making a liar out of me.'

The ladder was lowered to the floor as Titch shook with laughter. 'But yer are a liar, Ma!'

'Yes, I know that. And you know it, too. But yer've no need to let the whole bleedin' street know.' Aggie spread her hands out. 'It's not meself I'm thinking of, it's you. How would yer like to be walking down the street and hear a woman saying to her neighbour, "His mother's not half a liar. Yer can't believe a word what comes out of her mouth." '

'Ma, I'll do a deal with yer. I'll tell lies for yer, if you make a rice pudding for after our dinner. How does that sound?'

'Yer drive a hard bargain, son. But, yeah, it's a deal.'

Titch was on the landing preparing to lift the ladder down the top stair. Then over the rustling of the paper as the parcels were rewrapped, he heard his mother talking to herself. 'If he had eyes in his bleedin' head he'd have seen the rice in steep on the draining board. Still, he wanted a deal and he got one.'

'I heard that, Ma.'

'Oh, did yer now! Well, now yer know it's true what they say about listeners never hearing good about themselves. It's coming to something when an old woman can't have a decent conversation with herself without some nosy bugger butting in.'

'Well, this nosy bugger is on his way downstairs now to make a cup of tea for an old woman. She doesn't deserve it, like, 'cos she tells lies and all sorts of things. But I'll be lenient and make allowances for her age.'

'Sod off, Titch McBride.'

Steve opened the door and his face stretched in a smile. 'Hello, Mr Titch, it's nice to see yer. Come on in.'

'Is yer mam respectable?'

'Keep yer voice down, Titch McBride,' Olive called. 'Yer'll have the neighbours thinking there's times when I'm not respectable.'

'Only the bad-minded ones, Olive, only the bad-minded ones.'

Steve put a hand on his arm. 'I want to thank yer for

yesterday, Mr Titch, we all had a smashing time. And me new clothes went down a treat.'

'Think nothing of it, lad, it was my pleasure.'

Olive eyed the bag with suspicion. 'What's Aggie sent yer down with now?'

'Don't you start on me, Olive, 'cos me ma's had me up since the crack of dawn. The last Sunday of me leave and she drags me out of bed at ten o'clock.'

'And that's the crack of dawn, is it?'

'It is when yer've had a few drinks the night before.' Titch put the bag on the table. 'Me ma said yer know about these. They're things she's had for years and has no use for.'

'Don't tell me she's had yer in the loft this morning?'

'I haven't been in the loft, Olive.' Titch thought half a lie wasn't so bad. 'I just stood on the ladder and pulled out the first things that came to hand.'

'Can I have a look, Mam?' Steve's hand was already on the bag. 'We're not half getting a lot of surprises these days. Everyone's been very kind.'

'We shouldn't really take them.' But Olive's words were half-hearted. She was dying to see what Aggie had sent. 'I feel as though I'm scrounging.'

'Scrounging! Olive, me ma's got enough stuff at home to open a shop. Yer'd be doing her a favour by taking them off her hands.'

'I'll believe yer, Titch, because I want to.' Olive smiled into the weatherbeaten face. 'I feel like a little girl when she finds out Father Christmas has been.'

That was good enough for Steve, and his hand went into the bag. And as he and his mam showed their pleasure as each piece of paper was opened, Titch stood by and watched in silence. How little it took to make these two happy.

'There's a hammer in the bottom of the bag, Mr Titch.' Steve looked puzzled. 'Fancy carrying that around with yer, 'cos it's heavy.'

'I've got a nail in me pocket to go with it, lad. And strict instructions from me ma that I wasn't to go home until that picture was on yer wall. She said if I didn't do it, she'd come down and have a go herself. I didn't fancy letting her do that because I think she'd knock yer wall down in the process.'

Olive stood with a finger in her mouth, looking first at the sideboard and then the mantelpiece. 'I think the vase in the middle of the sideboard, and an ornament each end. What do you think, Titch?'

'Move them around until yer get them where yer think they look best. And while ye're doing that, I'll put the picture up. Which wall would yer like it on?'

There was no hesitation. 'On that wall, so everyone can see it when they walk in.'

Steve watched the pleasure on his mother's face and thought of how much they owed to the McBrides. Yesterday he'd felt equal to the other children because he was dressed as well as any of them. And he'd never forget the two people who'd made that possible.

Olive stood behind the table and looked across at the sideboard. Only a couple of weeks ago it had been falling to pieces, only fit for the scrapheap. Now, with the lovely runner, the ornaments and vase, it looked a treat. And the picture hanging over it was just the right finishing touch. The trouble was, the wallpaper didn't do them justice. Dark with age, and torn in so many places, it took the shine off the nice things. She didn't say anything, though, because it might sound as if she was dropping hints. 'Thank yer mam for me and tell her I'm thrilled to bits.' She pointed to a chair. 'Yer can sit down, yer know, we don't charge. Not even for the spring that'll stick in yer bottom and leave a mark.'

When Titch sat down he felt the truth of her words and grinned. 'No one will see it. I've been changing me own nappies for nearly forty years now.'

Steve was in his element having a man to talk to. 'How did yer party go, Mr Titch? I bet it wasn't as good as ours.'

'Well, the first couple of hours were interesting, and quite lively at times. But they were nothing to write home about. It was nearly ten o'clock when it really got going, after we were all well-oiled.' He lifted a finger and corrected himself. 'I should say when the men were well-oiled. Irene and me ma don't need drink to make a party go, and they had us in stitches.'

'How was Ruby?' Olive asked. 'Did she enjoy herself?'

'Least said, soonest mended, Olive.'

'Oh.' She had gathered from snippets of conversation with Aggie and Irene that Bob's wife wasn't very popular. Whenever she mentioned her name they changed the subject. So she now followed their example. 'When do yer sail, Titch?'

'I'm reporting on Tuesday, so we'll probably sail the day after. I was told it would only be a short trip, but yer can't rely on them. I didn't expect to be away four months on the last one. But when I get home, I'll be taking the Pollard boys and Lucy to the flicks one night. And yer'd be very welcome to join us, Steve, if yer want to.'

Steve was agog. If someone had given him a pound note he couldn't have looked any happier. 'Ooh, yeah! That would be the gear, Mr Titch, thanks very much.'

'Just look at the face on him,' Olive said, feeling so pleased for her son. 'That's all I'll be able to get out of him now, so yer'd better not be away for four months, Titch McBride, or he'll drive me round the bend.'

'I was going to suggest that yer come with us. That's if ye're feeling better, like. It would do yer good to get out.'

'Oh, please, Mam,' Steve said. 'That would be brilliant.'

Olive was flabbergasted. Her hand to her throat, she croaked, 'I couldn't go with yer, Titch, I haven't been over the door for nearly two years. Anyway, what would the neighbours say? They'd have a field day!'

'Don't be acting daft, Olive, I'll have four kids with me. And if it makes yer feel better, I'll get me ma to come along.' Titch leaned forward and rested his elbows on his knees. 'Anyway, what the hell's it got to do with the neighbours?

They don't pay yer rent for yer, or put bread on yer table, so why care what they say? I took Irene into town the other week, while her husband was at work, but there's been no gossip about us having an affair.' He grinned. 'Mind you, if George wasn't such a big feller, I might have tried me luck.'

'Let me think about it, Titch.' Olive didn't need to think about it, she'd already decided she wouldn't go. 'It's such a long time since I've been out, just the thought frightens me.'

'It's coming up summer, Olive. Hot, sunny days. Yer can't spend them in the house, it wouldn't be healthy.' Titch looked at his watch. 'I'd better get back, me ma will have the dinner ready. But will yer promise to give it some thought?'

'I will, I promise. Now don't forget to thank Aggie for me. And if I don't see yer before yer set sail, have a good trip and take care of yerself.'

'So Olive was pleased with the things, was she?' Aggie sat facing her son across the table as they tucked into a roast dinner. She'd already asked Titch half a dozen times since he came home. 'And the picture looked nice on the wall, did it?'

'Ma, the picture was a joy to behold. And Olive was so delighted she jumped up and down for joy.'

'There's no need for sarcasm, Titch. And as it's Sunday, keep a civil tongue in yer head if yer don't mind. Yer never hear me being sarcastic, or swearing, on the Sabbath.' She wiped a trickle of gravy from her chin before adding, 'Well, only in extreme circumstances, of which this will be one if yer give me any more lip.'

'A paragon of virtue, yer are, Ma, and no mistake.' Titch bit on the inside of his mouth to stop himself from smiling as he told her, 'By the way, I've asked Olive for a date.'

Aggie nearly choked on a piece of crispy roast potato. Swallowing hard, she gasped, 'What did yer say?'

'I've asked Olive to come to the pictures with me one night on me next leave.'

Aggie searched his face for a while then burst out laughing. 'Pull the other one, it's got bells on.' She laid down her knife and fork and sat back in the wooden chair. 'Oh, that was a good try, son, but yer didn't really think I'd fall for it, did yer?'

'If yer don't believe me, ask her yerself. Yer'll be seeing her tomorrow 'cos it's your turn to make them a dinner. Just ask her, casual like, and see what she says.'

'Will I heckerslike! The woman would think I've gone off me rocker. She'd die of embarrassment.'

His face still straight, Titch said, 'Well, she was alive and kicking when I left. She wasn't the least embarrassed when I asked her.'

'Titch, the joke's gone far enough.'

'Yeah, ye're right, Ma. What happened was, I told Steve I'd be taking the kids to the pictures one night next time I'm home, and I asked if he'd like to come with us. He was absolutely over the moon. Then it struck me that it might be one way of getting Olive out of that house, and I asked if she'd like to come with us. She said she'd think about it, but I know she won't come. Which is a pity, 'cos she needs fresh air. She needs to get out, even if it's only to the shops. Wouldn't you or Irene have a go at asking her?'

'We've already tried, with no luck. It was thoughtful of yer to ask her, and I'm proud of yer. But I think the reason she won't go out is because she's no clothes to go out in. It's never been mentioned, like, but I'll bet a pound to a pinch of snuff that the two washed-out dresses I've seen her in are all she possesses. And they're nearly falling off her back – she wouldn't want to be seen out in them.' Aggie picked up her knife and fork. 'This dinner will be stiff if we leave it any longer, so get stuck in.' She cut a potato in half and speared it with her fork. 'It's early days, yet, son, just give it time. Me and Irene will keep working on her, and George and Bob will do as much as she'll allow them to do. Only God can do more than that.'

Chapter Fourteen

Titch walked up the street with a swagger. With his seaman's bag slung over his shoulder, his navy-blue peaked cap at a rakish angle and a twinkle in his eye, he was feeling in high spirits. He'd been away for two months and was looking forward to seeing his mother. He had the key ready in his hand and was smiling as he imagined the delight he'd see on her face. And he knew his heart would lurch, as it always did, at the love that was plain to see in eyes moist with tears of emotion. He was about to insert the key in the lock when he heard a piercing whistle and turned his head to see Steve Fletcher running towards him, a hand waving in the air.

'Mr Titch, I've got a job!' Steve was breathless with excitement. 'I started two weeks ago. I've been dying for yer to come home so I could tell yer.'

'Good for you, lad.' Titch was highly delighted for the boy. 'Come inside and tell me all about it.'

'Nah, I won't come in. Mrs Aggie's been so looking forward to yer coming home, she won't want me in the way.'

'Yer know me ma better than that, Steve. She's always glad to see yer.'

'I'll wait here for five minutes, so yer can give her the kiss and cuddle she said she always gets. I don't want to spoil yer homecoming.'

'Okay, I'll leave the door open and give yer a shout when the coast is clear.'

Aggie was in the kitchen when she heard the key in the

lock. Her heartbeat quickened as she dried her hands on the corner of her pinny. She entered the living room at the same time as Titch came in from the hall. Her arms wide, she walked towards him. 'It's a sight for sore eyes yer are, sweetheart. Welcome home.'

He held her close and they rocked from side to side. 'It's good to be home, Ma. And I'm happy to say yer've got me company for at least ten days.'

'Oh, that's good. The last couple of leaves ye've had were a waste of time. Yer barely had time to unpack before yer were off again.'

'Listen, Ma, Steve's outside. Is it all right if he comes in? I told him it would be, but he wasn't having any. He said he didn't want to spoil yer kiss and cuddle.'

Aggie grinned. 'I told him yer were due about this time – he must have been watching out for yer. I'm not going to say anything, he'll want to tell yer the news himself.'

And Steve couldn't get his news out quick enough. The words tumbling from his mouth, he brought Titch up-to-date. 'Yer know Jack got a job at Dunlop's when he left school – well, he got an application form for me from the office. Mrs Pollard helped me fill it in, then she asked Mr Whittle from the corner shop if he'd give me a reference. He gave me a good one, too, and so did the headmistress at school. They must have done the trick because I got an interview and was told to start on the Monday.'

'I'm really pleased for yer, lad.' Titch eyed him up and down. 'Yer haven't half shot up in the last few months. Either that or I'm shrinking.'

'It's me what's growing, Mr Titch.' There wasn't an inch of Steve's face that wasn't smiling. 'Me mam had to let the hem down on the trousers.'

'I bet she's proud of yer, is she?'

'Not half! I had to work a week in hand, but I got me first wage-packet on Friday. I couldn't get home quick enough to see her face when I handed it over.'

'And he wouldn't take a penny back.' Aggie knew the lad wouldn't say it, so she did. 'He walks to work every day, there and back, to save the tram fare.'

Titch looked surprised. 'That's some walk, that is. How long does it take yer?'

'I can do it in half an hour. And I don't mind. If I went on the tram, there and back, six days a week, it would be two bob out of the seven and six I earn. Then there's me carry-out. Me mam has to buy that as well.'

This lad is a bloody hero, Titch thought. For years he'd been deprived of even the basic needs in life. Things other kids took for granted. But it hadn't made him bitter or resentful. He was healthy in mind and body, kind and caring, and appreciative of the good things that came his way. A son to be proud of. 'How is yer mam?'

'I think she's a lot better, Mr Titch. Don't you think so, Mrs Aggie?'

'It certainly seems that way. She's been out to the shops a couple of times and that's a good sign.' Aggie chuckled. 'Me and Irene pulled a fast one on her. Steve knows about it so I'm not telling tales out of school. We'd been taking turns getting her messages in, like bread and something for the lad's carry-out. But we decided that as long as we did that, Olive would never go out. So one day we told her we wouldn't be able to see her the next day until late, 'cos we were going to visit Irene's family. We both felt a bit mean about it, but it had the desired effect. If she didn't go to the shops, there'd be no bread for carry-out. And she wouldn't see her son go without, 'cos as we all know, she loves the bones of him.'

Titch clicked his tongue on the roof of his mouth. 'The older yer get, Ma, the worse yer get. Is it you leading Irene astray, or the other way around?'

'Six of one and half-a-dozen of the other, son. Me and Irene think alike, always have done. And that little trick paid dividends. Since that first day, Olive's been to the shops a few times. Once with me, once with Irene and once on her own. So things are definitely looking up.'

'I'll go and leave yer in peace now,' Steve said. 'I can smell Mrs Aggie's got a nice dinner ready for yer.' He hesitated for a second. 'How long are yer home for, Mr Titch?'

'Ten long, beautiful days, lad. Ten days of being spoiled rotten by me ma. And that dinner yer can smell is only the start.'

'I know what it is, but I'm not going to tell yer. Me and me mam had the same, thanks to Mrs Aggie.' There was fondness in the look he gave the woman who was like family to him. 'She's a smashing cook.'

'She's everything a mother should be, and more.' When Steve moved towards the door, Titch followed. 'I'll have a look down the paper tonight and see what's on at the pictures this week. Then we'll let the gang decide if they want to see a cowboys and Indians, a thriller or a comedy.'

'That's smashing. I don't care what we go to see.' Steve turned on the top step. 'Are yer going to ask me mam if she'll come?'

Titch pursed his lips. 'I don't think so, lad. She hasn't wanted to come the other times I've asked her, and I don't want to put her in an embarrassing situation.'

'She might do, this time. She's been out now, she hadn't before.'

'We'll see how the land lies, eh? Tell her I'll nip up and see her tomorrow. Tonight is my night for a drink with me mates. If I'm not mistaken, Bob's on night shift, so we might get a couple of pints in before he goes to work.'

'Okay, Mr Titch, I'll tell me mam.' Steve lowered his head to gaze down at his shoes. 'I don't know how we'd have managed if you hadn't come down to our house that day. I used to worry meself sick about me mam, but I didn't have no one to turn to. I could see she was really ill, but she wouldn't let me get the doctor 'cos we had no money. I knew we weren't getting enough to eat, that the house was a tip and

I was walking around like a tramp. None of that worried me, I didn't care what people said about me. But I did care what was happening to me mam, and I used to have nightmares that she was going to die and I couldn't do a thing to stop it.'

Titch put a hand on his shoulder. 'Listen to me, lad, all the neighbours in this street have nothing but praise for yer. Yer've come through that bad patch with flying colours. Put it behind yer and look towards the future. Ye're a working man now, with yer whole life ahead of yer.'

'Without you, Mr Titch, I wouldn't have had a pair of trousers to wear for the interview for a job. Without Mrs Aggie and Mrs Pollard, me mam wouldn't have been getting a decent dinner every day. She doesn't spend all her time lying on the couch now because she's got good friends that visit and have given her an interest in life.' His blue eyes told of a wisdom beyond his years. 'We've come through the worst of it, as yer say, but I'll never forget we didn't do it alone.'

'Ay, it's a good job me ma isn't here listening to yer, she'd be crying buckets. Life has made yer grow up quick, Steve, but yer've got the guts and courage to make a good life for yerself, and yer mam. And all yer friends are behind yer and dead proud of yer.' Titch punched him good-naturedly in the chest. 'Now will yer go on home before yer have me bawling me eyes out. Me ma thinks the world of yer, but if she thought yer'd made her lovely son cry, she'd be chasing yer down the street with the poker in her hand.'

He stood for a while watching the lad walk down the street, his back straight, his stride long. A young man with a purpose who deserved to get on in life. 'Olive might not have been able to give that lad any luxuries, Ma,' Titch said when he went back in the living room to find his mother setting the table, 'but she's given him something more important. She's taught him honesty and a respect for people. I think she's done a damn good job on him.'

'There's no doubt about that, son. There's not a better-mannered lad in this street.' Aggie bent over the table, straightening the knives and forks and making sure the condiment set was close to where her son would be sitting. 'Did I hear yer telling him yer'd be taking the kids to the pictures during the week?'

Titch chuckled as he pulled a chair out from under the table and sat down. 'My God, yer've got good hearing, Ma – yer don't miss a thing. Yes, I did say I'd be taking them to the flicks. They look forward to it, and so do I.'

'And are yer going to ask Olive?'

'There's not much point, is there? She'd only refuse.'

'Then I'll ask her. I'll say I want to go with yer but I don't fancy being the only female.' Aggie bustled out to the kitchen. 'Come and stand by the door so I can talk to yer while I'm putting the dinner out. Once yer go out to the pub, that's the last I'll see of yer until tomorrow.'

Titch leaned against the door jamb, his arms folded and his legs crossed at the ankles. 'Okay, Mam, let's have all the news. I've got a couple of months to catch up on.'

'We'll stick with Olive. She has improved a lot, although once she steps out of that house she gets very nervous. But that'll pass in time. Irene had some dresses that won't go near her now she's put weight on, and she told Olive she was welcome to them if she could alter them to fit. It turns out she's very handy with a needle and thread and she made a good job of them. That's why I suggested yer asked her to come to the pictures. Now she's got some decent clothes she might be glad of a night out.'

'She'd be more than welcome, Ma. I'd be made up to see her getting out and about. But I'd feel happier if you asked her.' Titch waited for his mother's agreement, then asked, 'What about the Pollards? Everyone well, I hope?'

'They're fine. Irene's still doing her morning job, she's saving up for some new furniture. They're pretty comfortable now with three lots of wages coming in, even though young

Jack thinks it's his few bob that keeps the house going. He takes after his mam, always with a smile on his face and a joke on his lips. They're a very happy family, the Pollards.'

'Shall I ask how the Mellors are, or would it put me off me dinner?'

'It's hard to say. Sometimes Bob looks as though he's got the troubles of the world on his shoulders, but he never mentions his wife's name. They don't go over the door together, so things haven't improved. But to give Bob his due, he keeps his worries to himself. I very seldom see Ruby. If we meet in the street we just walk past each other. I've no time for her and I'll not pretend otherwise.' Aggie drained the potatoes and put a knob of butter in the pan before plunging the masher up and down. 'Lucy is a little treasure. Every time I see her I want to give her a big hug to make up for the ones she doesn't get off her mother. She is always happy and cheerful, but I think deep down she's a sad child. She spends a lot of time in the Pollards', especially when Bob's at work. I think she confides in Irene, but I wouldn't like to say for sure. Irene's not one to break a confidence.'

Titch moved away from the wall and stretched his arms over his head. 'In other words, Ma, things are just the same as they were when I went away?'

'Not quite, son, not quite. I've got another wrinkle in me forehead, three more white hairs in me head and a hole in the heel of me stocking that yer could put yer fist through.' Aggie pointed the masher at him. 'I'm not complaining, mind. I wouldn't have mentioned them if yer hadn't asked.'

'Ma, yer've got steel-grey hair and there's not a white hair to be seen. Nor have yer got a wrinkle in yer face. What's more, I'll bet a pound to a pinch of snuff there's no hole in the heel of yer stocking. In all, I'd say ye're a remarkable woman for yer age. And now, while ye're dishing the dinner out, I'm going to give George and Bob a knock to ask them to be ready for half-seven. I'll be back in two ticks.' Titch was passing the sideboard when he heard his mother talking to herself.

'I'll have a little bet on the side meself. I bet that when the world comes to an end, my son will be sitting in a pub somewhere with a bleedin' pint glass in his hand.'

Titch crept up behind her. 'Ma, can yer think of a better way to go?'

Lucy was in the Pollards' when Titch called for George that evening. As soon as he walked through the door she flew to him and put her arms around his waist. 'I'm glad to see yer, Mr Titch.'

'And I'm glad to see you, sweetheart.' He stroked her hair, thinking here was a child starved of affection. Oh, Bob was affectionate with her, he idolised her. But she wasn't getting any from the one person, who above all, should be showering it on her. 'Are we all set for the pictures one night, gang?'

'Oh, yes please, Mr Titch.' Greg's face was one big smile. 'I'm looking forward to it.'

Jack stood up, and with his two hands in his pockets, sauntered across the room. 'I thought yer were never going to ask.'

'Ay, you,' Lucy said, 'where's yer manners?'

'I keep them in me back pocket so no one can pinch them. I got a lot of smacks learning those manners, so I'm not taking any chances on them getting nicked.'

'That's enough now, all of yer,' Irene said. 'I'm still waiting for me kiss.'

'Don't mind me, I'm only yer husband!' George said with mock indignation. 'It's getting to be too much of a habit, this kissing lark.'

'Take no notice of him, Titch.' Irene winked. 'Pretend he's not here.'

Titch wagged his head from side to side. 'Ooh, I don't know about that, he's bigger than I am.' He eyed the youngsters. 'I'll take a chance though, 'cos it's worth it. But hold the door open in case I have to make a quick getaway.'

Irene held her cheek up and Titch's mouth was two inches away when George banged his fist on the wooden arm of his chair. 'That's enough now. Don't be making a meal out of it.'

Titch was laughing so much he only managed a peck on the cheek. 'See what yer've done, mate? Two flaming months I've waited for that.'

George's hearty chuckle filled the room. 'Tomorrow's another day, mate, and I might be feeling more generous.' He pushed himself out of the chair and shook his trouser legs until the crease was straight. 'We'd better be off, Bob will have to leave just after nine.'

'Yeah, okay. I'll see yer all tomorrow.' Titch held his hand out to Lucy. 'Are yer coming home with us?'

The girl seemed to shrink from him. 'No, I'm staying here to have a game of cards.'

'I'll take her home when it's bedtime,' Irene said. 'We'll have a couple of hands, first.'

'Lucy always wins, yer know, Mr Titch,' Jack said. 'As sure as eggs is eggs, she'll end up with another eight buttons tonight. That's because me mam taught her how to cheat.'

'You big fibber! It's you what cheats, not me.'

'Come on, Titch, or we'll be here all night.' George led the way out of the house. 'Those boys of mine would talk yer into an asylum.'

Bob answered their knock and stepped into the street, banging the door behind him. 'Yer'll have to excuse the clobber but I'm a working man. I wish I could get a day job, but there's none going in our place and there's too many men out of work to look elsewhere.'

They fell into step for the short walk to the corner pub. George had a few bob in his pocket through the week these days, so he said he'd get the first round in. While he went to the bar, Titch and Bob found seats in a corner.

'How's the world treating yer, Bob? Okay?'

'It's ticking over, Titch.' Bob was on edge, hoping they

wouldn't mention his wife. He didn't want to talk about Ruby. He could lie, and say they were getting on fine, but the words would stick in his throat. 'Nothing exciting, like, but it's ticking over.'

'That's all we can expect, I suppose. There's always someone worse off than yerself, but then there's always someone better off.'

George was laughing as he put the three pint glasses down. 'There's an argument going on over the bar and it's a scream to listen to them. Yer know the old man from the top of the street – Bert? Well, he's trying to get a half-pint of stout on tick. And Alec's telling him he can't have it because he hasn't paid for the one he got on tick last week. Bert asked, "Which one was that? I don't remember getting half a pint on tick." Alec was very patient with him at first, explaining it was Friday night and he had it written on his slate. And if Bert couldn't pay him for one, he certainly wouldn't be able to pay for two. And d'yer know what the old man said? "If that's yer attitude, I'll have to take me custom elsewhere." '

Titch saw the funny side and turned in his seat to see the old man's head going as he argued the toss. Lifting his arm, Titch snapped his fingers to attract the manager's attention. Then he pointed to the old man's back and mouthed, 'Give him one. I'll pay for it.'

Alec shrugged his shoulders and reached up for a glass. 'There's one born every minute, so they say.' He filled the glass, put it in front of old Bert and nodded to where the three men were sitting. 'Yer can thank the bloke in the navy reefer.'

Bert turned with the glass in his hand and a smile that showed he didn't have a tooth in his head. 'Ye're a gent. Ta very much.'

'Ye're welcome, mate, enjoy it.' Titch swivelled back in his seat. 'Poor old bugger. We could end up like him one day. None of us knows what's in store for us.'

'My two lads say they'll look after me when I'm old and grey,' George said with a smile. 'They won't see me without a few coppers for me beer money.'

Bob nodded. 'Lucy must have heard them saying it because she said the same thing last week. I wondered what had put the idea into her head.'

'It doesn't say much for me, does it?' Titch said. 'I'll have to hope the manager who's here when I'm old is an easier touch than Alec.'

'The solution's in yer own hands, mate,' George told him. 'Get yerself a wife and family before it's too late.'

Bob drained his glass. He wasn't so much on edge now and told Titch, 'I'd give that very careful thought if I were you. Weigh up all the pros and cons.'

'Oh, don't worry, mate. To me it sounds like a choice between the devil and the deep blue sea, and I don't fancy either.' Titch scraped his chair back and reached for the empty glasses. 'Looking at old Bert though makes yer think, doesn't it? He mustn't have had any children.'

'What! Are yer joking?' George laughed. 'He only had six! Four boys and two girls. They're all married with children of their own, but I know they slip him a few coppers when they can, 'cos I've seen them. But he likes his stout, does Bert, and this isn't the only pub he frequents. He does the rounds and I'll bet he never goes home without a drink, even though he seldom has a penny to bless himself with. Ask the manager of the George – he'll tell yer all about the tricks Bert gets up to.'

'In other words, I've been had?'

'Well and truly, mate. Well and truly.'

Titch gave an exaggerated sigh. 'There's nothing down for me, is there? No wife, no kids and no ruddy brains.'

Ruby paced the floor after Bob had left, feeling really hard done by. What a bloody miserable life she was expected to lead. If he had his way, she'd be stuck in this house every night looking at four walls and she'd had enough. It had been like that for months now, and she was fed-up to the teeth with it. Every third week, when Bob was on the early shift, she had three nights out with her mates, but it wasn't good enough. She'd go stark staring mad if she thought this was how her life was going to be until she was too old to want some fun.

Not once did it enter Ruby's head that her life was of her own making. If she was friendly with the neighbours she'd have had plenty to do to pass the time away. Like the Pollards, where Lucy was now, playing cards. She could be in there if she'd put herself out to be friendly. But that wasn't what Ruby called having a good time. She wanted to be with her mates, sitting in a pub having a few drinks and being fawned over by Wally Brown. Now there was a man who appreciated her and made her feel like someone special.

She looked at the clock to see it was nearly eight o'clock. She'd give a knock on the wall in half an hour, a signal for Lucy to come home. And when the girl was in bed and fast asleep she'd take a chance and slip out for an hour. Bob would never know, and anyway she didn't give a monkey's whether he did or not. He couldn't expect her to live like a ruddy hermit.

With her mind made up, Ruby sat down and reached for her purse. Counting the money into her lap, she smiled. She had plenty to buy a round for everyone. Bob had never given her the extra five shillings housekeeping back, he'd reduced it to three. But with what she saved on food, it was enough for her nights out. She scooped the money up and put it back in her purse before running up the stairs to get changed. After that, she got the mirror out and began to apply thick layers of make-up.

'There's yer mam knocking for yer, sunshine.' Irene saw the look that always came to Lucy's face when it was time to go home. It was a look of disappointment mixed with fear. But she couldn't ignore the knock, otherwise Ruby would come banging on the door creating merry hell. 'It must be yer bedtime.'

Lucy put her cards down and pushed her chair back. Although she would never say it, she hated leaving this warm, happy house to go back to her home where there was never any laughter or smiles when her dad wasn't there. She hadn't done anything wrong, she always made sure she kept on the right side of her mother. But she knew something would be picked on as an excuse for a telling-off.

'We'll see yer tomorrow night, Lucy,' Jack said, hoping to bring a smile to the pretty face. 'It's a pity yer only won three buttons tonight, but yer luck might change tomorrow.'

'Yeah,' Greg grinned. 'And when yer've got enough to open a button shop, I'll be yer very first customer. Every time me mam washes a shirt, she manages to lose one of the pearl buttons. I don't know how she does it, but she definitely has the knack because all me shirts are missing a couple of buttons.'

'You cheeky beggar!' Irene put her arm across Lucy's shoulders. 'Take no notice of him, sunshine, he's pulling yer leg.'

'I know he is.' Lucy put out her tongue at the grinning face. 'Your mam looks after yer, she always has yer well turned out.'

'I'll come to the door with yer, sunshine, and make sure yer get in all right.'

The Mellors' front door was open and Lucy waved before stepping inside to be confronted by her mother. She was startled and took a step back, expecting a hand to lash out at her. But to her surprise and suspicion, there was a smile on the heavily made-up face. It wasn't a proper smile, but one that Lucy called a put-on one.

'I've made a hot drink for yer,' Ruby said, closing the front door and following her daughter into the living room. 'It'll warm yer up before yer go to bed.'

This was so out of character it put Lucy on her guard. 'I'll take it up with me and have it in bed.'

'Yeah, okay, if that's what yer want. But I'd like yer to do me a favour.'

Lucy took in the best dress, the made-up face and the sickly-sweet smell of cheap scent. Her mother was up to something. 'What d'yer want?'

'I've got a message for me mate Josie, and I want to slip round to her house for a few minutes. I won't be out long, just there and back. But yer know what yer dad's like, he'd do his nut if he knew. So it would be daft to tell him and start a row, wouldn't it? Just for the sake of half an hour at the most. So I want yer to be a good girl and not mention it to him. I'll give yer a ha'penny in the morning to buy some sweets on yer way to school.'

She's trying to buy my silence, Lucy told herself. But she needn't bother because for my dad's sake I wouldn't tell him. I know he'd get upset and there'd be a big row. And I wouldn't want that. 'I don't want any money for sweets, and I won't tell me dad unless he asks me.'

Ruby breathed a sigh of relief. Bob wouldn't ask, he had no reason to. He was stupid enough to think he had her under his thumb. 'I'll stay until ye're fast asleep, and I'll leave the light on for yer.'

Lucy didn't answer. She went down the yard to the lavvy, came back and washed her hands before pouring herself a cup of tea. She carried it through the living room and up the stairs without so much as a glance at her mother. And not a word was spoken.

When Alec called time, he motioned to Titch and George to stay put. He often did this, and would sit with the two mates and have a pint in the peace and quiet of an empty pub. He said it gave him time to wind down before clearing glasses and ash-trays. They just talked about things in general and had a good laugh. What the pub manager heard standing behind the bar counter was nobody's business and the three men would be in stitches. Until he called time on them, too.

Alec slid the heavy bolts back and opened the door. He peeped out to make sure the coast was clear, then stepped back to let the two men out. 'See yer tomorrow, eh, Titch?'

'More than likely, Alec. Goodnight.'

George was still smiling at something Alec had said which tickled his fancy. 'Yer wouldn't believe the stories he hears behind the bar, would yer? He should write a book about it.'

'Yeah, but as yer say, George, no one would believe it was the truth.' Titch suddenly took hold of his mate's arm and drew him into the darkness of the pub door. 'Not a word,' he said softly. Seconds went by before he let go of his grip. 'Yer can turn around now. Ruby Mellor's just gone past on the other side.'

George turned and watched the figure covering the ground quickly. 'What the hell's she doing out this time of night?'

'She certainly hasn't been on an errand of mercy, George, that's for sure. I'd say she's been up to no good.'

'She must have left Lucy on her own in the house. Bob will go mad when he knows.'

'He won't hear it from me, George. He's got enough worry on his plate without us adding to it. I think this is something we should keep between the two of us. I won't tell me ma, and I don't think yer should tell Irene. It's none of our business and it's not our place to interfere. That doesn't mean I condone it, far from it. I'd really like to give that woman a piece of my mind. But I don't think Bob would thank me for it.'

'No, ye're right, he wouldn't.' George had seen Ruby disappear into the house and knew it was now safe for them to walk up the street. 'I won't breathe a word to Irene because I know she wouldn't keep it to herself. She thinks the world of Lucy, and would go mad if she thought the girl was in danger. And she could be, yer know, Titch. All it would take is a piece of coal falling out of the fire on to the rug. Or even the gas mantle flaking, as they sometimes do, and a burning piece falling on to the tablecloth. Yer do hear of these things happening.'

They were outside the Pollards' house now, and Titch said, 'We'll talk about it tomorrow, George. Me ma will wonder where I've got to. She might even think I've met the only girl in the world that's good enough for me, and run off with her.'

George chuckled. 'Aye, and pigs might fly.' He inserted the key in the lock. 'See yer tomorrow, mate. Goodnight.'

'Goodnight, George.' Titch waited until his neighbour was in the hall before saying, 'Oh, will yer give Irene a kiss for me? The one I would have got earlier if you hadn't been so flaming miserable.'

Kate Brown looked across the canteen table at Bob. 'Did yer have a pint before yer came into work?'

'Yeah, I had two as a matter of fact. How did yer know?'

'I tell fortunes. And looking at the tea leaves floating on the top of yer tea, I can see yer sitting in a pub with a pint glass in yer hand.'

Silence descended on the table and all eyes were on Bob as he said, 'Ye're pulling me leg, aren't yer?'

Kate shook her head, feeling she was pretty safe in what she was saying. She'd come to know a lot about Bob in the last six months and knew he only ever went for a pint before work when his friend was home from sea. 'I can see yer as plain as day. Ye're sitting with a man who has some sort of peaked cap on his head and he's wearing a navy-blue jacket.'

Peg Butterworth stopped munching and her eyes were wide with excitement. 'Is she right, Bob?'

Bob looked mystified. 'Yeah, she is. Me mate, Titch, is home on leave.'

'Well, I'll be a monkey's uncle.' Down went Peg's butty and she lifted up her cup. 'Yer can read my cup, Kate, when I've drank me tea.'

'And mine.' Elsie Burgess wasn't going to be left out. 'Ooh, I don't half love fortune-tellers. I went to one in

Queen's Drive last year and yer should have heard some of the things she told me. She didn't half buck me up.'

Ada Smithson shook her head knowingly. 'I wouldn't have me fortune told, it's bad luck.'

Billy Gleeson had been listening with a smirk on his face. He could have told Bob what Kate did because he'd come to know his habits as she had. But he wasn't going to spoil the fun. 'You women would fall for the bloody cat. Thick as two short planks, the lot of yer.'

'Billy, ye're like a wet week,' Peg said, in between trying to drink tea that was too hot. 'If Aladdin had been as miserable as you, he'd have told the genie to sod off.'

Kate, after winking at Bob and mouthing that it had been guesswork, now looked on in amusement. She didn't know the first thing about telling fortunes but was game for a laugh. 'Don't blame me if I tell yer something yer don't like.'

Billy chuckled. 'Kate, be warned. If you tell Elsie something she doesn't like, she'll crack yer one.' He looked over to where the big woman sat. 'By the way, Elsie, this woman yer went to see on Queen's Drive, did the things she told yer come true?'

'Well, er, no they didn't. But she cheered me up for a week, so it was worth the tanner I'd paid.' The table began to bounce up and down as her mountainous tummy shook with laughter. 'Wait till yer hear this, Billy, it's a belter. She told me, all mysterious like, that she could see money around me: "I can't tell you exactly, but I think you're going to come into money. That's the message I'm getting through the cards." She spoke dead posh, as though she had a plum in her mouth. And she was right about seeing money. Yer see, ten days later I lost me purse with five bob in it.'

Peg nearly choked on her tea. 'Yer never told me that, Elsie Burgess.'

'Well, I don't tell yer everything, Peg. I mean, I don't say to yer that we've got three blankets on our bed. Or that the tap in the kitchen is leaking. And I wouldn't dream of telling yer that my feller kisses me every night and tells me how beautiful I am.'

'No, but ye're quick enough to tell me when ye're skint. Or like the time we were walking to work and yer said the elastic had snapped in yer knickers. I didn't know where to put meself when I looked down and there they were around yer ankles.' Memory of the scene had Peg rocking in her chair. 'I must have looked a right nit, standing there holding yer hand while yer stepped out of them.'

Everyone around the table went in a pleat, even Elsie. 'Yeah, it was funny that. It wasn't at the time, like, 'cos there were a lot of people about. But I had a good laugh afterwards and told my feller how funny it had been.'

'Elsie, the only thing I've ever seen that was funnier, was a Laurel and Hardy film. The only difference is, they get paid for making fools of themselves and you don't.' Peg leaned across her friend and handed her cup to Kate. 'Try and come up with something nice for me, girl. I need cheering up.'

'It'll have to be short if Elsie wants her reading as well. We haven't got that much time before the bell goes.' Kate pretended to concentrate, while her mind was trying to remember anything Peg had said that she could use. Then she had a brainwave. 'I'm probably miles out, but have yer bought anything recently, or are yer thinking of buying a dress or coat?'

'Well, I never!' Peg gaped. 'Yeah, I'm thinking of buying meself a new dress. Remember, Elsie, I told yer last week?'

Elsie was wide-eyed. 'Yeah, yer did, queen.'

Kate was glad her workmates had loud voices and she'd heard every word of their conversation. She turned the cup around and pretended to study the tea-leaves in the bottom. 'I think I see the colour blue.'

Well, that had Peg and Elsie banging on the table. 'That's the very colour I had in mind, girl! Isn't that right, Elsie?'

'It is, queen, I can vouch for that.' Elsie was by now convinced they had a fortune-teller in their midst and she wasn't going to be left out. 'Do mine, now, queen, before the bell goes.'

Kate was stumped. She couldn't think of anything she'd overheard. So she decided to go for a bit of fun. She turned the cup round and round, a puzzled expression on her face. 'I can't make this out. When yer were little, Elsie, were yer ever a May Queen?'

Elsie preened at the very thought, but had to admit it wasn't true. 'No, queen.'

'I don't know what it is, but it looks like a throne. And you're sitting on it, surrounded by light.' Kate had a funny ending in her head for this piece of fortune-telling, but it wasn't needed as Elsie had a funnier one.

Her chubby cheeks all screwed up and covering her eyes, Elsie shook her head as she tried to find a connection to what had been said to her. Then suddenly she blurted out, 'Bloody hell!' and every head in the canteen was turned towards her. 'Ay, queen, ye're not far out on that one. The throne yer see me sitting on is me lavvy. And the light around me comes from my feller having whitewashed the walls last week.'

When the laughter had died down, Peg said, 'Yer didn't tell me your feller had whitewashed the lavvy for yer.'

'Well, as I said before, queen, I can't remember to tell yer everything.'

Bob smiled across at Kate. 'You're not half coming out of yer shell lately. Yer used to be as quiet as a mouse.'

There was shyness in Kate's smile. 'Yer can blame yerself for that. I used to be as quiet as a mouse until you started sitting at our table. Yer must be having a bad influence on me, Bob Mellor.'

'I hope that's not true. I hold yer in very high esteem, Kate Brown.'

She lowered her eyes as a faint blush covered her cheeks. 'Then I'll have to try and live up to it, won't I?'

Chapter Fifteen

'It's a shame your Titch never got married,' Olive said, walking between Aggie and Irene, their arms linking hers. 'He loves kids and is so good with them.'

'Yeah, I know. I keep telling meself it's not too late, 'cos I'd like to see him settled down with a family. But he's either too bleedin' choosey or no one will have him.'

'Your son would have no trouble finding a dozen girls who'd be more than willing to marry him,' Irene said. 'He's a fine-looking man and if he was that way inclined he could have his pick.'

After much persuasion they'd finally talked Olive into coming to the pictures. She was worried because she didn't have a decent coat to wear, so Aggie had lent her a black knitted shawl to wear over a thick cardigan. It was a cold winter's night and there was a stiff breeze blowing, but cushioned between her friends, Olive was sheltered from the worst of it. 'He's got a lot of patience with kids. Just look at him now, they're all over him and he's lapping it up. Our Steve idolises him, I know that much.'

Titch was walking ahead with the youngsters, one hand holding Lucy's while the three boys walked on his other side. Their laughter was carried on the wind, bringing smiles to the faces of the three women. 'That's our Jack,' Irene said. 'I don't think he's stopped talking since we left the house.'

'Oh, I don't know,' Aggie said. 'They're all doing their fair share, even Lucy. She's not behind the door when it comes to getting her twopennyworth in.'

Olive saw Lucy look up at Titch with a smile on her face. She couldn't hear what the girl said, but loud laughter followed her words. 'I see what yer mean, Aggie. She's a beautiful-looking girl, I bet her parents are proud of her.'

There was no immediate reply to that, then Irene said, 'I'll tell yer what, Olive. You scratch my back and I'll scratch yours. If you say my two are handsome lads, I'll say the same about your Steve. Then we'll all be happy.'

'Oh, no we won't,' Aggie tutted. 'Yer seem to forget that I have a son, too. Now let's hear it for Titch. Is he handsome, or is he not?'

'Very, very handsome,' was Olive's verdict.

While Irene thought he was, 'Film-star handsome.'

'That's better. He may be forty, but he's still my little boy.' They grinned at each other before quickening their steps to catch up with Titch and company outside the picturehouse. The children had all opted for a comedy, *The Gay Divorcée*, starring Fred Astaire and Ginger Rogers. And it was hilarious. Jack got so carried away with mirth he kept banging his fist on the back of the seat in front of him, until the woman turned around and told him if he didn't knock it off she'd knock his block off. Lucy was captivated by the dancing, Steve was captivated by the changing expressions on her face, and Greg was too busy enjoying himself to worry about anyone else.

On the walk home, it was unanimously agreed that a good time had been had by all and the evening had been a great success. For Olive it had been more than that. It had been a much-needed tonic.

It was when they turned into their street that Titch noticed a change in Lucy. The smile had gone from her face and she seemed tense. 'Are yer all coming back to ours for a cup of tea?' he asked.

'No thanks, Titch,' Olive said. 'I'll go straight home if yer don't mind.'

'Me too.' Irene gathered her sons to her. 'It's nearly time for Greg to go to bed. But thanks for a lovely night, I thoroughly enjoyed meself.'

There was a chorus of thanks from the children. It was Steve, a gentleman at fourteen years of age, who held out his hand. 'Thanks, Mr Titch, it's been smashing.'

Titch shook his hand warmly. 'Ye're welcome, lad. We'll do it again, soon.' He put his arm across Lucy's shoulder. 'Are you coming in for a cuppa, sweetheart?'

'Oh no, Mr Titch. Me dad won't have left for work yet, so I'll be in time for me goodnight kiss. I wouldn't want to miss that.'

'Then I'll walk down with yer and have a short natter with yer dad.'

The group went their separate ways, leaving Titch with his mother and Lucy. 'Are yer coming with us, Ma?'

Aggie shook her head. 'No, I'll go in and put the kettle on. You see Lucy home.'

Bob had been watching out and the door was quickly opened. 'Good time, pet?'

'Oh Dad, the picture was lovely. It was very funny, but I liked the dancing the best.'

'Come in, Titch.' Bob threw the door wide open. 'I don't have to leave for half an hour, so there's time for a cup of tea.'

'I'll come in, but I won't stay for a drink, thanks. Me ma's gone in to put the kettle on.'

Ruby managed a smile. 'Was it a good picture?'

Titch looked to Lucy, expecting her to reply. When she didn't, he said, 'Yeah, it was great. Everyone enjoyed themselves.'

'I don't know how yer've got the patience to take a gang of kids out. Yer wouldn't catch me doing it, they'd drive me potty. It certainly wouldn't be my idea of a good night out.'

Titch saw the look of disgust on Bob's face. And he saw Lucy standing with her head bowed, a stranger in her own home. Leaning an elbow on the sideboard and injecting a note of interest in his voice, he asked, 'Oh, and what's your idea of a good night out, Ruby?'

'A couple of drinks in pleasant company. Friends yer can have a laugh and a joke with.'

'Yer won't get many of those nights with Bob being on shiftwork, will yer? I mean, when he's on afternoons and nights, yer won't manage to get out, will yer?'

There was something in the tone of his voice and the look in his eyes that caused Ruby to feel uncomfortable. He seemed to be goading her, as though he knew something. Could she have been seen on the two nights she'd been out? She'd been very careful, using the back entry when she went out. But she'd come home the front way because she didn't fancy the dark entry late at night. She hadn't given a thought to anyone seeing her because the street had been deserted on both nights. No, she told herself, he doesn't know anything, it's just my imagination. So she brazened it out. 'No, the only social life I get is when he's on mornings, worse luck.'

'Count yer blessings, Ruby, 'cos that's more than most women get.' Titch pushed himself up and stretched his well-built frame. 'I'd better be going or me ma will tell me off if the tea gets cold.' He gave Lucy a hug. 'I'll see yer, sweetheart.'

'Yeah, okay, Mr Titch, and thanks again.'

'I'll see yer out, then I'll have to put a move on meself.' Bob followed his neighbour to the door, 'I appreciate yer taking Lucy out, she doesn't half enjoy herself. I'm sorry to say me daughter doesn't get many treats in life.'

'She's got a lot of friends, Bob, that think the world of her. And she's got the best father anyone could ask for.' Titch began to laugh and pointed a finger. 'Just look at me ma, standing on the step shaking a fist at me. Anyone would think I was fourteen instead of forty. She used to do that when I was a slip of a lad and wouldn't come in when she called me.

I'd better skedaddle or I'll be getting a clip around the ear. Don't work too hard, Bob.'

Bob stepped down to wave to Aggie. 'Goodnight and God bless, Aggie. Sleep well. And you, Titch. I'll see yer.'

The night before Titch was due to sail, he went to say goodbye to Olive and Steve. He also went with a plan in mind.

'How long are yer away this time, Titch?' Olive asked. 'A couple of months?'

'Could be longer this time, Olive. That's why, if you don't mind, I'd like to ask Steve to do a job for me.'

'Of course I will, Mr Titch.' Steve would willingly run to the ends of the earth for this man. 'Just name it and I'll do it.'

'Only on certain conditions, Steve. I want to pay yer for it. Not much, mind yer, but I don't want yer to do it for nothing.'

'Steve wouldn't take money off you, Titch!' Olive protested. 'After all you've done for him, he wouldn't dream of it.'

'Me mam's right.' Steve was highly indignant. 'I wouldn't take no money off yer.'

'But it's a big job I'm asking yer to do, Steve. Yer see, I'm worried about me ma, now the winter has set in. I don't like the thought of her having to lug coal up the yard in freezing weather. I have visions of her slipping on the snow or ice and laying in the yard with no one knowing she's there. So I was going to ask if yer'd slip up there each night and fill her coal scuttle for her and make sure she's all right. I'd have an easy mind when I'm away if I knew she was being cared for.'

'I'd do that with pleasure,' Steve said, looking happy at just the thought. 'Yer don't have to pay me no money to look after Mrs Aggie.'

'I'll keep me eye on her, too,' Olive said. 'I won't go up at night, but I'll call in each day.'

This was what Titch had been hoping for. It was a good way of getting Olive out of the house. 'That's taken a load off me mind. But if I'm away for two or three months, it's a lot to ask of yer. So if yer won't take money off me, will yer let me do something for yer?'

Olive tilted her head and narrowed her eyes. 'Oh, aye, what are yer up to now? I don't trust you, Titch McBride.'

Titch winked at Steve. 'Will yer sit on yer mam for me, so she can't scratch me eyes out or wallop me one?'

Steve left the wooden chair to sit next to his mother on the couch. He put his two arms around her and held her tight. 'Safely anchored, Mr Titch.'

'What I've asked you two to do is a very big favour. Now I'd like yer to let me give a little back in return. It's not much, but it would please me to do it.'

'I don't like the sound of this,' Olive said. 'Spit it out and get it over with.'

'Promise yer won't hit me, fall out with me or throw me out?'

'In the name of God, what's the man up to now?' Olive managed to keep her face straight while asking herself how could anyone fall out with Titch when he had that huge smile on his face and mischief dancing in his eyes. 'Come on, out with it.'

'Well, now I know me ma's going to be well looked after, I'd like to think you two were happy and comfortable. So let me buy the wallpaper to brighten this room up.'

'You what!' Olive's voice was shrill. 'Not on yer blinking life.'

'Excuse me, Mrs Fletcher, but I haven't finished yet. There's more to come.' Titch wagged an admonishing finger. 'So be a good girl and listen before disagreeing with me. I knew I'd have trouble getting Steve to take money off me, so I went ahead and bought wallpaper for this room. I didn't pay full price for it because I've got a mate what's got a mate with a wallpaper shop. So I'm not being as generous as yer think. It only cost me a few bob. And George and Bob have said they'd be delighted to do the work.' Titch grinned before letting out a deep sigh. 'Now I'll ask Steve to keep tight hold of yer until yer've had time to think it over. But to help yer come to the right decision, close yer eyes and imagine how nice and cheerful this room would look for Christmas. And remember, I wasn't too proud to accept your help, so to keep things square, the least yer can do is accept mine.'

When Olive stayed stony-faced, her eyes fixed on the far wall, Titch wagged his head at Steve before asking, 'Is yer mam still breathing, lad?'

'I think so, Mr Titch, I can see her nostrils going in and out.'

'That's good. It means she hasn't gone and died on us.' He leaned forward and looked into the solemn face. 'I'm glad about that, 'cos I'd have been left with eight rolls of wall-paper and a lot of explaining to do.'

Without moving a muscle, Olive asked, 'What colour's the paper?'

His face as straight as hers, Titch said, 'Pea-green.'

'I'm not having no pea-green wallpaper on my walls, Titch McBride – yer can take it right back and change it.'

'How about a pale beige with little sprigs of pink flowers on?'

'That sounds more like it.' Olive faced him with a beaming smile. 'How soon can the workmen start?'

'Bob's on mornings, so he could do a bit in the after-noons. Then on Saturday him and George could go like the clappers and get a fair bit done. But you and Steve could help by stripping the old paper off and rubbing the paint-work down.' With a cheeky grin on his face, Titch reached into his pocket and brought out a scraper and two sheets of sandpaper. 'I've come prepared for any contingency. These for if yer said yes, and running shoes in case yer came after me with the poker.'

'It wouldn't have made a scrap of difference what I said, and you know it. I could have argued until I was blue in the face, yer'd still have got yer own way in the end.'

'Excuse me, Mr Titch,' Steve said. 'Can I let go of me mam now?'

'Just make sure she's not frothing at the mouth first. It's a bad sign that, frothing at the mouth.'

'I'll froth you at the mouth, yer cheeky beggar.' But Olive was feeling very light-hearted inside. It would be lovely to see this room nice and bright. 'I should tell yer off for being underhanded and arranging all this behind me back. But I'm not going to because I'm really delighted. I'm indebted to yer, Titch.'

'Ay, remember there's a price to pay for this. I'm relying on both of yer to look after me ma for me.' Titch wondered what his mother would say if she knew she'd been used as a weapon in his plans. She'd probably stand on a chair and box his ears for him. 'It means a lot to me, knowing she's being looked after.'

'I'll keep an eye on her, Mr Titch, I promise yer that. Me and Mrs Aggie get along fine together, we're good mates.'

'It does me heart good to hear that, lad. I know she thinks the world of you.' Titch stood up and put the scraper and sandpaper on the table. 'I'll take me leave of yer now 'cos I'm going for a pint with me two drinking buddies. It's me last night so I've got to make the most of it.'

'Well, look after yerself, Titch,' Olive said. 'Next time yer come we'll be all posh and yer won't get in unless yer wipe yer feet.'

Titch chuckled. 'I'm a clever bugger, Olive, but even I can't walk on walls.'

Olive raised her brows. 'Oh, no? According to Aggie yer can walk on the ceiling when yer've had one over the eight.'

'I wish me ma would stop bragging about me achievements, it's embarrassing. But if she ever tells yer I can walk on water, take it with a pinch of salt.' Titch glanced at the clock before holding his hand out to Steve. 'Look after yer mam, lad, take good care of her. And, of course, yer mate, Mrs Aggie.'

Steve felt ten feet tall. 'Yer can rely on me, Mr Titch. But I wish yer weren't going away, I'll miss yer.'

'We all will,' Olive said. 'Even if it's only for yer cheek.'

Titch bent and kissed the top of her head. 'Yer've come on a treat, Olive. Keep it up at this rate and I won't recognise yer when I come home.'

Mother and son felt sad when they heard the door close behind him. Tommy 'Titch' McBride had come into their lives like a ray of sunshine, and picked them up when they were down. They had much to thank him for.

'Me mate sails today,' Bob said, flicking a crumb from his lips. 'We had a cracking night out with him last night. Mind you, me and George can't keep up with his drinking. If Titch had had his way, neither of us would have been fit for work today.'

'When are we going to meet this mate of yours?' Peg Butterworth wanted to know. 'Tall, tanned and handsome, he sounds right up my street.'

Elsie Burgess, her plump elbows leaning on the table, looked sideways. 'Any man in trousers is right up your street, queen.'

'Ay, watch it, you!' Peg looked put out. 'Be careful what yer say about my good name, unless yer fancy wearing a black eye.'

'It's true! Everyone knows ye're man mad.' Elsie's elbow slipped off the table and her sandwich ended up in her eye. But, undeterred, she carried on: 'It's not so long ago that yer asked me about the milkman what was having it off with a woman in our street.'

'But the poor man wasn't having it off with the woman in your street, was he?' Billy Gleeson said. 'It was your bad minds. If he'd known what yer were saying about him, he could have had yer all up for defamation of character.'

Elsie's mouth gaped. 'What was that yer said, Billy?'

'He could have had yer all up for defamation of character.'

'Yeah, I heard that, but could yer say it in English, please?'

Peg gave her friend a dig. 'Don't show yer ignorance, girl. That *was* English.'

'Well, I didn't never learn nothing like that in my school. Some of it, yeah, but not that defation. I didn't never hear that word before.'

'The word is defamation, Elsie.' Billy was highly amused. 'It means he could have sued yer for every penny yer've got.'

Up and down went the table with Elsie's tummy. 'Blimey, if he can get his tongue around a big word like that, he'd deserve to take every penny I've got. But he'd have to do it on a Saturday, 'cos I've never got two ha'pennies to rub together the rest of the week.' Her face straightened. 'Anyway, clever clogs, Billy Gleeson, yer'd better be careful what yer say or I'll have you up for that deffy thing. We didn't do no wrong, it was a genuine mistake. How were we to know our neighbour was a friend of his missus? And that he stopped for a cuppa and a butty every morning? It was an easy mistake to make.'

Peg sat sideways in her chair and weighed her friend up. 'And what about the coalman? Was his missus a friend, too?'

'How the hell do I know!' Elsie was getting all het up. 'Yer'll be asking me next if the bleedin' horse was a cousin of hers.'

'Keep yer hair on, girl.' A glint came in Peg's eyes. 'Yer can't afford to lose any hairs 'cos yer haven't got many to start with.'

'Are you looking for a fight? If yer are, I'll give yer one,' Elsie said. 'I've got as many hairs on my head as you have, if not more.'

Peg pursed her lips. 'I'll bet yer any money yer haven't.'

'And I bet yer any money I have.'

'Okay,' Peg said. 'Put yer money where yer mouth is. How many hairs have yer got on yer head?'

Oh, she's not catching me out there, thought Elsie. She thinks she's clever, but she's picked on the wrong one. 'You tell me how many you've got first, then I'll tell yer.'

Peg's expression was superior to say the least. 'At the last count it was two million, three hundred thousand and twenty-five.'

Elsie managed to look astounded. 'Well, would yer believe it?' She gazed around the table. 'That's exactly the same number I've got.' She turned to her friend, and before Peg realised what she was up to, Elsie reached over and pulled out a few hairs that were sticking out from under her turban. 'Now yer've got three less than me.'

'That does it.' Peg banged her fist on the table. 'Prove it.'

Elsie looked blank. 'What d'yer mean?'

'Start pulling them out and count them. And we'll all sit here and witness that yer play fair. When yer've got to two million, three hundred thousand and twenty-five, if yer've still got a hair left on yer head, then you win.'

'Yer can sod off, you can! Yer must think I've just come over! It was you what started all this, so it's up to you to prove what ye're saying. Start counting, queen.'

'I haven't got time, girl, 'cos the bell will be going in ten minutes. So we'll call it quits, eh?'

'Yeah,' Elsie smiled, 'we're both winners.'

Peg delved into the pocket of her overall and brought out a threepenny joey, which she handed over. 'Here's yer winnings, girl.'

'Thanks, queen.' Elsie stared down at the small chunky coin nestling in her chubby hand. Smiling, she picked it up and held it out to Peg. 'And here's yours, queen. It was a good, clean, fair fight and we both deserved to win.'

Bob winked across at Kate. 'D'yer know, it's a pleasure to come to work. Apart from when I'm out with me mates, this is the only time I get a few laughs and some decent conversation. Plus the added bonus of having a pretty woman sitting opposite to me.'

Billy swivelled in his seat. 'Ay, I heard that.'

'Yer were meant to.' Bob chuckled. 'I don't see why all the

gossip should come from the women, so I thought I'd add a bit of spice to liven things up.'

'That's a good idea, mate. Just listen to this.' Billy leaned across the table and gestured for everyone to follow suit. Then in a loud whisper, he said, 'Don't any of yer repeat this, but Kate and Bob are having a clandestine affair.'

'Oh, the gear!' Peg said. 'That's something we can really get our teeth into.'

'I don't agree with it.' Little Ada Smithson's thin lips became a narrow line in her pale face. 'It's a sin, that is.'

'What did yer say Kate and Bob were having, Billy?' Elsie asked, not bothering to keep her voice down. 'I didn't hear yer properly.'

'A clandestine affair, Elsie.'

'What school did you go to, Billy Gleeson? It certainly wasn't the same one as me 'cos we don't speak the same language.' Elsie leaned her elbows on the table and looked along to where Kate was sitting. 'You speak English, queen, so you tell me. What are you and Bob having?'

It was with great difficulty that Kate kept her face straight. 'We're having an affair, Elsie.'

'Go 'way!' Elsie mulled the information over for a few seconds, then asked, 'What exactly d'yer mean, queen?'

'Me and Bob are having what you thought yer milkman and neighbour were having. Only they weren't and we are.'

The bell sounded then and chairs were scraped back. 'Why didn't yer tell us that earlier, Billy Gleeson?' Peg asked. 'Now we've got to wait until tomorrow for the next instalment.'

Bob stood at the end of the table and waited for Kate to pick up her belongings. 'I dropped yer in it there, I hope yer don't mind. I just thought it would be a laugh.'

'So yer think having an affair with me would be a laugh, do yer, Bob Mellor? Well, thanks for the compliment.'

Bob blushed to the roots of his hair. 'I didn't mean it like that, Kate. Any man having an affair with you would be a lucky man indeed.'

'Don't take it to heart, Bob, I was only pulling yer leg. And it was a laugh. But we'll never hear the end of it, so be prepared. Peg and Elsie will have a field day with this.'

'I'll sort it out with them tomorrow, then they won't embarrass yer. I should have had more sense, a man of my age.'

'Will yer stop worrying? Peg and Elsie are not soft, they'll know it was only a joke. They'll have a few laughs at our expense then it'll die a natural death. You mark my words.'

Kate turned off when they reached her section. 'I'll see yer tomorrow, Bob.' Then in a loud voice she called after him, 'I'll meet yer at eight, outside the Forum.'

He smiled and waved back. 'Don't be late, like yer were on Monday.'

Peg nudged her mate. 'Yer see, Elsie, I told yer it wasn't true. They're just having us on. The trouble with you is, yer'd fall for the bleedin' cat.'

'Which cat, queen? I haven't got no cat.'

Peg rolled her eyes. 'Why did I pick a friend what's got nothing between her ears only fresh air?'

When Bob came home from work on the Thursday he went straight into the kitchen to swill his hands and face. 'I'm going up to the Fletchers' after I've had a cup of tea. I want to get the room prepared for Saturday, so me and George can start hanging the paper.'

Ruby was by the stove, pouring boiling water into the tea pot. 'You men are bloody fools falling for a hard luck story. Talk about act soft and I'll buy yer a coalyard, isn't in it. Olive Fletcher is too lazy to do anything for herself, so she flutters her eyelashes, pretends she's sick, and has the lot of yer running around after her.'

Bob didn't answer as he dried his face on the towel. He refused to be drawn into an argument with someone who wouldn't get off her backside to help anyone. His wife didn't know anything about the Fletchers and the hard time they'd had. Even if she did, they'd get no sympathy from her. She didn't have a compassionate bone in her body.

'It would do yer more good to decorate yer own house,' Ruby said. 'Never mind wasting yer time up there.'

Bob hung the towel back on the nail behind the door. It wasn't twelve months since he'd papered the living room, but it wouldn't do any good reminding her. She'd set her mind against the Fletchers, and every other family in the street for that matter, and no amount of persuasion would alter that. 'I won't bother with a drink, I'll have one when I get up there. I'll be back at half-five for me dinner.'

'But I've made this pot of tea now!' Ruby followed him into the living room, intent on giving him a piece of her mind. But her mouth closed on the words when she saw him looking down at the *True Confessions* magazine she'd bought that morning. She bought one every week but never cracked on because he'd have a go at her for wasting money when Lucy needed clothes. She usually hid it behind the cushion on her chair but she'd slipped up today.

'I'm sure yer'll manage to get through a pot of tea while ye're reading this tripe.' Bob saw the price on the top of the magazine and was filled with hopelessness and despair. 'The cost of that would have bought Lucy a pair of socks.'

Ruby stared him out. 'I didn't buy it, smart arse. Me mate called round and lent it to me.'

'Telling lies is the only thing ye're good at, Ruby. Oh, and calling everybody fit to burn. I suppose I should feel sorry for yer really, but I can't. Yer see, where ye're concerned, I no longer have any feelings whatsoever. You killed them long ago.' With that, Bob turned on his heels and left the room. He told himself to put it out of his mind; getting upset wouldn't do him any good. So when he was knocking on Aggie's door, there was a smile on his face.

'I've come for the paper and paint, Aggie. I know there's a lot to be done before we can make a start, but seeing as me hands are empty I thought I'd carry it up and get it over with.'

'Come in, lad.' Aggie closed the door behind him. 'Yer can take the paint 'cos they're big tins and too heavy for me to carry. But yer can't take the paper or border 'cos it wants trimming. Me and Irene are going to make a start on it tonight, so it'll be ready when yer need it. Oh, and your Lucy's going to help. We're meeting at Irene's at half-six, when she's got the dinner out of the way.'

'A hive of activity, eh, Aggie? I'm glad to have something to do to occupy me mind.'

Aggie studied his face. He was still smiling, but it was an empty smile. And she detected a sadness in his eyes. 'Glad of a chance to get out of the house, are yer, Bob?'

Bob's nod came with a sigh. 'Yes, Aggie, ye're right. It's a terrible thing to say, but when Lucy's not there, there's nothing in that house for me. I must be the only feller in Liverpool that's glad to go to work. But as they say, I've made me bed and I must lie on it.'

'Yer shouldn't have to spend a lifetime in misery, lad, no one deserves that. Perhaps when Lucy's grown up yer can do something about it. There is such a thing as divorce, yer know.'

'I've thought of everything, Aggie, believe me. But a divorce is complicated and nasty. Ruby wouldn't consent to it anyway and she'd cause merry hell. I wouldn't want to put Lucy through that. But in a few years – well, who knows.'

'Yeah, ye're right, lad. God works in mysterious ways and none of us knows what's going to happen in the future. But I've got a feeling in me bones that there'll come a time when you and Lucy are happy and contented.'

'I hope so, Aggie. Now can yer show me where the paint is and I'll be on me way to Olive's and get some work done. George is hoping I'll have the room ready for papering by Saturday.'

'They're on the floor in the kitchen. Yer'll have to get them yerself, I can't lift them.'

★ ★ ★

Bob put the tins down and stared at the bare walls. 'I wasn't expecting this, Olive. Steve must have worked like mad to get this stripped.'

'Ay, Bob Mellor, I helped, yer know. Steve did the top, I did the bottom. The paper was hanging off anyway, so it was easy.'

'Right, I'll start rubbing the paintwork down, then. But is there any chance of a cuppa? I work better after I've had a drink and a ciggie.'

'I'll put the kettle on, but I've only got conny-onny. Is that all right?'

'I was brought up on conny-onny, Olive, it suits me fine.'

Bob started on the door leading to the hall. He was on his knees when Olive came through carrying two cups of piping hot tea. 'Come and get it. I've no saucers, I'm afraid.'

Bob pulled a chair out and sat facing her. 'Olive, I was brought up in a house with no saucers.' They were both laughing when there was a knock on the door.

Olive's hand went to her throat. 'I wonder who this can be?'

'It won't be a bogeyman – they only come when it's dark.' Bob laughed and stood up. 'I'll answer it.'

Olive sat with her ear cocked. She heard a man's laughter and her heart lurched. It sounded like Titch, but it couldn't be. He'd be on the high seas by now. 'Who is it, Bob?'

'I was wrong, it *is* a bogeyman. I'll let him in though, 'cos he looks harmless enough.'

Olive's eyes were on the door when Titch walked in. 'In the name of heaven, am I seeing things or is it a ghost?'

'The ship developed engine trouble and we had to turn back. It's in for repairs now, and they could take a few days. So ye're honoured with my company again.' Titch eyed the two cups. 'What are yer doing, Olive Fletcher, entertaining a strange man the minute me back's turned? A married man at that.'

'He's only been here about five minutes.'

'I know how long he's been here, 'cos I went home first and me ma told me. Anyway, where's my cup of tea?'

Bob chuckled. 'Only conny-onny, Titch, and no saucer.'

'Just the way I like it. And you can pour it out, Bob, while I fill Olive's heart with happiness by telling her I'll probably be home long enough to see this room decorated.'

'Yer'll be getting stuck in, mate, like the rest of us,' Bob told him. 'With everyone working flat out, it should be finished on Saturday.'

Titch grinned. 'In time for the pub opening, I hope.'

Chapter Sixteen

Bob and Titch worked like Trojans, and by half-past five all the paintwork had been rubbed down. 'That's a good job done,' Titch said. 'But with the best will in the world I don't see how we can get the room finished on Saturday.'

'It can be done.' Bob was more optimistic. 'If Olive will wash the paintwork down while we nip home for our dinner, we can start putting the undercoat on when we come back. I'll bring a brush and the two of us can get cracking. We should get it finished tonight, then the gloss can go on tomorrow.'

Olive looked uneasy. 'I don't want to stop Titch going for his pint.'

'Yeah, that's an important point,' Titch said, pursing his lips as his head wagged from side to side. 'A whole day without a pint doesn't bear thinking about.'

'Yer could keep telling yerself it's Sunday,' Bob said. 'And all the pubs are shut.'

'I've got a better idea. Every time I get a pang, I'll look at Olive and remind meself that even a pint of bitter with a frothy head on isn't as pretty as she is.'

'Will yer go home for yer dinner and stop embarrassing me.' Olive could feel herself blushing. 'Our Steve will be in soon and he'll want something to eat before he gives me a hand washing the paintwork.'

'Aren't some people ungrateful, Bob?' Titch slipped his arms into his reefer jacket. 'I sabotaged the engine for this woman, and that's the thanks I get.'

Olive pointed to the door. 'Will yer go now, the pair of yer?'

Bob chuckled as he grabbed Titch's arm and pulled him into the hall. 'We'll be back in an hour, Olive.'

As soon as she heard the door close after them, Olive bustled out to the kitchen where the mince and onions were simmering gently and the potatoes were ready for mashing. She turned the gas off but left the pan lids on to keep the food warm. An hour wasn't very long to eat a dinner, wash the dishes and then start cleaning the paintwork. But she was determined to do as much as she could. God knows, everybody was doing all they could to help her, the least she could do was pull her weight.

The sound of the key in the door had her reaching for two plates. 'Hurry up, son, we'll be having visitors soon.'

Steve gave her a hug and a kiss. 'Who's coming?'

'Mr Mellor and Mr Titch.'

'Mr Titch!' The lad's voice was high with surprise. 'Is Mr Titch home?'

Olive nodded as she spooned potato on to the plates. 'The ship developed engine trouble and had to turn back. He reckons he'll be home for a few days. Him and Bob have been here all afternoon, rubbing down. They asked if we'd make everywhere clean so they can start on the undercoating tonight.'

Steve took a plate from her and sniffed up. 'It smells good, Mam.'

'Yeah, thanks to Mrs Aggie. She brought the mince down early on and I only had to heat it up. But we'll have to wolf it down, son, 'cos they'll be here before we know it.'

The men were a quarter of an hour late, for which Olive was thankful. The extra minutes gave her time to wash up after their dinner and then really get stuck into the woodwork. She started one side of the room, her son the other.

Steve sneaked a look at his mother as she stretched up to

reach the top of the door. Just a few short months ago, she wouldn't have had the energy to do that. Even washing the dishes would have tired her out. So she really must be getting better. His spirits lifted, he went back to washing the windowframe with renewed vigour.

When the knock came, Olive said, 'This'll be them. Open the door, love.' She stood with the wet cloth in her hand and listened as her son welcomed his hero. But she was proud to hear Bob get as warm a welcome. She waited for the two men to enter, then said, with mock severity, 'You are late.'

'It's his fault,' Bob said, nodding at Titch. 'I called for him on time.'

'And I'd have been ready if it hadn't been for me ma. We had fish for tea, and didn't I go and swallow a bone this size.' He held his hands about two foot apart. 'I'm not kidding, I nearly choked to death.'

Steve, never happier than when he was in this man's company, chuckled. 'And the bone was really that big, Mr Titch? It must have been some fish.'

'I told me ma it must have been a whale, but she would have it that it was a piece of cod. And this'll tell yer how serious it was. When I was choking to death, instead of hitting me on the back to dislodge the thing, me ma was searching the sideboard drawer for the insurance policy.'

'Titch McBride, yer can't half tell some whoppers,' Olive said, shaking with laughter. 'And yer have to drag poor Aggie into it.'

' "Poor Aggie", did yer say? If that bone had finished me off, it would have been "rich Aggie". Mind you, she did say she was pleased when I coughed the thing up. And I know she meant it 'cos there were tears in her eyes.'

'I thought yer were having mince and onions for yer dinner.'

'Yeah, we did. But I had to have some excuse for being late and I couldn't very well say I'd choked on a bit of mincemeat. I mean, yer wouldn't have believed that, would yer?'

'No, not really,' Olive said, her face deadpan. 'The two-foot bone was far more believable.'

'We came to work, mate,' Bob reminded him. 'Or had yer forgot?'

And work they did. Stopping only once for a cuppa and a smoke. And by half-past ten, all the woodwork had been undercoated. Titch was as pleased as Punch. 'Not bad going, eh, mate?'

Bob nodded, satisfied they'd achieved their goal. 'Ruddy good going, mate.'

'It's brilliant,' Steve said. 'Yer've done wonders.'

'The room looks brighter already.' Olive was tired, but it was a nice tiredness. 'I didn't realise how horrible that brown paintwork was.'

'Wait until the room's finished, love, yer won't know yerself.' Titch was glad he'd be here to see her face. 'We'll make tracks now 'cos Bob's on early shift. But I'll make a start on the gloss paint in the morning and should have it in hand by the time he gets home from work. Would nine o'clock be too early for yer?'

Olive tutted. 'Titch, no woman looks her best at that time of the morning – at least, I don't. So could yer make it ten? I'll have tidied up by then.'

'Vanity, thy name is woman.'

'Okay, Titch, come at nine and take me as yer find me. But don't say I didn't warn yer, 'cos I'll look like death warmed up.'

Bob yawned. 'I'm off, folks, or I'll never get up in the morning. Goodnight and God bless, everyone. Sleep well.'

'Thanks for everything, Bob. I'll never be able to repay yer for what yer've done. And you, Titch, yer've been brilliant. Now go home and get yer beauty sleep. I'll see yer tomorrow.'

'I'll see them out, Mam, and bolt the door.' Steve was

afraid his mother might be overdoing it. 'You get yerself off to bed.'

When the two men stepped into the street, Titch said, 'That's right, lad, you take good care of yer mam.'

'I'll always take care of her, Mr Titch, because she's a good mam and I love her very much.'

Aggie was with her son when Olive opened the door next morning. 'I know it's early for visitors, queen, but I thought I'd bring yer up to date on what's happening.' Her basket in the crook of her arm, she marched through to the living room. 'Me and Irene trimmed all the rolls of paper yesterday and we're starting the border when she gets home from work. Oh, and young Lucy's been a great help. She made as good a job at trimming as any grown up could have done.'

'Ma, where's yer manners? Good morning, Olive,' Titch said with a wink.

Aggie snapped her fingers. 'Yer know, I knew I'd forgotten something. I left me manners on the table, and if yer don't behave yerself I'll send yer down to get them.'

Olive grinned. 'Titch, yer might know yer'll never get one over on yer ma. She's got an answer for everything.'

'I'll catch her one of these days, when she's not looking.' Titch folded his coat and laid it on the couch. 'I'll get the ladder out of the yard and make a start.'

'Yer said yer had to report to yer ship,' Aggie said. 'What time are yer going?'

'I'll go about one. I should have a fair bit done here by then. And I'll be back for when Bob arrives.' Titch shook his head, a look of doubt on his face. 'I still can't see us getting this room finished tomorrow.'

Aggie tutted. 'Oh ye of little faith. Would yer like to have a bet on it?'

'Not with you, Ma, 'cos I've tried that before. I never win.'

'I wouldn't take yer money off yer, son, 'cos it would be like taking sweets from a baby. Yer've never seen George

Pollard working, have yer? He's that fast, yer eyes can't keep up with him. And I'll be cutting the paper to size, 'cos this room's exactly the same as ours. So if you or Bob do the pasting, all George has to do is put it up. And as I've said, the man is like greased lightning.'

'I'll take your word for it, Ma. Now, if yer don't mind, I'm going to get the ladder. And once I make a start, I don't want no interruptions.'

'I'll be going anyway, I'm off to do some shopping. But before yer put the silence board up, can I just say one thing? I'll be down at half-twelve with some sandwiches for you and Olive. I can't have me one and only son working on an empty tummy.'

When Aggie had gone, Olive felt uncomfortable being alone in the house with Titch. He was busy working away, and she didn't know where to put herself. 'I'm going upstairs to give the bedrooms a clearout, Titch. If yer want anything, just holler.'

It was eleven o'clock when he shouted up the stairs. 'Ay, Olive! I know I said I didn't want any interruptions, but a cup of tea wouldn't go amiss. Everybody has a break this time in the mornings. Even ruddy slaves! Get yerself down here, woman!'

As Olive walked down the stairs, she was thinking how strange it was to have a man in the house. Strange, but somehow comforting. 'There's still only conny-onny, Titch.'

Titch, back on the ladder and painting the picture rail, said, 'If it's wet and warm, it'll do me fine. Yer should try the tea we get on the ship, it's so thick yer can stand yer spoon up in it. And yer won't hear one complaint from the crew because the cook's six foot six. And that's in his stocking feet.'

When they were facing each other across the table, Titch admired his handiwork. 'Not bad going in two hours, is it?'

'Yer've done well, Titch. I won't know meself when it's finished.'

'Well, at least you and Steve can sit in comfort. Ye're a lot better than yer were a few months ago, aren't yer? Yer've put a bit of flesh on yer bones and yer face has filled out.'

'I feel a lot better. I'm hoping to look for a part-time job soon. A few extra bob coming in would make a lot of difference. Me and Steve could both do with some clothes, and we need new bedding.' Olive grinned. 'Actually I could do with throwing every stick and stitch out, and starting from scratch. But we will get there, given time.'

'Of course yer will.' Titch looked at her over the rim of his cup. 'Yer don't have to hide yerself away upstairs, yer know. I won't eat yer.'

'I'm not hiding meself away! I just don't want to distract yer by walking in and out and generally getting on yer nerves.' Olive put her cup down. 'I'm not used to having a man in the house, yer see, Titch. I'm out of the habit of having someone to talk to.'

'Yer'll feel different when yer start getting out and about a bit. Ye're still a young woman, Olive, and a pretty one. The chances are yer might just meet a man and fall for him. Then yer'd never be lonely again.'

Olive shook her head. 'No, I'll never marry again, Titch. I had a good man in Jim, and nobody could ever come up to him.'

'I wouldn't be so quick to dismiss the idea, Olive, 'cos there might be a man out there yer could take to. Yer wouldn't love him as yer did Jim, but love comes in many different ways. So while I'm not saying yer should go out and look for him, I think yer should keep an open mind.'

'You're a fine one to talk, Titch McBride. Forty years of age and still unmarried. And yer can't tell me yer've never met a girl yer liked.'

'I've met dozens that I liked, but not one of them set my heart on fire.' Titch drained his cup and smiled across at her. 'And I believe that's what happens when yer meet the one that's meant for yer. I've been told that when yer lips meet, bells start ringing in yer head and yer see stars. Well, so far there's been no bells, stars or heart set on fire. But being an optimist, Olive, I'll keep on trying.' Titch stood up and leaned his two curled fists on the table. 'Mind you, falling in love doesn't sound very exciting, does it? Who in their right mind would want to see stars, have ruddy bells ringing in their ears and be dashing around for a bucket of water to put out the fire in their heart?'

'Go on with yer, Titch. Don't yer ever take anything serious?'

'I take this painting lark very serious, Olive. I've got an hour before me ma comes with some eats for us, so for that hour I'm going to go like the clappers. 'Cos after that I've got to get down to the ship to see what's happening. So I'll thank yer not to keep me talking like this, it puts me off me work.'

Peg Butterworth had barely planted her bottom down before asking, in a loud voice, 'How are the lovebirds today? Enjoying life to the full, are yer?'

Elsie gave her a dig in the ribs. 'Ay, you! You said they weren't having no affair.'

Peg gave a sigh. 'Yer don't get it, do yer, girl?'

'What is it I don't get, queen?'

'Yer see what I mean? Yer don't even know what it is yer don't get.'

'I will if yer tell me, queen.'

'I'll draw yer a bleedin' picture if yer like.' Then Peg shook her head. 'No, yer still wouldn't get it. Ye're as thick as two short planks, Elsie Burgess, yer haven't got the brains yer were born with.'

'Ay you! Of course I've got the brains I was born with.'

'Yeah, and they haven't developed since the day yer were born. Now will yer shut yer gob and listen?' Peg's expression became all sweetness and light as she looked along the table. 'Are you two still all lovey-dovey?'

Kate gave Bob a sly kick before answering. 'No, Peg, I'm sorry to say we're not. Yer see, our consciences were pricked when Ada said yesterday that it was a sin to have an affair. And because me and Bob don't want to commit no sin, we've decided to end what we had going.'

Peg leaned across the table until her nose was within an inch of Ada Smithson's. 'Ye're a miserable little sod. Why don't yer mind yer own business? That tale would have given us enough gossip to last a couple of weeks.'

'Ay, queen, what are yer shouting at Ada for?' Elsie put on a bewildered expression. 'It wasn't Ada what had an affair. Mind you, no one would blame her if she did. Not with the bleedin' husband she's got.'

Ada Smithson, the size of sixpennyworth of copper, sprang to her feet and shook a clenched fist in Elsie's face. 'You leave my husband out of this. He'd make six of yours.'

Elsie didn't flinch. 'Ye're right there, Ada. He's six times more bad-tempered, six times more tight with money and six times more handy with his fists. I won't argue with yer on that, queen, 'cos yer've got him bang to rights.'

Kate smiled across at Bob. 'I told yer it would blow over.'

Bob glanced at Billy to see if he was listening. But his mate was too interested in what was taking place at the other end of the table. 'I'm sorry, in a way. It would be very nice to have an affair with yer, Kate. Even if it was only a make-believe one.'

Peg didn't know what to do for the best. She could hear Kate and Bob talking and was eager to know what they were saying. But she had two women near who were spoiling for a fight, and she didn't want to miss that. So she jerked a thumb at Billy. 'You see what the lovebirds are up to, while I keep me eye on these two.'

'Nah, there's nothing doing down here. Besides, if those two come to blows I want to be ready to separate them before Elsie makes mincemeat of Ada.'

Kate winked across the table. 'In our dreams, eh, Bob?'

'Yeah, Kate, in our dreams.'

★ ★ ★

Six o'clock on Saturday came, and Olive didn't know whether she was on her head or her heels. She'd never known the house be so crowded or noisy. George was on the ladder hanging lengths of wallpaper and singing at the top of his voice. No one knew what he was singing because he was off-key, but he seemed to be enjoying his work. For such a big man he was very agile on the ladder, and its rocking from side to side didn't seem to bother him. But young Steve's heart was in his mouth a few times, so he took it upon himself to stand and hang on to the rickety ladder like grim death. Titch and Bob were kept busy pasting so that when one strip was up there was no delay in waiting for another. To say that George was quick and efficient would be the understatement of the year.

And the women weren't going to be left out, either. Irene had come up armed with cups, tea, sugar and milk, and she was busy in the kitchen brewing up every half-hour or so. Aggie's excuse was that she'd just nipped in to see how things were going. But really she'd come to supervise. 'George, sweetheart, there's a bubble in the paper, just above yer head.'

'I've seen it, Aggie.' When George turned, Steve's hands tightened on the ladder. 'If it weren't for yer age, Aggie, and the fact that I love the bones of yer, I'd tell yer to go and teach yer grandmother how to milk ducks.'

'And I'd do it, George, except for two things. Me grandma's been dead for fifty years and I haven't never seen no ducks in Kirkdale. I haven't seen no ducks anywhere, come to think of it. Wouldn't know one if I tripped over it.' Aggie lifted a finger. 'I'm sorry, George, but I tell a lie. I've seen them lying on slabs in the butchers' stalls in St John's Market. The poor buggers are dead, though, so it would be no good trying to milk them. They haven't even got no bleedin' feathers, never mind milk.'

'Ma, will yer let the man get on with his work?' Titch said. 'There's only three more pieces to put up, then the border, and the room's finished. Don't forget I've got to be back at the ship for ten at latest – we're sailing on the morning tide. And I dearly want to see the job finished.'

'If I had something to stand on, I could start putting the border up on this back wall,' Bob said. 'I wish we had another ladder.'

Irene came through from the kitchen. 'We've got a small stepladder. Would that be any use, George?'

'Yeah, that should do the trick. Bob's tall enough to reach on that. It's not as though he'd have the lengths of paper to fiddle with.'

'I'll nip down and get it.' Irene was nearly out of the front door when she called, 'The kettle's almost boiled, will yer see to it, Olive?'

Half-past seven the ladder was out in the yard, Steve was brushing the floor and Titch was helping Bob move the sideboard back into place.

'I never thought yer'd do it,' Olive said. 'Yer've worked wonders, all of yer.'

George had to bend his head to look her in the eyes. 'It's not finished yet, lass. If yer look up, yer'll see the ceiling laughing at the rest of the room. We wanted to get as much done as possible to please Titch, but I'll be back tomorrow to do the ceiling and frieze. And don't worry, I won't splash over yer new walls, I'm a clean worker.'

Titch came to stand next to her. 'George will finish the job off for yer, don't worry. But from what's been done so far, I think it's going to look a treat. Are yer happy with it?'

'Happy is one word I'd use, Titch. Along with thankful and grateful. I'm not very good at expressing meself, but I want yer all to know that me and Steve appreciate everything yer've done for us. And when I find meself a little job, and we're in the money, we'll throw a big party as a thank you to yer.'

'Are yer really going to look for a job, sunshine?' Irene asked.

Olive nodded. 'Not a full-time one, I couldn't manage that yet. Just a couple of hours a day to earn a few bob for things we need for the house.'

'Then hang on for a few weeks. I'll be packing my job in soon, so I could put in a word for yer with Alec. I've been paying off some new furniture and I reckon I've got another four payments to make. How would that suit yer, sunshine?'

Olive's face glowed. 'That would be marvellous, it's so close to home. But Alec might not think I'm suitable for the job.'

Titch grinned at George and Bob before saying, 'Oh, yer'll have no trouble with Alec. He'll be only too happy to give yer the job.' He didn't say that he would be having words with the pub landlord that night. 'And talking about the pub has made me realise me mates must be as thirsty as I am. So we'll get off now, 'cos I haven't got much time.'

'Ye're not going drinking on an empty tummy, me lad,' Aggie said. 'I've made a stack of sandwiches, enough for you, George and Bob. So come on, before yer tell me yer haven't got time to eat.'

'I'll have to go, as well,' Irene said. 'The boys will be starving.'

'You take care of yerself, Olive.' Titch kissed her cheek, causing her to blush and his mother to raise her eyebrows. 'I'll see yer next time I'm home.' He stretched his hand out to Steve. 'I don't need to tell yer to look after yer mam, 'cos I know yer will.'

'I will, Mr Titch.' Steve looked at each face to show his words were for everyone in the room. 'Like me mam said, we both appreciate what yer've all done for us. Ye're good people, and true friends.'

Olive and Steve stood at the door and waved their neighbours off. Then they went back to admire the white paintwork and bright wallpaper with little sprigs of pink flowers on.

★ ★ ★

'While you're putting the kettle on, Aggie, I'll slip home and take me overalls off,' Bob said. 'And I'll have to tell Ruby I'm going for a pint. She won't be too happy because Saturday is her night for going out with her mates.'

'Lucy can come to us if Ruby wants to go out,' Irene said. 'After all, yer won't be late home and it's Sunday tomorrow so no school for Lucy.'

'Thanks, Irene, I'll send her in. She'll be made up.'

When Bob got home it was to find Ruby with a face like thunder. 'Where the bleedin' hell d'yer think yer've been? It's turned eight o'clock and I've been walking the floor like a bloody fool.'

Lucy was sat at the table, as quiet as a mouse. She could see her mother getting more angry by the minute and had been careful not to speak or move in case the anger was directed at her. She had been expecting a full-blown row when her dad came in, so was surprised when he ignored his wife, and said, 'I'm going for a pint, would yer like to go next door for a game of cards, pet?'

Lucy scrambled off the chair. 'Oh yeah, I'd like that, Dad.'

'Go on, then. I won't be late because Titch has to leave at half-nine.'

Lucy was near the front door when she heard her mother, and she stood to listen. If she thought her dad was going to be upset, she'd go back in the room to him.

'I asked yer where yer've been until now. Yer know I like to be out by half-seven.'

'I don't ask you where ye're going, or who these mysterious friends of yours are, so I don't see why I should tell yer where I've been. Just go about yer business, Ruby, and leave me to mine.'

Lucy could tell by her father's tone that he wasn't prepared to argue, so she skipped the few steps to the house where she knew she'd be welcome and would never hear a voice raised in anger.

Ruby watched her husband step out of his overalls before

walking past her as though she wasn't there. His lack of emotion angered her even more and her fists curled in readiness to rain blows on his back. But a little voice in her head told her she would be unwise to start anything that would jeopardise her night out. Anyway, why bother? In half an hour she'd be with her mates having a good laugh.

The pub was packed and Ruby's eyes were everywhere, searching for her friends. Then she saw Wally Brown waving his hand in the air. 'Over here,' he shouted above the din. 'We saved a seat for yer.'

Ruby pushed her way through the crowd, flattered that he must have been watching out for her. She was surprised he wasn't married because he was a good catch – tall and slim, with fine sandy hair and deep blue eyes. He had plenty of clothes, too, and was always well dressed. She knew he was a flirt because he was always chatting the women up. But he'd told her it was only a bit of fun and they meant nothing to him.

'I'm a bit late 'cos I just missed a tram.' Ruby smiled at Jessie Armitage and her husband Harry. She'd gone to school with Jessie but had lost touch until they'd bumped into each other two years ago. It was a lucky encounter for Ruby, because the women had arranged to meet one night in the pub and through that came her escape from the boredom of married life. And it brought her into contact with friends of the Armitages, Mabel and Jim Bowler, and of course, Wally Brown.

'We thought yer weren't coming,' Jessie said. 'Didn't we, Harry?'

Harry merely nodded. He wasn't keen on Ruby and didn't know why his wife bothered with her. He knew she was married and couldn't understand why she came out drinking without her husband. She looked like a fly turn with her dyed hair and painted face, and he felt sorry for the bloke she was married to. And the way she wallowed in the compliments

Wally plied on her was pathetic. He was like that with all the women, but none of them took him seriously because it was so obvious he was a womaniser. All except the silly cow standing there waiting for a space to be found for her to sit down. And ten to one when she sat down it would be next to Wally. Then the flattery would start and Ruby would simper as her eyelashes fluttered, her bright red lips pursing and her giggle that of a teenager.

Harry picked up his glass and gulped down several large swallows of his bitter beer. They'd been enjoying themselves until this stupid woman came on the scene. Just looking at her was enough to put anyone off their drink.

'Can yer slide along a bit, Mabel, and make room for Ruby?' Wally asked. 'Just about six inches will do, she's only got a small bottom.'

Mabel gave her husband a dig. 'Shove up, Jim.'

Wally waited until she was seated, then bent down to smile into her face. 'What would the lady like to drink? Name it and it's yours.'

'I'll have a port, please, Wally. And the next round's on me.'

'There's no need for that, Ruby,' Jessie said, 'we've got a kitty going. We've put two bob each in.'

'If yer want to buy yer own drinks, yer can do,' Harry said gruffly. 'If not, throw two bob in that ashtray with our money.'

'I'll do whatever you're doing.' Ruby took her purse from her handbag. 'We're all pals together.' She tossed a silver coin into the glass ashtray then took a packet of twenty Capstan from her bag. 'Anyone like a cigarette?'

Both men shook their heads, but Jessie and Mabel leaned forward. 'Ooh, I'll have one,' Jessie said. 'It'll be a change from Woodies.'

'Yeah, not half.' Mabel drew deeply as Ruby held a match to the cigarette. 'I can only afford five Woodies a day.'

'Yer should consider yerself lucky yer can afford any,' Jim

said. 'With only my wages coming in, and two children to keep, I think yer do very well with yer five Woodies a day and at least two nights out.'

'Ye're dead right there, Jim,' Harry said. 'These two don't know they're born.' He gazed at Ruby's face for a few seconds before saying, 'Your husband must have a good job, yer never seem to be short.'

'Who never seems to be short?' Wally set the glass of port down. 'What am I missing?'

'You wouldn't understand, mate, being footloose and fancy free. The only one you've got to worry about is yerself.'

'My husband does shiftwork, so he probably earns a bit more,' Ruby said. 'And we've only got one child, that makes a difference.'

'I'm not complaining, love.' Jessie was on the plump side, with a round face, rosy cheeks and a happy disposition. She now linked her husband's arm and squeezed. 'I'm more than happy with what I've got, Harry. I wouldn't swap you for a big clock.'

'And I wouldn't swap you, Jim Bowler,' Mabel said. 'I know when I'm well-off.'

'Oh lord, listen to the lovebirds.' Wally winked at Ruby as though they were two of a kind and shared a secret. 'Make yer sick, wouldn't it?'

Conversation was general after that, until a bloke standing by the bar started to sing 'The Rose of Tralee'. This was what the crowd had been waiting for, and soon the rafters were ringing with the popular songs of the day. And the loudest voice belonged to Harry who, with his head thrown back, sang with gusto. And a fine voice he had, too. Requests were shouted from every corner of the room and there wasn't one song he didn't know. With his arm across Jessie's shoulder, he had everyone singing and swaying. Mabel and Jim couldn't sing for toffee, so they let themselves go by clapping their hands and stamping their feet.

When Harry stopped for a breather and a swig of beer, he noticed Wally bending down to whisper in Ruby's ear, while his hand rested on her knee. To hell with them, they're both as bad as one another, he thought, wiping the back of his hand across his mouth. They make a fine pair, neither of them are any bloody good. With that he put his glass down, cleared his throat and to everyone's delight, began to sing 'Wait Till the Sun Shines, Nellie'.

There were howls of disapproval when time was called, but the manager didn't fancy a visit from the police, so he was strict. 'Towels have been on for fifteen minutes now, plenty of time to finish yer drinks. Out yer get, before I lose me licence.' He held the door open while disgruntled customers filed out, then when the last one was through, he shot the bolts. Turning to the barman who was collecting the empty glasses, he said, 'There must be an easier way of making a living than this, Brian. I just wish I knew what it was.'

Standing on the pavement, Ruby said, 'I've had a smashing night, thanks very much. I'll see yer next week some time.'

'Yeah, okay, kid.' Jessie linked her husband's arm. He'd been looking at her with passion in his eyes for the last hour, and she knew he was eager to get home. 'We'll see yer.'

'Be careful going home, now,' Mabel said. 'Yer never know who's lurking about these dark nights.'

'I'll walk Ruby to the tram stop.' Wally cupped her elbow. 'I'll make sure she gets on the tram safely.'

'Come on, let's go.' Harry's mind was on bed and his wife's voluptuous body. 'Are yer coming, Jim?'

'Yeah.' Jim's mind was running along the same lines. Only Mabel wasn't voluptuous. She had slim legs, a neat bottom and a small waist. But she was well-endowed where it mattered. As he had once said to Harry, it was like nestling his head down on a feather pillow. 'I'm ready for me bed.'

As goodbyes were exchanged, Ruby and Wally began to walk in the opposite direction. 'I'll be all right, yer know. There's no need to walk with me.'

'I'm coming because I want to, not because I need to. We never get any time on our own, we're always in company.'

Ruby's heart quickened. 'There's not much we can do about that.'

'Of course there is, if we really wanted some time on our own. I know ye're married, Ruby, but I get the feeling you and yer husband are not exactly crazy about each other.'

'No, we're not. He's a good bloke, but dull and uninteresting. He's quite content to sit in every night, but I'm not. I want to get some fun out of life.'

'Then meet me one night and we'll go for a drink, just the two of us.'

'Oh, I couldn't do that. We might be seen, and then all hell would break loose.'

'But the idea appeals to yer, doesn't it?' Wally had decided that this was the night he'd make his move. He'd played her along until now, and felt sure she was ready to respond to his advances. 'Tell the truth.'

'Yeah, it would put a bit of excitement back in me life. But I wouldn't want to get caught.'

'Meet me one night next week and I'll take yer to a little club where no one will know yer. We can have a drink, just like friends. That wouldn't harm anyone.'

Ruby did some quick thinking. Was she prepared to take such a risk? The thought that Wally might walk away from her if she refused, was enough reason to say, 'Bob's on afternoon shift next week, he's home about half-ten. The most I could manage is an hour.'

'That's enough time for a drink and to get to know each other a bit better.' Wally was gloating inside. She was just the ticket for him. A married woman who wouldn't tie him down. He'd lived alone since his mother had died and left him a comfortably furnished house, and it suited him fine. He wasn't the marrying kind, he'd rather love them and leave them. 'How about eight o'clock on Wednesday, outside the Rotunda?'

'As long as it's only for an hour. I've got to be home by half-nine.'

'Yer have my word on it.' And Wally meant it. He had no intention of scaring her off by rushing things. He'd take it nice and easy until he had her eating out of his hand. 'Is that a date, then?'

Ruby thought of Lucy. She shouldn't have any problem there, 'cos the girl wouldn't tell tales for fear of hurting her father. 'Yeah, it's a date.'

Wally lifted her hand to his lips and kissed it, sending a thrill running down her spine as he knew it would. Here was a woman ripe for excitement, and he'd see that she got it. But all in good time. 'I'll look forward to Wednesday.'

Chapter Seventeen

Aggie came bustling through from the kitchen with a tea pot in one hand and a cup and saucer in the other. 'I told Irene I'd give her a knock when yer got home, so she can have a cup of tea with us and hear yer news first-hand.'

Titch had been away for four months, much longer than he'd expected, and his eyes had been following his mother's every move. He worried about her when he was away so long and was relieved to find her looking well and in high spirits. 'It's your news I want to hear, Ma. I'm sure yer wouldn't be interested in anything I've got to say, 'cos nothing much happens when ye're on board. The only thing of note that happened during the trip was that the skipper had a gumboil and was like a raving lunatic for a week. I did offer to punch him and burst the thing, but he didn't appreciate the offer.'

'A hot poultice is the best thing for that. It brings the boil to a head and draws the pus out.' Aggie put a cosy over the tea pot before making for the door. 'I'll give Irene a knock. She comes in every afternoon for a natter, 'cos with not working now she has plenty of time on her hands.'

Titch sat back and his eyes swept the room. Everywhere was spotless, as usual. Even the leaves on the aspidistra plant standing on a table in front of the window looked as though they'd been polished. His mother had always been house-proud and she hadn't let age change the habits of a lifetime.

'Well, here is the sailor, home from the sea.' Irene breezed in like a breath of fresh air. Her face was beaming and her arms open wide. 'Come and give us a kiss, sunshine. And seeing as my feller's not here, yer can take as long as yer like.'

'Oh, no he can't,' Aggie said, laughing. 'We'll have no hanky-panky in this house.'

Titch hugged Irene and pecked her cheek. 'One of these days we'll meet down a dark entry and I'll finally get to give yer a proper kiss.'

'In the meantime, will the pair of yer sit down while I pour the tea out?' Aggie said. 'Any longer and it won't be fit to drink.'

When Irene sat down facing him, Titch asked, 'Did Olive get the job when you packed it in?'

'Yeah, she's been there three months now.' Irene's brows drew together. 'Apparently someone told Alec that if he didn't give her the job he'd lose three good customers. Now I wonder who that could have been?'

'Don't be looking at me, I've been away for four months. I can only think it must have been your George, or Bob.'

Irene shook her head. 'No, Alec said good customers, and yer could hardly say George or Bob were good customers. The pub would shut down if it was relying on their couple of pints a week.' Again she shook her head. 'No, I think Olive has got a secret admirer.'

'Secret admirer or not, Alec isn't the type to do someone a favour. If she wasn't up to the job she'd be out on her ear.'

Aggie sipped her tea as she took it all in. It was funny that the first person her son should ask about was Olive. Was there an attraction there, or was he just asking out of interest for a friend? Well, he said he had three week's leave, that was plenty of time to find out how the land lay.

'She's doing fine. I went with her for the first week to show her the ins and outs,' Irene told him. 'There's so many jobs to do, I couldn't see her thrown in at the deep end. But she's taken to it like a duck to water and likes it. And the few extra bob a week certainly mean a lot to her. Her and Steve are not living in the lap of luxury, but there's a definite improvement in their standard of living. And it's brought her out of her shell. Yer'll notice a big difference to the last time yer saw her.'

'And young Steve has been a godsend to me.' Aggie nodded to emphasise her words. 'Every night without fail he comes up to get me coal in and see I'm all right for paper and firewood for the next morning. I was glad of him when we had snow six inches deep, I can tell yer. And he's never without a smile on his face. He's a cracking lad, one in a million. And Olive calls in every morning on her way home from work and has a cuppa with me.'

'So yer've not been short of company, Ma?'

'What! Sometimes this house has been busier than Lime Street Station. But that's the way I like it, son. Better that than sitting on me own looking at four bleedin' walls and talking to meself. Not that I don't enjoy a conversation with meself, 'cos as yer are well aware I can hold a very intelligent conversation with meself. The only thing is, it's very difficult to tell yerself to sod off and mean it.'

Titch put a hand over hers. 'I'll do anything for yer, Ma, yer know that. But telling yer to sod off is the exception.'

'I should think so!' Aggie huffed. 'That would be very disrespectful and would call for me to stand on a chair and box yer ears for yer.'

'Knock it off, you two,' Irene laughed. 'Anyway, Titch, aren't yer going to ask how I am?'

'How are you, Irene?'

'I'm fine, thank you. George is fine, Jack's fine and Greg's fine. Me new sideboard is beautiful and me new couch a dream. I was going to tell yer about me lovely new bedding, but I think Aggie would think it was disrespectful to mention the word "bed" and I wouldn't want to end up getting *my* ears boxed.'

Titch sat back in his chair feeling very contented. It was good to be home. 'So yer got everything yer were saving up for?'

'Yes, Mr McBride, I'm very happy to say I did. When yer call for George tonight yer'll think yer eyes are deceiving yer. Of course yer won't be allowed to sit on me couch, or lean yer elbows on me sideboard. If I let you get away with it, the boys would complain about me making them sit on the floor. So while yer can look, sunshine, yer cannot touch. Those are the rules of the house now.'

Titch thought it was hilarious. 'I'll stand on the step and wait for George to come out. From the sound of things, yer'd lay a duck egg if me coat happened to brush against yer sideboard. I bet George is having a dog's life.'

'Don't you believe it! He's as happy as Larry in his old fireside chair. He wouldn't part with that thing for all the money in the world. And my chair has been taken over by Jack. He says he's a working man now, and his wages entitle him to the same comfort as his dad.' Irene's laughter ricocheted off the walls. 'He's asked me to buy him a whip for his birthday, so he can crack it when I don't move fast enough for him.'

'Ye're well blessed with yer family, Irene. Good husband and good kids.'

'She certainly is,' Aggie said. 'But then she's a damn good mother.' Under her breath, she muttered, 'Not like some I could mention.'

'Does Lucy still come in for a game of cards?' Titch asked. 'And if she does, does she still win all the time?'

If there was a slight hesitation before Irene answered, it went unnoticed. 'Yeah, she still comes in, and much to Jack's disgust, she's still very lucky.' Then she quickly took the conversation away from Lucy. 'Yer won't be seeing Bob tonight, by the way, 'cos he's on afternoon shift. So it's just you and George. And please don't let my husband have too much to drink, he's the very devil to get up in the mornings.'

'Okay, we'll just have a couple of jars and save the serious drinking until Saturday, when Bob's with us.'

★ ★ ★

Lucy sat at the table and watched her mother combing her hair in front of the oval-shaped mirror over the mantelpiece. She knew if she said anything it would bring forth a load of abuse, but the burden of guilt she was carrying around with her was getting too heavy to bear. 'Ye're not going out again, are yer, Mam?'

Ruby swung around. 'And what if I am?'

'Me dad would go mad if he knew yer went out so often when he's at work. The first time yer went out and left me, yer said it was only for that one night. But that was months ago and now ye're going out more than ever. It's not fair on me dad.'

'The only way yer dad would know is if you told him.' Ruby forced herself to remain calm. 'And it would be daft to cause a row when I'm only going round to me mate's. I'm not doing anything wrong.'

'Then why don't yer tell me dad? He wouldn't mind if ye're only going to yer mate's, and I could go in next door instead of being in the house on me own.'

Ruby gritted her teeth. 'If you want to cause a big row, then tell yer dad if yer want. But I can't understand what all the fuss is about. I'm always in when he gets home from work and there's always something ready for him to eat. And as for you being on yer own in the house, well, at thirteen years of age yer should be old enough to put yerself to bed.'

'I'm not thirteen until next month. And yer know I've always been frightened on me own in the house. Why can't I go next door and play cards with them?'

'Because I say so, that's why. I don't want the whole bleedin' street knowing me business.' Ruby's temper was reaching boiling point. Her hand was itching to lash out at Lucy. But she couldn't take a chance on her daughter getting upset and running next door. If Irene Pollard found out what was happening, she could say goodbye to her nights out and to Wally Brown. 'Look, I've promised me mate I'd go tonight, and I don't want to let her down. But I won't go out again this week, honest. And as yer dad's on nights next week, I won't be able to get out at all, then.'

Lucy lowered her head, not knowing which way to turn. How could her mother look her straight in the face and tell barefaced lies? Lucy knew she went out when her dad was on nights because she'd heard her. Ten minutes after the front door closed on her dad, she'd hear the kitchen being closed and locked, footsteps down the yard, then the latch on the entry door being dropped. And it wasn't only one night, it was at least two in each week. The knowledge Lucy carried around with her was making her ill. She didn't know where her mother went or what she got up to, but she did know it was wrong for a married woman to behave in such a way. She also knew her mother was using her to deceive her father and that was the worst part because he didn't deserve it and she loved him so much. Many times she'd been on the point of telling him, but was afraid of the consequences. What if it were the straw that broke the camel's back and he walked out of the house for good? That didn't bear thinking about because she couldn't live without her father's love.

'Well, don't just sit there,' Ruby said, her hands on her hips. 'Are yer going to take yerself off to bed, or not?'

'Only if yer promise it will be the last night yer ever go out without me dad knowing. It's not fair to expect me to go along with your lies and I won't do it.'

'But yer haven't told any lies, have yer?'

'Not telling the truth is just as bad as lying.'

Ruby looked at the clock. Wally would be arriving at the club on the dock road any minute now, and he didn't like to be kept waiting. She'd promise anything rather than have him upset. 'I've told yer this will be the last night, and I mean it.'

Lucy kept her head down; she couldn't bear to look her mother in the face. 'I'll see meself to bed.'

Ruby's sigh was one of relief and anger. Fancy having to kowtow to a chit of a girl. If it weren't for the fact she had a sneaking feeling Lucy confided a lot in that cow next door, and Irene Pollard and Bob were as thick as thieves, she'd give her a good hiding and kick her up the stairs.

Ruby gave one last pat to her hair before leaving the room without a word or a glance at her daughter, who was still seated at the table. Her head was bowed and tears were trickling down her cheeks.

Wally Brown didn't look very pleased when Ruby hastened down to where he was sitting. 'Where the hell have yer been? I felt like a right mug sat here on me own.'

'I'm sorry, but me daughter kept me back. Yer know I wouldn't be late if I could help it. But she wouldn't go to bed and we had words.'

Wally wasn't at all happy with the way the affair was progressing. They still met on a Saturday night in the pub and sat with the Armitages and the Bowlers, but they were careful not to let their friends know they were meeting twice a week on the quiet. This seedy little club, frequented by sailors and women of ill-repute, was their meeting place. Wally hadn't expected to wait so long for what he was after from Ruby, but the furthest he'd got in four months was passionate kisses and fumbling down a dark entry. 'I don't know why yer won't let me come to your house. Once yer daughter was in bed she wouldn't know any different. I could come and go the back way so no one would see me, and I'd leave well before yer husband was due in from work. At least we'd have an hour to ourselves. I'm browned off coming to this dive, it gives me the willies.'

'Ooh, I don't know about that. Me neighbours are nosy buggers, and they wouldn't think twice about telling Bob. Besides, if Lucy heard us talking she'd be down like a shot and that would really put the cat amongst the pigeons.'

'I don't want to come to talk, Ruby – we've done enough of that in the last four months.' Wally resorted to flattery. 'I'm not made of stone, yer know. I can't be satisfied with the odd kiss, not the way I feel about yer. When we're together, I can hardly keep me hands off yer. I want to make love to yer and it's driving me crazy.' He ran a hand over her thigh. 'Yer said yer wanted some excitement in yer life and I can give yer that, and more. But I'm beginning to think yer don't feel the same about me.'

Ruby covered his hand. 'I do feel the same about you, Wally, yer know that. Otherwise I wouldn't be here tonight.'

'Then find a place where we can be alone, even if it's only for an hour. And let me make love to you like yer've never been made love to before.'

The nagging doubt in Ruby's mind fled when she felt her whole body thrill to his words. He'd practically said he loved her. She couldn't lose him now, she'd never find anyone else to please her the way he did. She'd be back to her boring life, with her boring husband and boring daughter. 'I'll do me best, Wally, I promise. Perhaps we can take a chance next week when Bob's on nights. If yer came about ten, Lucy should be fast asleep.'

Although he was gloating inside, Wally managed one of his smarmy smiles. It wouldn't have fooled any of the tough prostitutes sitting near them with sailors of every nationality, but it fooled Ruby. 'Yer won't be sorry, love, I promise. I'll please and satisfy yer so much yer'll be floating on air. And I'll show yer how to make me happy.'

'I'll write the day down, and me address, on a piece of paper and slip it to yer on Saturday in the pub. The entry door's got the number painted on it in white, so yer can't miss it. And I'll be watching and waiting for yer.'

Bob leaned across the canteen table. 'How old is your daughter, Kate?'

'Just a couple of weeks older than yours. Why?'

'I was just wondering. Has she changed at all? I mean, has she gone quieter, more withdrawn, like?'

'Not so I've noticed. She doesn't act daft like she used to, but yer can expect that when they're growing older. In twelve months, Iris will be leaving school, same as your Lucy. They won't be our little girls any more, they'll be working young ladies.' Kate could see this wasn't what Bob wanted to hear. He was obviously worried about his daughter. 'What is it? Is Lucy not well?'

'Oh, she's not sick or anything like that. It's just that she doesn't laugh as easily and is much quieter than she ever was.'

'Well, haven't yer asked her? That would be the best thing to do.'

Bob blushed. 'I wondered if it was her age. You know, a girl's body changes when she gets in her teens. And I couldn't ask her that because she'd get embarrassed.'

'I know things are not good at home, Bob, but surely it's her mother's place to tell her the facts of life. It shouldn't be left to you.'

'I know that, Kate, but yer see, my wife isn't a normal mother. She has no time for Lucy and I doubt if she's even noticed the change in her. All Ruby thinks about is her make-up, dyeing her hair, her ciggies and her nights out in the pub with her mates. She doesn't give a toss for me, I'm just the man who hands his money over every week. There are times when I feel like packing me bags and finding lodgings somewhere. But I'd have a job finding a place that would take me and Lucy. And I'd never leave her there, she's my whole life. I love her more than anyone else on this earth.'

'I wish I could help yer, Bob, but there's not much I can do. Lucy doesn't know me, and she wouldn't take kindly to a stranger asking her questions.'

'No, I realise that. I'll have a word with Irene, next door. Lucy thinks the world of her, so she'd be the best one to have a chat with her.' There came a loud burst of laughter from their workmates, and Kate and Bob leaned forward to see what was going on.

Peg Butterworth had her chin cupped in her two hands as

she glared at Elsie Burgess. 'Say that again, girl, but start at the very beginning.'

'All right, queen, I'll start from the night before last, when I put me washing in the dolly tub to steep overnight. Well, it was all me sheets and pillowcases, so I put some bleach in the water to bring them up nice and white. But when I took the clothes out of the tub yesterday morning, I found I'd accidentally put my feller's blue shirt in the wash. At least, it *was* my feller's blue shirt, but now it's his patchy grey one. I was beside meself, queen, 'cos he loved that bleedin' shirt more than he loves me. While I was getting the dinner ready for our Edna to put on, I was trying to think of what I could do to make amends. I'd peeled the potatoes and carrots and turnip, and I was just salting them when I had this brainwave.'

'You with a brainwave?' Peg said, tongue in cheek. 'That's a novelty.'

'Who's telling the tale, queen, you or me?'

'I'm sorry, girl.' Peg lifted her hands in surrender. 'My lips are sealed from now on.'

Happy she now had the undivided attention of all her mates, Elsie went on: 'I thought of a way to sweeten him up, so he wouldn't pulverise me when I showed him his shirt. I set a tray with a nice lace cloth on, filled me best glass sugar bowl, got out me china milk jug what hasn't seen daylight since Adam was a lad, and put them on the tray with his favourite cup. It looked a treat, dead posh and fit for the King. And I left a note for our Edna to make her dad a nice cup of tea before she put the dinner out.'

'Did it do the trick?' Billy Gleeson asked. 'Did it sweeten him up?'

'Well, it would have done if I hadn't gone and got meself all mixed up. What with all the worry and one thing and another, I'd filled the sugar bowl with salt and put sugar in the potatoes and carrots and turnip. And my feller takes three sugars in his tea, so yer can imagine he wasn't best pleased when he gulped half the cup down in one go before making a dash for the sink and spewing it up. Our Edna said he was drinking cup after cup of water until she put his dinner down to him. She said that was when all hell broke loose. Yer see, my feller doesn't only like a lot of sugar in his tea, he likes plenty of salt in his spuds and vegetables. And I'd gone and got them all mixed up, hadn't I?'

The howls of laughter were so loud, Elsie knew there was no point in going on because she wouldn't be heard. So she folded her arms across her tummy and waited for the noise to subside. Then she said, 'Well, anyone can make a mistake, can't they?'

Peg was pressing her hands to her cheeks which were stiff with laughing. But she couldn't resist a leg-pull. 'Anyone can make a mistake, girl, but very few could make as many in one go as you. It's beyond my comprehension how anyone can be so feckless.'

Elsie's eyes narrowed. 'Is she insulting me, Billy Gleeson?'

'Yeah.' Billy's eyes were red-rimmed with wiping away the tears of laughter. 'She said she can't understand why ye're so daft.'

'Yer mean that's all those big words meant?' Elsie looked down her nose at Peg. 'Ye're wasting yer time here, queen, yer should be standing behind the counter at Cooper's. That's the posh shop where all the rich people go, and they talk so far back yer can't hardly hear them. I think yer'd go down well there, queen, as long as yer remembered yer can't tell them to bugger off, like yer do me.'

Billy was getting impatient. 'Elsie, will yer get back and finish the tale off? What did your feller have to say?'

'Oh yeah, yer'll like this bit, Billy. I didn't, but you will. Yer see when I got home last night, I didn't know what I'd done, did I? So when Tiger put this dinner in front of me I thought he was being all lovey-dovey. "I've saved this for yer, petal," he said. "I hope yer enjoy it as much as me and the kids did." ' Elsie rolled her eyes and hitched her bosom. 'I thought my ship had come in, didn't I? So when I picked up me knife and fork, I was planning in me mind what to do, seeing as he seemed in a good mood. I'd finish me dinner, then sit on his knee, give him a big kiss and stroke his hair. Then I'd break the news about his shirt.'

Little Ada Smithson's eyes and mouth were twitching. 'I know what's coming next. Yer couldn't eat the bleedin' dinner 'cos yer'd ruined it.'

Elsie rested her soulful eyes on each of them for a second. Then in a dramatic voice that would have done credit to Bette Davis, she said, 'If I never move from this chair, I sat there and stuffed mouthful after mouthful in me gob. I could feel my feller's eyes on me and I tried to look as though I was enjoying it. But halfway through I had to give up. I looked at him and asked if this was his idea of a joke. Then of course, I got the lot thrown at me. I can't tell yer what he said because the air was blue. So suffice to say my dear husband was not in the least amused.' She looked at Peg with a haughty expression. 'Yer see, queen, ye're not the only one what knows big words. So if yer ever do get a job in Cooper's, yer can always put in a good word for yer best mate. And don't forget to tell them I'm house-trained.'

'I wish yer'd finish what yer started, Elsie.' Billy hated missing out on anything. 'What did your feller say about his shirt?'

'Ooh, he doesn't know, yet. The mood he was in I wasn't about to confess to another sin. Not ruddy likely, I wasn't.'

'That's daft, that is,' Peg said. 'Yer should have told him and got it over with. Come Saturday, when we're going to the pub, he'll be wanting to wear that blue shirt.'

'I'll have had time to think of something before then. In fact, queen, I was going to ask yer to lend me half-a-crown so I can buy him a new one. I'll pay yer back next week.'

'Blimey! If that's not cheek, I don't know what is. Yer ruin yer husband's best shirt, yer don't know the difference between salt and sugar, and yet it's Muggins here what's going to be out of pocket.'

'Don't shout at me, queen. What with all the carry-on, I've got a splitting headache. And I didn't get much sleep last night because my feller had to get up to go to the lavvy every half hour after drinking so much water.'

'I'll lend yer the half-crown, Elsie,' Billy said. 'The laugh we've had was worth that.'

'Yer will not!' Peg was highly indignant. 'You've got a cheek, Billy Gleeson. She's my mate, and if anyone's going to lend her half-a-crown, it'll be me. So there!'

Aggie glanced at the clock when a knock came on the door. 'This'll be Olive on her way home from work.'

'I'll go.' Titch was halfway out of his chair when his mother waved him back.

'Stay where yer are, sweetheart, I'll go.' She gave a cheeky grin. 'Me legs are younger than yours.' Aggie swayed along the hall with a smile on her face. Unless she was very much mistaken, her son's interest in Olive was more than friendship. He might not know it himself yet, but she could see the signs were there. He'd been clockwatching for the last hour without even realising he was doing it. 'Come in, queen, the kettle's on the boil.'

Titch sprang to his feet and grasped the hand Olive had extended. 'Hello, Olive, it's good to see yer.' He bent to kiss her cheek. 'And it's good to be home.'

'It's good to see you, Titch.' Olive cursed the colour she could feel rising from her neck to cover her face. Fancy a grown woman like her blushing because an old friend kissed her. In front of his mother, too. 'Aggie's been running around like a two-year-old since she knew yer were coming home. And Steve can't wait to see yer.'

Titch pulled a chair out for her. 'I'd have come down last night but yer know I always go for a pint with me mates. Or I should say mate, because there was only me and George.'

'I'll see to the tea while you two catch up,' Aggie said, humming as she went through to the kitchen. After pouring the boiling water into the tea pot, she leaned back against the sink. She knew she shouldn't let her imagination run away with her, but if a romance blossomed between her son and Olive, she'd be the happiest woman alive.

'Ma, have yer gone to China for that tea?'

Aggie shook herself out of her dreaming. She'd been miles away and had forgotten what she was doing in the kitchen. 'Keep yer hair on, son, I'm not a ruddy whippet.'

Olive pushed her chair back. 'I'll give yer a hand, Aggie.'

'I'll do it,' Titch told her. 'You stay where yer are, yer've been working hard.'

Well, well, thought Aggie as her heart began to sing. Things are definitely looking up.

'How's the job going, Olive?' Titch had already quizzed Alec last night, but he wasn't going to say so. 'D'yer like it?'

'It's great. Alec and Betty are very friendly and we have a good laugh. I found it hard going at first, but I'm used to it now.'

'I can see the likeness between you and Steve, now yer face has filled out. Same fair hair and bright blue eyes. He's got your mannerisms, too.'

'But he's got a dimple in his chin like Jim had, and he's got the same square jaw.' Olive turned to Aggie and winked. 'If your son tells me I've put a lot of weight on, I'll clock him one.'

Aggie grinned. 'I'll hold him while yer do it.'

'I wasn't going to say that at all,' Titch said. 'You women have a happy knack of jumping the gun. What I was going to say is that ye're just right now, Olive. Nice and slim but with a bit of flesh in the right places.'

'He's getting personal now, Aggie, and making me blush. I'm going before he tells me me hair needs setting and me eyebrows plucking.' Olive stood up and pushed the chair back into place. 'Next time I see yer, Titch McBride, it'll be me asking all the questions. Like what did yer get up to while yer were away? And have yer added any more conquests to yer long list of girlfriends?'

'Yer can ask me on the way down to your house, 'cos I'm coming with yer. Don't forget I haven't seen yer living room since it was finished.'

'Oh no, you are not! I don't have time to do me housework before I go out in the mornings and the place is a tip. I wouldn't dream of letting yer see it, I'd die of humiliation.'

'Olive, I'll only be looking at the walls! I'm not going to run me fingers over the dust on yer sideboard, or look under yer bed.'

'I know ye're not, 'cos ye're not getting the chance.'

Aggie put a hand over her mouth to hide a smile. That's right, queen, she thought, make him toe the line. Give him a run for his money and he'll come to his senses quicker.

Titch wasn't the least bit put out. 'What time is visiting time then, Mrs Fletcher?'

'Half past six, when Steve's had his meal.' Olive's face broke into a smile. 'He'll be made up to see yer, Titch. And so am I.'

Steve eyed his mother as he stood beside her at the sink. 'Yer hair looks nice, Mam, and the lipstick suits yer.' He dried the plate she passed over and reached up to put it on the shelf. 'In fact, yer look very pretty.'

'I had a spare half-hour so I put a few dinky curlers in.' Olive moved away from the sink and waved a hand down the figure-hugging, soft wool blue dress she was wearing. 'Does this look as though I bought it secondhand from Paddy's Market?'

'No! It looks smashing on yer, Mam, it really suits yer.'

'Yer won't tell anyone where it came from, will yer?'

'Of course I won't, I'm not that thick.' Steve put the last plate on the shelf and hung the tea towel behind the door. 'Did Mr Titch say yer looked well?'

Olive grinned as she dried her hands. 'Yeah, he said I've come on a treat. I must have looked ruddy awful before, 'cos everyone I meet tells me how well I look.'

Steve cocked an ear. 'There's the knocker, Mam. Shall I go?'

'Yes, please, son.' Olive scolded herself for being nervous. After all, Titch was an old friend and there was no reason for her tummy to be doing somersaults.

Titch came in with an exaggerated sailor's roll. 'I gave me ticket in to the man at the door. He didn't give me half back, so I mustn't be getting a cup of tea in the interval.'

'Go on, yer daft nit. I'll have yer know that not only are yer getting a cup of tea, but there's fresh milk to put in it.'

Steve was hopping from one foot to the other. 'What d'yer think of the room, Mr Titch?'

'It looks grand.' Titch tore his eyes away from Olive. 'Yer wouldn't think it was the same room, it's made such a difference.'

'Yeah.' The cleft in Steve's chin deepened with his smile. 'For the first week I kept thinking I'd come into the wrong house.'

'It's not only the room that's changed,' Titch said. 'Look at yer mam! She looks like a film star.'

'You start that, Titch McBride, and I'll send yer packing.' Olive didn't possess a full-length mirror, so while she knew the dress was a good fit, she had no idea it showed off every curve of her body. Or that the colour accentuated the blue of her eyes. 'Sit down and behave yerself.'

'I'll swap yer a list of my conquests for a cup of tea.'

'That should be interesting,' Olive said. 'I'll put the kettle on.'

'What conquests are they, Mr Titch?'

'Yer mam thinks I've got a girl in every port, and she wants to know how many new ones I got this trip.'

'Oh.' Steve looked puzzled. 'Yer haven't, have yer?'

Titch shook his head. 'No, but I don't want to disillusion her.'

'If we go to the pictures while ye're home, Mr Titch, I can pay for meself this time.'

Olive hurried through from the kitchen. 'Steve, don't be so forward.'

'He's all right love, don't be getting at him. As a matter of fact, I was going to suggest we all go on Saturday night. That's yerself, me ma, Irene and all the kids. It would have to be first house because of Lucy and Greg, but I thought the grown-ups could go for a drink afterwards. Just to the corner pub, like. We could meet up with George and Bob.'

Steve's face was a joy to behold. 'That would be the gear, Mr Titch.'

'Excuse me,' Olive said. 'But have yer forgotten I work in the pub?'

'What difference does that make? Yer don't work there at night. And if you came, I'm sure we could persuade Irene and me ma to come. The children would be all right in the Pollards' for an hour or so. Jack and Steve are old enough to see the others don't come to any harm.'

'Go on, Mam,' Steve urged. 'Yer never go out for a drink.'

Her son's face looked so eager, Olive didn't have the heart to refuse outright. Anyway, she was probably reading more into this than there really was. Irene always got a peck on the cheek off Titch when he came home, and he called her love. It was just his way of being friendly, that's all. 'See what Aggie and Irene say first. If they go, I'll come too.'

Chapter Eighteen

Rhoda had her arm across Lucy's shoulder as they turned the corner of the street. 'Are yer playing out after?'

'I don't know yet. I'm not playing skipping or hopscotch, though, 'cos we're too big for that now.'

'Well, come over to ours and have a game of Ludo, if yer like. But it'll have to be after we've had our tea and me mam's cleared away.'

'We'll see, eh?' Although Lucy didn't feel in the mood for games, the prospect of staying in the house all evening with her mother was even less appealing. 'I'll call for yer after tea and see what we want to do.' They stopped opposite Rhoda's house and Lucy watched her friend skipping over the cobblestones. 'See yer later.'

Irene Pollard stepped from her doorway and into Lucy's path. 'I've been watching for yer, sunshine, I want to have a word with yer. But yer better go home first to see if yer mam wants yer for anything. I'll leave the door ajar, so just walk in.'

'Yeah, okay, Mrs Pollard.' A smile came to Lucy's face. 'Did Mr Titch get home?'

Irene nodded. 'He came yesterday, but he didn't call to yours with yer dad being at work. He asked about yer, though, and he's looking forward to seeing yer.'

'I can't wait to see him. I love Mr Titch, he always makes me laugh.'

'He has that effect on everyone, sunshine. Like his mother,

he can turn any situation into a joke. He wouldn't let yer be miserable, even if yer wanted to.' Irene thought the word 'miserable' summed up Lucy's life. They never heard laughter coming through the wall of the Mellors', only Ruby's bawling and screeching. And this pretty girl standing in front of her deserved better than that. She deserved to be loved and cherished. 'I'll tell yer what, sunshine, I'll come up to Aggie's with yer when we've had our talk. Then yer can see yer heart-throb. How does that sound to yer?'

'Oh, yes, please! But I'd better go and see if me mam wants me first.'

'I'll leave the door open for yer.'

Irene was seated in the chair, her hands in her lap when she heard the front door crashing back against the hall wall. 'I'm home, Mam!'

'I gathered that, sunshine. I hope the front door's still on its hinges?'

Greg grinned. 'The door's fine, Mam. There's a big hole in the wall, like, but as I say, the door's fine.'

'Listen, son, I want yer to go on a message for me. And I want yer to take at least half an hour over it.'

'Where's the shop yer want me to go to, Mam? In Scotland?'

'I haven't got time to explain, son, except to say I need a quiet word with Lucy. And I want you out of the way. So I'll give yer a penny for some sweets and yer can go and play with yer mates and annoy the neighbours.'

Greg held out his hand. 'Sounds like a fair exchange to me, Mam.'

There was a timid knock at the door. 'It's me, Mrs Pollard.'

'Come in, sunshine. Greg's just going on a message for me.'

'Hi, Greg!'

'Lucy, the button millionaire.' Greg patted her cheek. 'I'm going to marry you when I grow up, just so I can get me buttons back.'

'Chance is a fine thing, Greg Pollard. When I get married it'll be to someone handsome and rich.'

'Yer need look no further, 'cos he's standing in front of yer. At the moment I'm only handsome, but one day I'll be rich as well.'

Irene tutted. 'Will yer get going, son, I've got a lot to do before yer dad gets in.'

When her son's footsteps had died away, Irene moved to the couch and patted the seat next to her. 'Come and sit down, love, I want to have one of our little discussions.'

'What about, Mrs Pollard?'

'It's about you, Lucy. Yer look so miserable and sad lately that I'm worried about yer. And anything that is said in this room will go no further, yer know that.'

Lucy looked down at her hands and laced her fingers. 'I'm all right, Mrs Pollard. I feel a bit fed up sometimes, but it's nothing, really.'

'I'm sorry, Lucy, but I don't believe yer.' Irene put a finger under the girl's chin and lifted her face. 'I thought you and me were friends, and yer trusted me.'

'Oh, we are, Mrs Pollard, ye're me very best friend. And I trust yer more than anyone, except me dad.'

'Then tell me what's worrying yer. And don't say ye're not worried because I know full well that yer are – and have been for months now. I give yer me solemn promise I will not say or do anything about it, but I need to know to set me mind at rest. And don't forget, sunshine, a trouble shared is a trouble halved. Yer'll feel a lot better if yer get it off yer chest.'

'It's me mam,' Lucy said in a quiet voice. 'She's been going out at night when me dad's at work. And I've been real worried because I feel I'm doing wrong by not telling me dad. I know I should have told him in the beginning, but she said I'd only cause trouble and I was frightened.'

Irene's temper was rising but she kept her voice calm. 'And is she still doing it?'

'I pulled her up about it on Tuesday night when I saw her

dolling herself up. I said if she didn't stop I would tell on her. She promised she wouldn't do it again, but I don't believe her. I know I shouldn't say things like that about me mother, but I'd be lying if I said otherwise. She's a married woman and she shouldn't be going out drinking when me dad thinks she's at home minding me. That's cheating, and she's making me into a cheat as well.' Lucy's voice became stronger with emotion. 'Me dad's a good husband to her but she hasn't got a kind word for him. And that makes me sad because he's a lovely man and I idolise him.'

'Yer dad *is* a lovely man, one of the best. And I know yer dote on each other. As for yer mother – well, we'll just wait and see if she keeps her promise, eh?' Irene had no intention of setting the girl against her mother, that wouldn't be fair. So her thoughts on Ruby stayed in her head. 'Perhaps one day yer mam will come to her senses and realise what a good husband and daughter she's got. So forget about it, sunshine, and see how things go.'

'D'yer really think she will change, Mrs Pollard?'

If Irene were to be honest, she'd have said there wasn't a snowball's chance in hell of Ruby Mellor ever changing. But she hadn't the heart to extinguish the light of hope she could see in the girl's eyes. 'Only time will tell, Lucy. But if yer'll take my advice yer'll put it out of yer mind for now. There's no point in making yerself ill over it, that wouldn't solve anything. And yer've got yer dad to think about. If he sees you're unhappy, it's going to make him unhappy as well. I'm sure yer don't want that, do yer?'

'I would never do anything to make me dad unhappy, never.'

'Then let's see a smile back on yer pretty face and the laughter back in yer voice. Then everyone that loves yer will be happy.' Irene held out her arms and Lucy moved into the shelter of them as though it was the most natural thing in the world.

'Yer really are me very best friend.' She looked up into

Irene's face. 'And I do feel better now I've told yer what's been worrying me.'

'I said yer would, didn't I? So in future, don't keep things bottled up inside yer.' Irene held the girl away from her. 'Now, let's go and see your Mr Titch. I won't be able to stay long because I'll have to put the dinner on soon.'

Titch saw them passing the window and had the door open before the knock had even sounded. His face creased in a smile as he held his arms wide. 'My little sweetheart.'

Lucy seemed to fly through the air. 'I don't half love it when ye're home, Mr Titch.' Her arms around his waist, she grinned up at him. 'And I'm not so little any more. See, I'm up to yer shoulder now.'

'That's 'cos I'm bending down, soft girl.' He stretched to his full height. 'Another couple of inches, then yer'll be up to me shoulder.'

Aggie's voice called out, 'Will yer come in so I can hear what ye're saying? I'm sitting here like a bleedin' stuffed dummy, straining me ears.'

Titch pushed Lucy towards the living room and waited for Irene to follow before closing the door. 'Yer haven't missed anything, Ma.'

'That's for me to decide.' Aggie moved to the side of her rocking chair to make room for Lucy to sit beside her. 'If I don't hear what's said, I won't know whether I've missed anything, will I?'

'I'll tell yer what Mr Titch said, Mrs Aggie.' The rocking chair wasn't made for two people and when Lucy turned she could feel her bottom slipping off the seat. So she held on to Aggie's arm for safety. 'He said he was going to take me back to the ship with him and hide me in one of the lifeboats until the ship was hundreds of miles out at sea. He'd bring me food every day, of course, and make sure I was warm enough. Then when we were that far out the skipper couldn't turn back, Mr Titch would pretend he'd found a stowaway.'

'Well, I never!' Aggie's eyes were wide. 'He told yer all

that in a couple of minutes? He's a fast talker, is my son.'

'Yer've got to be fast these days, Ma,' Titch said. 'All the prettiest girls get snapped up in no time. If I don't watch out I'll be left on the shelf.'

'And what did yer tell him, queen?'

Lucy giggled. 'I told him I would give it serious consideration.'

'Well, now yer've had time for this serious consideration, queen, thank him for his kind offer, but say that unfortunately yer'll have to decline. If he wants to know why, tell him yer have too many friends here who wouldn't be without yer.'

Lucy played her part well. With a hand over her heart, she said, 'But he'll be broken-hearted, Mrs Aggie.'

'He'll get over it, queen. I mean, he can always give Irene a kiss if he's feeling lonely. That's as long as George doesn't catch him at it.'

'Ay, hang about, Aggie!' Irene said. 'If any of the neighbours heard yer say that, they'd think there was something going on between me and Titch.'

Titch chuckled. 'I should be so lucky.'

'Sod the neighbours, Irene, they shouldn't be so bleedin' bad-minded.' Aggie thought it was time to throw another name into the pot. 'Anyway, ye're not the only one me son has taken to kissing. Olive's on his list now, as well.'

'Go 'way!' This wasn't news to Irene, but she pretended it was. 'Well, you fickle thing, Titch McBride. Here's me thinking I was yer one and only.'

'And I thought yer were waiting for me to grow up.' Lucy put a sob in her voice. 'Ye're a flirt, Mr Titch.'

'Oh dear, I'm in the doghouse now.' Titch sat down and held his head in his hands. 'I can see I'm better to conduct me love-life in another country. The girl in Rotterdam, now she's a nice quiet little thing – I wouldn't get any trouble from her. Or there's Anna, a beautiful Chinese girl. And I mustn't forget my French girlfriend, Giselle. Now there's a beauty if ever there was one.'

'Don't yer be bringing no foreign girls to this house, me lad. I'm too old to be learning to speak Chinese or bleedin' French.'

'Yer'd have no trouble with the Dutch girl, though, Ma, 'cos yer speak double Dutch all the time. Yer'd get on like a house on fire with Bertha.'

'Listen to me, buggerlugs, there's enough English girls around for yer to choose from.' Aggie was really enjoying herself. And part of her enjoyment came from seeing a genuine smile on Lucy's face. 'If yer can't find one of yer own kind to marry, then all I can say is ye're too bleedin' hard to please and yer deserve to stay a bachelor for the rest of yer life.'

'See what yer've started, Lucy?' Irene asked, her face straight. 'If yer'd told Titch right away that yer didn't want to be a stowaway, none of this would have happened.'

'It's been funny, though, hasn't it, Mrs Pollard? Especially the part about Mr Titch and his girlfriends.'

'Yes, it has, sunshine. But I'd better get home and put the dinner on. My feller won't see the funny side if his meal's not ready for him. He says he's got no sense of humour when his tummy's empty.' Irene waved goodbye. 'I'll see you folks later.'

Lucy slipped from the chair. 'I'd better go as well.'

'Hang on for a few minutes, sweetheart, while I tell yer what we've got planned for Saturday night. Then yer'll have something to look forward to.'

Aggie patted the chair. 'Sit down again, queen.'

Lucy was wide-eyed as Titch's plan unfolded. 'We're all going to the pictures, first house. That's me ma, Irene and the two boys, Olive and Steve and yerself. And after the pictures, the grown ups are going to the corner pub for a drink, while you youngsters can amuse yerselves playing cards in the Pollards' house. I saw yer dad this morning before he went to work to make sure it was all right with him.'

'It sounds wonderful, Mr Titch, I really will look forward

to it.' There was mischief in Lucy's eyes. 'Can I just say that no matter how beautiful yer Dutch and Chinese girlfriends are, they can't have yer. I mean, how could yer take us to the pictures if yer were living in China? Yer couldn't travel on the twenty-two tram, 'cos it doesn't go any further than the Pier Head terminus.'

'D'yer know, sweetheart, I hadn't thought of that. Oh well, I'll have to say goodbye to Anna, Bertha and Giselle. They were nice while they lasted, but they'll have to go.'

'D'yer see how fickle he is, Lucy? Now he won't marry anyone who doesn't live on the twenty-two tram route. That narrows the field down to about ten thousand.'

When Lucy had left, Titch kept looking at his mother. Then he finally plucked up the courage to ask, 'Why did yer mention me kissing Olive, Ma?'

'Did I do wrong, son?' Aggie looked the picture of innocence. 'I wasn't to know yer wanted to keep it a secret.'

'It's not a secret, Ma, I just wondered why yer mentioned it.'

'Well, I said yer kiss Irene, so what's the difference? After all, they're both just good friends so there's no harm in yer kissing them. Is there?'

'No harm at all. As yer say, they're both just good friends.'

'Now I've got a question for you, son. Who the hell are these girls yer mentioned? This Anna, Bertha and Giselle? I always thought a giselle was an animal.'

'A gazelle is an animal, Ma. And the three girls I mentioned don't exist. I picked their names out of thin air. So does that answer yer question?'

'I'll mull that over in me head, son, while I'm seeing to something to eat. I'll come back to yer if I find yer answer unsatisfactory.'

'You do that, Ma,' Titch laughed. 'While ye're at it, I'll think up another three answers to be on the safe side. Then yer can pick which one yer find acceptable.'

★ ★ ★

Titch walked ahead with the youngsters while the three women walked behind. He had hold of Lucy's hand as she walked between him and Steve – an arrangement that didn't suit Jack one little bit. 'What are yer walking on the outside for, Steve? Yer should be with me and Greg. All boys together, like.'

'I like walking beside Lucy, she's prettier than you and Greg.' Steve glanced along the line, a smile on his lips. 'Yer don't mind, do yer?'

'I do, as a matter of fact.' Jack was wearing a new shirt and trousers, and he strolled along feeling all grown up and a real toff. 'Ye're not the only one to appreciate a pretty face, yer know. I mean, even I can see the difference between Lucy and our Greg.'

'Thanks a bunch, our kid.' Greg looked really put out. 'If I'm stuck with your ugly mug, it's only fair you should be stuck with mine.'

Jack took his hands from his pockets so he could spread them out for effect. 'Yer see, he admits himself that he's no oil painting. So come on, swap over.'

'Not on yer life. That's like expecting someone to swap a bull's-eye for a slab of Cadbury's. I'm quite happy here, thank you very much.'

Ho, ho, thought Titch, there's rivalry for the fair maiden's hand. Friendly rivalry at the moment, but would it be so in a couple of years' time? 'I hope ye're not going to come to blows over this. We're supposed to be out to enjoy ourselves.'

'I've got the perfect answer,' Greg said. 'And none of yer can say it's not fair. Let Steve carry on walking with Lucy now, then our Jack can walk beside her on the way home. And as I'm the one who sorted yer problem out, I get to sit next to her in the pictures.'

'You can go and take a running jump,' was Jack's answer to his brother's solution. 'And preferably into the River Mersey.'

'Yeah,' Steve agreed, 'and without a lifebelt.'

'That's charming, that is.' Greg put on a pained expression. 'Our kid knows I've got me best kecks on, and he saw me polishing me shoes until I could see me face in them, yet he wants me to go for a swim and get them all wet. That's brotherly love for yer. So I've decided that if him and Steve want to fight dirty, I'm more than a match for them. When we get to the Astoria, it's every man for himself.'

'Don't mind me,' Lucy said, 'I'm only here to make the numbers up. I can think for meself, yer know. And I'm sitting next to Mr Titch and Mrs Aggie. So there!'

Walking between Irene and Olive, her arms linking theirs, Aggie chuckled. 'Thirteen next week and she's got three suitors. Not bad going, eh?'

'Our Steve thinks the world of Lucy,' Olive said. 'When we were down on our luck, he used to say she was the only one who had time for him.'

'I think our Jack's got his eyes on her, too. But the one to watch is our Greg. He might be an outsider at the moment, but very often it's the outsider that wins the race.'

'They're young yet. They've got years ahead of them before they even think of courting.' Aggie saw the group outside the picturehouse, and as she quickened her step she noticed the young girl clinging to Titch's hand. 'I hope when Lucy starts going out with blokes she doesn't pick a wrong 'un, like her dad.'

'I'll go along with yer on that, Aggie,' Irene said. 'I vote we form a committee and vet every feller that looks sideways at her.'

Titch waited for them to catch up before marching in and buying the tickets. He passed the sweet counter because his mother had eight bags of sweets in the large handbag she carried. Mr Whittle from the corner shop had made them up for her with a mixture from the wide selection of jars that lined a shelf in a shop that sold everything from food, to gas mantles, firewood and small bags of coal.

The first-house performance hadn't started and the lights

were still on when Titch passed the tickets to the usherette. But the performance in the aisle was well in hand. Jack had given Steve the nod, and they frogmarched Lucy down the aisle to a row where there were enough empty seats for them all. And when Titch turned around with the torn tickets in his hand, it was to see Lucy sat between the two boys, giggling her head off. So he now had to manoeuvre himself into the position he wanted. 'Greg, you go in and sit next to Jack. Ma, you go next.' Then, horror of horrors, Olive followed Aggie and then Irene pushed herself past him. He was left standing at the end of the row with his plans lying in shreds at his feet. 'Blow that for a lark,' he muttered. 'The kids have got more nous than I have.'

Aggie noticed his predicament and chuckled softly. 'What are yer standing there for, son? The lights will be going down in a minute and yer might find yerself sitting next to a strange woman. It does happen, yer know, there's some queer folk around.'

It was the opening Titch needed. 'In that case I'm not sitting at the end. Irene, let me get between you and Olive, before some strange woman tries to take advantage of me.'

So it ended up with everybody being pleased with the seating arrangement, except Greg. He was plotting his revenge when the lights went down, but he put his thoughts to one side for the time being while laughing loudly at the antics of Charlie Chase. The big picture was *Annie Oakley*, a Western with Barbara Stanwyck. And while the boy watched open-mouthed as guns blared and there were dead bodies everywhere, he forgot the girl called Lucy Mellor who was being plied with sweets from both sides, even though she had a bag of her own on her lap.

Aggie was nearly cross-eyed as she tried to watch the film without missing anything that went on beside her. Not that there was anything going on. Olive was sitting as stiff as a board with her hands clasped on her knee, while Titch sat with his arms folded staring at the screen as though he'd never seen such an exciting film. He's too bleeding slow to catch cold, Aggie thought. I bet he's late for his own ruddy funeral.

Meanwhile, Titch was quite content with the way things were going. Last time he was on leave, four months ago, Olive had said she would never marry again because there'd never be anyone to come up to Jim. It hadn't bothered Titch at the time because although he knew he was attracted to her, he thought it was friendly affection and didn't amount to anything more serious. But the whole time he was away, she was never far from his mind. And when the ship was homeward bound, he found himself counting the days until they sailed into Liverpool. He'd always welcomed the sight of the Liver Birds, but never as much as he had this trip.

'She's a good actress, isn't she?'

Titch blinked rapidly as he turned to Olive. 'What did yer say, love?'

'I said she's a good actress, isn't she?'

'She is that. One of the best.'

Aggie hadn't missed a word. 'She can act all right, but I don't like her eyes. They're too close together for my liking and she's always got them screwed up.'

Olive and Titch looked at each other and laughed. 'Ye're there, are yer, Ma?'

'Of course I'm here, yer daft nit. Didn't yer see me coming in with yer?'

Irene leaned across Titch to say softly, 'For the money she's getting, Aggie, I'd screw me eyes up too, if that's what they wanted.'

Greg flopped back heavily in his seat. 'I wish yer'd all shut up, I can't hear what they're saying. I've a good mind to go and ask for me money back.'

'It wasn't your money,' Jack hissed. 'It was Mr Titch what paid.'

A man sitting behind Greg tapped him on the shoulder. 'Do us all a favour. Go and get yer money back and toddle off home. Then perhaps the rest of us can enjoy the film.'

Lucy's giggle brought a loud tut-tut from the man's wife. 'I think some people only come to the pictures to stop others enjoying themselves. For two pins I'd call the manager and have them put out.'

Greg slid down in his seat and there wasn't a peep from him until the lights went up.

Ruby left the house at seven o'clock, while Bob was upstairs getting changed. She'd decided to leave early so she could meet Wally on his way to the pub. It was too dangerous to slip him a piece of paper while they were sitting with Jessie and the gang. Especially when she knew full well Jessie's husband didn't like her and was only looking for an excuse to tell her to get lost. He'd made it quite clear he didn't approve of married women being in pubs without their husbands and she didn't want to upset the apple-cart.

Ruby didn't know where Wally lived, but she knew the direction he came from. So she walked past the pub, crossed a few side streets, then took shelter in a shop doorway. There was no fear of bumping into the Armitages or the Bowlers because they got to the pub very early to get decent seats.

Wally's expression changed three times in as many seconds when Ruby stepped out of the shop doorway into his path. Shock registered first, then annoyance, followed by slyness. 'What on earth are you doing here?' he asked.

'I thought it would be safer this way. We can't make proper arrangements for next week with the others looking on.'

Wally's mind was working overtime. 'I don't live far from here – just two streets away, actually. Would yer like to come and see my house, seeing as we're so near?'

'The others might think it's queer if we're both late.'

'We won't be late. Ten minutes is all it'll take to show yer where I live. Then you can go to the pub and I'll follow five minutes later. They won't think anything of it.'

'What about yer neighbours?'

'They don't bother me and I don't bother them. Besides, they don't know you, so why get all het up about it?'

'It's your good name I'm thinking of.'

Wally grinned. 'What makes yer think I've got a good name? Come on, we're only wasting time standing here.'

Ruby kept her eyes lowered until she was standing in the hallway of the small two-up two-down house. 'I felt as though I was running the gauntlet.'

Wally didn't tell her the neighbours were so used to him bringing women home they wouldn't give it a second thought. Cupping her elbow he ushered her through to the living room. 'Just a quick look around then we'll go.'

Ruby's face showed her surprise. The room was spotless and very comfortably furnished. 'You don't clean this place yerself, do yer?'

'No, I have a woman comes once a week and cleans it right through. And seeing as there's only me, and I'm a tidy person, the place doesn't get untidy or dirty.'

'Yer've got a nice home, it's a credit to yer.'

Wally led her through to the well-fitted kitchen where, once again, everything was clean and in its right place. 'Now a quick look upstairs and then yer can make yer way to the pub.'

The two bedrooms each held a double bed, covered with expensive eiderdowns. And the wardrobes and dressing tables were of good quality. 'I think yer've got a very nice home, Wally,' Ruby said as she made her way down the stairs. 'Ye're better off than most people.'

She didn't go back into the living room, but went towards the front door. 'I'll be on me way and see yer later.'

Wally put his hand on the door to stop her from opening it. 'Yer haven't told me what's happening next week.'

'D'yer know, I'd forget me head if it was loose.' Ruby brought a piece of paper out of her pocket. 'Here, yer can read it for yerself.'

Wally's eyes scanned the note. *Monday, around ten,*

number painted on yard door. He folded the paper and handed it back to her. 'I've got a better idea, and we wouldn't be on pins in case yer daughter woke up and caught us. You come here instead of me coming to you. We could enjoy ourselves without worrying about being heard or seen.' He saw the indecision on Ruby's face and coaxed, 'Come on, love, yer must admit it would be a hundred times better. I don't want to have our first taste of intimacy ruined by worrying about whether yer daughter's going to walk in on us. I'm not one of these blokes who's satisfied with a quickie down an entry. I want to take me time and show yer what it's like to be really loved.'

He loves me, Ruby thought. He really loves me. I can't let him down now. If I start raising objections he'll think I'm childish and get fed up with me. 'Okay, I'll come on Monday night. If I can get here before ten I will, depending upon Lucy and if I don't have to wait for a tram.'

'Yer won't be sorry, I promise yer.' Wally opened the door for her. 'I'll follow in five minutes.' He went back into the living room and lit a cigarette. God, but she was gullible. She believed every word he said. Still, he had a feeling she'd be very good at what he wanted her for. If she wasn't, it would just be a one-night stand and goodbye Ruby.

Chapter Nineteen

'Mrs Pollard, would yer mind if Rhoda came over for a game of cards?' Lucy asked. 'It would save me being the only girl and I know she'd love it.'

'I wouldn't mind in the least, sunshine, as long as her mother will let her stay out until ten o'clock. D'yer think it would be better if I asked Mrs Fleming?'

'Ooh, yes please, if yer would.'

'Right, I'll be back in two shakes of a lamb's tail. I told the others I'd follow them on, so I'll have to be sharpish.'

When his mother had gone, Greg said, 'I don't know why yer want that Rhoda here, she's as soft as a brush.'

'She is not!' Lucy was quick to defend her friend. 'She's always near the top of the class so she can't be that soft.'

'Which is more than can be said for you, our kid.' Jack was at the sideboard drawer getting the packs of cards out, and he turned to wink at Lucy before adding, 'I think yer were third from the bottom, weren't yer?'

Greg was speechless for all of two seconds. 'I was third from the top, and you know it. If you'd ever got so far up yer'd have been dizzy 'cos yer don't like heights.'

'Who doesn't like heights?' Irene came through the door with a very happy-looking Rhoda in tow. 'I hope you two are not fighting.'

'Me fight with our Jack? I wouldn't do that, Mam! He's me ever-loving brother and no one fights with their ever-loving brother.'

'Well, see it stays like that. I'm relying on the two working men to see there's no shenanigans.' Irene gave a quick glance in the mirror before bustling out. 'Enjoy yerselves but don't go mad.'

'Yer don't need to worry, Mrs Pollard,' Steve called after her. 'Me and Jack will make sure nothing gets broke.'

'Does that include noses?' Greg contorted his face to look vicious. 'Because if anyone cheats tonight, that's what they'll get.'

'Take no notice of him, Rhoda,' Lucy said. 'Come and sit down.'

'Yeah, make yerself at home, Rhoda.' Jack believed that when his dad wasn't at home, he was the man of the house. So what he said went. 'Ignore the face on our kid, he couldn't burst a hole in a paper bag, let alone someone's nose.'

'I'll sit next to you, Lucy.' Rhoda plonked herself down on the chair coveted by the three boys. With a shy look on her face, she said, 'Hello, Steve.'

He gave her a bright smile. 'Welcome to the gang, Rhoda.'

'We'll have to play with two packs tonight, seeing as there's five of us.' Jack placed two packs of cards on the table. 'I'll shuffle, then Steve can cut.'

'I've never played with two packs before,' Lucy said. 'Is it just the same?'

'Exactly the same, but yer stand more chance of getting the cards yer want 'cos there'll be two of everything.' Jack shuffled the cards and pushed the pack over to Steve. 'You cut and Lucy can deal.'

Greg was eyeing Rhoda. 'Have yer ever played cards before?'

'Of course I have.' When Rhoda nodded, her long mousy hair bounced on her shoulders. 'Me and me mam often have a game of Snap.'

Greg's grin was one of pure delight. Oh boy, they were going to have some fun tonight. His anticipation of seeing her beaten in every game made him magnanimous. 'I'll tell yer how to play.' So while Lucy dealt, Greg outlined the rules. 'It's easy-peasy when yer know how.'

'We're not playing for buttons tonight,' Jack told them in his capacity of man of the house. 'I'll buy the winner of the first game a tuppenny slab of Cadbury's.'

Rhoda was still sorting her hand out when it was her turn to go. 'Ooh, er, can yer help me, Lucy? I've got three twos, but they're not the same suit.'

'Of course they're not the same suit, soft girl.' Greg nearly swallowed his Adam's apple. Then he consoled himself by thinking it was beginner's luck. 'There's only one of everything in a pack of cards, so how could yer get three out of two packs?'

'Leave her alone, you!' Lucy said. 'Go on, Rhoda, yer can put them down.'

The first hand went to Rhoda, the second hand went to Rhoda and she ended up winning the game comfortably. 'Aren't I lucky? And Cadbury's is me favourite chocolate.'

'She's cheated.' Greg looked disgusted. 'I don't know how, but she's cheated.'

'I have not!' Rhoda looked indignant. 'I'm going to tell me mam on you.'

'There's nothing worse than a bad loser, Greg,' Steve said. 'Yer should act like a gentleman in defeat.'

'Yeah, she won it fair and square,' Jack said. 'So behave yerself.'

'How could she win fair and square?' Greg wasn't going to give in without a fight. 'She said she only ever plays Snap with her mam.'

Lucy was laughing inside as she listened and waited for the truth to emerge. Greg was about to get his eye wiped.

Rhoda's face was set and her hazel eyes sending out sparks as she leaned across the table and glared at Greg. 'Yeah, I do play Snap with me mam every night. That's until me dad has finished reading the *Echo*. Then we all play Rummy, or Whist.'

Jack, Steve and Lucy were convulsed with laughter. The expression on Greg's face was a picture no artist could paint. His voice came out as a high squeak. 'Whist! Yer mean yer can play Whist?'

Rhoda tossed her head. 'Yeah, of course I can. And I can play Patience, as well.'

'Then she should be disqualified.' Greg glanced towards his brother. His look was fierce, but anyone who knew him well would have seen the laughter lurking beneath the surface. 'She was playing under false pretences. A professional among amateurs.'

'Ye're only jealous, Greg Pollard,' Lucy said. 'Why don't yer be a good sport?'

Jack nodded. 'Yeah, take it like a man.'

Steve came up with, 'Give in gracefully and admit yer were wrong.'

'Go on, give in.' Rhoda gave Greg a beaming smile. 'If yer give in I'll share me slab of Cadbury's with yer.'

Greg pretended to perk up. 'Well, that puts a different light on things. Did yer say yer'd share yer slab of chocolate with me?'

Rhoda nodded. 'Yeah, and I always keep me promises. When I've eaten the chocolate I'll give yer the silver paper.'

'Now that's what I call having a heart of gold.' Greg wasn't half enjoying himself. Rhoda wasn't so daft after all. 'And for being so generous, if yer win the next game I'll give yer the silver paper back.'

'Ye're not soft, are yer? Yer haven't got the paper yet.'

'You haven't got the chocolate yet. And if I know my brother, yer never will have. Yer see, he's one that never keeps a promise.'

'You watch where ye're flicking yer ash, Titch McBride,' Olive said, wagging a finger. 'I'm the one who has to clean this floor.'

'I'll ask Alec for a brush before we go if yer like.' Titch

was sitting opposite, between George and Bob. It was a position he'd chosen deliberately, having decided that he stood much more chance with Olive if he let things take their course. She seemed to be happy in his company and was always glad to see him. That was good enough to be going on with and he'd work on what he had. 'Why pick on me, anyway? Why don't yer have a go at these two. They're dropping ash all over the place.'

'Then they can hold the shovel while you brush up.' Olive had been apprehensive about coming to the pub, but Alec and Betty had greeted her like an old friend and she was soon at ease and soaking up the atmosphere. 'That's if the three of yer aren't legless by the time the night's over.'

'I've never seen George legless,' Irene said. 'I don't know whether I'd see the funny side or hit him on the head with the poker.'

'Oh, I think yer'd see the funny side, queen.' Aggie took a swig of her milk stout. 'As long as it wasn't yer rent money he got drunk on, then I doubt yer'd be laughing.'

George stubbed his cigarette out before leaning his elbows on his knees and smiling across at his wife. 'You've never seen me legless, but I've seen you.'

'I beg your pardon?' Irene looked flabbergasted. 'I have never been drunk in me life, and you know it.'

'Oh, I've seen yer blind drunk, love. And I should know because it cost me enough to get yer that way.' George let out his hearty chuckle. 'It was the night I asked yer to marry me and I was making sure I got the right answer.'

Irene's bonny face lit up as she and her husband exchanged that special look that said they were as much in love now as the night he proposed. 'D'yer know, I've often wondered what I was thinking about, marrying you. But ye're telling me now I wasn't capable of thought.' She leaned towards him. 'I wasn't drunk that night, love, but the girl sitting next to me was. She must have thought it was her birthday, 'cos every time you went to the bar I passed me drink over to her.

So yer see, sunshine, I was as sober as a judge and knew perfectly well what I was saying. And never for one minute have I regretted it.'

'You two are lucky,' Bob said. 'I think I must have been drunk the night I proposed and I have lived to regret it.'

There was a trace of sadness in Aggie's smile. 'I've told yer, Bob, there's happiness in store for you and Lucy. Don't ask me how I know, I just do. Yer'll not spend the rest of yer life as yer are now.'

'I think me ma's right,' Titch said. 'Something will blow up one of these days and yer'll say enough is enough. And yer'll be free to start a new life. There's plenty of good women around who'd make yer a good wife, and be a good mother to Lucy.'

'I know that, I've already met one.'

Silence descended as the news was digested. Then Irene found her voice and asked, 'Yer mean yer've already met a woman yer'd like to spend the rest of yer life with?'

'It's a bit premature of me to say it, but yes, I could quite easily spend the rest of me life with her. That's if she'd have me, of course. We sit on the same table in the works canteen, with about eight other people. That's the only time I see her. Her name's Kate, she's a widow with a girl the same age as Lucy. And yer'd go a long way to meet a nicer person.' Bob wasn't usually a talker, but tonight he just wanted to bring his feelings out into the open. 'I think she likes me, but never by word or deed have either of us shown our feelings.'

'Yer just talk to her in the canteen?' Titch asked. 'Is that as far as it goes?'

Bob nodded. 'That about sums it up. But she's kind and caring, everything that Ruby's not. There is a spark between us, I can tell, but that's the way it'll stay as far as she's concerned. And I wouldn't expect, or want her to be any different. I'm just telling yer because ye're me friends and I wanted yer to know. I don't have to pretend to you that I have a happy marriage, and everything in the garden's rosy, 'cos yer know different. If I was on me own I'd walk away tomorrow and breathe a sigh of relief. But Lucy's too young to have her life turned upside down, so I'll have to stick it out until she's old enough to understand.'

'Lucy's not soft,' Titch said. 'She probably understands a lot more than yer give her credit for.'

'Oh, she understands all right. In fact, I believe my daughter knows more about the underhanded antics of my wife than I do. But nevertheless I think the shock of the family splitting up would be too much for her. So I'll leave things as they are for a while, at least until she leaves school.'

'This woman at work,' Aggie said, 'what's her name?'

'Her name's Kate Brown, and yer'd get on with her like a house on fire, Aggie. She's very shy until she gets to know yer, then surprises yer with her quick sense of humour.'

'Never mind all that.' Titch was eager to learn more. 'What's she like to look at? Is she pretty and has she got a figure like a film star? If she has, then she sounds as though she'd be right up my street and yer can introduce me to her.'

'Oh dear, oh dear, oh dear,' Aggie tutted. 'There's that son of mine at it again. It's coming to something when he can't get a girl of his own and has to resort to asking his mate to fix him up with a blind date.'

Bob laughed. 'I wouldn't need to introduce him – Kate knows more about him than he knows himself. In fact, if she walked in here now, she'd greet yer all by name because she's heard so much about yer.'

'That's scuppered my chances then, before I've even met her,' Titch said. 'I suppose yer've told her I've got a girl in every port?'

'No, I told her yer were a bachelor at the moment. But I said that one of these days yer'd meet a woman and yer'd fall for her like a ton of bricks.'

Olive sat back on the bench and laced her fingers over her tummy. 'It'll take a good woman to catch Titch McBride.'

Titch met her eyes for the first time that night. 'It's a good woman I'm after, Olive. D'yer know of one?'

She blushed and lowered her eyes. 'I'll keep a look-out for yer and let yer know.'

George had been sitting very quietly supping his beer and taking it all in. They say life is full of surprises, he thought, and Bob had certainly dropped one on them tonight. Not that they should be surprised, because God knows, the man had put up with more than anyone should have to put up with. He was a nice bloke and deserved some happiness in his life. So good luck to him.

There'd been another surprise for George in the last hour. One that had sneaked up on him unexpectedly. He might be wrong of course, but if the relationship between Olive and Titch wasn't developing into something more than friendship then he was a monkey's uncle. They hadn't said a word to confirm his belief, but that in itself was what made it more obvious. It was as if they were deliberately being cool with each other. Oh well, George thought, perhaps they don't know it themselves yet. But if I had anyone to bet with, I'd have a little flutter on them getting together in the near future.

'Tell us more about this Kate Brown,' Aggie said. 'Don't forget, she's got to pass our inspection to see if we think she's good enough for yer.'

Bob knew it was all wishful thinking on his part, but he wanted to talk about Kate and surely there was no harm in that. 'Let's see. She's got a round, pretty face, mousy-coloured hair, hazel eyes and strong white teeth. She doesn't wear make-up, at least not in work and that's the only place I see her. Since her husband died she hasn't had an easy life. She works to support herself and her daughter, and her mam helps her out by minding the girl and doing odd jobs for her. If I was asked who she reminded me of, I'd say Irene. I've always thought of Irene as the perfect wife and mother. She's pretty, always got a smile on her face, keeps her home like a palace, is sensible with money, always willing to help anyone out, and is wonderful with the boys. And I bet George is the most contented husband on this earth.'

Irene put her hands to her cheeks. 'Ay, Bob, yer've got me blushing. Anyone would think I was a saint, and I'm far from it.'

'You are to me, love,' George said. 'Ye're everything that Bob said yer are, and more. If he's found a treasure like you, he'd be a fool to let her slip through his fingers.'

Aggie was wishing they had rocking chairs in pubs. Words seemed to come easier to her when she was rocking back and forth. 'Bob, in all the years I've known yer, I've never heard yer talk so much. This woman must be having quite an effect on yer.'

'Aggie, I've never had anyone to talk about before. And I haven't really got the right to be discussing Kate like this when I've only ever seen her in the canteen, with a yard of table separating us. For all I know she might think I'm a dead loss.'

'Yer don't really think that, do yer, Bob?' Irene asked.

'No, I don't. I honestly believe that if I wasn't married, me and Kate would have got together ages ago.'

'Ay, I'm beginning to feel left out with all this talk of love and marriage,' Titch complained. 'Yer'd better find me a good woman soon, Olive. If yer haven't found one by the time I come back off me next trip, yer'll have to marry me yerself.'

'Yer cheeky thing! Did yer hear that, Aggie?' Olive turned to see Aggie grinning all over her face. 'He just wants to get married so he won't feel left out, so anyone will do. He must think I want me bumps feeling.'

'Why, is that what happens?' Titch looked the picture of innocence as he faced George. 'When yer get married, mate, do yer get yer bumps felt?'

'Don't yer dare answer that, George Pollard,' Irene said. 'Unless yer want a bump on yer head the size of a football after I've clouted yer with the poker.'

George chuckled. 'Surely yer wouldn't begrudge Titch

feeling a bump on me head? I mean, it wouldn't be neighbourly to refuse.'

'Ho, ho, very funny.' Irene pointed to the table. 'Have yer not noticed me glass has been empty for the last half-hour?'

'I'm sorry, my love.' George stood up and collected the ladies' glasses. 'It was Bob's fault, he took me mind off things with his startling revelation. And now Titch, of all people, is on the look-out for a good woman. If they both get their wish, we'll have to put an order in with Alec for a bigger table. We'll not get many more glasses on this fiddling little thing.' He began to walk away, thought of something and came back. 'D'yer realise it'll take a full week's wages to buy one round of drinks?'

Titch chuckled. 'I never thought of that. It does put a different complexion on things. Unless the women find themselves a job to pay their way. Or they could take in washing.'

'Yer can sod off, Titch McBride,' Irene said. 'My working days are over.'

'And I'll have a job finding yer a good woman, Titch,' Olive said. 'It's no good me singing yer praises and then saying yer'd stipulated that the woman ye're looking for has to go out to work. I think ye're doomed to stay a bachelor.'

'And yer can count me out, 'cos my dreams are too good to come true.' Bob spread out his hands. 'So we won't be needing a bigger table after all, George.'

Bob lay in bed staring at the ceiling. Ruby wasn't home yet so he was free to let his thoughts wander. And he was going over what he'd said in the pub. Perhaps he should never have mentioned Kate because now his friends would be asking about her and he'd have nothing to tell. They wouldn't ask out of curiosity, or because they were nosy, but because they really cared about him and Lucy. He'd be a very lonely man indeed without his good neighbours. It was his loneliness that had brought about his outpourings tonight. He was always the listener, as his friends talked about their wives, husbands and families. But apart from his beloved Lucy, he had no one to talk about. He couldn't talk about his wife because there was nothing good he could say about her. She lived her own life and didn't give a damn about him. Like tonight – she'd gone out without even telling him. Where she got to, God only knows, and he'd reached the state where he didn't even care. So just for once, when Irene and George were telling of their love for each other, he had felt the need to have someone in his life that he could talk about.

Stretching his arms high, Bob laced his fingers and put his hands behind his head. This was one of the times he craved the love of a woman. Someone whom he could hold, who would cuddle up in bed beside him and tell him she loved him. Surely that wasn't too much for a man of thirty-eight to ask for? And he knew without any doubt that the woman he wanted was Kate Brown. But it would take a miracle to bring them together, and miracles were few and far between.

Bob heard the key in the front door and glanced at the alarm clock on the tallboy. The illuminated hands told him it was a quarter to twelve. Where the hell had his wife been until this time of night? He gave a deep sigh and was about to turn on his side when he heard a clatter on the stairs, followed by a loud thud. Then the bedroom door was pushed open to bang against the wardrobe and Ruby walked into the end of the bed. Cursing under her breath, she felt her way round to the side she slept on and, so drunk she couldn't stand, she fell on the bed. The smell of alcohol filled the room and Bob felt sick. He'd been in the company of three women tonight, and two drinks each was all they'd had. Sherry for Irene and Olive, and milk stout for Aggie. Yet his wife, this drunken woman who wasn't even capable of undressing herself, must have had ten times that amount to get in this state. And where had the money come from to pay for it?

The smell was overpowering, and filled with disgust, Bob

moved as far away from Ruby as the bed would allow. There was no movement from her now, and he assumed she was too drunk to undress herself properly and had fallen asleep on top of the bedclothes. But minutes later he could feel the mattress on the bed being pushed down and knew Ruby was trying to sit up. At this rate he wasn't going to get a wink of sleep tonight. He could feel his temper rising, but knew it was no use trying to talk sense into her, she was far too drunk. It would end up in a blazing row and Lucy would be disturbed. The best thing he could do was sleep on the couch.

Bob pushed the bedclothes back and was about to slip his legs over the side of the bed when he heard a match being struck. He turned his head to see Ruby trying to light a cigarette. Her eyes wouldn't focus and the hand holding the match was waving all over the place. 'Oh no, you don't.' He quickly rounded the bed, and seeing the matchbox lying on the eiderdown he picked it up before taking the flickering match from between her fingers. 'I don't mind yer setting yerself on fire, but yer'll not set the house on fire.'

Her words slurred, Ruby said, 'Give them here.' She hiccuped several times and the stench caused Bob to step backwards. But he didn't move fast enough, and as she made a grab for him her nails raked the back of his hand. 'Ye're a bleedin' miserable swine, that's what yer are. Call yerself a man, do yer? Ye're not a man, ye're a bleedin' little sissy.'

Bob didn't answer. He knew if he didn't get out of the room quick he wouldn't be responsible for his actions. So, keeping the box of matches in his hand so she couldn't cause any damage, he walked out and crept down the stairs, hoping Lucy had slept through the last fifteen minutes.

But Lucy had been wakened by the noise her mother made coming up the stairs and had heard every sound and word. Tears welled up in her eyes and she felt like running down the stairs after her dad. She wanted to put her arms around him and tell him how much she loved him. But it would upset him to know she'd heard what had gone on. So she pulled the sheet over her head and curled up like a baby. All her life she'd tried to win her mother's love. She'd done everything to try and find favour with her. But right now, her heart filled with sadness for the father she adored, the girl knew she would never again crave the love of a woman who said such wicked things to hurt him. He had never wronged her, but she thought nothing of cheating on him.

Lucy sniffed up and used the sheet to dry her eyes. You were supposed to honour your mother, but how could you honour someone who couldn't speak without using bad language? Who came in drunk at this time of night, and who told terrible lies? No, she couldn't honour the woman whom she could hear muttering drunkenly in the next room. She wasn't a real mother. Not like Mrs Pollard and Mrs Aggie, who loved their children. And Steve's mam, who loved him to bits.

Downstairs, Bob put a match to the gas mantle and the room flooded with light. He blinked for a few seconds until his eyes became accustomed to the brightness, then gazed down at his hand. There was blood running from three deep scratches and dripping on to the floor. Shaking his head, partly in anger and partly in sadness, he went to hold his hand under the tap in the kitchen. He'd need to find something to use as a bandage to stem the bleeding for tonight. Then tomorrow he'd see if the corner shop had any large plasters to cover the back of his hand completely. If they couldn't be seen he could always say he'd injured himself while doing a job in the house. He'd rather tell a lie than admit to the truth.

Bob opened the cupboard that was set in the recess at the side of the hearth and took out a pillowslip. After folding it, he wrapped it around his hand several times. The cuts were stinging like mad, but he knew there'd be no ointment in the house so there was no point in looking. Ruby didn't believe in spending money on the likes of that. 'No,' he muttered softly as he brought his coat in from the hall, 'but she can find money for booze.'

After placing two cushions at the end of the couch, Bob put the light out and lay down. He shivered as he pulled his coat around him and the cold lining came into contact with his bare skin. Taking a deep breath, he spoke softly to the empty room. 'What sort of a life is this? I can't stand much more of it and one of these days I'll just snap. Then Ruby won't know what's hit her.' He moved his position to try and find comfort, but the couch wasn't made to accommodate his long frame and his feet were hanging over the side. 'I won't say anything to her tomorrow, I'd only be wasting me breath. But one thing I can do is cut her money again. It won't change her attitude but it will stop her from coming home blind drunk.' His eyes closed tight, he said, 'May God forgive me, but I wish she would go out one day and never come back. And if I'm wicked for saying so, then it's her who's made me wicked.'

Kate was already seated in the canteen when Bob sat down. And right away she noticed the plasters on his hand. 'What have you been doing with yerself?'

Billy Gleeson answered her. 'I bet he's hit his hand with a hammer, the silly bugger. I've told him to lay off the whisky.'

'Ye're wrong, as per usual,' Bob said. He'd had time to think clearly and he knew the scratch-marks would be there for weeks, long after the plasters came off. 'Not wrong about me being a silly bugger, 'cos I'm that all right. And I'm paying the price for it. A flaming shelf in the kitchen fell down yesterday, and soft lad here,' Bob poked a finger in his chest, 'stood it up against the wall with the nails sticking out. Well, yer can guess the rest. I raised me arm and scratched meself to blazes on the nails.'

'Ay, ye're not the only wounded soldier,' Billy said. 'Look at the black eye on Elsie. It's a real beauty.'

'I heard that, Billy Gleeson.' Elsie glared at him. 'Yer don't miss much, do yer?'

'Don't miss much!' Billy grinned. 'Blimey, anyone would

have to be blind to miss that. Who the hell did that to yer?'

'I walked into a door, if yer must know.' Elsie definitely didn't think it was funny. 'Not that it's any of your business.'

Peg Butterworth was struggling to keep her face straight. 'Which door was it, girl? The lavvy door?'

It was difficult for Elsie to put on a haughty expression because her eye was almost lost in the swelling of the angry black and blue bruise. But to her eternal credit she did her best to look down her nose at her friend. 'I've already told yer what happened, so d'yer mind if we forget about it?'

'The only way I can forget about it, girl, is if I stop looking at yer altogether.'

Elsie bit into a sandwich. 'Then don't look at me. Nobody's forcing yer to.'

'But I want to look at yer. Ye're me best mate, aren't yer?' Peg put an arm across the wide shoulders. 'I always thought yer liked a bit of fun and a joke.'

'I do like a joke, queen, yer know that.'

'Then why don't yer loosen up and see the funny side of what happened?'

'The funny side!' Elsie's voice was shrill as she pointed to the offending eye. 'Yer expect me to see the funny side of this?'

'No, girl, 'cos that's not a bit funny.' Peg's tummy was shaking. 'But how yer got it is bloody hilarious. The funniest thing I've heard in years.'

'Yer can sod off, Peg Butterworth. And if yer say one word, I'll never speak to yer again as long as I live.'

'Oh, I wouldn't say anything, girl, 'cos nobody can tell a story like you. But yer have to admit that being on night shift is miserable, and a good laugh would cheer us all up.' Peg gave the shoulders a squeeze. 'And I don't know anyone who can make us laugh like you do.'

'Ooh, I don't know, queen.' Elsie was beginning to weaken. 'I'd feel daft.'

Bob had spent the day in a house where the atmosphere

was so tense you could almost touch it. A good laugh right now would be a tonic to him. 'Elsie, never a day has gone by that yer haven't livened up our dinner break. Yer really cheer us up, and not once have we ever thought of yer as being daft. In fact, you are anything but daft.'

The buttons nearly popped off Elsie's overall as her chest expanded with pride. That was praise indeed, and she'd have to remember every word so she could tell her feller.

Peg could tell they were nearly there, so she added a little more pressure. 'Go on, girl, tell them what really happened. And I bet by the time ye're halfway through it, yer'll be laughing yer bleedin' head off.'

'Okay, queen. And before yer say it, I will start at the very beginning.' Elsie shuffled her bottom on the chair and hitched up her bosom. 'It was on Saturday teatime and I was in the kitchen getting our eats ready. Tiger had gone to find the bookie who owed him a couple of bob from the day before, and the kids were playing in the street. Then suddenly I heard this screaming and our Rosie came dashing in, crying her eyes out and holding her nose. When I asked her what had happened, she said Joan had punched her in the face.' Elsie stopped for a second, then said, 'By the way, Rosie is me next to youngest – she's seven. Anyway, I did no more than dash out into the street. I found Joan Craven playing with a mate outside her house and I was that mad, I grabbed hold of her arm and started shaking her. I told her if she ever hit me daughter again I'd give her a good hiding. The next minute her mam, Annie Craven, came flying out of the house screaming, "Take yer bleedin' hands off my daughter before I brain yer." I was going to say I wouldn't let go until the girl had said she was sorry, but before I got the words out, this fist came flying through the air and nearly knocked me over. Yer think I'm big, but yer want to see Annie Craven. She's as big as a ruddy six-roomed house. Anyway, the pair of us were going at it hammer and tongs, and we had an audience by this time. Half the flaming street was out and the neighbours were egging us on. "Go 'ed there, Annie!" they were shouting, and: "Get stuck into her, Elsie." The next thing I know, our Rosie's pulling at me skirt and screaming, "What are yer fighting for, Mam?" '

Elsie couldn't say any more for laughing. She covered her face with her two hands and her whole body shook with laughter. 'Yer were right, queen,' she spluttered, 'it is bleedin' funny.'

'Ah, ay, Elsie, come on.' Billy was sitting on the edge of his seat in anticipation. 'What happened next?'

Elsie wiped her chubby hands across her eyes, savouring the words that were to come from her mouth. 'Well, in between trading punches, I told our Rosie I was trying to get Joan to apologise for hitting her. And Rosie started jumping up and down like a jack-in-the-box. "It wasn't this Joan what hit me, Mam, it was Joan Smedley." '

In the midst of all the laughter, Bob felt like giving Elsie a big kiss. This time last night, lying on the hard couch, his mind in turmoil, he thought he would never laugh again. 'Elsie, you are one good sport.'

'I thought I was a good boxer, too, until I came up against Annie Craven. She can't half pack a punch, believe me. The tops of me arms are black and blue.'

Ada Smithson's thin lips were working overtime. 'It serves yer bloody well right for jumping to the wrong conclusion.'

Elsie leaned across the table. 'I might not be a match for Annie Craven, but a little one like you I could make mince-meat out of. So just watch it.'

'Yer must have landed a few punches, though, Elsie,' Billy said. 'I mean, ye're capable of handling yerself.'

'Oh, I landed more than a few, Billy. But the crafty cow made sure she kept her bleedin' face out of the way. Still, she took it in good part and we shook hands to make up. And the neighbours didn't half enjoy it – they fell about laughing. I met a woman this morning who said she laughed that much she wet her knickers.'

'What did yer husband have to say about it?' Kate asked. 'Did he think it was funny?'

'Did he hell's like! He ranted and raved until me head was splitting. "Fighting in the street like a fishwife! Only women as common as muck do that." ' Elsie's round face beamed. 'But I got round him in bed with some sweet-talking and a few other things, and he went to sleep with a smile on his face. And another good thing came out of it. If the kids in the street break every bone in our Rosie's body, she'll never come crying to me again.'

Bob smiled across at Kate. 'I could do with Elsie in our house. I bet there's never a dull moment when she's around.'

'She is a case, there's no doubt about that.' Kate leaned her elbows on the table. 'I didn't have you down as someone careless enough to cut yerself on nails that yer knew darn well were sticking out of the wood. It doesn't sound like you, somehow.'

Bob made sure Billy was still listening to the women talking before replying: 'It's my story and I'm sticking to it, Kate. Except to you. I'm not going to lie to you. My wife came home on Saturday night at a quarter to twelve, rotten drunk. She could barely walk or stand up. I'd been out for a drink meself, with the neighbours, but we got home just after ten, when the pubs close, and I was in bed when Ruby came in. We don't even speak to each other now, so I turned on me side and was going to leave her to get on with it. But I heard her striking a match to light a ciggie, and the condition she was in, I was afraid of her setting the house on fire. So I took the matches from her for safety. She made a grab for them and scratched the back of me hand in the process. They're quite deep scratches, too, 'cos she has her nails very long and painted a bright red.' Bob gave a hollow laugh. 'It's a good thing for me that she was too drunk to stand or she'd have made for me face.'

Kate pursed her lips and blew out her breath. 'That's

terrible, Bob. I don't know what to say, except I really am sorry.'

'Can yer imagine what this lot would say if I told the truth? I'd be a laughing stock.'

Kate nodded. 'Stick to yer story. They'll believe yer 'cos they've no reason not to. It's just that I've come to know yer so well over the months, I can tell when yer've got something on yer mind.'

Bob puffed on his cigarette and made a smoke ring. He watched it rise towards the ceiling as his heart urged him to say what was on his mind. 'Kate, I want to ask yer something. Yer don't have to answer if yer don't want to, but whether yer do or not, I'm asking yer not to fall out with me over it.'

'What is it, Bob?'

'If I was a single man, and I asked yer to come out with me one night, for a drink or to the flicks, would yer come?'

'If yer were single, Bob, yes, I would go out with yer.'

'Thanks, Kate, yer've made me a very happy man. I'm not in a position at the moment to take yer up on it, but who knows what the future holds?'

Chapter Twenty

'Last day of yer leave, eh, son?' Aggie rapped her fingers on the wooden arm of her rocking chair. 'Are yer sorry it's over, or will yer be glad to get back to the sea?'

Titch shrugged his shoulders. 'All good things come to an end, Ma, whether we like it or not.'

'That doesn't answer me question, son. Will yer be glad to get back or not?'

Titch looked uncomfortable. 'Yeah, I suppose so. Although I've got to say I've enjoyed being home. We've had some good laughs, haven't we?'

'We certainly have. Particularly on Lucy's birthday when we all went to the flicks. I don't think I ever seen anyone as happy as she was that night. She was beside herself with excitement. I think she looks on yer as a second father when Bob's on shiftwork. She won't half miss yer when yer've gone.'

'I'll miss her, too, she's a lovely kid. I'll miss you most of all, though, Ma, but that goes without saying. And the rest of the gang, they're real good mates.'

Oh God, Aggie thought. It's like trying to get blood out of a stone. But she had to bring it up now, 'cos he'd be gone tomorrow. 'Isn't there someone in particular that yer'll miss more than anyone else?'

'Yeah, I've just told yer. I'll miss you the most.'

'Well, seeing as I'm yer mother, I'd expect that.' Aggie raised her eyes to the ceiling and asked the Good Lord to give her patience. 'But what about Olive?'

While Titch's face turned the colour of beetroot, he stared at Aggie as though he didn't understand the question. 'What about Olive?'

'Listen, son, I might be old in years, but I'm still sound in mind and body. And there's nowt wrong with me bleedin' eyes or ears, either. Every morning yer've been sat at that table, all spruced up, waiting for Olive to call in on her way home from work. Am I right?'

'Well, yer wouldn't want me to sit here all scruffy, would yer? Yer'd soon have something to say if I did.'

'Can we stop beating about the bush, son? Have you, or have yer not, taken more than a passing fancy to Olive? And don't start humming and hawing, otherwise yer bleedin' ship will be sailing off without yer.'

Titch dropped his head back and roared with laughter. 'Ma, yer have a very delicate way of phrasing things. No formalities for you, yer believe in getting right down to the point.'

'I'm getting on in years, son, I don't have time to hang around. And I'm not waiting three or four bleedin' months to find out if I'm right, so come on, out with it.'

'I hope this conversation isn't going to be repeated to the lady in question? If it is, then my lips are sealed.'

'I said I was getting on in years, son, I didn't say I was going senile. Ye're all I've got in life, so it's natural I want to share everything with yer. I want to know what's going on in that head of yours and what yer hopes and plans for the future are.'

'There's not much to tell, Ma, I'm afraid. But as I know yer won't be satisfied with that, I'll tell yer where I'm up to. Last year, when we were all trying to get Olive back on the road to recovery, I told her to start getting out and about and meeting people. I said she was young and attractive enough to meet a man who she could come to care for. She told me plainly that she would never marry again because no one would ever take the place of Jim. I can't remember the exact words, but I said something like she shouldn't be so quick to dismiss the idea. Anyway, it was a friendly conversation, and as far as I was concerned, Olive was just a good friend, nothing more.'

Titch smiled at his mother who was leaning forward in her chair, her eyes filled with expectation. 'Are yer with me so far, Ma?'

'Hanging on to every word, son. Ye're taking yer bleedin' time about it, but I'll forgive yer for that as long as the ending is the one I want to hear.'

'That's just it, Ma, I haven't got an ending for yer. But I'll tell yer what my feelings are and yer can figure it out for yerself. As I said, when I went back to sea that time, as far as I was concerned Olive was like Irene, just a friend I was fond of. Then I found meself thinking about her a lot, and when the ship docked in Liverpool I was like a young boy, eager to see her. And I still feel the same way. But I'm afraid of saying anything in case I frighten her off. So I'm just biding me time and waiting for a sign that tells me she feels more for me than friendship.'

Aggie sat back in her chair and for a while her face was serious. Then came a smile and chuckle. 'Here's me thinking yer were too slow to catch a ruddy cold. But ye're right, son, about taking yer time. That's the best way to do it, and it'll come out right in the end. But yer know, sometimes the onlooker sees more of the game than the people taking part. From what I've seen, I'd say that Olive has a definite leaning towards you. And as I'd like yer to go away with hope in yer heart, I'll let yer into a little secret. When Olive comes here every morning for her cuppa she's always got a turban on her head, an old pair of slippers on her feet and there's definitely not a trace of lipstick. Then when you come home it's a different story. The hair's nicely combed, she has a pair of shoes on and her lips are more red than nature intended. So I'd say yer were both dressing up for each other. And that to me, my dearly beloved son, is a very good sign. Ye're both moving forward slowly, and when the time is right, yer'll meet each other halfway.'

'Ye're a sucker for romance, aren't yer, Ma? Ye're wasting yer time, yer should be writing love stories.'

'That's as maybe. But I'm also impatient. So don't be dragging yer heels with Olive.' Aggie rubbed a finger up and down the side of her nose. And trying to sound casual, she asked, 'By the way, are yer seeing her tonight?'

'I'll be going over to say goodbye, yes. Why?'

'Well, always being one who liked to help the course of true love, I'll wangle it so yer have a bit of time on yer own. Just tell Steve I've got a little job for him to do, and that will get him out of yer way for a while.'

'What job's that, then, Ma?'

Aggie shook her head and clicked her tongue. 'It won't be whitewashing the bleedin' yard wall, yer daft nit. But I'll think of something. And if Olive is looking her best, with her hair nice and lipstick on, then take it from me that she's dressed herself up just for you. So don't waste time sitting there twiddling yer ruddy thumbs, make the most of the time yer've got. Drop a few hints and sow a few seeds. That'll give her something to ponder on while ye're away. If ye're too slow, yer might come home to find she's married the flaming coalman.'

Titch smiled. How lucky he was to have this woman for his mother. 'Ma, the coalman's married with half a dozen kids.'

'Which just goes to show he was a damn sight quicker off the mark than you are.'

'Yer've got an answer for everything, Ma, so would yer like to come down to Olive's with me? Yer can tell me what to say and when to say it.'

'Blimey! Would yer like me to hold yer hand and wipe yer nose for yer?'

Titch left his chair and went to kneel in front of Aggie. He held his arms wide and said, 'Give us a hug.'

Locked in each other's arms, Aggie whispered in his ear, 'I

only want what's best for yer, son. And I don't know anyone who would make yer a better wife than Olive.' She moved back so she could look into his face. 'And I'd have a daughter and a grandson that I couldn't love any more if they were me own.'

'Don't be counting yer chickens, Ma, 'cos I'd hate to see yer disappointed.'

'I won't be, son, so don't worry.' Aggie had a good feeling about this and her heart was singing. 'Whatever happens I'll still have you.'

'Hello, Mrs Aggie.' Steve was growing more handsome by the day. He was still wearing the clothes Titch had given him and always looked immaculate. He and his mam were still struggling for money, but they took good care of the things they had. 'Mr Titch said yer wanted to see me. He said yer had a job for me.'

'Ah well, that's not strictly true.' Aggie waved him to a chair. 'In fact, sweetheart, it was a downright lie.'

Steve's dimple appeared when he smiled. 'What are yer up to, Mrs Aggie?'

When Aggie sat down and folded her arms, there was mischief glinting in her eyes. 'Whatever it is I'm up to, sweetheart, I want you to be up to it with me. I'd say we'd make good partners, don't yer think?'

'Mrs Aggie, ye're not thinking of robbing a bank, are yer?'

'No, yer need guns for that, son. And I lent mine to Edward G. Robinson for his latest gangster picture. So I can't offer yer anything so exciting.'

'In that case, count me in, partner.'

'I need a promise from yer first, Steve. That this will be our secret and yer won't tell anyone, not even yer mam. In fact, especially not yer mam.'

Steve made a sign on his chest. 'Cross my heart and hope to die.'

Aggie smiled. 'Right then, down to business. I asked yer to

come up here so Titch and yer mam could have some time together. Yer see, I've got a sneaking feeling that they like each other.'

'Ye're not the only one, Mrs Aggie, 'cos I think so, too.'

'There yer are, then! I think it and you think it. The only ones that won't admit it are the two silly beggars involved. And that's because they're both afraid of showing their feelings.' Aggie was thinking that as soon as Steve left, her teeth were coming out. How could she think properly when the damn things were getting on her nerves. Vanity was one thing, being miserable was another. 'Tell me, sweetheart, what makes yer think they like each other?'

'Because they're at great pains not to show it. But me mam is a different person when Mr Titch is home. She takes more pride in her appearance for one thing, and she's like a cat on hot bricks when she's expecting him down. And she never used to be shy in his company, but she is now.'

Aggie banged the palm of her hand on the arm of the chair. 'That's exactly how I see things. And we can't both be wrong, can we? So tell me, how would yer feel if they did start courting, serious like?'

'Mrs Aggie, I'd be over the moon. I'd have a permanent smile on me face for the rest of me life knowing me mam was happy.' Steve had a question in his head he had to have answered. 'Does Mr Titch really like me mam?'

'Oh, I think so, son.' Aggie wasn't prepared to say more. 'But we can't force them to do anything just because it's what we'd like. So all we can do is try and help the romance along. And that is why ye're sitting here right now. To help the romance along.'

Unaware that they were the subject of a conversation just down the street, Titch and Olive sat back in the fireside chairs either side of the fireplace. 'How long will yer be away this trip, Titch?'

'I haven't a clue. It depends upon where the cargo's bound

for. It could be one month, or it could be four.' Titch thought on about what his mother had said about him being so slow he'd come back and find she'd married the coalman. And while the coalman, with his wife and six kids was no threat, there were plenty of single blokes around. So he took his courage in his hands. 'Why, will yer miss me?'

When Olive nodded, Titch put a hand to his ear. 'I didn't hear what yer said, Olive, I must be getting deaf. Will yer miss me?'

Olive plucked nervously at her skirt. 'Yes, of course I'll miss yer.'

'Will yer miss me like a headache, or miss me 'cos yer like me?'

'Titch McBride, why do yer say these things to make me blush?'

'Well, yer do look pretty when yer blush, but that's not why I asked if yer'd miss me. Ye're not the only one that's shy, yer know. And even though I know me face will turn purple, I'm not going to let it stop me from saying I'll miss you.'

Olive chuckled. 'That'll be the day when you blush, Titch. I hope I'm there to see it.'

'Yer can see it right now 'cos I'm going to ask a favour of yer.'

'If it's about yer mam, yer've no need to ask. Yer know me and Steve will keep an eye out for her. In fact, yer'd have a job stopping me son from going to see his beloved Mrs Aggie. Visiting her is the highlight of his day.'

'I'm glad yer son gets on with my ma, Olive, but will yer stop making things difficult for me? Even me ruddy toes are blushing now. The favour I was going to ask has got nothing to do with me ma, it's for meself. And if I don't get it out now, I never will.' The words came tumbling from Titch's mouth. 'I want to know if yer'll come out with me one night next time I'm home? Just the two of us.'

'Just the two of us?'

'Yeah. You and me, together, like.'

The blush on Titch's face was obvious now, and it chased Olive's nerves away. She began to giggle. 'Yer really are shy, aren't yer?'

'I've never been shy in me life until this minute. And if yer say yer won't come out with me, I'll probably burst out crying.'

'Oh, we can't have that, can we? So I'll have to accept your offer. What was it now? Let's see if I've got it right. Just the two of us. You and me, together, like.'

'Olive Fletcher, I do believe yer've been having me on. Here's me, going through agony, and you've been enjoying me discomfort.'

'Your face was a picture, Titch. But I wasn't having yer on, honest. I felt like a sixteen-year-old girl being asked out on her first date, and you looked like the shy seventeen-year-old boy asking her.'

'I feel seventeen now. I had visions of yer turning me down.'

'Why would I turn yer down? You and me are very good friends, aren't we, Titch?'

'Yes, you and me are very, very good friends, Olive. In fact, I'd go as far as to say you and me are very *close* friends.'

When Steve finally opened the front door he heard them laughing and thought that was a very good sign. They were still in the same chairs they'd been in when he left them, but he detected a difference in their attitude to each other. They were more at ease, more light-hearted. He'd have to tell Mrs Aggie about that tomorrow, she'd be very pleased.

Titch didn't stay long. He'd seen Bob this afternoon with him being on the early shift, but he hadn't said goodbye to the Pollards yet. And he had to be up with the larks in the morning. 'So I'll see you two when I get back – which I hope won't be long.'

Olive got to her feet. 'I'll see you out, Titch.'

Steve's eyebrows shot up in surprise. His mam had never done that before.

He'd have been more surprised if he'd heard Titch asking, 'Do I get a farewell kiss?'

'Of course.' Olive lifted her cheek, but as Titch's face came near, she cupped it in her hands and planted a fleeting kiss on his lips. 'Thank you for giving me me life back, Titch.'

On those softly spoken words, Olive closed the door, leaving Titch looking bewildered. Then a smile lit up his face and he walked away with a spring in his step. He gave a glance up and down the street to make sure there was no one around, then he punched the air with a clenched fist. Nothing had really been said about an understanding between them, but he was certain in his mind that when he came home again there would be a woman waiting to welcome him. Two women, really, because he must never forget his ma.

Titch was going to walk past his house to get to the Pollards', but changed his mind. He had his mother to thank for the progress he'd made tonight, because if Steve had been home he'd never have got the chance to say what he had. So she deserved to share his happiness.

He gave a loud knock on the door and waited for it to open. 'I'm not coming in yet, Ma, I've got to see the Pollards first. But I thought yer'd like to know I've got a date with a certain lady for when I come home.'

'Oh, I am glad, son. I'll sleep happy tonight.' Aggie, minus her false teeth, grinned. 'I owe meself a tanner now.'

'What d'yer mean, yer owe yerself a tanner?'

'I had a feeling tonight was going to be yer lucky night, so I had a little bet with meself.'

'Oh Ma, what am I going to do with yer?'

'Yer can put a move on, that's what. Get yerself settled down, so that when me time comes I can die in peace. I don't want to be standing at the Pearly Gates arguing the toss with St Peter that he had no right to take me until I'd settled all me affairs.'

'Ma, if St Peter knows what's good for him, he won't take yer until ye're too old to argue. And that won't be for another thirty years.'

'Oh well, if I've got that long to wait, I may as well go and make meself a pot of tea and drink to a long life. Then I might take meself off to bed and have an early night. So don't make a noise when yer come in.'

'In that case, I'll come in for a minute now. I want to sort something out with yer and I might not have time in the morning.' Titch ran straight up the stairs to his bedroom and was back down again within seconds with an envelope in his hands. 'Ma, there's thirty pounds in here and I want yer to mind it for me.'

Aggie's jaw dropped. 'Thirty pounds! In the name of God, son, where did yer get that much money from?'

'I'm not the spendthrift yer think I am, Ma, I always keep a bit aside for a rainy day. Not usually this much, but I'm not taking any back to the ship with me. If I haven't got it, I can't spend it. And yer never know, I might be looking for money sometime in the future.'

Aggie took the envelope from him, muttering, 'Think of all the milk stouts I could buy with this. I could be sozzled every day until yer come home again.' Then she smiled up at him. 'This will be safe under me mattress, son, until yer want it. Now go and visit yer mates.'

Titch put his arms around her and kissed her soundly. 'Goodnight and God bless, Ma. I don't half love yer.'

'And I love you, too, son.' Aggie was always emotional the day before her son left to join his ship, but he was so happy tonight she didn't want to spoil things for him. So she did what she always did, she resorted to humour. 'Which is a good job, really, 'cos life wouldn't be worth living if we couldn't stand the bleedin' sight of each other.'

Lucy finished her dinner and carried her plate out to the kitchen. After washing it in the bowl of water in the sink she left it to drip on the draining board. It was April and the nights didn't start getting dark until late, so on the way home from school, she and Rhoda had decided to go for a walk and do some window shopping. They enjoyed pressing their noses against the shop windows and pointing to what they'd buy if they had the money.

'I'm going over to Rhoda's, Mam.' Lucy walked through to the living room where her mother was sitting reading the *Echo* with a cigarette dangling out of the corner of her mouth. 'I won't be late.'

'Yer better hadn't be, yer little faggot. I want yer back in this house by half-seven.' Ruby turned a page of the paper, her eyes screwed up against the smoke swirling upwards from her nostrils. 'And not a minute later.'

'I'm not coming in at half-seven, I'm too big for that now.' Months had passed since the night Ruby had come home drunk, but Lucy had never forgotten or forgiven. Her dad said he'd cut his hand on a nail, but the girl knew better. And she never spoke to her mother unless it was absolutely necessary. 'Yer seem to forget I'm turned thirteen and will be leaving school in seven months.'

'Don't be giving me any of yer bleedin' lip, my girl, or yer'll be sorry. I said half-seven and if yer know what's good for yer, yer'll be in this house by then.'

Lucy was stung by the injustice. Children of eight and nine were allowed to stay out later than that. 'I won't, Mam, 'cos ye're not being fair.'

Ruby threw the paper on the floor and rounded the table to where her daughter stood. 'Yer'll do as I say.' She poked a stiffened finger in Lucy's chest. 'Half-seven in this house, eight o'clock bed. Yer heard what I said, yer haven't got cloth ears.'

Lucy was shaking with fear, but she stood her ground. 'I won't do as yer say, 'cos ye're mean and wicked.'

Ruby grabbed hold of the front of Lucy's gymslip and pulled her forward until their noses were nearly touching.

'Don't have me start on yer, yer little faggot. 'Cos if I do, yer'll be sorry yer signed.'

Lucy never knew where she got the courage from, but she couldn't have stopped the words even if she'd wanted to. 'I know why yer want me in bed early. It's because me dad's on afternoons and yer have to meet yer mates early so ye're back in time to make supper.'

Ruby was dumbstruck. She stared at Lucy for a few long seconds, then dropped the hand holding the gymslip. 'What are yer talking about, yer stupid bitch? I'm not going out! I only go round to me mates when yer father's on early shift.'

'Mam, why do yer tell so many lies? My bedroom is at the back of the house, remember, and I hear yer closing the kitchen door and the yard door. Yer go out at least twice a week when me dad's on afternoons and nights. Don't deny it, 'cos I don't only hear yer, I've seen yer creeping down the yard when yer think I'm fast asleep. It's been going on for months now, and I have thought of telling me dad but I don't want to add to his worry. He doesn't have a happy life, my dad, and it's all your fault.'

Ruby's mind was in a spin and her temper was raging. But she was crafty enough to know her daughter had her over a barrel and could make life very difficult for her. She was going to Wally's house tonight and he'd go mad if she let him down, so she did something she never thought she would, she crawled. 'Look, I'm sorry if I've upset yer, I didn't mean to. And I do only go to me mates', I swear. I can't be expected to stay in this house day and night, it's not fair. And I'm not doing any harm just sitting in me mates' for a couple of hours having a chinwag and a bottle of stout.'

Lucy turned her head away. She was filled with disgust and didn't believe a word her mother said. But she would never tell her dad, for fear of losing him. 'I'm going out now and I won't come in until I'm ready. You can please yerself what yer do, I'm quite capable of seeing meself to bed.' There was a cardigan hanging over the back of a chair and Lucy picked it up and slipped her arms into the sleeves. She was halfway to the door when she spun round. 'I'm not going to say anything to me dad, but it's not because I'm on your side. Yer see, just because ye're me mam doesn't mean I've got to like yer, 'cos I don't. And me dad will find yer out for himself one of these days.'

When Lucy left the room, little did she know how soon her words were to come true.

'Hello, Mrs Aggie.'

'Hello, queen.' Aggie was standing on her doorstep taking advantage of the nice weather. 'Ye're looking very pleased with yerself. Like the cat what got the cream.'

Lucy giggled. 'I'm happy 'cos I'm going to the pictures with me dad. I've just been over to tell Rhoda I won't be seeing her tonight.'

'That's nice for yer.' Aggie stepped back into the hallway. 'Come in for a minute, queen, and keep an old woman company.'

'Okay, me dinner won't be ready for another fifteen minutes.' Lucy was so full of beans she skipped into the living room. 'I like going out with me dad, just the two of us together.'

'Like a courting couple, eh, queen?'

Lucy tilted her head and fixed her large green eyes on the woman rocking back and forth in her chair. 'Would yer think I was cheeky if I asked yer something, Mrs Aggie?'

'Now how can I answer that if I don't know what it is ye're going to ask me? Go ahead and ask, and then I'll tell yer whether it was cheeky.'

'Is Mr Titch courting Steve's mam?'

The rocking stopped and Aggie sat forward. 'I'll tell yer what, queen. Why don't you and I put all the facts together and see what we come up with, eh?'

'Well, I know he took her to the pictures when he was home on leave last time.'

'Twice he took her. And as yer know he was only home for a week. So what does that tell us, queen? D'yer think it means they're courting?'

'Ooh, I don't know, Mrs Aggie. But he's never done it before, has he? So I suppose it must mean something.'

'Ye're not jealous, are yer, Lucy?'

'Of course not, silly!' Lucy's giggle filled the room. 'I love Mr Titch, but I think he's a bit too old for me. I hope he is courting Mrs Fletcher 'cos I think she's lovely. I did ask Steve, being nosy, like, but he said it's too soon to say.'

'For a lad of fifteen he's very sensible, is Steve. And what a handsome lad he's turning out to be, eh? He'll turn a few heads in another year or so.'

Lucy looked surprised. 'But Steve's always been nice-looking, Mrs Aggie. At least, I think he has. And Jack, next door.' She leaned forward and lowered her voice. 'I'll tell yer who else is nice-looking – that Andrew Bentley from the top of the street. The one whose mother tries to speak posh and thinks she's better than anyone else.'

Aggie chuckled. 'So, yer've got three smashers lined up to choose from when ye're a little bit older. That can't be bad, can it?'

'Ooh, not Andrew Bentley, thank yer very much. He's nice to look at but not nice inside. Every time he sees me he tries to get me to stop and talk to him, but I always say I'm on a message and haven't got the time.'

'He's working now, isn't he?'

'Yeah, he's fifteen, the same age as Steve and Jack.'

'Yer know, queen, yer can't take it out on the lad because his mother's a snob. It wouldn't be fair because he can't help what his mother is.'

This brought a frown to Lucy's face. She'd never thought of it like that before. And she should have done, because she wouldn't like anyone to think that she took after her mother. 'Ye're right, Mrs Aggie, he can't help what his mam is. But he's a bit of a snob himself on the quiet.' She began to giggle.

'Rhoda calls him Andy, and he goes mad.'

'She's very outspoken, your friend. If she thinks it, she says it, and to hell with the consequences.'

'I know, I keep telling her about it. But she says it's better to say what yer think than be polished with someone and then talk about them behind their back.' Lucy glanced at the clock. 'I'll have to go, Mrs Aggie, or I'll get told off.'

'Off yer go, then, queen, and enjoy yerself. Come in tomorrow night and tell me what the picture was all about.'

'Where shall we go, pet? Would yer like to see Claudette Colbert and Robert Young, or Jean Arthur and Ray Milland?'

'Ooh, Robert Young, Dad. He's one of me favourites.'

Ruby pricked up her ears. If these two were going out it meant she could get away early. 'Yer haven't forgotten this is one of me nights out, have yer?'

'I don't see what difference that makes to me taking Lucy to the flicks.' Bob speared the last bit of potato and popped it into his mouth before pushing his plate away. 'We'd better make a move, pet, if we don't want to miss the short comedies.'

Ruby waited until she heard the door close behind them before allowing a smile to appear on her face. The silly bugger thought taking his daughter to the first-house pictures was a big deal. He didn't know what real enjoyment was, but she did. Wally had taught her. And she'd be getting an extra half-hour of it tonight in his bed under the feather eiderdown. He was a real man, was Wally, he knew how to make a woman happy.

Bob glanced in the window of the corner shop as they were passing, and asked, 'Would yer like some sweets, love?'

'Can yer afford it, Dad?'

Bob smiled and ruffled the dark curly hair. He was three shillings a week better off now, since he dropped Ruby's housekeeping money. 'I wouldn't ask yer if I couldn't afford it.' He passed a penny over. 'You get what yer want, I'll wait here for yer.'

Steve was in the shop carrying bags of coal in from the storeroom. He came every night straight from work and at the end of the week Mr Whittle gave him a few bob. His face lit up as it always did when he saw Lucy. 'Hi-ya.'

'I'm going to the pictures with me dad.' Lucy sounded very proud. 'And he's given me a penny for some sweets.' She saw the shopowner waiting to serve her and gave him a broad smile. 'Can I have a ha'porth of mint imperials and a ha'porth of jelly babies, Mr Whittle, please? And can I have them in two separate bags?'

'With a smile like that, how could I refuse?' George Whittle was in his sixties and had owned the corner shop for as long as anyone could remember. Small of stature, he had wispy white hair, kind blue eyes and a deeply lined face. He was very popular in the neighbourhood but he had his favourite customers, and two of them were in the shop now. As he weighed the sweets out, he smiled at the girl he thought had the face of an angel. 'Let me guess. The jelly babies are for yer dad.'

'No, silly! They're for me.' Lucy watched the coloured jelly sweets being tipped on to the scale and said wistfully, 'The red ones are me favourites.'

So it was, as she waved goodbye, Lucy had a bag of white mints for her father and a bag of all-red jelly babies for herself. And as she took her father's hand she thought her happiness was complete.

The picture was a romantic comedy, and Lucy was sighing with pleasure when they came out of the cinema. 'I enjoyed that, Dad. Robert Young's dead handsome, isn't he?'

'I've got to admit, pet, that Claudette Colbert is more my cup of tea.'

When Lucy giggled, Bob put an arm across her shoulders. 'How about getting a pennyworth of chips each to eat on the way home?'

'No, Dad, yer've spent enough. Yer'll leave yerself short of yer ciggie money.'

'I'm not that daft, pet. It's not often I take yer out so I want yer to enjoy yerself. Besides, it's ages since I ate chips from the paper. Me mouth's watering at the thought.'

When they got to the chip-shop, Bob said, 'D'yer think they'd mind if I asked them to wrap them separate? Or would they think I had a cheek?'

'Shall I go in? They know me because I often come for Mrs Aggie.' Lucy held out her hand. 'Yer money or yer life.'

She was still giggling when she came out of the chip-shop with two parcels wrapped in newspaper and letting off steam. 'I asked for plenty of salt and vinegar and he doused them.'

Bob made a hole in the paper and put in a finger and thumb. He pulled out a long chip that was so hot he had to wave it about before popping it into his mouth. With a smile on his face he sighed with bliss. 'Just like I remember. We'll have to do this more often.'

'Next time ye're on mornings, eh, Dad?'

They were eating the last of the chips when they reached home. Lucy took the paper from her father and squeezed it into a ball with hers. 'I'll put these in the bin and then make us a nice cup of tea. We might as well finish the night in style.'

When they were sitting facing each other across the table, talking about the film and things in general, Lucy thought what a wonderful life it would be if it was always like this. No shouting, no sarcastic remarks, no tension. There was nothing in this room tonight except love. Just like the Pollards next door.

It was nine o'clock when Lucy took herself off to bed, and Bob sat down to read the evening paper. He smoked a couple of cigarettes and felt at peace with the world. The silence was soothing and after a while he could feel his eyelids becoming heavy. He looked up at the clock to find it was ten o'clock. Time to hit the hay, he thought, 'cos he had to be up at a quarter to five. So he lowered the gas-light and made his way upstairs. After getting undressed he climbed into bed and was asleep as soon as his head hit the pillow.

Bob thought he'd been asleep for hours when he felt the bed sag. His eyes blinking rapidly, he looked at the alarm clock. A quarter past eleven. He was too drowsy to wonder where his wife got to until this hour, but he was niggled that she had no consideration for him. She knew he had to be up at the crack of dawn.

When Ruby had finished undressing and bent to turn the bedclothes back before getting into bed, the smell of drink wafted over to Bob. He tried to push it from his mind, but he couldn't help asking himself where she got the money from. Then he thought, Oh, what the hell, forget about it. What's the point in going over old ground again?

He grabbed hold of the bedclothes, intending to pull them up to his nose to blot out the stench of drink, at the same time as Ruby climbed into bed. And with the movement of the clothes there came another smell. It was a body odour, but certainly wasn't one he associated with his wife. And after sleeping with her for nearly eighteen years he should know. He couldn't make it out. What the hell was it?

Ruby moved nearer to the middle of the bed and the smell became stronger. And then the truth came to hit him like a blow between the eyes. He caught his breath, and the bile churning in his tummy rose to burn his throat. He knew what the smell was now. It was the smell made by two people whose bodies are joined together in lovemaking. His wife had been with a man. And he knew with a certainty he couldn't understand, that it wasn't the first time. Whether it was one man or ten, made no difference to him now. He would never again share a bed with her. He'd put up with everything she'd thrown at him, but not this.

Bob got out of bed and felt for the clothes he needed for work the next morning. He put them over his arm then dragged the eiderdown off the bed and put a pillow under his arm.

'What the bleedin' hell d'yer think ye're doing?' Ruby asked. 'Yer stupid bugger.'

Bob bent over the bed and kept his voice low. 'You slut. You dirty, cheap slut.' With that he made his way downstairs where he threw everything on the couch before dashing out to the grid in the yard to be violently sick.

Chapter Twenty-One

As soon as Bob sat down in the canteen the next morning, Kate could see there was something amiss. 'You look terrible, Bob. What on earth is wrong?'

For the benefit of Billy, who was listening, Bob said, 'I've got an upset tummy. I must have eaten something that didn't agree with me because I've been up all night vomiting.'

'Yer look like death warmed up, mate,' Billy said, not unsympathetically. 'Yer should have taken the day off and stayed in bed.'

'I would have done if I could have afforded to lose a day's pay. But I'll be all right, me tummy will settle down.'

'What's that I hear?' Peg called. 'Is Bob not well?'

'He's got a tummy upset,' Billy told her. 'Been up all night vomiting.'

'Ooh, er, that's terrible, that is.' Elsie Burgess nodded her to head to emphasise how terrible it was. 'I had it the other week, and d'yer know what?'

Billy decided Elsie's troubles were bound to end up in a laugh, so he turned his back on his workmate. 'Oh, aye, Elsie, do tell.'

This gave Bob his chance. 'Kate, my world's fallen apart and I'm out of me mind. Could yer spare me five minutes when the shift's over? I need to talk to yer.'

'I'll hang around the cloakroom until all the girls have gone, then I'll meet yer outside. You really do look dreadful, Bob.'

'I feel worse than I look, believe me. I never, ever thought it would come to this – I'm at my wits' end.'

'I notice yer've got no carry-out.'

'I couldn't eat anything if yer paid me, Kate. The mere thought of food makes me want to be sick. I'll explain to yer later and yer'll understand the state I'm in.'

'Okay. Ten past two outside.'

They stood in a small side street by an end shop and Kate leaned back against the wall. 'Go on, Bob, get it all off yer chest. I'm a good listener.'

His head down and his voice thick, Bob briefly outlined how his life had been for the last ten years. How it had worsened over the last year to such an extent Ruby lived her own life and had no time for him or Lucy. The way she belittled him in front of his friends, came home the worse for drink and laughed at him when he asked her to try and make a go of it for their daughter's sake.

After a brief pause, Bob went on to the start of last night's events. 'I took Lucy to the pictures last night, and we really enjoyed ourselves. We walked home eating chips out of the paper and I was happier than I've been in a long time.'

'Didn't Ruby go with yer?'

Bob shook his head. 'My wife was out boozing. Who with, God only knows. She wouldn't dream of coming out with me or Lucy, she says we're dull. And I'm a fuddy-duddy who doesn't know how to enjoy himself. Anyway, Lucy went to bed about nine, and I followed an hour later. I was well away when Ruby came in at a quarter past eleven and woke me up getting into bed.' Bob met Kate's eyes, 'I hope I don't embarrass yer with what I'm going to tell yer, but it's the truth and I want yer to know.' It wasn't easy to find the right words and he only managed by keeping his eyes to the ground. When he heard Kate's sharp intake of breath, he looked up to see the colour had drained from her face. 'Not a pretty story, is it?'

'Not a pretty life for you or Lucy, either. I'm very sorry, Bob, I don't know how yer've put up with it all these years.'

'Neither do I, or me friends. But last night was the last straw. I'm getting away from her and I wondered if yer know anybody who takes in lodgers?'

Kate shook her head. 'They're all two-up two-down houses where I live, and you'd need two bedrooms if Lucy's with yer. My mam's got a spare room and she's taken a few lodgers in over the years. But, as I say, it's only the one room, and a small one at that. I will ask around for yer, though, and I'll get me mam to keep an eye open.'

'Thanks, Kate. I bet ye're sorry me and Billy ever came to sit at the same table as yer. I've done nothing but burden yer with me troubles.'

'I don't mind, I really don't. If I could help yer at all I would, 'cos I think ye're a good man, Bob, and I don't like to see yer unhappy. Your wife must be a very stupid woman not to know when she's well off.'

'She might be stupid but she's the one that's going to be left with the house and all the furniture: me and Lucy will end up with nothing. But I've got to get out, I can't live in the same house as her. We haven't lived like a married couple for years, but right now I can't even bear the thought of looking at her face, never mind sharing the same bed. And while I can manage sleeping on the couch for the odd night, I don't fancy doing it for ever. So yer can see how desperate I am. If I had somewhere to go, I'd walk out today, even though it means leaving all me best friends behind.'

'Something will turn up for yer, Bob, I'm sure.'

'Oh, I know it will because I'm going to make it. As soon as I'm out of that house I'm going to make some enquiries about how to go about getting a divorce. I believe it takes a few years but I'm determined not to let her ruin me whole life for me.'

Kate reached out and touched his arm. 'Now, I might be able to help yer there. Yer see, I'm the poor one of the family.

Me mam had two daughters, and our Audrey hopped in lucky and married a solicitor. At least he was only training when they got married, but he's a fully fledged solicitor now. They live in a big posh house in Allerton. But he's a nice bloke, Howard, and I'm sure he wouldn't mind giving yer some advice.'

'Ye're an angel, Kate. I feel better already, just talking to yer. If yer wouldn't mind having a word with yer brother-in-law, I'd be grateful.'

'Are yer sure it's what yer really want, Bob? It's a big step to take.'

'It's a step I should have taken years ago. Instead, I put up with being humiliated, degraded, and taunted by a wife who says I'm not a man, but a mouse. And for good measure she adds that she has no feelings for me, or our daughter. I've put up with all that, but I will not put up with a wife who goes with other men. Yer wouldn't expect me to, would yer?'

Kate shook her head. 'No, I wouldn't. I don't think any man would. But I don't want to interfere, you must make up your own mind.'

'I have made it up, Kate, and I'll not change it. So I beg of yer to ask around for some decent lodgings. The sooner I'm away from her the better.'

'I will, I promise. And if I hear of anything I'll give yer the nod in the canteen and we can meet here after work. Now I must go – me mam will wonder where I've got to.'

'Yeah, I'd better scarper, too. I want to call in to see a couple of me friends. They've been good to me and it's only right I tell them what's going on. I'll see yer tomorrow, Kate, and thanks for everything.'

Bob's hand was shaking as he knocked on Aggie's door. It gave him no pleasure to talk about his wife to others, but she'd brought it on herself. And he couldn't just disappear one day without telling his friends the reason.

Aggie beamed when she saw him. 'Have yer had something to eat already?'

Shaking his head, Bob didn't wait to be asked in. He passed her, saying, 'No, I haven't been home yet.'

The wise old eyes noted his pallor and agitation. There was something radically wrong here. 'What's happened, son?'

'I want to talk to yer, Aggie, and Irene. I wonder if yer could give her a knock for us. I don't want to go in, in case Ruby's looking out of the window. The last thing I need now is a slanging match with her.'

'Are things as bad as you look, Bob?'

'Much worse, Aggie.'

'Right, I'll go and get Irene. You sit yerself down.'

Less than five minutes later the two women walked in, worry on both their faces. 'Nothing has happened to Lucy, has it?' This was Irene's first concern.

'No, Lucy's all right. But what I've got to tell yer will affect her as much as meself.'

'I should offer to make a pot of tea,' Aggie said. 'But I can see yer want to get something off yer chest so I'll leave it till later.' She motioned to Irene to sit down while she settled in her rocking chair. 'What is it, Bob?'

'I'm leaving home and taking Lucy with me.'

The enormity of his statement rendered the women speechless. They stared at him, then at each other. Irene was the first to find her voice. 'This is sudden, isn't it? What happened to make yer think of anything so drastic?'

'After years of being taken for a sucker, Irene, I've finally had enough. I did intend waiting for Lucy to leave school, but last night altered all that. Yer see, I found out my wife has been sleeping with another man. I doubt they did much sleeping, but I used the word to spare my embarrassment and your blushes.'

Aggie fell back in her chair, shaken by Bob's words. 'Well, I've always thought the worst of Ruby, but even so I never thought she was that bad.'

Irene too was shaken. 'How did yer find out?'

Choosing words that wouldn't cause offence, Bob related the events of the night before. 'I've been a fool not to have twigged what she was up to before now.'

'Are yer sure ye're not mistaken, son?' Aggie asked.

'Of course he's sure.' Irene couldn't remember ever being as angry as she was now. If Bob moved away they would lose a good friend, and they'd lose Lucy. All because of a woman who wasn't fit to wipe their shoes. 'I'm sorry, Bob, but I've known for ages that Ruby was gadding about when you were on afternoons and nights. Perhaps I should have told yer, but I didn't want to interfere. I've seen her a few times slipping out the back way when Lucy's been in bed asleep.' Irene would never give the girl's secret away. Bob would never find out from her that his daughter knew, and was ill from the worry. 'I didn't know she was seeing a man, though, but I can't say it surprises me.'

Aggie was wishing Titch was home. He would think of some way whereby Bob wouldn't have to leave his home. 'Does Ruby know that yer know?'

'Oh, yes. Before I went down to sleep on the couch, I told her she was a slut. A dirty, cheap slut.'

'And she didn't deny it?'

'She couldn't, Aggie, 'cos it's the truth. Ruby thinks I'm stupid, she's told me often enough, but she knows I'm not that thick.'

'And ye're determined to move out and take Lucy with yer?'

'For the sake of my sanity, I've got to.'

'Does Lucy know?'

'Not yet, Aggie, and I'm not going to tell her until I've found digs for us. I've got a few people looking around for me, so when it's settled I'll tell Lucy. That way she won't be worrying and wondering.'

Irene was feeling sick inside. Bob and Lucy were very dear to her, she didn't want to lose them. 'All these years yer've worked hard to build that home up, Bob, it's not fair that you should be the one to leave. And Lucy won't like being moved away from her friends.'

'Don't think I haven't gone over all this in me mind a hundred times, Irene. I don't want to move away from you and George, and Aggie and Titch. We've been best mates for years and it'll break me heart to leave yer. But there's no alternative. I'm so full of bitterness towards Ruby for what she's done to me and Lucy, I can't bear the thought of being in the same house as her.'

Aggie coughed to clear her throat, because tears weren't far away. 'There is an alternative, Bob. It's your name on the rent book, not Ruby's. So let her move out. She's the one who's wronged you, not the other way round.'

'I haven't got it in me to throw her out, Aggie, and I can't see her leaving of her own free will. There'd be blue murder and I can't take any more, I've had a bellyful.'

But Aggie was still determined to talk him out of it. 'If your name's down as the tenant, it's you who'll be responsible for paying the rent. Ruby won't pay it, that's a bleedin' dead cert, so it's you they'll come after.'

Bob sighed and ran a hand across his brow. 'I'll pay the rent, Aggie, but I won't give it to Ruby, I'll pass it in to the office. I won't give her money to keep herself though, so she'll have to find a job.'

'I've never heard anything so ridiculous in all me life,' Irene said heatedly. 'Your wife is a bitch and a cheap tart. Any other man would have thrown her out years ago and said good riddance. But you don't throw her out, yer throw yerself and yer daughter out instead! I can see neither sense nor reason in that.'

'Me neither,' Aggie said. 'I wish Titch was here to drum some sense into yer. Why don't yer go home now and tell her to pack her bags and go to the bloke she was with last night? She might just surprise yer and do it.'

'Aye, and pigs might fly.' But Aggie's words set Bob's

brain in motion. Everyone would think he was a weak fool for leaving an adulterous wife sitting pretty in a fully furnished house, while he made himself and his daughter homeless. And if he didn't even put up a fight, they'd be right. He didn't think there was much chance of Ruby doing what Aggie said and packing her bags, but to prove to himself that he wasn't the spineless creature she took him for, he had to at least try. He spread out his hands and gave a faint smile. 'However, seeing as pigs have nothing to do with this, Aggie, I might just do as yer say. And because I don't want Lucy involved in any fighting, I'll get home now before she comes in from school.'

'I'll stand at the door and wait for her, Bob,' Aggie said. 'I'll bring her in here and keep her talking for as long as I can.'

'And I'll stay with yer.' Irene was so mad her heart was beating fifteen to the dozen. 'We won't let on, so don't worry. But we'll be on pins wondering how yer got on, so will yer give a knock tonight and let us know?'

Bob pushed himself up out of the chair. 'Of course I will.' He looked from one worried face to the other. And with a catch in his voice, said, 'I can't imagine life without you two.' With that he strode from the room before they saw the moisture of tears in the corner of his eyes.

Rhoda was going to her grandma's straight from school so, being on her own, Lucy used the back entries for quickness. When she opened the yard door, she could hear raised voices coming from the living room. Her heart sinking, she stayed close to the side wall where she couldn't be seen, and stood on the kitchen step. She was in two minds what to do. If her mother was having a go at her dad, she'd go in without hesitation. But if they were discussing something private, it might be better if she went back out again. When she heard her father speaking, though, her feet were rooted to the spot. She didn't intend to eavesdrop, but his words brought fear to her heart and she couldn't move.

Bob and Ruby were facing each other across the table, their faces red and their eyes blazing with anger.

'Who was the bloke yer slept with last night?' Bob asked. 'That's if yer even know his name.'

'Don't be so bleedin' stupid. Ye're away with the mixer, you are, imagining things in that thick head of yours. They'll be putting yer away one of these days.'

'I'm not imagining things, I know for certain that yer slept with a man last night. It's probably not the first time, either, but I can't be sure of that. I can be sure of last night, though.'

Ruby was taken aback. Somebody must have seen her. She was always very careful but Bob was so sure of himself, she must have been seen. She opened her mouth to deny it, then changed her mind. Why bother lying when he couldn't do anything about it, anyway? An evil smile crossed her face. 'Okay, I was with a bloke. So what? If I can't be entertained to my liking here, what's wrong with looking elsewhere for it?'

'I wouldn't lower meself to answer that question. Ye're a bitch, Ruby. A scheming, cruel, heartless bitch. And I want yer to pack yer bags and get out of my house, right now. I don't want to ever set eyes on yer again.'

Ruby's hard laugh rang out. 'Some hope you've got, soft lad. This is my house and no one is going to shift me from it.'

'Wrong! It's my house and I want you out of it. I'm surprised yer want to stay, anyway, seeing how little yer think of Lucy and me. I bet we never entered yer head when yer were being so well entertained last night.'

'Ye're bleedin' right there! Mind you, yer never do enter me head. I wouldn't care if I never saw either of yer again. But this house is a roof over me head and no one will budge me from it. Certainly not you, ye're not man enough.'

Bob was determined to knock that cocky smile off her face and the sarcasm from her voice. 'I've made arrangements to see a solicitor with a view to starting divorce proceedings, so while I'm at it, I'll find out whether you have any legal right, as an adulteress, to remain in my house.'

His words did knock the cocky smile off her face, but not for long. 'Who are yer trying to kid? Yer stupid bleedin' fool, yer don't expect me to fall for that, do yer?'

'Please yerself. But tonight is your turn to sleep on the couch. And I warn yer, I'll not hesitate to throw yer down the stairs if yer make any effort to get in the bedroom.'

Lucy was devastated as she made her way silently out of the yard and walked up the entry to the main road. She wasn't worried about her mother, she wished she would pack her bags and leave. It was her dad she was worried about because she knew her mother was brazen enough to stay put. Nothing would make her move, even though she knew her husband had found out what she was up to.

Lucy sighed as she turned into her street as she normally did each night when she was with Rhoda. What was going to happen to them? Because they couldn't pretend to be a family, not now. She was so deep in thought, she didn't see Aggie standing on her step talking to Mrs Pollard, until she was on top of them.

'Ye're late, sweetheart, where've yer been? We were beginning to think yer'd got lost, weren't we, Irene?'

Irene smiled. 'We nearly had the police force out looking for yer, sunshine. Our Greg got home ages ago.'

'Rhoda was going straight to her grandma's, so we stood talking for a while outside the school gates.' Lucy was wishing her tummy would settle down and her heart stop racing. She just wanted to crawl away somewhere and give way to her sadness with tears. 'Why, did yer want me for anything?'

'Not for anything in particular, sweetheart, we just wanted to see yer pretty face. And we did start to get worried when yer were so late.'

'Aggie's right, sunshine,' Irene said. 'Yer see, when yer

love someone, yer can't help but worry about them.'

'And yer do love me, don't yer?' Deprived of love all her life by the one person who should love her more than anyone, Lucy needed reassurance. 'I mean, really love me?'

'Of course we do, don't yer know that?' Irene sensed the girl's unhappiness and was puzzled. Lucy couldn't know what was happening because she hadn't been home yet. 'I'd go as far as to say yer must be the most loved person in this street. What do you say, Aggie?'

'Oh, without a shadow of a doubt. Yer've got yer dad, me and Titch, Irene and all her family and Steve and his mam. That's besides Rhoda and the other neighbours.'

'There yer are, yer see. One thing yer've got plenty of, sunshine, is love.' Irene held out her hand. 'Come on, yer dad will be wondering what's keeping yer. And it's time I thought about what to give my lot for their dinner.'

Lucy took her hand. 'I'll see yer, Mrs Aggie.'

'Yer can count on it, sweetheart. Ta-ra for now.' Aggie watched them walk away with sadness in her heart and tears in her eyes. She dreaded what the future had in store for the girl whose pretty face should never be without a smile. And whose life should never know anything but kindness and affection.

Lucy was reluctant to release the hand that gave her comfort and a feeling of safety. But she had no excuse to cling to it. She was afraid of going home because of what she might find, but knew she couldn't put it off for ever. 'I'll probably see yer later, Mrs Pollard.'

'I hope so, sunshine. And yer know what I've told yer hundreds of times, just knock if yer want a game of cards or fancy a natter. Don't ever forget that.'

'I won't.' Lucy's legs were as heavy as lead as she walked the few steps to her front door. She didn't have a key, so she lifted the knocker hoping her dad would open the door.

'Ye're late, pet.' Bob had never found it so hard to keep a smile on his face. 'I was beginning to worry.'

'I've been talking to Mrs Aggie and Mrs Pollard. Yer know yer don't have to worry about me, Dad, I can look after meself.'

'I know yer can, pet, but it doesn't stop me from worrying. Yer mind plays funny tricks on yer when someone's late, and yer start imagining all sorts of things.' Bob glanced towards the kitchen where Ruby was frying bacon and eggs for their tea. There had been a deathly silence since the flare-up; not one word had been exchanged between them. It wasn't the sort of atmosphere for a young girl to spend any time in. 'Are yer playing out with Rhoda when yer've had yer meal?'

Lucy shook her head. 'She's gone to visit her grandma and won't be back till late. I might go next door for a game of cards to pass the time away.'

'Yer know, I might just come with yer. D'yer think Mrs Pollard would mind?'

'I'll go and ask.' Lucy was out of the room like a shot, and Bob was just as quick making it to the kitchen.

'If yer start acting up in front of Lucy, I won't hesitate to tell her what yer've been up to. And then I'll go and tell all the neighbours. And don't underestimate me this time, Ruby, because I mean every word I say.'

Ruby moved away from the stove and the spurts of fat shooting out from the frying pan before fixing him with her eyes. She didn't say one word, but her look spoke volumes. Bob knew if her thoughts were put into words, they would be to tell him he was a stupid bugger and to sod off. And her dumb insolence brought his blood to the boil. 'Another thing,' he said. 'You don't go over this door tonight. If yer do, yer'll not get back in because I'll bolt up before I go to bed.'

Bob entered the living room as Lucy came in from the hall. 'Mrs Pollard said to tell yer yer'll be very welcome. But yer've got to take six buttons with yer.'

'Oh, dear. I'll have to empty all the drawers and see what I can find.'

'I'll lend yer them, Dad, 'cos I've got loads. Yer see, I win more than I lose.' Lucy put her arms around his waist and hugged him. 'Yer'll enjoy yerself 'cos we do nothing but laugh.'

Bob could hear Ruby muttering in the kitchen. He couldn't make out what she was saying but knew whatever it was wouldn't be complimentary to him or their daughter.

Ruby was snoring on the couch when Bob crept through the living room the next morning and he closed the kitchen door quietly behind him so as not to wake her. After striking a match under the kettle he cut two slices of bread and put them under the grill to toast. While he was waiting for the kettle to boil, he swilled his hands and face in the sink, donned his working clothes and combed his hair. Then with a cup of tea in one hand and a piece of toast in the other, he leaned back against the wall. What a way to start a working day, standing up in the kitchen eating his breakfast. Still, he'd had the comfort of the bed to himself, even if he didn't get much sleep. With his mind being so active, it must have been one o'clock before he'd managed to drop off.

Draining his cup, Bob put it in the sink before slipping on his jacket. Then he looked around for his carry-out box. He spied it on the small larder-shelf next to the stove and reached for it. As soon as he picked it up he knew it was empty. But not wanting to believe it, he opened the lid. There wasn't even a crumb inside. He closed his eyes and counted to ten, trying to calm himself down, but it was no use, his temper was too high. She was deliberately provoking him, going out of her way to anger him. But how did she expect to get away with it? Surely she must know that one day he'd snap.

With the box in his hand, he went through to the living room and shook Ruby's shoulder. 'Where's me carry-out?'

Her eyes heavy with sleep, she gazed at him as though she didn't know what was going on. Then it all came back to her, the reason for her being on the couch. 'What?'

'I said, where's me carry-out?'

'Oh, I forgot.' Ruby turned on her side, away from him. Not for one moment did she think he'd do any of the things he said he would. Wasn't Wally always telling her how beautiful she was, with a wonderful figure and personality? And how lucky her husband was that she'd married him when she could probably have had her pick from hundreds of men? His constant flattery had filled her head with grand ideas about herself, and had her believing that Bob was indeed a lucky man to have her. And he knew it. That's why he wouldn't carry out his threats. 'Do it yerself, it won't kill yer. Ye're big and ugly enough.'

Bob stood looking down at her curled-up form, his empty carry-out box in his hand. There was something mentally wrong with his wife. There had to be, the way she was acting. No one in their right senses would behave like her and expect to get away with it. He sighed as he quickly made his way back to the kitchen to cut some sandwiches to take to work.

Elsie Burgess glanced across to where Bob was sitting. 'How's the old tummy today, lad? Still got the collywobbles, have yer?'

'No, it seems to have settled down now, thank goodness. I hope so, anyway, because it's not to be recommended.'

'Ye're telling me! I told yer I had it, didn't I? And it was bloody awful. I put it down to some corned beef I got from the corner shop.'

'But the rest of the family didn't have it, did they?' Peg Butterworth said. 'Yer all had the corned beef, so it couldn't have been that what caused it.'

Elsie's look was one of disdain. 'Excuse me, queen, but who was the one what was vomiting every five minutes, you or me? And who, pray, is the one telling the bleedin' story, you or me?'

'Oh, all right, be like that!' Peg huffed. 'Pardon me for breathing.'

'I don't mind yer breathing, queen, as long as yer do it

silently and it doesn't interfere with me talking. Nothing puts me off me stroke more than someone butting in.' Convinced there would be no further distractions from her friend, Elsie turned her attention to Bob. 'I was in a right mood when I went back to the shop and told Tom Black it was his corned beef what had made me sick. I said I wanted me money back or the goods replacing. I must have raised me voice a little, yer know how yer do. Anyway, his wife Sheila came through from the back room and stood next to her husband. "That's funny," she said, all sarcastic like. "There was nothing wrong with your feller when he came in for his ciggies. And I've seen all the kids playing out, looking happy and healthy." '

Elsie took a mouthful of tea before picking up the thread of her story. 'I told them it hadn't affected the others, but it had made me really ill and I wanted me money back or the goods replacing. Sheila opened her big mouth, ready for a fight, when Tom put his hand on her shoulder. "Leave it, I'll give her the corned beef. It's not worth arguing over." I was over the moon, thinking I wouldn't have to worry about what to have for our tea. I watched Tom pick up the corned beef and take it to the slicing machine. Then he cut one slice off, put it on a piece of greased paper and brought it to where I was standing. I thought he was showing me how nice and lean it was, and I said it would do fine. The next thing I know, he's wrapped the slice up and was handing it to me. Well, I blew me top, didn't I? I said I'd bought six slices of the meat and I wanted six back. And d'yer know what the smart arse said? "Ah, but there was nothing wrong with five of the slices. And I've only your word that there was anything wrong with the one you had. I'm only giving you this as a goodwill gesture." '

Another mouthful of tea was required before Elsie could continue. 'I was hopping mad and said I had a good mind to wrap it round his bleedin' neck. As cool as a cucumber, he said, "In case yer haven't noticed, Elsie, I take a size eighteen collar. That slice of corned beef would just about cover me Adam's apple." '

When Elsie delved into her box, brought out a sandwich and proceeded to chew at it, Billy Gleeson looked most put out. 'Come on, Elsie, yer didn't leave it at that, did yer?'

'The shop had filled up while this was going on, Billy, and everyone was having a good laugh. So I laughed with them, 'cos by this time I could see the funny side of it. I told Tom he was a gentleman, grabbed me slice of meat and legged it home before he changed his mind. After all, I couldn't prove it was his meat made me sick. I could just as easy have been the fried egg I had for me breakfast. When I cracked it open I thought it ponged a bit, but I ate it just the same. I mean, yer can't waste food just because it doesn't smell as sweet as honey, can yer?'

'Elsie Burgess, yer should be ashamed of yerself.' Peg clicked her tongue on the roof of her mouth. 'Yer've let the whole street think that Tom sold yer meat that was off. I think yer should tell him the truth.'

The table began to bob up and down as Elsie's body shook with laughter. 'Wouldn't make no difference, queen, 'cos I bought the bleedin' egg off him too!'

Bob was wishing he had Elsie's capacity for laughter when he saw Kate trying to catch his attention. She gave a brief nod and he nodded in reply.

'Me mam doesn't know anybody who takes in lodgers, not with two spare bedrooms, anyway. But she said she'll keep her ears open. Sometimes people put cards in shop windows for that sort of thing, so we'll both be looking out. What I wanted to tell yer was that our Audrey and Howard visit me mam every Sunday without fail. So I'll make it me business to go round and have a word with Howard. Unless, of course, yer've had a change of heart?'

'I'm more determined than ever, Kate.' Bob related the blazing row he'd had with his wife. How she had admitted going with a man and wasn't a bit ashamed or repentant. And how she'd laughed in his face when he told her to pack her bags and get out of his house. 'Then when I asked her this morning where me carry-out was, she told me I was big and ugly enough to do it meself.'

'Do yer mind if I tell Howard all this? Just to put him in the picture?'

'He'll have to know, won't he? Otherwise he won't know whether he can help me.'

'Have yer told Lucy, yet, Bob?'

'No, I thought I'd leave it until something turns up.'

'I don't think ye're being fair to her. She has a right to know. Yer can't just take her away from her friends, and the school she goes to, without giving her some advance warning. And yer should ask her how she feels about it. After all, she's not a child any more, and she might not take kindly to being uprooted from everything she's used to. It's her life, too, and I think she should have some say in the matter.'

'I've thought of all that, Kate, but I wouldn't know where to start. Lucy knows Ruby's not a good mother and leads us both a dog's life, I don't need to tell her that. But how to explain the reason and the urgency for me wanting to leave her so suddenly – well, I don't know. How do I explain that her mother's done something so bad I can no longer stand being in the same house as her? Perhaps I'm a coward, Kate, but I just couldn't bring meself to explain that to a thirteen-year-old girl.'

'What about yer friends, Mrs Aggie and Irene? They know Lucy well and could perhaps give yer some advice. But don't just leave things as they are, Bob, because yer might find yer daughter will come to resent yer if yer turn her life upside down and don't even bother telling her why. And I know yer love her too much to want that to happen.'

There was understanding and sympathy in Kate's eyes as she moved away from the wall of the corner shop. 'Do it, Bob, or yer might regret it for the rest of yer life.'

Chapter Twenty-Two

'So, there yer have it. Word for word.' Bob pushed his finger along Aggie's green chenille tablecloth, causing the tufts to form a furrow before springing back up again. He'd just finished repeating the conversation he'd had only half an hour earlier with Kate and he looked now to Aggie and Irene for their reaction. 'I think what Kate meant was that I was being selfish for not taking Lucy's feelings into account.'

'If she knew Ruby, she wouldn't think yer were selfish, Bob. I don't know any man who would have been as patient as you've been.' Aggie leaned her elbows on the table. 'But I'll go along with her on everything else she said. Of course yer should tell Lucy, she's got every right to know.'

'I agree.' Irene kept clasping and unclasping her hands with nerves. 'I've thought about nothing else since last night. Yer can't just spring something on the girl like that, it wouldn't be fair.'

Bob sighed. 'I know yer couldn't say anything when we were playing cards last night, Irene, but did yer get a chance to mention it to George?'

'When we were in bed.' Irene nodded. 'We were still talking about it at midnight. He got the shock of his life when I told him, but he's of the opinion that what ye're thinking of doing is crazy. He said if he was in your position he wouldn't be asking Ruby to pack her bags, he'd pack them for her and then throw them in the street. Any woman who was unfaithful to her husband would get short shrift from George.'

'I should bleedin' well think so,' Aggie huffed. 'Anyway, are yer going to tell Lucy?'

'As I told yer, Kate thought I should talk to you and Irene. She knows yer think the world of Lucy, and that she loves and trusts both of yer. So I'm doing as she advised and asking yer to help me do what's right for me daughter.'

'The right thing would be to put her in the picture straight away. I think yer'll find she knows a lot more than yer think,' Irene told him. 'She's quite grown up for her age, and she'll understand what yer've had to put up with. But as for yer taking her away from here, well, I think she'll be devastated. It'll break her heart.'

'I realise that, Irene. But is Lucy grown up enough to understand that her mother has committed the worst sin any woman can commit against her husband? And that is why just being in the same room as Ruby makes me feel physically sick? That is something Lucy would have to be told so she doesn't think I'm disrupting her whole life through spite or childishness. But I don't think I've got the guts to tell her.'

Irene glanced at Aggie, her eyes questioning. It was her neighbour's slight nod that caused her to say, 'Me and Lucy get on well together. We tell each other secrets and share confidences. Nothing of any consequence, like, but she trusts me. And she trusts Aggie. How about if we have a word with her? I could say you'd called in on yer way home from work and told us, and me and Aggie thought we'd get to her first so she wouldn't be embarrassed when you speak to her. We'd be very diplomatic, we wouldn't upset her.'

Bob ran his fingers through his mop of dark hair. That he was a man in torment could be seen in his brown eyes. 'I know yer wouldn't upset her, Irene, or you, Aggie. She loves the bones of both of yer. But d'yer think my letting yer do me dirty work for me, makes me what Ruby said I am – spineless?'

'Don't be stupid, Bob Mellor,' Aggie said with feeling. 'The only trouble with you is ye're too much of a bleedin' gentleman. Any other feller, Ruby would have been out on her backside ages ago. Anyway, with regards to Lucy, I think it would be better coming from me and Irene. Woman to woman, like.'

'And we'll do it today and be done with it,' Irene said. 'When it's all out in the open and we see how Lucy takes it, I might be able to get some sleep tonight.'

'We'll watch for her coming home from school.' Aggie turned to glance at the clock. 'It won't be long now, so I suggest yer take yerself off, Bob, and come back about a quarter to five. That should give us plenty of time.'

It was Aggie who opened the door to Bob. As he stepped into the hall she raised her brows and whispered, 'Ye're in for a shock, lad.'

He didn't have time to question her before Lucy came flying out to put her arms around him. She stood on tiptoe to kiss him. 'I love you, Dad.'

'And I love you, pet.' Bob could see she'd been crying and was filled with guilt. He should never have let things get this far. A firm hand had been needed with Ruby years ago, but he'd opted to put up with her antics for an easy life. 'Let's go in and sit down, me feet are killing me. I've been walking the streets for the last hour.'

Aggie's voice was high with surprise. 'Yer mean yer haven't been home?'

'I can't stand being in the house when Lucy's not there. We'll go home together when we've finished here.'

Irene was sitting hunched up at the table, her hands clasped tightly. 'I've got me dinner on the stove on a low light, so I'm all right for a while. Greg's going to keep an eye on it to make sure it doesn't burn.'

Aggie set her rocking chair in motion. 'We've had a good talk with Lucy, haven't we, sweetheart? And I think she's got something to tell yer.'

'I can see yer've been crying, pet,' Bob said, from his seat on the couch. 'I'm sorry yer've been upset, yer know I'd do anything rather than hurt you.'

Lucy had chosen to sit on one of the wooden chairs next to Irene. 'It's not your fault, Dad, I'd never blame you. It's me mam what's caused all this, she's been horrible to yer.'

'So yer understand why I've got to get away, then? I can't stay with her any longer, pet, you must see that. And if I threw her out, which is what she deserves, she'd cause ructions in the street. And I wouldn't put it past her to come and cause trouble for me at work. You know her well enough to know that we'd never have any peace from her. I don't want that for meself, and I don't want it for you.'

'I understand all that, Dad, and I can see why yer don't want to live with her any more. But it's not only you she's treated badly. She's never been a proper mother to me, always shouting at me and hitting me. I can't ever remember her once, in all me life, saying anything nice to me. I've never told yer all this because I knew yer had enough to put up with. But I've had bruises all over me body where she's hit me, and scratches. And me head's been sore where she's pulled at me hair. She's very sneaky, she never hit me where you would be able to see the bruises. It was always on me body, where no one could see. But Mrs Pollard's seen them, haven't yer, Mrs Pollard?'

Irene looked down at her hands. 'Yes, I've seen them, sunshine. But yer told me in secret and made me promise not to tell yer dad.'

Bob was sitting forward on the edge of the couch, shaking his head in disbelief. 'In the name of God, pet, why didn't yer tell me?'

'Because yer always looked so sad and unhappy. She doesn't hit me now, hasn't done for ages. We had a big row last week and she came at me to give me a belt. That's when I told her I knew she was slipping out the back way at night when she thought I was asleep. She got worried then, and she actually smiled at me. That's never been known before. She didn't get round me though, and I told her so. I said I wouldn't tell you 'cos yer had enough worries, but that one day yer'd find her out for yerself. And yer have, haven't yer, Dad?'

'It seems I'm finding out a lot of things, pet. I must have been going around with me eyes closed not to have realised how bad things were for you. But now yer can see that the sooner we get away from her the better.'

Lucy shook her head. 'No, Dad, I don't see that, or understand. I don't see why it's us that has to move. That house is our home and I think we should stay there.' There was a tremor in her voice, but determination in her heart. She couldn't say she'd overheard her father saying he was seeing about getting a divorce, but if he did then he wouldn't be married to her mam any more and she'd have no right to live in the house. But if they left now, they'd never get it back. 'I don't want us to leave, Dad, please?'

'It's not as easy as that, Lucy. There's grown up things ye're too young to understand.' Bob was wondering what he'd ever done to be punished in this way. Because seeing his beloved daughter like this was indeed a punishment. 'But we'll be all right. I've got the feelers out for some decent digs for us, until I can find us a proper house.'

'Dad, don't take me away from this street and all me friends, please? I wouldn't be happy anywhere else.'

Irene could see the girl was near to tears. And Bob looked like a man who had reached breaking point. 'Look, sunshine, yer've told yer dad how yer feel, so why not give him time to think it over? He's only trying to do what's best for yer.'

'I know that, Mrs Pollard.' Seeing the look of despair on her father's face, Lucy left her chair in such haste it would have toppled over if Irene hadn't caught it in time. Sitting on his knee she laid her head on his chest. 'I don't like to see yer looking so unhappy, Dad, because it makes me unhappy. Let's not talk about it any more now; you take yer time to think things over. Me mam's done bad things to both of us, but she can't part us. No matter what happens we'll always have each other.'

'You and yer dad will never be alone, sweetheart,' Aggie said, trying to swallow the lump in her throat. 'Yer've got lots of good friends and we'll do anything to help yer.'

'I know yer would, Mrs Aggie.' And hoping to bring a smile to her father's face, Lucy asked, 'Can me and me dad come and lodge with yer?'

'Nothing would please me more, sweetheart, if I had the room. I'd be in me bleedin' apple-cart, and that's a fact.' Aggie grinned. 'I can just see Titch's face if he came home and found you sleeping in his bed. He'd think yer were that princess in the storybooks what was asleep for donkey's years and got woke up when a handsome prince kissed her.'

Lucy's giggle brought a smile to each of their faces. 'Yeah, he'd be struck dumb.'

'Ooh, I don't know about that. It would take more than a sleeping princess to rob my son of his powers of speech. He was born with the gift of the gab. The midwife what delivered him said that when she lifted him up by his legs and smacked his bottom, he opened his eyes and said if she did that once more he'd hit her back.'

Now the mood was lighter, Irene pushed herself up from the chair. Greg was very good at watching the stove for her, but he wouldn't think of giving the stew a stir so it wouldn't stick on the bottom of the pan. 'I'm off, folks. Will yer be calling in tomorrow afternoon, Bob?'

'If it's convenient for Aggie. I wouldn't go home anyway, I'd hang around and wait for Lucy to come. To be greeted with a sneer when yer walk in yer own living room after working an eight-hour shift, isn't exactly the best of welcomes.'

'Ye're welcome here, lad,' Aggie said. 'I was going to go to the Adelphi Hotel for afternoon tea, but I'll give it a miss for once.'

'Ooh, ay, Missus,' Irene laughed, 'the state of you and the

price of fish! The Adelphi Hotel indeed! That's a new one on me.'

'It's one of my little secrets, queen.' Aggie left her chair and stretched to her full height. 'I'm very well-known in social circles, but it's not something I brag about. I'm not a snob and I wouldn't want my friends to get an inferiority complex.'

'I've already got one, Aggie.' There were the makings of a smile on Bob's face as he pushed Lucy to her feet. 'But you didn't give it to me.'

'Don't let anybody put yer down, lad.' Aggie followed them to the door. 'Ye're as good as anybody and better than most.'

Lucy gave the old woman a kiss before taking her father's hand. 'I won't see yer tonight, Mrs Aggie, 'cos I've promised Rhoda I'd go over there after I've had me tea. But I'll see yer tomorrow. And you, Mrs Pollard.'

'You and yer mate are welcome to come and have a game of cards,' Irene said as they reached her house. 'The boys would enjoy that.'

'Thanks, Mrs Pollard, but I might not go out at all. I think I'll stay in and keep me dad company.'

'He's welcome to come, too, sunshine.'

'Not tonight, Irene, but thanks all the same.' Bob squeezed Lucy's hand and smiled down at her. 'I'm going to have an early night in bed and do some serious thinking. Eh, pet?'

'Yes, Dad.' Lucy pulled him towards their door. 'We'll go to bed at the same time.'

After dinner was over and the dishes washed, Ruby picked up her handbag and left the room. Lucy's eyes followed her, and as she heard footsteps mounting the stairs she knew in her heart her mother was getting ready to go out. How has she got the nerve, the girl asked herself, when me dad's told her he knows what she's up to? She doesn't seem to care what he thinks.

Bob lowered the paper he was reading and looked across at his daughter. 'I'm thinking the same as you, pet. She's going out again.'

'Are yer going to tell her she can't, Dad?'

'No, it's no use, love, and anyway, it's too late for that now. At least we'll have the house to ourselves.'

Lucy bit on her bottom lip. Her dad did look very tired, but she had promised her friend. 'Can I ask Rhoda to come over here for half an hour, then? I promised I'd try and do something with her hair. Not that I'm any good at it, but she thinks because mine's curly I can make hers the same. It's only for a laugh, Dad, and we wouldn't get in yer way. I always feel mean not asking her in here, 'cos I'm in her house nearly every day. But she's only been in here once or twice in all the years we've been friends. Me mam wouldn't let her in.'

'Of course she can come over.' Bob's smile turned into a yawn. He was so weary he felt like falling into bed and sleeping for a week. 'But only for an hour, pet, I do want to have an early night.'

When Ruby came into the room, the smell of cheap scent came with her. Her face was caked with powder and rouge, and her lips were scarlet. 'I'm going out.'

'I gathered that,' Bob said, without looking up from his paper, while Lucy pretended to be so intent on pushing the skin back from her cuticles, she didn't hear. But as soon as the front door closed she was off her seat. 'I'll go and get me mate.'

Bob was staring into space when he heard the girls' laughter and he quickly fixed a smile on his face. 'Hello, Rhoda.'

'Hiya, Mr Mellor! How yer doing? And don't say ye're doing everyone because me mam got there before yer.'

'I always was slow on the uptake, love. Anyway, you've changed a lot. Yer used to be a lot bonnier than yer are now.'

There was a look of bliss on Rhoda's face. Bob's words were music to her ears. 'I've lost a lot of me fat, Mr Mellor, like me mam said I would. Mind you,' the girl pursed her lips and her look was comical, 'she was eight years out in the timing. I was six when she said it was puppy fat, and here I am nearly fourteen.'

Bob grinned at the girl who had been Lucy's steadfast friend since they were toddlers. 'Yer look well, Rhoda, very pretty.'

'I'm not as thin as yer daughter yet, but I'm working on it. And I haven't got curly hair like hers, but I'm not working on that, she is.'

'Don't expect miracles,' Lucy told her. 'I'm not a hair-dresser.'

'If yer make a mess of it, yer won't be able to blame the tools.' Rhoda placed a bag on the table. 'Me mam's pipe cleaners are in there, together with a brush and comb. So there's no excuse if I don't end up with curls like yours. If I don't, yer'll have me mam to answer to.'

Lucy raised her hands in mock horror. 'Oh no, not yer mam! Let me answer to yer dad instead, please, I beg yer.'

'Shut up and get on with the job.' Rhoda pulled a chair from the table and plonked herself down. 'And I'll be counting the curls when yer've finished. If I haven't got as many as you there'll be skin and hair flying.'

Bob went back to his paper, but not to read. For the next hour he had a real, genuine smile on his face as he listened to his daughter and her friend. They never stopped talking and laughing. When one wasn't rattling off about one thing or another, the other was. And it did Bob's heart good to hear young voices and laughter in the house. This was how life should always have been for Lucy. And Bob was grateful for this short period of normality.

'There yer are, there's thirty pipe cleaners in now.' Lucy put the comb down on the table. 'And if yer hair's straight in the morning I'll eat me hat.'

'Ooh, er, how am I going to sleep with these in? I'll have to sit up all night.'

'Don't be daft! Put a scarf on yer head before yer go to bed and it'll keep the pipe cleaners in place. Anyway, yer've got to put up with some discomfort if yer want to be glamorous.'

'Okay, kid, don't be getting obstreperous.'

Lucy's jaw dropped. 'Don't be getting what?'

'I ain't repeating that! It took me all me time to get it out the once.'

'Well, what does it mean?'

'How the heck do I know? I was in TJ's one day and some kid was screaming his head off. His mam dragged him out of the shop telling him not to be what I've just told yer.'

'I'm going to ask our teacher tomorrow what it means,' Lucy said. 'And if it means something bad I'll clock yer one.'

'What are yer going to ask her?'

'What that word means.'

'What word?'

'The one yer've just used.'

'Can yer say it, then?'

Lucy sent her curls swinging as she shook her head. 'Of course I can't say it. But you can.'

'I'm staying out of it,' Rhoda said, picking up her bag. 'And another thing, I'm staying away from T.J. Hughes' and screaming kids. If I'd known the miserable little blighter was going to cause me this much bother I'd have hit him meself.'

Bob couldn't help laughing aloud. He knew these two had been mates for years, but had no idea how close they were. He was sorry when Rhoda said it was time to go. 'Thank you for a very entertaining hour, Miss Fleming. I sincerely hope yer head is one mass of curls in the morning.'

'Oh, it will be, Mr Mellor. Yer see, Lucy's coming over to ours early in the morning to take the pipe cleaners out and roll me curls for me.'

Lucy gasped. 'I never said I'd do that.'

'No, you didn't say it, I did.' Rhoda pushed her friend into the hallway. 'And don't yer start getting obstreperous with me, Lucy Mellor, or I'll give yer a thick lip.'

Ruby huffed when she walked into the living room at eleven o'clock that night. Why did he have to lower the gas every time she went out? It made the room look miserable, and all for the sake of saving a copper. She pulled the chain at the side of the gas-light to brighten the room, while calling her husband all the tight-fisted buggers she could think of. It was when she was taking her coat off that she saw the blanket and pillow on the couch. 'Oh no,' she said aloud. 'If he thinks I'm sleeping on there again he's got another think coming.'

Wally's lovemaking and flattery had filled her with confidence, and the belief that she was far too good for her husband. And the drink he'd plied her with clouded her judgement. She hung her coat on a hook in the hall, then picked up the blanket and pillow. Without making any effort to be quiet, she climbed the stairs, threw the bedding on the bed and waited for Bob to stir. 'If yer think yer can get away with that, ye're dafter than I thought yer were.'

Bob lay still for several seconds to collect his thoughts. Then, with a deep sigh, he pushed the clothes back. Gathering the blanket and pillow in his arms, he said quietly, 'You will not sleep in my bed.' He started to walk out of the room, intending to throw the clothes down the stairs, but Ruby barred his path. Her two hands pushing him backwards, she yelled at the top of her voice, 'Who the bleedin' hell d'yer think yer are? Yer can't be right in the head if yer think yer can make yer wife sleep on the couch.' All the time she was pushing and beating Bob's chest with her fists. And when he didn't reply, her language became that of the gutter.

Lucy woke with a start and shot up in bed. She heard her mother screaming like a wild woman and was sickened by the swearwords. Then she heard her father speaking in a low voice. 'Will yer move out of my way?' His words sent Ruby into a rage and her screaming intensified.

Lucy scrambled from her bed and flew into the next room. She saw her mother lashing out at her father with both hands and was horrified. 'You leave my dad alone.' She stood behind her mother and began to pummel her back with clenched fists. 'Ye're wicked, you are. Now leave him alone.'

Ruby turned around, pulled her arm back and delivered a stinging slap to the side of Lucy's face. 'Get back to bed, yer little faggot.'

Bob closed his eyes. To think it had come down to this. His daughter trying to protect him from a wife who was clearly not in her right mind. And the neighbours both sides must be able to hear the row. He laid the clothes down on the bed, put his arms around Ruby's waist and lifted her from the floor. 'You either sleep on the couch or walk the streets all night. The choice is yours.'

Lucy stepped away from the thrashing arms and legs as her mother was carried screaming from the room. Holding a hand to her cheek which was smarting from the slap, she watched as her mother clung to the bannister like grim death, screaming like a wild woman as her father tried to carry her downstairs. And, sick at heart, the girl knew that what was happening now had put paid to any thought of her dad staying. It wouldn't be fair to expect him to, either.

'Go back to bed, Lucy,' Bob said. 'I'll handle this.'

'Will yer be all right, Dad?'

'Yes, I'll be all right. You go back to bed, there's a good girl.'

Bob waited for a few seconds, then took an arm from around his wife's waist. He let it fall before bringing it up sharply under her arms and wrenching her away from the bannister. He managed to get her down the stairs and into the living room, where he dropped her on to the couch. She was still shouting and blaspheming as she tried to push herself up, and it was then that Bob saw red. With the sound of Lucy's face being slapped still ringing in his ears, he had come to the end of his tether. 'Shut up, woman, before I make you.'

'That'll be the day,' Ruby sneered. 'Yer haven't got the bleedin' guts. Ye're not man enough.'

Bob had always sworn never to raise a hand to a woman, but he had taken enough humiliation from this loud-mouthed, so-called wife of his. He didn't put his weight behind the slap he gave her, but it was hard enough to bring a startled cry from Ruby. 'You bleedin' sod! I'll get yer back for this.'

'That slap was for Lucy. And if yer don't keep that filthy mouth of yours shut, I'll be happy to give yer one from me. And I won't pull me punch next time. So it's up to you. Yer can go upstairs, very quietly, and bring down the blanket and pillow for yerself, or yer can take a chance on me belting yer one before throwing yer out on the street.'

Ruby had sobered up quickly. She had never seen her husband like this, but she could tell by the anger in his voice that he was more than capable of carrying out his threat. However, habit wouldn't let her give in to him. 'I'll be quiet if you sleep on the couch.'

'My terms are not up for discussion, Ruby. Take it or leave it.'

She still wasn't ready to give in. 'And how long is this lark going to go on for – me sleeping on the couch?'

'Oh, not long, Ruby. Not long at all.'

'How d'yer mean, not long? What's going on?'

'I don't have to tell you anything about my private life. You don't tell me anything, never have done. I don't know where yer go or who yer see. I was going to say I don't know what yer get up to, but I know that now.' Bob's sigh came from deep within him. 'I have an eight-hour shift in front of me, I'd like to get some sleep. So go and fetch the bedding if yer don't fancy a night walking the streets.'

Ruby left the room without a word. And when she came down, Bob climbed the stairs hoping to get a few hours' much-needed sleep. Tomorrow was another day. A day in which he had to sort his life out once and for all.

'What in the name of God went on last night?' Irene asked as Bob walked into Aggie's living room the next day. 'The whole street must have heard yer.'

'They wouldn't have heard me, Irene, or Lucy. I was fast asleep when Ruby came home at eleven o'clock. She must have been with her fancy-man and was the worse for drink. I'd left a blanket and pillow on the couch for her because I'd told her I'll never sleep in the same bed as her. If she hadn't gone out, or was home at a reasonable time, I might have slept downstairs meself. But I can't sit up until she decides to roll home, I've got a job to think of.'

'She is one bitch,' Irene said with feeling. 'Shouting her head off, and the language out of her was terrible! What was it all in aid of?'

'She came upstairs with the blanket and pillow and said she was getting into bed whether I liked it or not. Well, I didn't like it. And that started the whole thing off. The noise woke Lucy and she came dashing in to see her mother beating me with her fists. Of course the girl was upset and began to hit her on the back, telling her to leave me alone. The next thing, Ruby turns around and gave Lucy such a belt across the face it must have really hurt. Anyway, it brought me to me senses and I told Lucy to go back to bed while I somehow managed to drag Ruby down the stairs.'

Aggie had been shaking her head and tutting. The more her temper rose, the quicker the chair was rocked. 'Has the woman no shame? A married woman coming home drunk at eleven o'clock at night! And after being told that yer know what she's up to! If yer ask me, she wants horse-whipping.'

'I don't know about horse-whipping, Aggie, and I'm not exactly proud of meself, but I did give her a slap. She just wouldn't shut up when I finally got her downstairs, saying I wasn't a man and I didn't have the guts to do the things I was threatening to do. Like giving her a good hiding and throwing her out into the street. Anyway, I finally lost me rag and slapped her face. I told her that one was for Lucy, but if she didn't shut up I'd give her one for meself and I wouldn't be as gentle.'

'About bleedin' time,' Aggie said. 'Yer should have done it years ago.'

'It must have done the trick, Bob, because all went quiet about half-eleven.' Irene's pretty face was wearing a troubled expression. Last night, through the bedroom wall, she and George had heard a little of what Bob had had to put up with all these years. And it had given her plenty to think about. He was a nice, decent, hardworking bloke who wouldn't do anyone a bad turn. He deserved a good life and she for one wouldn't blame him for walking away from a living hell. 'What happens now?'

'I'm getting out, Irene. Kate and her mam have been looking round for digs for me and Lucy, but haven't come up with anything yet. Her mam's got a spare room, but she couldn't take both of us. I'm just hoping a place turns up quick, or I'll end up doing something I don't want to, and that's doing Ruby an injury.'

'If it helps, I'll have Lucy until something turns up,' Aggie said. 'Then yer could take the room that this Kate's mother's got. It probably wouldn't be for long, so I'm sure Lucy wouldn't mind. I mean, yer could see her nearly every day. There's nothing to stop yer coming home whenever yer've got the time, it's still your house.'

'I couldn't do that to Lucy. Besides, Ruby would give yer a dog's life. You have no idea just how bad she can be. She'd torment the life out of yer.'

'Oh no, she wouldn't, lad! I'm more than a match for that

little madam. If she knocked on me door once, she'd never do it again unless she wanted me boot up her backside.'

'Yer wouldn't have to worry on that score, Bob,' Irene said. 'I don't think Ruby would fancy a set-to with me. I'd skin her alive for what she's done to you and Lucy.'

'I couldn't leave Lucy, it would break my heart. She's never had a mother to speak of, and if I walked out on her it would scar her for life.'

'Don't be daft, it would only be for a few weeks. We get on fine together and it would be like a little holiday for her.' Aggie had it all worked out in her head. 'Besides, instead of looking for digs for the two of yer, why don't yer try and get a little house around here? That would mean we wouldn't lose our friends, and neither would you or Lucy.'

'And how would I furnish this house, Aggie? I'll have to pay the rent on the house I've got now, and pay me digs. I won't have much over, and it takes a lot of money to furnish a house.'

'Not if yer take yer furniture with yer. It's you what owns the bleedin' stuff! Just leave the queer one a bed, table and chair. Let her fend for herself.'

'Why don't yer let Lucy decide?' Irene said. 'At least wait until yer ask her thoughts on the matter.'

'Ooh, aye, she'll be home any minute.' Aggie pressed her hands on the wooden arms of her chair and pushed herself up. 'I'd better stand at the door and watch out for her.'

'No need, Aggie,' Bob said. 'Yer can bet yer sweet life she won't go straight home, not after last night. She'll call here first.'

And Bob was proved right ten minutes later when Aggie opened the door to Lucy. 'Come on in, sweetheart, we've been waiting for yer.'

Lucy made straight for her father. 'Are yer all right, Dad? She didn't scratch yer or hurt yer, did she?'

'No, pet, I'm fine.' Bob reached for her two hands and held them in his. 'A bit tired, perhaps, but that's about all.'

'Yer should have seen me mam last night,' Lucy looked over at the two women, 'it was awful. She was screaming and shouting her head off, using bad words. And she was punching me dad with her two fists, saying terrible things to him. She had no right to do that because he never did nothing.' The girl's emotions were running high. Concern for her father was uppermost in her mind, but anger wasn't far behind. 'I want yer to leave, Dad, 'cos I'm afraid she might do something really bad to yer when ye're asleep or something. She's wicked is me mam, and when she's had too much to drink yer never know what she'll do. I want yer to go 'cos I'm frightened for yer.'

'It's not that easy, pet. We have nowhere to go.'

Irene decided to step in. She too was afraid that one day Ruby might go too far. After hearing her last night it was easy to believe she was capable of anything. 'Yer dad knows someone who's got one bedroom, but it wouldn't be enough for both of yer. Aggie has suggested that yer dad takes that room, and you could stay here with her until something comes up where yer can be together.'

There was determination in the shaking of Lucy's head. 'No, I'll stay at home. You take that room, Dad, but I'm not moving. I'm not frightened of me mam, so I'll stay there until yer come back again.'

'Lucy, love, there's no way I'll ever come back to that house once I leave. It'll have to be a clean break.'

In her mind, Lucy didn't agree. She had this feeling that one day her mother would leave, and she and her dad would be back together in their own home. If there was any justice in the world, that's what should happen. But she thought it was wise to keep her thoughts to herself. 'Okay, Dad, we'll do as yer say. If you've got the offer of lodgings, then take it while yer've got the chance. If yer let it go, yer might be ages finding somewhere else. But I'll stay at home until yer've found a place for us to be together.'

'Yer can come here, sweetheart,' Aggie said. 'I'd love to

have yer, yer'd be company for me.'

'Thanks, Mrs Aggie, but I'd rather stay put. Yer see, that's my home, and I'm not letting me mam drive me away from it.'

The three adults exchanged surprised glances. Lucy was showing a strength and determination she'd never shown before. And each of them knew that if they talked to her until they were blue in the face, they wouldn't change her mind. Aggie was silently applauding the girl for standing firm. For the old woman still stood by the prediction she'd made – that Bob would one day find true happiness. And she'd never thought his happiness would be anywhere else but in his own little house. 'I'd give it a try, Bob, if that's what the girl wants. After all, me and Irene would always be close at hand.'

Lucy slipped her arm through Bob's and squeezed. 'Yer see, Dad, I wouldn't come to no harm with all me friends around. In fact, Mrs Aggie and Mrs Pollard will be sick of the sight of me before long.'

'That's something that will never happen, sunshine,' Irene said. 'I could take a lot of you without ever getting fed up.' She cast her eyes on Bob, who looked as though he didn't know what to do for the best. 'Give it a go, Bob, and see how it works out. After all, it's not as though yer'll never see each other again.'

'I'll tell yer what. It's Saturday tomorrow, me last morning shift. And you haven't got to go to school, pet, so we could go together to see what this room's like. And to find out what sort of a landlady I'd have. I believe some of them can be real strict. Mind you, if she's anything like her daughter she'll suit me fine.'

'Ooh, yeah, I'd like that, Dad.'

'I'll come home and get changed, 'cos I've got to make a good impression, haven't I? Then we'll pay the lady a visit.'

'Can we come?' Aggie asked. 'Me and Irene would like to meet this Kate.'

'I don't think so, Aggie. Some other time perhaps. If I turned up with you two, the woman would think I couldn't look after meself.'

'Is the lady who's going to be yer landlady called Kate, Dad?'

'No, pet, I don't know the lady's name. Kate is her daughter.'

Chapter Twenty-Three

'I'm not half nervous, Dad, me tummy's turning over.' Lucy was walking along Stanley Road with her father, their joined hands swinging between them. 'And me teeth are chattering like mad.'

'Yer'll be all right, pet. The woman I work with, Kate, said she'd try and be there with her daughter. She's the same age as you, so yer'll have someone to talk to.' Bob stopped at the end of a side street and checked the name sign on the wall. 'Primrose Street, this is it. Now we need to look for number twenty-three.'

Lucy pulled on his hand. 'Dad, I think that woman's waving to us.'

A smile crossed Bob's face when he saw Kate standing on the pavement outside a house about eight doors away. 'That's the woman I work with, pet, the one I was telling yer about.'

'Ooh, er, me nerves have gone mad.'

'After the first two minutes yer'll be wondering what yer were worried about.' Bob put his arm across her shoulders and coaxed her along. 'Kate, this is me daughter, Lucy.'

'Oh, I've heard a lot about you. Yer dad's always talking about yer.' Kate held out her hand. 'It's nice to meet yer at last.'

Lucy liked her on sight. The smile was so warm and friendly it calmed her nerves, and the chattering of her teeth slowed down. She gripped the outstretched hand. 'I'm very pleased to meet yer, Mrs Kate.'

'Come inside and meet me daughter, Iris. And me mam, who's been polishing the furniture so hard she's nearly worn it away. It didn't need cleaning 'cos she keeps it like a new pin, but she's a real fussy boots. As soon as I told her yer were coming, out came her mobcap and her polish and dusters. Plus loads of elbow grease.'

Bob held his daughter's hand tightly as they stepped into the tiny hall, then into the living room. He was feeling a bit nervous himself, but not for the world would he let Lucy see. In the two seconds it took for the older woman to leave her chair, his eyes had taken stock of the room. It reminded him of Aggie's. Spotlessly clean and tidy, yet homely. A room where a speck of dust would love to settle and make itself comfortable, but wasn't allowed to.

'Bob, this is me mam, Nellie Carson.'

'It's nice to meet yer, Mrs Carson.' Bob smiled at the small, stocky woman whose hair was steel grey and had a natural wave. He could see where Kate got her looks from, they were very alike. 'I hope yer didn't go to any trouble on my behalf.'

'Not at all, lad! I've only been up since the crack of dawn slaving away with me mop and bucket and me dusters.' There was a twinkle in the hazel eyes. 'I hope yer didn't stand on me step on yer way in, 'cos that got the scrubbing of its life at seven this morning.'

Bob rolled his eyes. 'Oh dear, I might have done.'

'Don't take any notice of her, Bob, she's pulling yer leg,' Kate said, giving her mother a fond look. 'Anyway, Mam, this is his daughter, Lucy.'

'Hello, queen. My, ye're a pretty little thing, aren't yer? And there's another pretty girl been waiting to meet yer, but the cat got her tongue all of a sudden and she's hiding in the kitchen.'

'Come on in, Iris,' Kate called. 'Don't be silly.'

'Shall I go out there to her?' Lucy asked. 'She might be

shy.' And without waiting for an answer, she walked on through to the kitchen while the three grown-ups, as though by silent agreement, stood and listened.

'Hiya! I'm Lucy. Me dad said you and me are the same age.'

'Yeah, me mam told me. My name's Iris.'

'That's a lovely name, that is. It must be nice to be called after a flower, and live in a street what's got a flower's name, too.'

'Oh, this is me nan's house, I don't live in this street. Me and me mam don't live far away, though, only two minutes' walk.'

'What school do yer go to, Iris?'

Three faces grinned. 'They'll be all right now,' Nellie said. 'We'll leave them for a while to get to know each other, then I'll put the kettle on. In the meantime, Bob, would yer like to see the bedroom?'

'If it's not too much trouble, Mrs Carson.'

'Call me Nellie, lad, everyone else does.'

Lucy appeared at the kitchen door. 'Can I call yer Mrs Nellie, please?'

'Of course yer can, queen. I'd like that.'

'Yer see, yer remind me of one of the neighbours in our street. I call her Mrs Aggie, and she's one of me very best friends.'

'Well, seeing as yer've privileged me by calling me Mrs Nellie, perhaps you and me can become very best friends.'

'Yeah, I'd like that.' Lucy grinned. 'I'll go and talk to Iris while me dad looks at the bedroom.' My father would be well looked after here, she thought. They're nice, kind people and they'd take good care of him until he can come home again. 'I'm sure he'll like it.' With that she disappeared into the kitchen and the two girls could be heard chattering away in good style.

'I'll stay down here,' Kate said, knowing she would feel embarrassed if Bob decided to take the room and asked what the weekly charge was. 'It's not a big room and three in there would be a crowd.'

'Come on, lad.' Nellie jerked her head. 'Yer'll have to be patient 'cos me legs are not as young as yours, and the stairs are narrow and steep.'

She gripped the side bannister with both hands and pulled herself up each stair. When she reached the landing she stood for a moment to get her breath back. 'This is the room, lad.' She threw open one of the two doors and waved Bob inside. 'It's nothing to write home about, but it's any port in a storm, eh?'

There was a small, iron single bed with wooden headboards facing the door. To the side of it was a tallboy, and behind the door a single wardrobe. The furniture was old but so highly polished you could see your face in it. It was easy to see it had been tended over the years with loving care. 'It's just the job, Nellie,' Bob said. 'Just what I wanted.'

'I haven't got enough bedding, I'm afraid, but Kate said she'll help me out.'

'There's no need,' Bob told her. 'I can bring a pair of sheets, a blanket and a pillow with me. And a couple of pillowslips. So we'll manage all right.'

Nellie looked at him through narrowed eyes. 'Kate's told me a bit about yer. She said yer've been having a bad time.'

'That's putting it mildly. My life's been hell for years now, but recently my wife has stepped over the boundary of decency and I can't accept that.'

'I should bleedin' well think not!' Nellie put a hand over her mouth. 'I'm sorry, lad, I don't usually swear. Not in front of visitors, anyway. Our Kate would have been mortified if she'd been here and heard that.'

'Then we won't tell her, eh? Anyway, that's nothing to what I'm used to. My wife can't open her mouth without cursing and blaspheming.' Bob gazed around the room once more. 'Can I ask how much a week it'll be?'

'D'yer want full board? Breakfast, carry-out and dinner?'

'I don't want yer to be put to too much trouble, Nellie, not on my account. If I can have the room, I'll fend for meself for food. I know yer help Kate a lot, so yer've got yer work cut out as it is, without me adding to it.'

'Don't be daft, lad! What's a couple of rounds of toast in the morning? And if I'm making a pan of stew, one extra won't make no matter.' Nellie cupped her chin in a hand and looked thoughtful. 'How about eight shillings a week, all found? That's yer bed, food and washing.'

Bob shook his head. 'That's not enough. Yer'd be out of pocket.'

'Not on yer life I wouldn't. I'm not daft, lad, I know what I'm doing. I get me dolly tub out every Monday, but it's hardly worth the effort with the few things I've got to wash. So it'll cost me nothing to throw yours in as well. And Kate will tell yer I'm very good in the kitchen. I can make a dinner out of practically nothing. So I'll be making a few bob on yer, lad, and I'll be able to get blind drunk every night.'

Bob chuckled. Kate was always talking about her mother, so he knew more about her than she thought. 'So, yer like a drink, do yer?'

'Aye, I do that, lad, and yer can't beat it. A nice cup of strong tea with two sugars in. Best drink in the world.' Nellie studied him for a brief moment. He was handsome all right, just as Kate said he was. And she knew enough about people to know the man who was standing in her bedroom, who she hoped was going to be her lodger, was decent through and through. 'Well, are my terms acceptable to yer, Mr Mellor?'

'More than acceptable, Mrs Carson. When can I move in?'

'Whenever yer like. Apart from a bit of bedding which yer said yer could bring, the room's ready for yer.'

'Would tomorrow be too soon? I'm off work now until I start afternoon shifts on Monday, so I'd have all day tomorrow to bring me bits and pieces and settle in. That's if it's all right with you?'

'It's fine by me.' Nellie wondered whether to mention what

she was thinking or leave well alone. But Bob didn't look the sort to get offended, so she said, 'Yer could kill two birds with one stone, if yer did that. Kate said yer'd like some advice off Howard – well, him and Audrey will be here tomorrow afternoon so yer could have a word with him yerself. They come for tea every Sunday.'

'Wouldn't that look a bit cheeky? First I ask Kate for help, then you, and now this Howard is being dragged into me problems.'

'If he can help yer, he will. He's a lovely bloke, is Howard. Speaks frightfully far back, like, but yer can't blame him for that. It was the way he was brought up.' Nellie made her way to the top of the stairs. 'Let's go down and tell Kate the news. I know she'll be on pins.'

Kate was sitting on the couch with her hands folded on her knees. When her mother told her it was all fixed up for the next day, her mouth turned up at the corners in the gentle smile that Bob looked forward to seeing every day as he faced her across the canteen table. 'I'm very glad for yer, Bob.'

'And I'm very grateful to you, Kate, and to yer mother. I think I've really hopped in lucky.' Bob glanced towards the kitchen where he could hear the two young girls still nattering away. 'Lucy, will yer come in, please?'

There was some hurried whispering, then Lucy came in leading Kate's daughter. 'This is Iris, Dad, and she's dead shy.'

Bob looked at the girl who was the same height and build as his daughter. He was expecting to see some resemblance to Kate, but there was none. Iris had long blonde hair and deep blue eyes. Then Bob remembered the day they'd been talking about Kate's dead husband, and she'd told him her daughter was the spitting image of her father. 'Hello, Iris, I'm very pleased to meet yer. You and me will be seeing a lot of each other, because I'm coming to live with yer nan.'

Lucy flung her arms around his waist. 'Yer've taken the

room, Dad? Ooh, I don't know whether to laugh or cry. I'm glad yer've got somewhere as nice as this to live, but I'm not half going to miss yer. Promise me yer'll come and see me as often as yer can.'

'I will, pet.' Bob stroked her hair. 'Except when I'm on afternoon shift, I'll see yer every day, I promise.'

'Yer can come here as often as yer like to see yer dad, queen,' Nellie said. 'The door will always be open for yer.'

Kate beckoned to her daughter to come and sit beside her on the couch. She put her arm across the girl's shoulders. 'I'm sure Iris would like yer to come, wouldn't yer, sweetheart?'

Iris smiled for the first time. 'I've already given Lucy me address and she's going to come and see me. We leave school on the same day, yer know, Mam. And when we start work we're going to the pictures together.'

Lucy brushed a tear away. It was all right trying to be brave and say she didn't mind her dad leaving home, but she did mind, very much. She wasn't going to say so, though, because that would upset him. 'And me friend Rhoda's coming with us.'

Bob put a finger under his daughter's chin and raised her face. 'Yer mustn't give any addresses to Rhoda, pet. I wouldn't want a certain person to know where I'm living.'

'I understand that, Dad. Rhoda's me best friend and I love the bones of her. But I know she can't keep anything to herself. She opens her mouth and lets it all out, whether yer like it or lump it.'

Bob happened to glance at Iris as the girl smiled. She may have inherited her father's looks, he thought, but that smile is definitely from her mother. 'Rhoda's a smashing girl and a good friend to have, love, but for the time being don't breathe a word to anyone.'

'What time can I expect yer tomorrow, then Bob?' Nellie asked. 'Shall I peel an extra spud and yer can have yer dinner here?'

Bob was dreading the next couple of hours. He had to tell Ruby he was leaving and knew she'd be like a raving lunatic. Especially when he told her she'd have to find a job to keep herself. But if he could get away early in the morning it would mean tonight would be the last time he'd have to listen to her screaming and her bawdy language. 'I would like that very much, Nellie, as long as it's not too much trouble.'

'Kate and Iris will be here for their dinner, so as I've said, lad, all I'll have to do is put another couple of potatoes in the roasting tin.'

Bob could sense Lucy looking up into his face and he asked himself if he could go through with this. Could he leave his beloved daughter with a woman who wasn't in her right mind? Then he asked himself what the alternative was. There wasn't one, not for the time being. But he'd move heaven and earth now to find a place where they could be together. 'Thanks, Nellie, ye're an angel.'

'Oh, these are not wings on me back, lad, they're me shoulders what have rounded with old age. I've got a halo somewhere, though, but I couldn't put me hand on it just this minute. I'll give me drawers a clean-out one day and find it to show yer.'

Lucy's titter turned into a giggle. 'Ye're just like Mrs Aggie. I'm going to tell her all about yer next time I see her.'

'Don't tell her about the halo, Lucy,' Iris said, getting into the spirit of things. 'It's only a piece of tinsel I put on me nan's head last Christmas.'

Nellie wagged her head from side to side. 'Did yer have to go and give the game away, Iris? I think I'd make a good angel.'

'Yer would, Nellie, yer certainly would.' Bob picked up Lucy's hand. 'We'll have to go, pet. I've got some unpleasant business to attend to and the sooner I get it over with, the better.'

Kate, with her daughter and mother, followed them to the

door. 'I hope everything goes all right for yer, Bob. We'll see yer tomorrow.'

'Yes, Kate, I'll see yer all tomorrow.'

After they'd walked a few steps, Bob and Lucy turned around to see the trio still watching them. They exchanged waves then carried on walking, Bob's arm over his daughter's shoulder.

'They're really nice people, Dad. Mrs Nellie will take good care of yer.'

'Yes, I know, pet. But I'm not happy leaving you at home. Why don't yer stay with Mrs Aggie until I sort something out?'

'No, Dad, I'm staying at home. Everything will work out fine, you'll see. I'll be all right and it's not going to be for that long.'

Bob sighed as his eyes went heavenwards. Please God, let that be true.

It was when they turned into their street that Bob said, 'Listen, pet, I'm going to knock and ask Mrs Pollard if she'll give yer a bite to eat and let yer stay there until I call for yer. I've got to tell yer mam I'm leaving tomorrow and I'm expecting her to create blue murder. I don't want you to have to go through that, ye're best staying out of it.'

'I'd rather come with yer, Dad. If she takes off on yer I can always help.'

'No! As far as yer mother's concerned, yer know nothing. Yer weren't with me this afternoon, and you haven't a clue where I'm going to live. Otherwise she'll be on yer back all the time and yer'll get no peace. Believe me, pet, it's the only way.'

'Okay, Dad, I'll do as yer say. If she asks, I'll tell her I've been in Rhoda's all afternoon playing cards.'

Irene answered their knock and held the door wide. 'Come in.'

'I won't come right in, Irene, I'll just step in the hall.' Bob pulled the door to behind them so anyone passing couldn't hear what was being said. 'I've been to see that room I told yer about, with Kate's mam. And I've taken it – I'm moving in tomorrow. But I wondered if yer'd do us a favour and have Lucy for an hour or two? I'm going in now to tell Ruby I'm leaving and I don't want anyone there when I do it.'

Irene put a protective arm across Lucy's shoulder. 'Of course she can stay. We're having a late tea so she can have something to eat with us.'

'Thanks, Irene, ye're a pal. I'll bring yer up-to-date with everything when I come back. Ruby's bound to go out, I'm certain of that. Me leaving home isn't going to make a blind bit of difference to her enjoyment. I've got a few things to tell her that she won't like, and I'm expecting verbal and physical abuse, but it won't stop her gallivanting. I'll lay odds she's got a heavy date and she'll be out of the house before eight o'clock.'

'We'll see yer later, then. And don't worry about Lucy, we'll look after her.' Irene reached to open the door. 'Go and get it over with, Bob, and good luck.'

Lucy grabbed his arm. 'Dad, yer know what me mam's like when she gets into one of her tempers – she lets fly with her hands and feet. Don't just stand there and let her get away with it, like yer always do, 'cos she could really hurt yer.'

'Don't worry, pet.' Bob bent to kiss her cheek. 'The days of me just standing there and letting her use me as a punch-bag are over. I'll see yer at eight o'clock and I promise I'll be all in one piece.'

Ruby turned on him as soon as he walked through the door. 'Where the bleedin' hell d'yer think yer've been all afternoon?' And without waiting for an answer, she went on, 'And where's that faggot of a daughter of yours?'

Bob stood by the sideboard, looking a lot calmer than he felt. He weighed his wife up, taking in the best dress, the heavy make-up and the cheap smell. All ready for a night out and annoyed that he'd had the nerve to keep her waiting. 'Lucy is probably with Rhoda, or even next door. Then again, she could be with Mrs Aggie. I really don't know. I do know where I've been though, if you interested.'

Ruby sneered. 'That'll be the day, when I'm interested in anything *you* do.'

'Oh, I think yer might just be interested in this. I've been looking at some lodgings and I've found a place to suit me. I'm moving out of here tomorrow.'

She looked at him as though he'd gone crazy. 'Pull the other one, yer stupid bugger. If yer think yer can put the wind up me by coming out with daft things like that, well, ye're sadly mistaken. And I haven't got time to listen to a load of rubbish, I'm going out. I haven't made yer no dinner, yer can see to it yer bleedin' self.'

'Ye're not setting foot outside this room until I've told yer what I intend doing. Then yer can't say I didn't warn yer. I am moving out of here tomorrow, into digs. Lucy will be staying until I can find suitable accommodation for both of us. I will pay the rent on this house for the time being, seeing as my name is on the rent book. But I'll not be giving you the money, I'll pay it into the office.'

Ruby was beginning to realise he wasn't joking. Still she wasn't worried. It was good riddance as far as she was concerned. 'As long as I get me housekeeping I couldn't give a sod where yer go. Let some other poor bugger put up with yer miserable gob for a change.'

'Ah, but yer won't be getting any housekeeping.' Bob leaned his elbows on the sideboard and told himself he needn't feel pity for this woman who had ruined not only his life, but their daughter's. He'd given her more than enough chances to change, but she chose not to. 'If you want to eat, light the gas or have a fire, then yer must find yerself a job to pay for them because I am certainly not. And of course there's yer ciggie money, the make-up, the magazines and the nights out with yer mates. In future, if yer want them, then yer must work for them. I've kept yer long enough.'

Ruby still didn't believe this of the man who had let her walk all over him since the day they got married. He wouldn't have the nerve to do it. 'If yer are leaving, which I couldn't care less about, yer'll still have to give me housekeeping. A man's got to keep his wife, that's the law.'

'Not an adulterous wife, Ruby. Adultery is against the law and grounds for a divorce. And that is something I'll be setting in motion very soon.'

'What about Lucy, eh? What about yer dearly beloved daughter? Is she supposed to live on bleedin' fresh air?'

'I haven't had time to work that out yet. But yer've had this week's housekeeping which includes the money for her keep. I'll pay for Lucy after that, but it won't be to you. I won't be handing you a penny.'

It was then Ruby went for him. 'You bastard! You bleedin' bastard!' Her hands were outstretched, her palms towards him and her nails on a line with his face. If he hadn't been alert, his face would have been scratched to ribbons.

Bob made a grab for both her wrists and pushed her arms high, while pressing her backwards towards the couch. Her rage was such she fought with superhuman strength and it took Bob all his time to keep her pinned down. All the time she was screaming like a woman possessed. 'I'll get yer for this, yer bleedin' bastard. Yer can't do this to me and expect to get away with it. Yer'll live to regret this, yer swine.' And so it went on and on. 'I'll find yer, no matter how far away yer go. I'll go down to yer works and tell all yer mates about yer, you see if I don't.'

'Don't threaten me, Ruby. You are the last person anyone will believe when I tell them exactly why I'm leaving. Yer'll get no sympathy from my mates, I can assure yer. And if ye're still intending to go out tonight, I suggest yer stop slobbering because yer lipstick is all smudged. I don't think yer'd like yer fancy-man to see yer like this, would yer?'

This incensed Ruby and she lashed out with a foot,

catching Bob on his shin. And when he let out a sharp cry of pain, she laughed hysterically. 'Hurt yer, did it?' Again her foot came out, but Bob was prepared and stepped back, managing to keep his grip on her wrists.

'I'm going to give yer one last warning, Ruby, and yer'd do well to listen. If yer don't stop this right now, I'll be down to the rent office on Monday and tell them I'm leaving. And seeing as I'm the tenant, you would be evicted and find yerself without a roof over yer head. If that happens, yer'll have no one to blame but yerself. And the warning stays in place even when I'm gone. If yer give Lucy a hard time I won't hesitate to have yer put out.'

If looks could kill, Bob would have been dead on the spot. But the expression in her eyes was the only opposition Ruby put up. Whether he would ever carry out his threat, or if his words were just hot air, she wasn't prepared to take a chance. But she remained defiant to the end. 'Let go of me hands, I want to get ready to go out and meet me friends.'

After releasing her hands, Bob pulled a chair from the table and sat down. He was a bundle of nerves. It wasn't in his nature to threaten, but there was no other way of doing it. 'I'll be sleeping on the couch tonight. And if yer come home drunk, full of Dutch courage and bravado, don't bother trying to get in this room because I'll have a chair behind the door so yer can't open it.'

Ruby picked up her bag and left the room without a word. And Bob stayed where he was until, fifteen minutes later, he heard her coming down the stairs then the front door close behind her. Only then did he start putting his plans into action. He rooted out an old battered suitcase from under the stairs, put it on the couch and opened the lid. It was as old as the hills and smelt musty, but there was nothing else, so needs must when the devil drives, he thought. He took a pair of sheets and two pillowslips from the cupboard in the recess and laid them on the bottom of the case before gathering his belongings together. There wasn't much, just his clothes, razor and overalls. And when he'd finished, he looked down with sadness. 'Not much to show after working for twenty-five years,' he said as he closed the lid. 'Me mother would turn in her grave if she saw me now.'

Bob looked around to see if he'd forgotten anything, then took the stairs two at a time to the bedroom. He stripped a blanket off the bed and put a pillow under his arm. All he had to do in the morning was wrap the pillow in the blanket, pick up his case and walk away. The thought gave him no pleasure. It wasn't easy to walk away from a house that had been his home for nearly twenty years. He remembered the day he'd moved in with his new bride, looking forward to a life of happiness. And the day Lucy had been born, in this very room, he thought there was nothing he could wish for that he didn't have. Little did he know then what the future held in store for him. If he had known, would he have acted differently? Would he have been stricter with Ruby? No, he knew he wouldn't. It wasn't in his nature to lay the law down, not to the woman he'd married. And when he finally did wake up to reality, the rot had set in and it was too late. Too late for him, too late for his beloved daughter, and too late for Ruby to change.

Bob sighed deeply as he made his way downstairs. He'd made the break now and nothing would alter that. Better to have few possessions and be happy, than live a life of misery.

Aggie was firmly settled in Irene's fireside chair when Bob arrived. She noted his pale face and haunted eyes and her heart went out to him. But she was wise enough to know sympathy was the last thing he needed now. 'I know ye're thinking I'm a nosy old cow, Bob, but I didn't want to hear all yer news secondhand. And I'm not nosy, lad, it's because I care what happens to yer; we all do.'

George motioned for Bob to sit on the couch. 'Park yer carcass, mate. Have yer had anything to eat?'

Bob shook his head. 'No, but I'm not hungry. Me tummy's

too upset to eat.' Before sitting down, he crossed to where Lucy was sitting at the table, facing Jack and Greg. He bent to kiss her. 'All right, pet?'

'Never mind me, Dad. Are *you* all right?'

'Yes, I'm all right, love.' Bob dropped wearily on to the couch. 'But I wouldn't like to go through that again for all the money in the world.'

'We could hear me mam shouting and I was worried,' Lucy said. 'Did she take off on yer like she always does?'

Irene stepped in before Bob could answer. 'No questions yet until yer dad's had something to eat. I'll do yer a poached egg on toast, Bob, it'll fill a hole. Yer can't go on with an empty tummy, it's not good for yer.'

When Irene bustled out to the kitchen, George asked, 'Are yer coming for a pint later?'

'I could do with one. In fact, I could do with half-a-dozen. As long as it's all right for Lucy to stay here till we get back?'

'Of course it is!' Greg said, with feeling. 'We're going to have a game of cards and it wouldn't be the same without Lucy.'

'And don't forget,' Lucy reminded him, 'yer mam said Rhoda could come over as well.'

'Yeah, well, that's all right. She's not so bad once yer get to know her.'

Jack, in his role of a grown-up working man, looked over at Bob. 'Yer don't have to worry about Lucy, Mr Mellor. We're all going to watch out for her.'

Irene came in carrying a plate and knife and fork. 'Move away from the table, lads, while Mr Mellor tucks into this. The kettle's on the boil so it'll be tea all round in five minutes.'

Bob didn't think he was hungry, but the toast was a lovely golden brown and the egg lightly cooked and runny, just as he liked. The plate was empty in no time. 'By, that was good, Irene. Just what the doctor ordered.'

'Yer needed it, sunshine – a grown man like you can't go without food. Now the tea's ready so we'll all sit quietly and drink it, while Bob tells us as much as he wants to. And before he starts I hope I don't have to remind yer that not one word leaves this room. When Rhoda comes, I don't want to hear a peep out of yer. Have yer got that?'

Greg pulled a comical face. 'Mam, when Rhoda's here no one can get a word in edgeways. She never stops talking. After she's been, me mouth's set from lack of use and I have to exercise it when I go to bed.'

'That's one of Rhoda's good points, sunshine. She's the only one I know who can shut you up.' Irene lifted a finger for silence. 'Now let's hear what Mr Mellor has to say.'

It wasn't a word for word account, because Bob wouldn't use bad language in front of the children. He told them of his terms for Ruby being allowed to stay in the house, and his threats. All the time he was talking, Aggie was nodding her head in agreement. If she'd been in her rocking chair it would have been going like the clappers.

'Good for you,' George said when Bob had finished. 'I still think ye're a fool for not throwing Ruby out, but that's your business. It's always easy to tell someone else what to do when, in their position, yer might do exactly the same yerself.'

'It won't be for long, Mr Pollard,' Lucy said. 'I bet any money me dad will be back home again soon.'

'Don't be banking on that, pet,' Bob said. ''Cos it's not going to happen.'

Aggie tutted. 'Leave the girl be. She could be right for all yer know. Don't forget, God moves in mysterious ways, His wonders to perform.'

'I'll go along with that,' Irene said, giving Bob a look that told him he shouldn't rob his daughter of her dreams.

'Me too!' Jack was gazing at Lucy's pretty face. 'I don't want Lucy ever to move away from next door.'

'Me neither,' Greg said. 'She's like a sister to us.'

Lucy tilted her head and looked at her father. 'Yer see, Dad, there's so many people wishing for it, it's bound to come true.'

'Then I hope you're all right and I'm wrong, pet. Yer see, I don't want to leave all me friends any more than you do.'

George pushed himself from his chair. 'I need something to whet me whistle. Let's go and get that pint, mate. It might be the last one we have together for a while.'

'Don't you believe it.' Bob smiled at his daughter when he saw her face drop at George's words. 'Yer'll be seeing as much of me as yer ever have.'

Bob woke up at seven the next morning, but didn't stir from the couch. It was far too early to be up and about, particularly as he didn't want to make a noise. He'd said a tearful goodbye to Lucy last night, promising faithfully he'd come as often as he could. It was heart-breaking and he didn't want to put her, or himself through that again. She usually got up on a Sunday between nine and half past, so he wanted to be away by then. Ruby never saw daylight before eleven, not after a night out drinking, so there was no fear of having to face her. He'd heard her come in last night and was waiting for her to try the door, but she'd made her way straight up the stairs.

It was eight o'clock when Bob put his pillow in the middle of the blanket and folded the sides over. He left them on the couch, with the case beside them, while he went into the kitchen to get a good wash down in the sink. Then he made himself a pot of tea and two rounds of bread and jam before donning his best clothes. He'd brushed his suit down and polished his shoes last night, wanting to make a good impression on his new landlady. So now he was all ready to leave. He'd go the back way, so he wouldn't be heard.

Halfway down the entry, Bob stopped. He was filled with despair and hopelessness. There didn't seem to be any light at the end of the tunnel. He was a man who'd worked since the day he left school at fourteen, had never asked for much from life, yet he was sneaking down a back entry like a thief in the night, with all his worldly goods in a battered suitcase and a blanket. He felt like sitting down on the cobbled stones and crying his heart out. But he couldn't afford that luxury, not now. Perhaps in bed tonight.

Nellie opened the door with a smile on her face. 'I've had the kettle on the hob for the last hour, so the tea will be up in no time.'

'Thanks, Nellie.' If she only knew I've walked all the way here to pass the time, she'd go mad. But I didn't like knocking on her door at nine in the morning. 'I could just go a cuppa.'

'Throw yer things on the bed for now, I'll help yer make it up later.'

When they were facing each other across the table, Nellie could clearly see the pain in Bob's eyes. It was naked, there for all to see. 'It's not easy, is it, lad?'

He was afraid to speak because the lump in his throat was growing so big it hurt. He was trying to keep his emotions in check but they didn't want to be bottled up, they wanted to be free. 'No, Nellie, it's not easy.' A lone tear trickled down his cheek and he wiped it away. 'I'm sorry, I can't – I can't . . .' He covered his face with his hands as sobs shook his body. Then he pushed his chair back, and in a voice thick with unshed tears, he said, 'I'd better go upstairs. Yer must wonder what sort of man I am for crying like a baby.'

Nellie rounded the table in a trice. 'Stay where yer are, lad. Yer don't want to be sitting on yer own with yer head filled with all sorts. Talk about it and get it out of yer system. And cry as much as yer want, 'cos I wouldn't think yer were much of a man if yer couldn't cry over what's happened to you and yer daughter. Yer've had yer whole life turned upside down; no one expects yer to walk round with a permanent smile on yer face.'

So Bob talked and cried as he unburdened himself, while

Nellie listened. She said very little, only to cluck sympathetically when he said he couldn't get the picture of Lucy out of his mind. She asked no questions, didn't pry. And it was then that a bond was cemented between Bob and his landlady.

Chapter Twenty-Four

Nellie said Kate and her daughter usually arrived between twelve and half-past, and as the clock ticked towards the hour of midday Bob began to get jittery. He'd been for a walk to buy a Sunday paper, hoping the fresh air would take away some of the redness from his eyes. He'd feel so stupid if Kate knew he'd been crying. But he had to admit his tears had eased the throbbing in his head and he was thinking more clearly. He would be eternally grateful to Nellie for her patience and understanding. When he'd knocked on her door he'd been at the lowest point in his life. He felt so useless and helpless. But in a kindly way, she'd told him to snap out of it. Feeling sorry for himself wouldn't get him anywhere, she'd said. He had to start thinking of making a new and happy life for himself and Lucy. And her words had worked wonders. He now felt able to start planning for the future.

When the knock came, Bob quickly folded the paper. 'Shall I go, Nellie?'

'If yer would, lad, 'cos I'm just turning the spuds in the roasting tin.'

Bob opened the door and raised his brows. 'Can I help you?'

'Go on, yer daft nit.' Kate smiled as she let Iris walk ahead of her. 'Been here five minutes and yer've taken over already?'

'If only I was that domineering, Kate, I wouldn't be in the mess I'm in now.'

She smiled up into his face. 'I don't like domineering men.'

'I'm glad about that, Kate,' Bob said as he closed the door and followed her into the living room. 'At least someone doesn't think I'm a spineless idiot.'

Kate crossed to her mother to give her a hug. 'How's the new lodger, Mam? Is he behaving himself?'

'No complaints so far, queen.'

'Me nan's been telling yer some of her funny stories, hasn't she, Mr Mellor?' Iris asked with a grin.

Bob was at a loss. 'Funny stories?'

'I know she has! I can tell yer've been laughing 'cos yer eyes are all red.'

'Now listen to me, sweetheart,' Nellie said, hitching up her bosom before smoothing her pinny. 'I've got funny stories for young girls like yerself, and I've got funny stories for grown ups. And the ones I've been telling Mr Mellor are not for young ears, so don't be pestering him.'

'Okay, Nan.' Iris clamped her lips and narrowed her eyes as she gazed at Bob. 'Your Lucy calls me nan Mrs Nellie. And she said there's a woman in your street she calls Mrs Aggie. Is that right?'

'Yes, that's right, love.'

'Well, can I call you Mr Bob, then?'

Kate wagged a finger. 'Don't be so forward, Iris.'

'She's not being forward, Kate, she's being straight.' Bob smiled at the girl. 'I'd be very happy for yer to call me Mr Bob.'

'D'yer think I could go and see this Mrs Aggie? Lucy said she's very funny.'

'Ask yer mam to take yer one day. Aggie would be delighted.'

'Ooh, will yer, Mam, please?'

Kate looked flustered. 'We'll see, but I'm not making any promises.'

Once again Nellie's bosom was hitched. 'I'll go with them.

This Mrs Aggie seems right up my street. Next time yer see her, ask if it's all right. And tell her if she hasn't got enough cups to go round, I'll bring some with me.'

Bob chuckled. 'Aggie's got a son who goes away to sea, and he's always bringing her things back from foreign countries. I bet she's got more cups than the Kardomah.'

Iris was hopping from one foot to the other. 'Lucy told me about Mrs Aggie's son what goes away to sea. She said he's dead funny, like his mam. And his name's Mr Titch.'

Nellie could smell the dinner which, if it wasn't served soon, would be ruined. And she prided herself on her cooking. 'Will yer all sit down, please, ye're making the place look untidy. Except you, Iris, you can set the table.'

'I'll give yer a hand with the dinner, Mam,' Kate said. 'Yer've got an extra one today.'

'I can count, queen.' Nellie jerked her head in disgust. 'I haven't lost me bleedin' marbles yet.' She wrinkled her nose. 'Sorry, queen, it slipped out. On a Sunday, too. And in front of a stranger. Oh dear, oh dear, oh dear, whatever next?' She was chuckling as she made her way to the kitchen. 'I don't need any help, Kate, you keep Bob company. But for crying out loud park yer backside when ye're doing it.'

'What would yer do with her?' Kate smiled as she took a seat on the couch while Bob sat in the fireside chair which Nellie had said was his for as long as he stayed with her. 'Yer never know what she's going to come out with next.'

'That's the beauty of her, isn't it, Kate? Yer know exactly where yer are with her. She'll never go behind yer back to say what she thinks about yer.'

'I know that, Bob, and I love the bones of her. I don't know what I'd have done without her the last few years. She was my rock to cling to when things were so rough I never thought I'd make it.'

In the kitchen, Nellie had a secret smile on her face as she jabbed a fork in a roast potato. Kate had had a hard time since her husband died. She had no friends, no social life.

Just bed and work, the same old monotonous routine every week. She idolised her daughter, but she couldn't burden young Iris with her heartache and problems. She needed someone mature to talk to, someone who had known sadness in their own lives. Now Bob had come along and Nellie thought they'd be good for each other.

'Kate said yer were a good cook, Nellie, but I never expected yer to be *so* good. That dinner wouldn't have been out of place at Buckingham Palace.' Bob licked his lips and rubbed his tummy. 'It was delicious.'

Nellie looked as pleased as Punch. 'I'm glad yer enjoyed it, lad. I hope yer've left a bit of room for some rice pudding?'

'I'll not say no, Nellie, even though me trousers are tight now.' It was a long time since Bob had been offered a sweet after his dinner. Ruby bought as little food as possible. She said she couldn't afford it on the money he gave her, but Nellie seemed to manage, even though she must be living on a pittance. 'Don't think yer have to cook special for me, Nellie, 'cos I'm the easiest person in the world to feed. Yer can't afford to be giving me meals like this every day.'

'If I can afford it, lad, then yer'll get a decent meal. If I'm hard-up, yer'll be getting conny-onny butties put in front of yer.'

Kate clicked her tongue on the roof of her mouth. 'Take no notice of her, Bob. Me mam would go mad if she had a man in the house and couldn't feed him properly. We don't go short because we share. When I'm on mornings and nights, and every Sunday, me and Iris have our dinner round here, so I share the cost with me mam. And I've got to say she's a wizard in the kitchen. She can make a dinner out of practically nothing.'

Nellie was lapping up the praise. 'Well, queen, as I've told yer, there's them what can, and there's them what can't.'

'I've learned that the hard way, I'm afraid.' Bob looked

across at Kate, but carried on talking to her mother. 'D'yer know what, Nellie? Until yesterday, I didn't know yer daughter had legs. I've only ever seen her from the waist up, across the canteen table.'

Iris began to giggle and it was like a knife turning in Bob's heart. She sounded so like Lucy. What was his daughter doing now? How had Ruby been towards her? He wouldn't be able to see her all week, with working afternoons and her being at school. The earliest would be Saturday morning before he went to work, and it seemed a lifetime away.

Nellie had seen Bob's expression change, and although she wasn't to know the cause of it, she did know his mind was elsewhere. 'Come on, Kate, let's get these dirty dishes out,' she said briskly. 'The rice pudding will be going dry in the oven.'

Kate was on pins. Her sister and her husband were due any minute, and she was worried about how to approach Howard regarding advice for Bob, when Audrey, her mam and Iris were sitting there listening. That was the worst of two-up two-down houses, there was never any privacy. She had been hoping to have a word with her brother-in-law before he met Bob, but things had happened so quickly it hadn't been possible. Catching her mother's eye, Kate nodded towards the kitchen.

'I'll start getting the dishes out, ready for tea,' Nellie said. 'Come and give us a hand, will yer, Kate?'

In the kitchen they went into a huddle. 'Mam, I'm going to the corner of the street to wait for Howard's car. I want to explain about Bob, 'cos yer can't expect the poor man to pour his heart out in front of strangers. It won't be so bad if Howard is put in the picture, and our Audrey knows what's going on. So I'm going to tell a little fib to get out, is that okay?'

'Of course it is, queen. Yer can tell a ruddy big whopper for all I care. You do what yer think best.'

Kate knew she couldn't look someone in the eye and tell a lie without blushing, so she made sure it didn't happen by walking straight through from the kitchen into the hall. 'I've got a horrible feeling I've come out and left the stove on,' she called over her shoulder. 'I'm just nipping home to put me mind at rest.'

'I'll go for yer, Mam,' Iris offered. 'I can run there and back.'

'No, it's all right, love.' Kate was gripping the round handle ready for pulling the door shut. 'I'll be back before yer know I'm gone.' She waved as she passed the window, then pelted it hell for leather to the bottom of the street. Howard always came this way in his little black four-seater car, so she wouldn't miss him. He'd caused quite a stir the first time he came in it, because cars were a rare sight in their street. The neighbours who didn't come out to gape, peeped through their curtains. And the kids would have swarmed all over it if Howard hadn't told them off in his posh voice.

When the car turned the corner Kate stepped into the gutter and waved both hands for it to stop. Howard wound the window down, a look of concern on his rather serious face. 'Is there something wrong, Kate?'

'No, I just want a word with yer before yer go in the house.' Kate opened the back door and scrambled on to the seat. She found her sister twisted round and glaring at her.

'You frightened the life out of me, I thought something terrible had happened to Mother.' Audrey's Liverpool accent had all but disappeared since she'd met Howard. The only time she allowed it to come to the fore was when she was angry and couldn't help herself. But she wasn't a snob. Born and raised in this narrow cobbled street, she never pretended to be anything she wasn't. Two years younger than Kate, she loved her family and was always there to help. So far her marriage was a childless one, but whether that was due to nature, or a deliberate decision taken by her and Howard, she had never said. And her time for childbearing was running out. 'What is it, Kate, that's so important we can't talk in front of Mother?'

'Oh, we can talk in front of me mam 'cos she knows all about it. But I want Howard to help a friend of mine with some advice and he's in the house with me mam and Iris. Would yer mind if I tell yer the whole story, very quickly, so you and Howard don't get it in bits and pieces?'

'Is this person a good friend of yours, Kate?' Howard asked.

Kate nodded. 'He's one hell of a nice feller and he desperately needs advice.'

'Then carry on, Kate.'

Kate told them everything, from the first time Bob had sat facing her in the canteen. And she ended by saying, 'Me mam offered him her spare room and he moved in yesterday.'

Audrey took a deep breath then blew it out. 'Well, that's some story. Are yer sure it's all true, Kate, or is he taking advantage?'

'It's true – I've seen his hand scratched to pieces where his wife had gone for him. He's a quiet man, and he's put up with it for years. Anyway, Audrey, would yer say me mam was a good judge of character?'

Her sister nodded. 'I've never known her to be wrong.'

'And he wants advice on how to go about obtaining a divorce?' Howard tapped his fingers on the steering wheel. 'It's a messy business, divorce, and it can take years.'

'Would yer talk to him about it?' Kate was gripping the back of his seat. 'He's only a working bloke and doesn't know where to turn.'

'I'll be only too happy to help a friend of yours, Kate. But isn't it going to be rather difficult in your mother's house? I would need to ask very personal questions which the man would find hard to answer in front of Iris, Audrey and yourself.'

'I know, but I can't think of any other way.' Kate sighed. 'When yer meet him, and yer've been in his company for a while, yer'll understand why I want to help him.'

Howard was conscious of the fact that this was the first time Kate had ever asked him or Audrey for help. Several times they'd offered to help out financially when they knew she must have been desperate, but each time she'd smiled and said she could manage. It was because of this he was prompted to say, 'Leave it to me, Kate, I'll think of something.'

Bob was nervous at first because he thought solicitors were a cut above the rest, like teachers and doctors. But he soon learned that even if the King came to Nellie's house he would be expected to muck in like everybody else. She didn't stand on ceremony, did Mrs Carson. Howard might be a solicitor, and she thought the world of him, but when he was in her house he was treated the same as everyone else. Even when her tongue slipped and a swearword came out, she merely pulled a comical face and said, 'That came out of its own accord, our Audrey. I had nothing to do with it, so don't be giving me daggers.'

Bob happened to catch Howard's eyes and they exchanged smiles. 'Yer've been blessed with a good mother-in-law, Howard.'

'Yes, I know. And I appreciate it. It was only when I met Nellie that I realised my teacher at school had taught me only half of the English language. It was Nellie who taught me the rest. I can't use it, of course, but I'm indebted to her for widening my horizon.'

'One good turn deserves another then, don't yer think?' Nellie asked. 'Yer can come and help me get the plates ready for the tea while Iris sets the table.'

'Mother!' Audrey looked horrified. 'That's not a job for Howard! Kate and I will help you with the dishes, like we always do.'

But Howard knew there must be a motive behind the very strange, and unusual request. 'Stay where you are, Audrey, this should be interesting. I think your mother wants to widen my horizon still further.' So in his immaculate navy-blue pinstripe suit, pure white shirt with stiff collar and a plain grey tie secured with a gold tie-pin, the man who spent most of his life behind a desk followed his mother-in-law into the tiny kitchen.

'Well, I declare,' Audrey said, then lapsed into her Liverpool accent. 'What's got into me mam? I mean, it's not funny, is it?'

'Don't worry, he won't reign long,' Kate told her. 'I'll give him two minutes at the most.'

Bob took the chance to study the sisters. They had the same facial features, but there the resemblance ended. Audrey looked every inch the woman about town. Her clothes were expensive and fashionable and she carried them well. Her stockings were pure silk and her black court shoes boasted a two-inch heel. And her hair was perfectly waved, as though she'd just come from the hairdresser's.

'Oh, get back inside,' Nellie said, pushing Howard into the room. 'Ye're about as much use as our cat.'

'Mother, you haven't got a cat.'

'I know that, queen. But if I did have it would be more use in the kitchen than Howard. At least I could kick it out of me way if it got under me feet.'

It was while they were sitting around the table having their tea that the sisters understood the reason for their mother's behaviour. With an angelic expression on her face, Nellie asked, 'Have yer seen Howard's car, Bob?'

'I've glimpsed it through the window, that's all.'

'Yer'll have to get him to show it to yer after. It's his pride and joy, that car. He'd take it to bed with him at night if he could, wouldn't yer, lad?'

Howard was of medium height and build, his complexion was pale through spending his working life in a stuffy office, and his hair was receding at the temples. But when he smiled he looked almost boyish and showed a set of strong white teeth. 'Before you drop me in deep water, Mother-in-law, may I say the car is my *second* pride and joy. Audrey is my first. And the car has a perfectly good garage to sleep in, where it's safe and warm.'

'It told yer that, did it?'

Iris giggled. 'It would do if it could talk, wouldn't it, Uncle Howard?'

'It can talk, dear. Except you wouldn't understand it because it's more of a splutter. On a very cold morning, when I switch the engine on, it splutters to tell me it would much prefer to stay in the garage than venture out into the cold.'

'Now I've heard everything.' Nellie placed her palms on the table. 'You go and show this amazing talking car to Bob, while me and the girls clear away and wash up.'

The men had only been out of the room for five minutes when Howard came back in. 'I'm taking Bob for a short spin. We won't be long.'

Nellie had a very satisfied smile on her face when she winked at Kate. Everything had worked out a treat.

Howard had stopped the car in a quiet spot and for half an hour he'd asked questions and listened carefully to Bob's answers. 'Your wife admitted to adultery, then?'

'Oh yes, she sounded quite proud of herself.'

'Do you know the name of the man she's involved with?'

Bob shook his head. 'I never asked because I knew she wouldn't tell the truth. All I know is she goes out two or three nights a week and usually comes home the worse for drink.'

'It would help if you could find out the man's name in case she denies it. Proof is needed rather than hearsay. I can set the wheels in motion if you'll come down to my office one day and fill in some forms. But I must warn you, it's a very lengthy process.'

Bob flushed with embarrassment. 'Howard, can we leave it for a short while? Yer see, I'm going to be strapped for cash with paying the rent on the house, my daughter's keep and my board and lodgings. I will start saving as much as I can, though, because I need to sort life out for meself and Lucy. I won't be happy until I've got her with me again and Ruby's out of our life for good. So if yer'll give me an idea of what I'll need to start the ball rolling, I'll make an appointment to see you as soon as I've got the cash.'

'You're a friend of Kate's, and I promised I would help you.' Howard smiled. 'She said when I met you I'd know you were a decent man, and she was right. So I'll get the proceedings under way without you coming in to my office. I'll ask Kate to bring you to my home one night and I'll have the forms there ready for you to fill in. That way you will be making the application yourself and my partners need not be involved. There may be a legal charge in the future, but we'll cross that hurdle when we come to it. At least you will have set the ball rolling.'

Bob hung his head. 'I don't know what to say. I seem to be asking so much and giving nothing in return. Kate has been a good friend to me, always ready to listen. Nellie has taken me, a complete stranger, into her home and is treating me like one of the family. And now you are offering to help a man yer have never seen in yer life before.'

Howard could see Bob was choked with emotion and hastened to say, 'Bob, Kate needed someone she could confide in, and from what I hear she found that someone in you. And she really wants to help you. As for Nellie, she's told me she's over the moon having you to keep her company. Her actual words were, and I quote, "He's the nicest and most handsome bleedin' lodger I've ever had. The neighbours will be green with envy." '

Bob raised his head and smiled. 'I can just see her saying that.'

'So, because these ladies are very dear to me, I want to make them happy by doing what I can for you. I'll get Kate to bring you to my home one night, when it's convenient for you, and we'll start writing a new chapter to your life.'

★ ★ ★

Four weeks later, Aggie was sitting in her rocking chair when she heard the key turn in the lock. She jumped to her feet and was standing by the table when Titch came into the room. 'Did yer call to Olive's first?'

Titch dropped his seaman's bag on the floor. 'Now, Ma, I might be living in hope that Olive will become me intended, but until we're married it'll always be you I come to first.'

Aggie didn't know where to start. 'Yer'll never believe what's been happening while yer've been away.'

'Ma, don't I even get me welcome-home kiss?'

'Oh, I'm sorry, son, I'm all hot and bothered.' She put her arms around him and kissed his cheek. 'Bob's left home.'

'What!' Titch held her away from him. 'What did yer say?'

'I said Bob's left home. Four weeks ago it was. He found out Ruby had been sleeping with some bloke and he packed his bags and left. He's down here nearly every day, though, except when he's on afternoons. And Lucy goes to visit him. He's got good digs with the mother of that Kate he told us about. And he's started divorce proceedings as well.'

'Whoa, there, Ma, I can't keep up with yer. Sit down and start at the very beginning.'

'I'll make yer a cup of tea first. I can't have yer coming home without even a drink ready for yer. The dinner's in the oven, it'll be an hour yet.'

Titch leaned forward and rested his elbows on his legs, a cup and saucer in his hands. 'I can't believe it. Yer mean Ruby actually admitted she'd been sleeping with a bloke?'

Aggie nodded. 'As bold as brass. And to see her walking up the street with her nose in the air – well, it's enough to make yer sick. She's had to take a part-time job in some laundry 'cos, although Bob pays the rent, he won't give her any money.'

'And what about Lucy in all this? Doesn't Ruby take it out on her?'

'Lucy has most of her meals in Irene's. Bob pays her a few

shillings a week. And Ruby daren't look sideways at Lucy because Bob threatened to stop paying the rent and she'd be turfed out. Besides, the girl isn't the least bit frightened of her mother now. She's turned out to be very strong-willed. She's got it into her head that her dad will come home again one day, so she's making sure the house is kept right for when he does.'

'Bob won't come back – he'd never be able to lift his head up if he did.'

'No, he won't come back if Ruby's there, Lucy knows that. She's of the opinion that her mother will up sticks and leave. And before yer say anything, I think the girl's right. I don't know why I think that, it's just a gut feeling I've got. I pray to God every night that we're both right. The whole sorry mess is taking its toll on Bob. He's lost weight and his face is haggard. He's pining for his daughter, which is only natural.'

'Fancy me being away and missing all this.' Titch shook his head slowly. 'I'm sorry for Bob, he's as nice a feller as yer'll ever meet. And yer say he's already put in for a divorce?'

Aggie nodded. 'Someone related to Kate is a solicitor and he's helped him with all the rigmarole. He wanted to know if Bob knew the name of the bloke Ruby's been sleeping with, but no one knows that.'

'It shouldn't be too hard to find out. Someone could follow her one night. If it's down on the divorce papers that she's been unfaithful to Bob, he could be asked to prove it.'

Aggie sighed as she got to her feet. 'What a bleedin' awful life. I'll be really upset if Bob and Lucy go to live miles away, I wouldn't half miss them.' She sniffed up. 'I'll get the dinner moving 'cos I suppose ye're dying to see Olive.'

'Yer could say that, Ma, seeing as she's me intended. And I'd like to see young Lucy before the day's out.'

'She calls in here every afternoon after school, before she goes to Irene's, so ye're bound to see her. Anyway, if she knows ye're home yer won't need to go looking for her, she'll find you.'

Olive opened the door and held her arms wide. 'Where've yer been all this time? I saw yer passing the window hours ago and I've been sitting on the edge of the chair waiting for yer.'

Titch held her tight, his kisses warm and eager. 'Oh, this feels so good, sweetheart. I've really missed yer this trip. I only intended to call at me ma's for five minutes, but she had so much news for me I couldn't get away.'

Olive took his hand and led him through to the living room. 'Yer've heard all about Bob's troubles, then?'

'Yeah, I only wish I'd been here.' Titch sat close to her on the couch and slipped an arm across her shoulders. 'Not that I could have done anything to prevent what happened, but at least I could have lent him an ear.'

'From what I've heard, Kate and her mother are marvellous with him. Lucy is quite taken with them. She said Mrs Nellie, that's what she calls Kate's mother, is just like yer ma. Always ready to put the kettle on and forever telling jokes.'

'I'm concerned for Lucy. I wouldn't have thought it safe to leave her in the house with Ruby. The woman's as mad as a hatter – she's capable of anything.'

'Don't worry about Lucy, she's being watched over night and day. She has her dinner with Irene and stays to play cards until it's her bedtime. Steve goes there after he's visited yer ma, and when it's time for her to go home, he takes her and waits until she's at the top of the stairs before closing the door. Then the Pollard boys take over. They sleep in the back room and it's only a thin wall separating them from Lucy's. Jack's told her to give a knock at the least sign of trouble and they'll be with her in seconds.' Olive chuckled. 'Greg said he'd come waving a rolling pin. Luckily, Bob gave Irene a spare key just in case, so they'd have no trouble getting in.'

'To think a woman would cause so much heartache to her husband and family.' Titch sounded disgusted. 'And me ma said she walks round as bold as brass.'

'Oh, yeah! She goes out nearly every night, and she doesn't bother using the back entry now. She walks up the street as though she owns it. Dolled up to the nines and enough make-up on to sink a ship.'

'She'll get what's coming to her one of these days, mark my words. And I hope that day comes sooner rather than later.' Titch removed his arm to take her hands in his. 'Anyway, my love, tell me about how much yer've missed me.'

'What? And give yer a big head! Not likely.' Olive nestled closer and kissed his cheek. 'I've missed yer more than yer'll ever know, love.'

Titch blew little puffs of breath into her ear. 'Have yer made up yer mind when ye're going to marry me, then?'

The reply came quickly. 'In six months' time. That's how long it'll take to save up enough to get the house as I want it, and to buy the clothes to get married in.'

'I've told yer over and over again yer don't have to worry about money, love! I've got enough for everything yer need.'

'And I've told yer over and over that after we get married, yer can keep me. Until then I'll hang on to me pride and independence.'

Titch knew it would serve no purpose to argue. They'd been over this ground dozens of times. 'Have it your own way, love. Six months it is.'

The knock on the door brought a look of surprise to Olive's face. 'I wonder who this can be? Steve's not due in till after half-five.'

'Only one way to find out.' Titch got to his feet. 'I'll go and chase whoever it is away. How dare they interrupt us when I've just got home? Have they no tact?'

When Olive heard him say, 'Hello, sweetheart,' she knew who would be coming through the door clinging to Titch's hand.

'Mrs Aggie said if I didn't get an answer the first time, I

wasn't to knock again 'cos yer'd be kissing and cuddling.' Lucy's face was one big smile. 'And she said I wasn't to stay long 'cos yer had to make up for lost time.'

'Oh, did she now?' Titch put his hand around her waist and lifted her from the floor. Smiling up into her face, he asked, 'And how's my girl, then?'

'I'm all right, Mr Titch, but I don't half miss me dad. Mrs Aggie told yer what happened, didn't she?'

'Yes, she did, sweetheart, and I'm very sorry. But don't be too unhappy – look on the bright side and tell yerself it won't be for long.'

'We keep telling her that,' Olive said. 'And I know something that will make her very happy. But ye're to keep it to yerself, Lucy, until Titch tells Mrs Aggie himself.'

Lucy's face was agog. 'Cross my heart, Mrs Fletcher, I won't say a dickie-bird.'

Olive glanced at Titch. 'Do you want to tell her, or shall I?'

'I'm sure you'll do it much better than I would, love.'

'Ye're getting married.' Lucy could barely contain herself as she clapped her hands. 'Oh, I bet that's what it is.'

'Yes, we are getting married, but not for another six months.' Olive wanted to give this young girl something to look forward to. 'What I wanted to tell yer, or rather to ask yer, is would yer like to be me bridesmaid?'

Titch felt like hugging Olive for being so caring and thoughtful, but Lucy beat him to it. She threw herself at Steve's mother, tears of happiness rolling down her cheeks. 'Oh yes, yes, yes! And thank you, thank you, thank you! Wait until I tell me dad, he'll be over the moon. I've never been to a wedding, never mind being a bridesmaid.'

'I'll tell yer what, sweetheart,' Titch said. 'I'll ask me intended if she'll come with me now to tell me ma. Then yer won't have to keep it to yerself. Yer can tell the whole world if yer like.'

'I wouldn't tell the whole world, Mr Titch. Just everyone in the street and all the girls in me class at school. I'll be that proud there'll be no keeping up with me.'

Titch was feeling excited himself now that arrangements were finally being made. He reached for Olive's hand. 'Let's go and make me ma as happy as Lucy is. I can't wait to see her face.'

Lucy walked between them, her arms linking theirs. 'How long are yer home for, Mr Titch?'

'Only a week, sweetheart.'

Olive brought them to a halt. 'A week! Ye're only on leave for a week?'

'That's the bad news, love. The good news is that I'll only be away a month on the next trip, then it's two weeks' leave.'

Lucy's mind went back to the wedding. 'Six months isn't long, it'll soon pass. And I'll be a working girl by then.'

'It's half-past nine, sunshine, time for you and Rhoda to be going to bed.'

'I won't be able to sleep, I'm that excited.' Lucy began to gather the cards together. 'Your mam is lovely, Steve, for asking me to be her bridesmaid.'

'I've never been a bridesmaid,' Rhoda said. 'D'yer think if I asked her nicely she'd consider having two?'

'No chance.' Steve grinned. 'It's only going to be a quiet wedding.'

'I'd fit in, 'cos I'm only a quiet girl.'

'Just listen to her!' Greg said. 'She gabs more than anyone I know. I bet a pound to a pinch of snuff that she talks in her sleep.'

'She wouldn't be the only one, would she?' Jack winked at Rhoda who was giving his brother daggers. 'You talk in yer sleep every night.'

Irene banged her fist on the table. 'That's it for tonight. Come on, girls, take yerselves off home to bed.'

Jack scraped his chair back. 'I'll see Rhoda to her door while you see to Lucy, Steve.'

George looked up from his paper. 'Remember, no goodnight kisses until the girls have left school.'

'You're awful, Mr Pollard,' Lucy said, giggling. 'But ye're awful in a nice way.' She pecked his cheek before flinging her arms around Irene. 'I'll see yer tomorrow.'

'Goodnight, sunshine. And yer'll make a lovely bridesmaid.'

When Lucy opened her front door, she said to Steve, 'If me mam's not in I won't go straight upstairs, 'cos I want to wash me hands and face.'

'I'll wait here until yer make sure.'

Lucy was back within seconds. 'She's gone out. I'll be all right now, Steve, thanks very much. I'll see yer tomorrow.'

'Okay, but don't forget to knock next door if she comes in and tries anything.'

'I won't. Goodnight, Steve.' Lucy closed the door and made her way through the living room to the kitchen. She had a headache with excitement and a swill in cold water might help shift it. She didn't waste any time because she didn't know when her mother would be in and she didn't fancy coming face to face with Ruby. After what she'd done to her dad, the less she saw of her the better.

Lucy was halfway across the living room when she happened to glance at the fireplace. She stood with her chin in her hand, wondering why she thought it didn't look right. Then it struck her. The carved wooden candlesticks were missing from the mantelpiece. She frowned as she tried to think where they could be. They'd been there this morning before she went to school. Then she spied the bag at the side of her mother's chair. It was a big bag, one her mother took to work with her overall in.

Without thinking, Lucy did something she'd never done before; she lifted the bag on to the chair and moved the newspaper that was spread over the top. And there lay the candlesticks that she knew meant a lot to her dad because they'd belonged to his mother. What on earth were they doing in the bag? Where was her mother taking them? She had no right to move them, they weren't hers. There was only one way to find out, Lucy told herself, feeling very angry, and that was to ask.

Ruby came home at half-ten to find her daughter sat at the table with the candlesticks in front of her. 'What the hell are you doing up at this time, yer little flamer?'

'Waiting to ask yer where yer were taking these.'

'I'm taking them to the pawnshop, yer hard-faced faggot. Now get up them stairs to bed and mind yer own business.'

'It *is* my business. They are not yours to pawn, they belong to me dad.' Lucy got to her feet and picked up the candlesticks. 'I'm taking them upstairs with me so yer can't get yer greedy hands on them.'

'If yer bleedin' father gave me enough to live on, I wouldn't have to pawn anything.'

Lucy wrinkled her nose. 'Yer smell of drink. It's funny how yer can always find the money for that. But if yer take anything out of this house that you haven't paid for, I'll tell me dad on yer.'

There was rage on Ruby's face, but she was crafty enough to know how far she could go. 'One of these days I'll give yer the hiding of yer bleedin' life, yer snotty-nosed little faggot. It's something I should have done years ago.'

'There's lots of things yer should have done years ago, but yer didn't and it's too late now. I used to pray that yer'd love me like a mother should, but I don't bother any more. That's because I've realised yer don't know what the word love means. I suppose I should pity yer, really, but I can't even bring meself to do that.' Lucy turned on her heels and left the room.

Chapter Twenty-Five

Lucy jumped down from the step of Rhoda's house then spun around to gaze up at her friend with a face that was full of excitement and joy. It had been a very hectic but happy day for both of them. It was their last day at school and they'd been allowed time off to go for an interview at Vernons Football Pools. To their delight they'd both been taken on and were to start work on Monday morning at the football pools office in Linacre Lane.

'I can't get over it, can you?' Lucy asked, hugging herself. 'I bet my dad will be as glad as your mam was that we're going to be working together.'

'Is yer dad coming down tonight?'

'Yeah, he said he'd come to see how I got on. He'll be dead pleased for me.'

'No sign of him finding a place for both of yer?' Rhoda pulled a face. 'I don't know why I keep asking yer that, because I hope he never does. Especially now when we can travel to work together.'

'He hasn't found a place he can afford. With needing two bedrooms, the people he's been to see are asking a lot of money.' Lucy looked down at the ground and kicked the step with the toe of her shoe. 'I don't tell me dad because he gets upset about it, but I don't want to leave here. I thought me mam would have moved out by now, but there's no sign of it. She seems quite happy because she's got the house, no one to answer to, and can come and go as she pleases.'

Rhoda always said what was in her mind, and she grinned now at what she was thinking. 'With a bit of luck she'll fall and break a leg and end up in hospital. And with a lot of luck she'll manage to break both legs. Then she'd be in hospital for ages and ages.'

Lucy tutted. 'Ye're terrible, you are, Rhoda Fleming.'

'No, kid, I'm just honest. And yer know what they say about honesty being the best policy.'

'That's not always the case,' Lucy said. 'Anyway, I'm going to tell Mrs Aggie the news before I go to the Pollards' for me tea. Me dad won't be here until about eight o'clock, so I'm going home after tea to sort me clothes out. I'll be wearing me skirt and blouse to start work in, so I want to make sure they're cleaned and pressed over the weekend.'

'Don't forget yer'll need long stockings.' Rhoda was nodding her head. 'If yer turn up in short socks I'll pretend I'm not with yer.'

'Okay, okay! I'll ask me dad for the money tonight. And I'm going now 'cos I can't wait to see Mrs Aggie's face when I tell her I've got a job. She'll be over the moon for me.'

Rhoda watched her friend running across the cobbled street and shouted after her, 'Er, yer wouldn't forget to tell her I've got a job too, would yer? I don't see why you should be allowed to hog all the limelight.'

Lucy turned after knocking on Aggie's door. 'Keep yer hair on, I won't forget.'

Rhoda wanted to make sure all her neighbours knew her good news, so at the top of her voice, she shouted, 'Talking about hair, Lucy, don't forget I want yer to do mine for when we start work on Monday.'

Lucy was grinning when Aggie opened the door. 'What am I going to do with that mate of mine, Mrs Aggie? She'll get me hanged one of these days.'

'I heard what she said, sweetheart. The interview went well, then, did it?'

'The interview was the most terrifying thing I've ever gone

through in me life, Mrs Aggie. We had to go to the main office for it. You know, the one in Aintree, near the Old Roan? There were about ten girls there beside me and Rhoda, and they all looked as frightened as I felt. Our names were called out one at a time, and by the time my turn came, me legs were shaking so much I thought I'd never be able to stand on them. I had to follow this woman to an office, and there was a small, oldish woman seated behind a desk. I was told her name was Miss Jones. She didn't half look strict, and I never thought I'd get taken on 'cos I was stammering and stuttering. She asked me all about meself after she'd read the reference I'd got off the headmistress, and she wrote everything down in this big book. Not a smile crossed her face the whole time, and I nearly fell off the chair when she said I could start on Monday in the Linacre Lane branch.'

'I'm made up for yer, sweetheart. And Rhoda got taken on too, I gather?'

Lucy nodded. 'Yeah, we'll be able to travel to work together every day. I'm glad she'll be with me, I won't feel so shy.'

'Wait until yer dad knows, sweetheart, he'll be so proud of yer.'

'Yeah, it's a bit of good news for him for a change. And I'm not bigheaded, Mrs Aggie, but I've got to say I'm dead proud of meself. I'll be a working girl earning a wage. I won't get any money the first week, like, 'cos it's a week in hand, but I will the week after. And that'll make things a bit easier for me dad.'

'Are yer going to tell yer mam?'

'Not likely! She'll want to take me wages off me. She's bound to find out – I mean, I can't go out every morning, come home at night, and her not know what's going on. But she won't hear it from me, nor will she get a penny of me money. I'll hand it all over to me dad and he can give me whatever pocket money he can afford.' Lucy hunched her shoulders and pulled a face. 'I've got to cadge off him tonight when he comes. Rhoda said if I turn up on Monday in short socks, she'll disown me.'

Aggie chuckled. 'She would say that. Sounds as hard as nails sometimes, but her heart's in the right place. I bet if you knock on her door on Monday morning in short socks, by the time yer get to Vernons yer'll both be wearing one stocking and one short sock each.'

Lucy could see it in her mind's eye and she giggled. 'I wouldn't put anything past my mate, she's got the nerve for anything.' The giggle got louder until it filled the room. 'D'yer know what the daft nit told me? That Miss Jones was as nice as pie with her and gave her a cup of tea and a biscuit. Having seen Miss Jones, I can see the funny side, 'cos the woman never cracked her face.'

'At least she gave yer the job, sweetheart. Better that than someone who smiled sweetly at yer and said she was sorry but yer weren't suitable.'

'Ye're right, Mrs Aggie.' Lucy couldn't sit still, she was so highly strung. 'I've got a lot to look forward to, haven't I? Starting me first job and earning money, then in a couple of months I'm to be a bridesmaid. I'm a very lucky girl.'

'No more than yer deserve, sweetheart. Yer can start making up for lost time now.'

'If only me dad could come back home, then I wouldn't ask for anything else in the whole world. I still miss him terrible, Mrs Aggie. I know I see him often, but it's not the same as him living in the house. We're not like a family any more.'

'Let's hope yer dad has a run of good luck, like you have. Yer know what they say about things happening in threes.' Aggie began to rock slowly, thinking that with the number of prayers she'd said, something good should have come along for Bob by now. Either God hadn't heard her prayers or He had a lot on His plate. Even so, He should give everyone a fair hearing. 'Have yer told Irene yet?'

'No, I'm going there when I leave here. Mr Pollard and

Jack will be in from work then, so I can tell them all at once and get it over with. Otherwise I'll be telling it in dribs and drabs and it'll take all night. And I want to go home before me dad comes so I can look through me clothes and get them ready for Monday.'

Bob always met his daughter in either Aggie's or Irene's. He'd only been back home the once since he left, and that was to pick up a couple of things he'd forgotten to take with him.

'Are yer all right for clothes, sweetheart?' Aggie asked. She would have loved to have bought the girl something as a leaving-school present, but was afraid of upsetting Bob.

'I've got a skirt and blouse, and one dress that'll be suitable. They'll see me through until I can save up for another blouse to change into.' Lucy looked at the clock and scrambled to her feet. 'I'd better go – Mr Pollard and Jack will be home any minute.'

Aggie walked her to the door. 'I'll see yer later, with yer dad. Ta-ra, sweetheart.'

Mealtimes were always noisy at the Pollards', but tonight everyone was talking at once and it was chaotic. It had been the last day at school for Greg, too, and they couldn't get a word in edgeways with him. What he was going to do, and what he wasn't going to do was nobody's business. He had an interview at the woodworks on Monday, and to hear him talk he had no intention of starting on the bottom rung of the ladder, it was a supervisor's job he was after.

Irene put a hand over her ears. 'Will yer all shut up for a minute, me head's splitting with the din ye're making.'

'There's only one person making a din, Mam,' Jack said, jerking his head towards his brother. 'It's talk a bit, here. He's never closed his mouth once since me and me dad came in. He's making more noise than a steam train chugging into Lime Street Station.'

Greg was so happy at never having to go to school again,

nothing would have upset him. No more getting the cane for staring out of the window when he should have been doing his sums, or for answering the teacher back. He wouldn't know he was born without the threat of that blinking cane hanging over him. 'I can remember the day you left school, our Jack, and the day yer wore yer first pair of long kecks. Yer really thought yer were somebody, you did.'

'You'll be in long kecks on Monday, son,' George said. 'So yer can expect to have as much fun poked at yer as Jack did. And I hope ye're man enough to take it in the same spirit he did.'

Greg took that as a compliment. 'I will, Dad. Yer can laugh at me as much as yer like, and I'll laugh with yer.'

'Well, now that's settled to everyone's satisfaction,' Irene said, 'can we hear a bit more about how Lucy's day went?'

So Lucy had the floor to herself without any interruptions. She was very good at imitating people and had them in stitches over Miss Jones. The serious, straight face, the cool voice and the dismissive wave of her hand as she told Lucy, "You may go now." Then came Rhoda's joke about the cosy chat she'd had with the woman who'd interviewed them, and the tea and biscuits she'd been served.

'That's not fair, that,' Greg said, his face unsmiling as he pretended to believe what Lucy had said. 'She shouldn't have given Rhoda tea and not you. Mind you, that Rhoda would talk her way into anything. She was probably given the tea to shut her up.'

'I wish yer wouldn't keep pulling my friend to pieces,' Lucy said. 'She's never done you no harm, so I don't know why yer dislike her.'

'I don't dislike her.' Greg speared the last piece of sausage on his plate and popped it into his mouth. He banged the end of his fork on the table until he'd chewed the sausage sufficiently to be able to speak. 'She's just like the other girls, I suppose. Yer all talk too much and yer love bossing people around. That comes with playing with dolls when yer were kids. Dolls can't answer back, yer see, so girls grow up thinking no one should answer them back.'

'Well, fancy that now!' Irene pinched on her bottom lip. 'I wouldn't have thought of that meself, but I'll put it to the test.' She leaned towards her son and held his eyes. 'Clear the table, Greg, and take the dishes out to the kitchen.'

'Ah, ay, Mam! What's wrong with Lucy or our Jack?'

'This may come as a surprise to yer, sunshine, but I was a little girl once. And I used to play with dolls. So according to your theory, I don't expect to be answered back.'

Lucy giggled. 'Nice one, Mrs Pollard.'

'Yeah, yer've got him stumped there, Mam,' Jack said. 'Look at his face, yer've taken the wind out of his sails.'

'Yer dropped yerself right in it, son,' George said. 'Now take a bit of advice from one who learned the hard way. Never, ever, try and get the better of a woman 'cos yer don't stand a snowball's chance in hell. If she says a thing is black, then agree with her. It could be sky-blue pink with a finny-haddy border, but if she says black, then black it is. That's if yer want an easy life, like. Otherwise she'll come at yer with both guns blazing and yer won't know what hit yer.'

'Ah, yer poor thing, me heart bleeds for yer.' Irene wiped away an imaginary tear. 'Sure there's not a sorrier sight than a henpecked husband.'

Greg had recovered his voice by this time, and his sense of fun. 'Lucy, when you and me get married, yer won't henpeck me, will yer?'

'I won't be henpecking yer, Greg Pollard, 'cos I won't be marrying yer. Any girl what marries you would want her head testing.'

'Too true they would.' Jack nodded. 'He only left school today and he wants to put the banns up to get wed!'

'I don't intend to hang around like you,' Greg said. 'Ye're turned sixteen and haven't even got a girlfriend yet.'

'That's what you think.' Jack tapped the side of his nose. 'I don't tell you everything.'

'I don't blame yer for not telling him anything,' Irene said, 'but I'd expect yer to tell yer mother. Come on, who is she?'

'I'm not telling yer, Mam. All I will say is that she's very pretty and yer'll like her.'

'He's pulling yer leg, Mrs Pollard,' Lucy said, collecting the plates. She didn't want to hear any more. If Jack had a girlfriend then soon everything would change, and she didn't want it to. 'I'll take these out and wash them. Then I want to nip home to get me blouse and skirt. I need to make sure they're all right for Monday.'

'Leave those, I'll do them,' Irene told her. 'You go and get yer skirt and blouse and bring them back here.'

Lucy didn't need telling twice. 'I'll take the key and let meself in. I won't be a matter of minutes 'cos I don't want me mam asking me questions. That's if she's in, of course.'

Lucy stepped into the hall, and as she was taking the key from the lock she thought she heard voices coming from the living room. This was unusual because her mother never had visitors. So instead of going straight upstairs as she'd intended, the girl opened the door of the living room, and became rooted to the spot. There was a strange man sitting in the chair by the fire, and he seemed quite at home with a cigarette in his hand and his long legs crossed.

'Who are you? That's my dad's chair ye're sitting in.'

Ruby had jumped to her feet in surprise. Lucy never came back from the Pollards' until it was time for bed. 'Well, yer dad's not here now, is he? And don't you be so bleedin' impudent, yer little madam.'

'Watch your language, Ruby,' Wally Brown said, before turning his eyes back to Lucy. 'My name's Wally Brown, my dear, and I gather you are Lucy.'

'I don't care what yer name is, yer have no right to be sitting in me dad's chair.' Lucy had taken an instant dislike to him. He was too smarmy for her liking. As Mrs Aggie would say, he was too sweet to be wholesome. And seeing him sitting in her dad's chair was making her feel sick and angry. 'What are yer doing here, anyway?'

'Mind yer own business,' Ruby said, trying to remember not to swear because Wally didn't like it. 'And mind yer manners.'

'She has every right to ask what a strange man is doing in her home,' Wally said, thinking he'd never seen such a beautiful young girl in his life. With those huge green eyes set in a heart-shaped face, topped by the mass of thick, dark glossy curls, she really was a stunner. 'I came to see your mother on some business, that's all. I'll be leaving very shortly.'

Ruby was beside herself with rage. She'd been so sure that she and Wally would have the house to themselves for a couple of hours, now this little faggot had gone and spoilt all her plans. She'd belt her one if it wasn't for Wally. He wouldn't like it and she wouldn't do anything to upset him. He treated her like a slave and she lapped it up. She was obsessed with him.

'I'll say goodbye to yer now then,' Lucy said with as much dignity as she could muster. ''Cos yer'll be gone when I come downstairs in about fifteen minutes.'

'Take no notice of her,' Ruby said, when her daughter's footsteps had died down. 'She can't do anything about it. I'm entitled to have visitors – it is my home.'

'Let's take things slowly, Ruby. You flying off the handle isn't going to help. Of course the girl would get a fright finding a strange man in the house, it's only natural. So I won't come again for a few weeks; we'll use my place as usual. The next time Lucy sees me it won't be such a surprise, and eventually she'll get used to me.'

'Whatever you say, love,' Ruby said meekly. 'Shall I come home with yer now?'

Wally shook his head. He enjoyed the power he had over her. She catered to his every whim and he loved to be the one pulling the strings. 'No, leave it until tomorrow night.' To keep her sweet, he said softly, 'I promise we'll have twice as much fun to make up for tonight.'

When Lucy came downstairs it was to see her mother leafing through a magazine. There was no sign of Wally Brown.

'I'm very proud of yer, pet.' Bob was sitting on the couch, holding his daughter close. 'Mind you, the thought of having a daughter working makes me feel a lot older.'

'Ye're not old.' Lucy smiled into his eyes. 'Ye're just the right age for a dad.'

'Ye're not the only one what's proud of her,' Aggie said, comfortable in the chair she'd claimed off Irene as soon as she'd walked in. 'We're all proud of her.'

'She's had quite an exciting day all round,' Irene said, her bonny face creased in a smile. 'Got her first job, and her first marriage proposal.'

George's deep chuckle ricocheted off the four walls. 'Don't jump out of yer seat, Bob, she turned it down.'

'She won't be getting offered it again, Mr Mellor,' Greg said. 'She didn't only turn me down, she insulted me into the bargain.'

'Try again in about four years, Greg,' Bob told him. 'I'm not parting with her until I have to. And then it'll be under protest.'

Lucy was smiling while this was going on, but her mind was active in another direction. Would she be doing right in telling them about Wally Brown? Or would it cause trouble? Her father was looking so happy she really didn't want to spoil it. But she knew he'd been asked if he knew the name of the man her mother was going with, and told that it would help. So surely it would be wrong not to tell him.

'Dad, would it upset yer if I talked about me mam?'

'Of course it wouldn't, pet. Why, what's she been doing to yer?'

'Well, didn't yer want to know the name of the man she was seeing?'

The room was so silent you could have heard a pin drop. 'What made yer suddenly ask that, Lucy?'

''Cos I know it.'

Five people leaned forward as their eyes widened in surprise. This was definitely not something they expected, and they waited with bated breath.

'How d'yer know it, pet?' Bob asked.

Lucy took a deep breath, hoping she was doing the right thing. 'He was in our house before, and when I asked him who he was he said his name was Wally Brown.' When her father took his arm from around her shoulders and went to stand up, she held him back. 'He's not there now, Dad. He'd gone by the time I came downstairs.'

'Well I never!' Aggie said. 'The bleedin' cheek of him!'

'The cheek of her, yer mean.' Irene ground the words out. 'She must have invited him in. My God, but she's got some nerve.'

'Tell us exactly what happened, love,' Bob asked her quietly. 'I want to know everything he said and what he looked like.'

'He was dressed all right, but he's not nearly as nice-looking as you are, Dad.' Lucy then began at the beginning and repeated everything that had been said. 'And as I told yer, he'd gone when I came downstairs.'

Aggie was rubbing her hands with glee. 'Did yer really tell him he had no right to be there, sweetheart?'

Lucy nodded. 'Well, he didn't, did he, Mrs Aggie? It's me dad's house and me mam can't be asking strange men into it.'

'I'm proud of yer, sunshine,' Irene said. 'I would have loved to have seen your mother's face when you walked in.'

'She would have belted me one if she'd got the chance, I could tell by her face. But she's frightened of upsetting this Wally Brown. He told her to watch her language and she never said a wrong word after that. He's the boss and what he says goes. But he's not nice, Dad. He's one of these smooth-talking fellers, all sweet and honey on the outside. But I wouldn't trust him as far as I could throw him.'

'Then don't have anything to do with him, pet. If he comes again, get out of the house as fast as yer can.' Bob was worried. There were some evil men in the world and he didn't want one of them near his daughter. And this bloke was no saint, he'd been going out with a married woman for God knows how long. 'I'll take yer home later, in case yer mam's got anything to say. But don't worry, I won't start a row. I'm too disgusted to look her in the face, never mind talk to her.'

'Steve usually comes down to take me home, Dad. He'll be here soon.'

'I'll take yer, just for tonight, pet. Then I'll sleep easy in me bed.'

'How come you and Kate come to work together these days, Bob?' Elsie pushed the turban out of her eyes. 'Yer live miles away from each other.'

'We used to, but we don't now.' Bob and Kate had been expecting this and were prepared. 'I've moved in with her family.'

'Go 'way!' Elsie's sandwich was put back in the box. 'Did yer hear that, Peg?'

'I'm all ears, girl. Go on, you're the nosy one, find out what's going on.'

'Oh I will, queen.' Elsie's bosom was hitched and her nose scratched. 'D'yer mean, like, that yer've moved in?'

'That's what I said, Elsie. I'm part of Kate's family now.' Bob didn't care any more that people knew about his marriage break-up. That's why he and Kate had decided to walk to work together instead of splitting up when they got near the factory. It was bound to come out sometime, they couldn't keep it a secret for ever. 'And very comfortable I am, too.'

Never one to mince words, Elsie asked, 'Yer mean ye're living over the brush?'

'What does that mean, Elsie?'

Billy Gleeson didn't know whether this was a legpull or not. It was something he would expect of Elsie, but Bob wasn't one for telling jokes. And he couldn't read anything from Kate's face; she was half-smiling and didn't seem to be uncomfortable with the way the conversation was going. But, nah, she wasn't the type to live tally with a feller. So he waited for Elsie's answer.

Elsie and Peg had their heads together, whispering. 'He doesn't know what living over the brush means, queen, so how else can I put it?'

'Yer'll think of something. Go on, girl, ye're doing fine.'

Elsie racked her brains but couldn't think of any other way to put it. 'Are the pair of yer living in sin?'

'Good heavens, no!' Bob was quite enjoying the exchange. 'How can yer think such a thing? I'm surprised at yer being so bad-minded, Elsie.'

'It was you what said yer'd moved in with Kate's family.' Elsie was getting flustered. 'So don't you be saying I'm bad-minded.'

Peg tapped her on the arm. 'Move over, girl, and let an expert have a go.' She looked across at Bob. 'Are yer living at Kate's, then, Bob?'

'No, Peg, I'm living with her mother. She was kind enough to offer me lodgings when I left home.'

Elsie nearly fell off the chair. 'Ooh, er! Yer've walked out on yer wife, have yer?'

Billy scratched his head. If this was a joke, it was a bloody long one.

'Yes, I walked out on me wife when I discovered she was having an affair with another bloke. I've put up with a lot from her, but that was the last straw.'

'I hope yer gave her a good hiding before yer left, Bob,' Peg said. 'I can't stand women who cheat on their husbands.'

'Yer wouldn't say that if yer got the chance to have a bit on the side with Robert Young, would yer, queen? I remember yer telling me once that if yer were in bed with Robert Young yer wouldn't be lying there counting the cracks in the ceiling.'

Peg chuckled. 'I was just thinking the same thing, girl. Bob's as handsome as Robert Young any day. And he's more available.'

When Elsie jerked her head in one direction, her chins went the other way. 'I've always said yer were man mad, queen, and yer'll get yerself into trouble one of these days.'

Kate spoke for the first time. 'She won't be getting into trouble over Bob, Elsie, 'cos he's spoken for. I saw him first.' Because she was laughing, nobody took her seriously. Quiet Kate, who'd run a mile if a man looked sideways at her.

'Yer wife wants her bumps feeling,' Peg said. 'There's not many fellers as good-looking or as nice as you. But perhaps he's loaded and it's his money she's after.'

'I couldn't tell yer, Peg. He could be a tramp or a millionaire for all I know. He does exist, me wife admitted to sleeping with him, but that's all I know. Oh, and his name's Wally Brown.'

Elsie's elbow slipped and her chin came crashing down on the table, but she was too excited to feel any pain. Pushing herself up and straightening her turban, she squeaked, 'Did yer say his name's Wally Brown?'

Peg put a hand on her arm to silence her. 'What's yer wife like to look at, Bob? Is she fair, dark, redheaded, blonde or what?'

'Nature intended her to be dark, but she's a bottle blonde.'

'Her name wouldn't happen to be Ruby, would it?'

Bob looked puzzled. 'Yeah. How did yer know that?'

'Me and Elsie go out every Saturday night with our fellers. We don't go to the same pub every week 'cos we like a change. But our local is Wally Brown's local, and he's there every Saturday with a blonde called Ruby. Unless it's a million to one coincidence, his Ruby and your Ruby are one and the same person. And I'll tell yer what, Bob, ye're well out of that marriage. Wally Brown's never married, but he didn't need to – he gets all the fun he wants and none of the worry. He's been with more women than you've had hot dinners.'

Bob nodded. 'So yer've seen them together?'

Peg turned to her mate. 'Am I telling the truth, girl?'

'Yes, queen. Thick as thieves they are. Can't keep their hands off each other. And from what I've heard, he doesn't need no cracks in his ceiling.'

'I don't suppose yer happen to know where he lives, do yer? Yer see, I've put in for a divorce on the grounds of my wife's adultery, and his name will be down on the application as co-respondent. It would help if I had his address.'

'I'll have it for yer tomorrow, Bob, without fail. I'm not quite sure of the number of his house and it's no good guessing. I even know his flippin' neighbour! I see her at the shops a couple of times a week and we always have a good natter. She'd tell yer some tales about the queer feller and the women he's had at the house since his mother died.' Peg turned to her mate with some impatience. 'What the hell are yer digging me for? I'll be black and blue tomorrow.'

'What is Wally going down on the application as, queen?'

'Yer mean yer've cracked six of me ribs to ask me that! If yer hadn't sagged off school so often, yer wouldn't need to keep asking me questions. The word is co-respondent.'

'What does that mean, queen?'

Peg sighed. 'It means he's the one what's been having it off with Bob's wife.'

'Why can't they just say that, instead of using big words what no one can understand? I'll have forgotten that by the time I get home.'

Bob smiled across at Kate. They'd been apprehensive about telling their workmates, but it was out in the open now and he felt relieved. And some good had come from it. Tomorrow he'd have the address for Howard.

Lucy and Rhoda were linking arms and laughing as they turned into their street. They'd been working for two months now and loved it. They didn't sit near each other at work, so they always had plenty to talk about on the way home. 'That Vera must get a lot of pocket money to spend on herself,' Rhoda said. 'She reeks of Evening in Paris and has a different coloured nail varnish on every day. Yesterday it was pink, today it was bright red. And she always wears lipstick to match.'

'She's older than us, so she's bound to earn more.' Lucy squeezed her friend's arm. 'Our day will come, kiddo, have patience.'

They came to a halt when Andrew Bentley stepped from his house and barred their path. 'Hello, Lucy. How's the job going?'

'Fine, thank you, Andrew.' The girls moved sideways to walk around him but he moved with them. 'Can we get past, please?'

'I was going to ask if yer'd come to first-house pictures with me one night?'

Lucy shook her head. 'I always go out with Rhoda, but thanks for asking.'

'Surely yer can go without her one night? You're not joined together at the hip or anything.'

'I said no, Andrew, and I meant it. I don't want to go to the pictures with yer.' Lucy tugged on Rhoda's arm and they stepped into the gutter. They'd only gone a few steps when the boy's voice brought them to an abrupt halt.

'I don't know where you get your airs and graces from. You've got nothing to be stuck up about. Your father's left home and your mother is no better than a common prostitute.'

Lucy closed her eyes and froze. But Rhoda moved like a

bullet from a gun. She jumped back on the pavement and laid into Andrew with her fists. 'Don't yer dare talk to my mate like that, you stuck-up, snotty-nosed little pig.'

Steve had turned the corner of the street a minute after the girls and he'd seen Andrew stop them. They seemed to be chatting and he thought nothing of it, until he heard Rhoda shouting as she attacked the boy with both fists flying. Then Steve took to his heels and covered the ground between them in no time. Andrew was bent down and had his arms across his face for protection against the blows that were raining down on him.

'Stop it, Rhoda.' Steve put his arms around her waist and pulled her away. 'What's all this in aid of?'

Andrew straightened up and growled, 'She's mad! Crazy! If she wasn't a girl I'd knock the stuffing out of her.'

'Yer haven't got the guts,' Rhoda said, struggling to get free. Her face red with anger, she twisted her head around. 'Let me go! I'll kill him for what he said to Lucy. No one talks to my friend like that and gets away with it.'

Steve then noticed that Lucy was standing with her back to them, as still as a statue. 'What did yer say to Lucy, Andrew?'

'Nothing! Take no notice of her, she's crazy.' Andrew didn't fancy getting on the wrong side of Steve, he was a big bloke. 'She can't take a joke, that's her trouble.'

'Shall I tell yer his idea of a joke, Steve?' Rhoda said, nearly in tears. 'Because Lucy said she didn't want to go to the pictures with him, he asked her where she got her airs and graces from. She had nothing to be stuck up about because her dad had left home and her mother was a common prostitute.'

Steve stared so hard at Andrew that the boy lowered his head. 'I'll see you later, and what yer said to Lucy yer can repeat to me.'

'You come near me and I'll tell my mother.'

'You won't need to. I intend to have yer mother present when yer repeat what yer said to Lucy. Your mam might be a snob, Andrew, but she's not wicked.' Steve carried Rhoda to where Lucy stood and lowered her to the ground. 'Come on, girls, he's not worth bothering about.' Then he noticed Lucy's silent tears. 'Come on, love, don't let him see he's got to yer.' He gave Rhoda a nod and they placed themselves either side of the girl who was trying hard to stem the tears. And they walked her to Irene's, where they knew there would be two loving arms waiting to hold her.

'I think he should be pulled up over it,' Irene said. 'And his mother should be told. Otherwise, who's to stop him from shouting his mouth off to everyone?'

'I'll have a word with his mother, if yer like, love,' George said. 'The boy needs a ticking off, no doubt about it. They weren't the sort of things yer'd expect to hear from the lips of one so young.'

'I told Andrew I would be calling to see his mam.' Steve was sat on the floor next to the chair Aggie was sitting on. When Lucy hadn't knocked as usual on her way home from work, the old lady had come down to see if there was anything wrong. And she was hopping mad when she heard what had transpired.

'I'd like to take him over me knee and smack his backside so hard he wouldn't be able to sit down for a week.' Aggie looked at Lucy's red, tear-stained face and thought the boy deserved to be hurt as much as he'd hurt her young friend. Still, she didn't agree with what she'd heard. 'But, much as I'd like to give him a hiding, I think it would be far better to just let the matter drop. The whole street would know about it in no time, and yer'd only be filling their mouths. Someone would be bound to mention it to Bob, thinking he'd know, and he'd be very hurt and upset.'

'Mrs Aggie's right. I wouldn't want me dad to know.' Lucy sniffed up. 'Anyway, I should have given him a go-along meself, instead of standing there crying like a baby. I shouldn't have left it to Rhoda to stick up for me. The trouble is, I've been too soft. All me life I've been too soft. But not any more. I'm going to start sticking up for meself – be hard instead of soft. Then the likes of Andrew Bentley, and me mam, won't be able to hurt me.'

Jack and Greg had listened in silence, each thinking that if they ever met Andrew in an entry, he'd come out with two black eyes for the unhappiness he'd brought to the girl who was like a sister to them.

'Oh, don't say that, sunshine!' Irene said. 'We all love yer and don't want yer to change. We wouldn't want the kind, sweet Lucy we know to become hard and bitter.'

'No, we wouldn't.' Jack dared to speak out. 'You just stay as sweet as yer are, Lucy Mellor, or me and our Greg won't play cards with yer no more.'

'There yer have it, sweetheart,' Aggie said. 'Yer've been outvoted.'

'Yer can't change now, love,' George said. 'Not even yer hairstyle.'

'Lucy will never change,' Steve said. 'It isn't in her nature.'

Looking around at the faces who were so dear to her, Lucy asked herself why she should let a little twerp like Andrew Bentley upset her. She had more than he would ever have.

Steve knocked on the Flemings' door on his way home. And when Jessie answered, he looked shy. 'I'm sorry to knock so late, Mrs Fleming. I hope yer don't mind?'

'Not at all, lad, it's only just turned ten.'

'D'yer think I could have a word with Rhoda? That's if she's in.'

'Oh, she's in all right. And calmed down a bit. She was in a right state when she got home, crying and calling that lad from the top of the street fit to burn. Mind you, he was way out of order, saying what he did.'

'Your daughter sorted him out, Mrs Fleming. I think he'll have a few bruises to show for it tomorrow.'

'D'yer want to come in, lad?'

'No, I won't if yer don't mind. Yer see, me mam's on her own.'

'Okay, I'll get her for yer.'

Rhoda looked surprised but pleased. 'If I'd known yer were coming I'd have combed me hair and put some lipstick on. Just my luck to be caught on the hop.'

'I just want to say I think yer were great for sticking up for Lucy the way yer did. Ye're a good friend to her, Rhoda, and I'm glad yer were there when she needed yer.'

'I'll always be there when she needs me, Steve. We've been mates for twelve years now, and we'll carry on being mates all our lives. I know I'm outspoken, even rude at times, but not where Lucy's concerned. I love her to bits.'

'You proved that tonight. She'll tell yer tomorrow how proud she was of yer. And I was proud of yer, too. Anyway, I just wanted to thank yer. I'll be on me way now 'cos me mam will be wondering where I've got to.'

As he turned away, Rhoda stepped down on the pavement and caught his arm. 'I've been wanting to bring this up for years now, but never had the nerve. Remember the time I said I didn't want yer to help me and Lucy because yer were dirty? Well, that wasn't the case at all. I was jealous because it was her yer offered to help and not me. Childish, wasn't it? I've had many a nightmare over it, I can tell yer. But I've got it off me chest now and can face yer with a clear conscience.' She turned and walked back into the house. 'Goodnight, Steve.'

'Goodnight, Rhoda, and thanks again.'

Chapter Twenty-Six

Aggie came in from the yard with a shovelful of coal and was about to carry it through to the living room when she sensed a movement in the hall. 'Oh, my God, someone's broken in.' She put the shovel down on the tiled floor and quickly glanced around for something to use as a weapon. Her eyes lit on the flat iron on the stove and she made a grab for it. 'No one's going to rob from this house if I've got anything to do with it. I'll kill the bugger.'

With the iron held high, she marched into the living room to face Titch coming through the door leading from the hall. 'In the name of God, son, yer frightened the life out of me. I thought yer were a burglar.' She sighed with relief as she placed the iron on the table before giving him a hug and kiss. 'Why didn't yer let me know yer were coming home?'

''Cos I didn't know meself until half an hour before I left the ship. We're only in port for two days, just long enough to unload and load up again. I asked the skipper if I could have the two days off to make all the arrangements for the wedding and he told me to scarper but be back before the ship sails.' Titch pulled a chair out and sat down. 'The banns have to be called for three weeks, so there wouldn't be time if it's left until I come home again.' His grin was that of a young boy. 'This wedding lark isn't as easy as yer think, is it, Ma?'

'It'll all work out, sweetheart, so don't be worrying. It's not going to be a big wedding, not with Olive having been married before, so once yer've seen the priest about having the banns called, there's nothing else for you to do except get yerself a new suit.'

'There's the flowers to think of, and we'll have to have some sort of reception afterwards. I'm not getting hitched without having a bit of a do for me friends.'

'Me and Olive will sort everything out while you're sailing the high seas. When yer get home everything will be organised. Women are much better at this than men. We can have things done while the bleedin' men are still scratching their heads and thinking about it.'

'I've just called into Olive's, and when I said we were going to see the priest tomorrow I could see her nerves go. But when she realised her son would be walking her down the aisle, she was soon happy and smiling. And Steve looked so proud, his face was a joy to behold.'

'Ah, God bless them,' Aggie said, trying not to let him see she was filling up. 'I'm going to have to take half a dozen hankies to this wedding of yours.'

'I've got a problem over me best man, though, Ma. Me two mates are Bob and George. How to ask one without hurting the other?'

Aggie frowned as she pinched on her bottom lip. Then her face lit up. 'I've got it! Yer could put it to them that yer've been agonising over it, not wanting to upset either of them. But with Lucy being a bridesmaid, yer thought it only fair the Pollards should be represented, and you'd be honoured if George would be yer best man. Bob certainly won't get upset 'cos he's so delighted over Lucy. It'll be a big day in the girl's life.'

'Sounds good to me, Ma. That way I don't upset anyone.'

'If yer want to go away with an easy mind, son, why don't yer get it sorted out right away? Bob's in the Pollards' now, so go and get it over and done with.'

'I'll do that, Ma.' Titch left his seat to cup her face in his two hands. 'Yer could make all the arrangements for this wedding standing on yer head, couldn't yer, Agnes McBride?'

'I'll certainly see it all goes off without a hitch, son.' Aggie smiled, and her eyes were full of the love she felt for him. 'It'll be the third happiest day of me life. The first was when I married your dad, the man I adored heart, body and soul. The second was the day you were born. I loved yer from the minute yer were put into my arms, and I've loved yer ever since. Now my life is going to be enriched with a new daughter-in-law and a grandson. There's nothing more I could ask for.'

'Hey, Ma! Yer'd better bring an extra six hankies to the wedding, I think I'm going to need them. I can see me standing at the altar blubbering like a baby.'

'You do, and I'll have yer life! Yer wedding day is one yer'll look back on in later years with fond memories. And one of those memories won't be of you standing there blowing yer nose all through the ceremony.'

'I'd be the talk of the washhouse, would I, Ma?'

'What! The washhouse, the poorhouse and every bleedin' alehouse from here to the Pier Head. Yer'd never be able to show yer face in the street again. And me – well, I'd be that ashamed I'd have to move house.'

Titch chuckled. He'd been a nervous wreck for weeks, thinking of all the things he had to do in a few days. But now he'd calmed down, thanks to his mother. Nothing would go wrong on his wedding day, she'd make sure of that. 'I'd better go and see Bob and the Pollards. That'll be one worry off me mind.'

'Yer'd better put a move on then, son, because Bob sometimes goes for a pint with George.'

Titch was whistling a sea shanty when Irene answered his loud rat-tat on the door. 'Well, I'll be blowed! Aggie never mentioned yer were coming home.'

'She didn't know.' A couple passing on the opposite side of the street turned when Titch let out a roar of laughter. 'She thought there was a burglar in the house and nearly crowned me with the flat iron.'

'Come on in and tell us what we owe this pleasure to.' In the hall, Irene lifted her cheek and said in a loud voice, 'Kiss me out here, so my feller doesn't go all jealous and get a cob on. Yer know what he's like.'

'As long as it's a secret and me intended doesn't find out.'

'I won't tell Olive if you don't tell George.'

'Get in here, woman!' George yelled. 'If there's any kissing to be done, I want to see it's all above board.'

Lucy flung herself at Titch as soon as he entered the room. 'This is a nice surprise, it's lovely to see yer.' She moved back to grin up at him. 'It won't be long now, will it, Mr Titch?'

'No, sweetheart, only about seven weeks.' He smiled a greeting at the eager faces who were waiting for his news. 'The ship's only in port for two days, it's a quick turnaround, and the skipper said I could have the time off to start making arrangements for the wedding. So me and Olive are going to see the priest tomorrow about having the banns read.'

'Ooh, it's all happening now, isn't it?' Irene beamed. 'Is it still at St Anthony's on Scotland Road?'

Titch nodded. 'That's what Olive wants. And Steve is going to give her away.'

'That's just how it should be,' George said. 'I bet the lad's over the moon.'

'I'd say that was the understatement of the year, George. I think he's got seven weeks of sleepless nights in front of him.' Titch told himself to make a start and get it over with. 'I was thinking about me best man, and with you and Bob both being me mates, I didn't know what to do. But I figured that if Lucy was to be bridesmaid, it would be fair to ask George to do me the honour of being me best man.'

'Of course it would!' Bob said. 'And a fine handsome best man he'll be too.'

Titch put a hand to his mouth and gave a slight cough. 'He

hasn't said he would be, yet, Bob. But I can see he's thinking about it.'

George was a big man, but right now he looked twice his size. And the smile on his face was so bright it would have lit up a dark room. 'Yer didn't think for a second I'd refuse, did yer? I'll be highly delighted, and honoured. It's not often I get the chance to show off in me best bib and tucker.'

'Will I be getting a new shirt?' Greg asked, looking pleadingly at his mother.

Irene tutted. 'Yer'd get anyone hanged, you would! Yer haven't been invited to the wedding and it's manners to wait until ye're asked.'

'Ye're all invited, every one of yer,' Titch said. 'As though I'd get married without all of me friends around me.'

Jack was beginning to feel a stir of excitement. He'd never been to a wedding. 'Does that include me, Mr Titch?'

'Most definitely!' Then Titch remembered what Steve had told him about the Andrew Bentley incident, and how Rhoda had rushed to her friend's defence. 'And Lucy can ask her mate if she'd like to come.'

'Oh, I've no need to ask her, Mr Titch, she's always going on about how lucky I am. I'll go over after and ask her.'

'I'm very happy for yer, Titch,' Bob said. 'Yer couldn't have chosen a better woman for yer wife than Olive. She's a lovely lady.'

'I know how lucky I am, Bob.' Bearing in mind Bob's unhappy circumstances, Titch left it at that. 'Anyway, I'm off now. Me and Olive have got a lot of planning to do. We've got a busy day ahead of us tomorrow, then it's back to the ship for me the morning after. I'll let yer know the date and time before I go back, though, because of yer jobs.'

'We'll all fit in with your arrangements, mate,' George said. 'If necessary we'll take the day off. What do you say, Bob?'

'I'd have no problem with that. I can't remember the last time I took a day off, so the boss could hardly complain.'

'What about me and our Greg, Mam?' Jack asked. 'Would we be able to stay off?'

'We've got seven weeks, yet.' Irene kept her face straight. 'That's plenty of time to think of what illness yer can have that'll keep yer off work for a day. Perhaps you can have the measles and Greg the chickenpox.'

'Ah, ay, Mam!' Greg looked disgusted. 'Only little kids have the chickenpox!'

'So they do.' Irene was laughing inside at the expression on his face. 'It'll have to be something a grown up gets, then. I know, you can have a sore throat and Jack can have an upset tummy.'

'Neither of those are as bad as a broken neck,' Titch said. 'And that's what I'll be getting off Olive if I don't put in an appearance pronto.'

'I'll see yer out, mate.' George pushed himself out of the chair. 'Then me and Bob are going for a pint.'

Titch winked at Irene before asking, 'Ay, George, when we're married, d'yer think Olive will let me off the leash now and again to go for a pint with yer?'

'If yer train her properly from the very start.' George nudged his friend towards the door. 'Like I did, with my missus.'

The cushion Irene threw fell well short of the mark. 'Never mind, I'll get him later,' she told Bob. 'He's not getting away with that.'

'Me mam said she'd buy me a new dress.' Rhoda didn't have her mind on the game and she'd already thrown the four of diamonds away before she realised she'd played right into Greg's hands. She watched him snaffle up the card with the look of a victor on his face and shrugged her shoulders. 'If you win this game, Greg Pollard, it won't be because ye're clever, but because I let yer.'

'Because yer talk too much, yer mean?' Greg laid three fours down with great aplomb. 'You and yer flippin' new dress, it's all yer can think about.'

'Oh, aye?' Irene raised her brows. 'So ye're not really interested in the new shirt and tie ye're after? Yer were full of it before.'

'Of course I want a new shirt and tie, but I'm not talking about it all the time.' Greg wasn't going to give them the satisfaction of knowing that in his mind he could see himself dressed to the nines in his navy-blue trousers, a new white shirt and a pale blue tie. 'It's nearly ten o'clock and we're still on the second game. All because the girls won't give their mouths a rest.'

'I'd rather talk about the clothes we're wearing for the wedding,' Lucy said. 'I mean, I've got to look nice, being a bridesmaid.'

'And I'm an invited guest,' Rhoda said, with more than a little pride in her voice. 'So I've got to look nice, as well.'

'I'm sure yer'll both look lovely.' Irene too had been wondering what colour dress to buy for herself. Something in blue, perhaps, or a deep lilac? 'And I'll make sure my two don't let the side down. They'll look like film stars.'

Greg grinned. 'Yeah! I'll be George Raft. He's always dressed to kill.'

'He's a gangster, yer daft nit,' Jack said. 'He doesn't only dress to kill, he carries a flippin' gun around with him.'

'What about you, Steve?' Lucy asked. 'Ye're very quiet, and you've got to look nicer than anyone 'cos yer'll be walking down the aisle with yer mam.' She giggled. 'I don't mean yer've got to look nicer than the bride, though. I bet yer mam will look lovely.'

'I won't let me mam down, don't worry.' Steve's grin hid the excitement he felt inside. Titch had brought a suit home for him and he was thrilled to bits. It was in a dark navy and fitted him to perfection. He was as tall as Titch, but not as stocky, so it was easy for his future step-dad to get the fit right. He said the words over again in his mind, relishing them. 'My step-dad.' Never had he known such happiness.

'Yer'll see me in all me finery on the day.'

'I bet yer'll look dead handsome,' Rhoda said, glaring knowingly at Greg. 'More like Randolph Scott than George Raft.'

'Who shall I be?' Jack scratched his head. 'Who's more handsome than those two?'

Lucy didn't hesitate. 'Robert Young. He's me favourite.'

Irene heard the key in the lock. 'Here's the men. Get the cards back in the packs and take the cups and saucers out. It's time yer were going home, Rhoda, or yer mam will start to worry.'

'Okay, Mrs Pollard, and thanks for having me.'

Bob came in rubbing his hands. 'Have yer won a fortune, pet?'

George chuckled. 'She's in the wrong house for that.'

'We've hardly played cards, Dad, we've been talking about clothes for the wedding. At least me and Rhoda have, the boys couldn't care less.'

'Well, let's get yer home now. Nellie waits up for me and I don't want to be too late.' Bob noticed Rhoda making her way to the door. 'Hang on, love, I'll see yer home once Lucy is safe in the house.'

'That's all right, Mr Mellor,' Steve said. 'I've got to pass her house on me way home. I'll hang on until she's inside.'

Lucy tossed and turned in bed, her mind too active for sleep. She was telling herself to put everything out of her head and count sheep, when she heard the front door open. Her mother was home. Then she heard a man speaking in hushed tones and she shot up in bed. It was Wally Brown, she could recognise the smooth, silky voice even though he was whispering. What was he doing here this time of night? It was nearly eleven o'clock. Then the voice faded and Lucy fell back against the headboard. They must be in the living room, but why would her mother bring him here so late at night? She had no right to, and her dad would go mad if he knew.

It was impossible to sleep now, with that man in the house. So Lucy drew her knees up to her chin and pulled the bedclothes around her. She'd stay awake until he'd gone. And she'd have something to say to her mother in the morning. The alarm clock on the chest of drawers ticked away, the only sound in the house. Until Lucy heard whispering at the bottom of the stairs. Alert now, she could make out her mother's voice. 'Don't go up, she'll scream the house down if she sees yer.'

'I'm only going up to see if she's asleep.' Wally's low voice carried up the stairs to the now terrified girl. 'She won't even know I'm there.'

Lucy knocked on the bedroom wall. And when she heard the footsteps reach the landing, she knocked again, harder.

Greg shook his brother's shoulder. 'Jack, Lucy's just knocked.'

Jack was wiping the sleep from his eyes when the knocking was repeated. The two boys scrambled out of bed and rushed down the stairs. 'Mam, Lucy's been knocking. There must be something up for her to do that.'

Irene and George were enjoying a cup of tea before going to bed, and they both looked startled at the sight of the boys. 'What did yer say, sunshine?' Irene asked.

'Lucy's been knocking.' Jack was impatient at their slowness to understand. 'There must be something wrong. Twice she's knocked.'

By the time he'd finished speaking, Irene had taken the key for next door from the glass dish on the sideboard and George was on his way out of the front door. The boys followed quickly on their heels.

Ruby was standing at the foot of the stairs when her front door was opened, and she looked bewildered when she was pushed aside by George, who took the stairs three at a time.

'What the hell d'yer think ye're doing?' Ruby was very worried now. 'Get out of my house.'

Irene passed her without a word. And she reached the bedroom just as her husband grabbed the man who was standing at the side of Lucy's bed. 'You dirty swine,' George roared. 'I'll flay yer alive for this.'

'Who the hell are you?' Wally blustered, knowing he didn't stand an earthly with the size of this bloke. He could only try and talk himself out of it. 'I only came up to see if Lucy was all right.' He saw Ruby hovering near the doorway. 'Tell this maniac to take his hands off me, will yer?'

Ruby came into the room, but made sure she kept out of Irene's reach. 'He's a friend of mine and you have no right to be in here.'

George, still holding Wally by the throat, asked, 'Oh, so yer allow men to come into yer daughter's room, do yer?'

Ruby lowered her head, lost for words. So it was up to Wally to bluff his way out of it. 'It's all a misunderstanding. Let's go downstairs and I'll explain.'

Irene looked at Lucy, who was backed against the headboard, her eyes wide with fright. 'Lucy, did you want this man to come into your bedroom?'

'No! I don't like him, he's horrid!'

'Then this is a police matter,' Irene said. 'You,' she gave Ruby a push which sent her flying against the wall, 'are not fit to be a mother. You allow a dirty old man to come into your daughter's bedroom, and the police wouldn't take kindly to either of yer. Yer'd both be locked up. I'll make sure neither of yer are allowed near Lucy again.'

'Oh, come on!' The thought of involving the police scared the life out of Wally. 'I didn't mean no harm. Yer've taken it the wrong way. Leave go of me and let me go home.'

'Ye're not moving from this spot until the police come.' George tightened his grip. 'But before I send me son to the police station, just tell me why yer came into this room?'

'I told yer! Just to make sure she was in bed and asleep!'

'Rubbish!' Irene said. A plan had formed in her mind and she prayed to God she could pull it off. 'There's only one way yer can crawl out of this, without us calling the police. And that's if yer walk away from here now, and take Ruby with yer. Not just for tonight, but for good. If either of yer show yer face around here again, I'll make sure yer go to jail. That's if the neighbours don't lynch yer first. It's up to you, so make up yer mind.'

'Yer can't do that to me,' Ruby cried. 'This is my home.'

'Wrong,' said George. 'It's Bob's house, he only lets yer live in it. We already know this evil bastard has his own house, and when yer visit him yer behave like a married couple, so I suggest yer go and live with him.'

Wally couldn't think any further than getting away from the huge hands around his throat. 'Go on, Ruby, put yer coat on and let's get out of here.'

'Not so fast!' Irene said. 'Ruby won't be allowed back for any of her belongings, so she'll be a while packing. George will sit with you downstairs and I'll stay here until she's got everything together. This is the last time either of yer set foot in this house. That's if yer've got any sense.'

The boys moved into the front bedroom out of the way of their father, who was literally carrying a struggling Wally down the stairs. No way was he going to be allowed to scarper without taking Ruby with him.

'Come in here and sit with Lucy, boys,' Irene called. 'So I can keep me eye on what's going on.'

'Mrs Pollard.' Lucy grabbed her arm to stop her from moving away. 'Does this mean me mam won't ever be coming back?'

Irene sat on the side of the bed and held her close. 'That all depends, sunshine. I've taken a lot on meself by telling her to leave because, after all, I'm only a neighbour and shouldn't really be interfering. If this situation hadn't come up, Ruby would have been within her rights to tell me to mind me own business. But that man was wicked to come into yer bedroom, and yer mam was as bad for not stopping him. I wouldn't trust her after that, and there was no way I was going to let her stay in this house tonight with you. Your dad will be very upset and angry when he knows, and I know he'll agree with me and George about throwing them out. But it depends upon how you feel, sunshine. She is your mother, after all. So think about it carefully, and be sure in yer mind. Would yer be very unhappy if yer thought yer were never going to set eyes on her again?'

Lucy plucked nervously at the bedclothes. 'I'll probably spend the rest of me life being unhappy because me mother never ever loved me, Mrs Pollard. And I'll always wonder why. But she's hurt me so much, and me dad, and I know she'll never change. Yer can't make someone love yer if they don't want to. So I'd rather she left so me dad can come back home again.'

'Are yer sure, sunshine?'

Lucy nodded as she wiped the tears away with the back of her hand. 'I'm sure, honest I am. I want me dad back 'cos I love him and he loves me. We'll be happy together, just the two of us. Me mam spoiled things for us, always skitting, telling lies and cheating. And there was never any comfort or laughter in the house.'

Irene put a finger under the girl's chin and lifted her face. 'In that case, I think yer dad's in for a very pleasant surprise tomorrow. We'll talk about it later, when yer mam and her friend have left. And there's nothing for yer to worry about because I'm certain neither of them will have the nerve to show their faces in this street again, not after me and George have given them a good talking to. And I'll be sleeping with yer tonight in case ye're a bit nervous. We'll cuddle up and keep each other company.' She beckoned to her sons who were hovering near the door. 'Yer can come and sit with Lucy for a while, now. I know ye're missing yer beauty sleep, but it'll soon be all over.'

'We don't mind that,' Jack said. 'As long as Lucy's all right.'

'I'm fine, now.' Lucy pulled the sheet up to her chin. 'I've got to admit I was terrified when I heard that man walking up the stairs, though. I knew he was coming 'cos I heard him and me mam talking in the hall. She told him not to come, but when he took no notice of her she didn't even try and stop him. And she should have stopped him. Even if she doesn't love me, she should have stopped him. But it's over now, and I do feel a bit better knowing me dad will soon be back home.'

'Yeah, in a couple of days when you and yer dad are settled down, yer'll be fine,' Jack said. 'And we can come in your house for a game of cards, for a change.'

'And don't forget we've got the wedding to look forward to.' Greg wanted to see the smile back on Lucy's face. 'Yer'll have yer dad here to make sure ye're the prettiest bridesmaid this street has ever seen. And he'll be so proud of yer.'

Before the smile came to Lucy's face, she allowed time to finish what she was thinking. That one day, when she was a bit older, she'd go and see her mother. Just to ask why she couldn't find it in her heart to love her husband and her daughter.

Ruby struggled to keep up with Wally while carrying three big, heavy bags. He was walking with his hands in his pockets, his anger showing in every step he took. Not once did he offer to help by taking one or two of the bags from her. 'What a bloody performance,' he growled. 'For two pins, that big feller would have marched us off to the police station and we'd have been in big trouble.' Not for a second would he allow himself to admit to being in the wrong. He'd only gone up to Lucy's room to take a peek at her. To stroke her long hair, or her pretty face, perhaps. He only wanted to touch her, not hurt her.

'I did tell yer not to go upstairs.' Ruby daren't raise her voice or say that everything that had happened was his own fault. 'I told yer what she's like.'

'Oh, shut up, woman!' Wally needed a scapegoat, someone

to vent his anger on. Gone now were the words of flattery as he looked sideways at her. 'If ye're coming to live with me, there's going to be some big changes. D'yer understand?'

'Yes, Wally.'

'For a kick-off, yer get yerself a full-time job to pay yer way. I'll get rid of the cleaner and you can do the housework – that'll save me a few bob.' Wally was beginning to think he might be on to a good thing here. More money coming into the house and his own personal servant who would cater to his every whim. And she'd put up with it because she was crazy about him. He'd be waited on hand and foot, and she'd be there for the taking, any time he felt like it. 'And another thing – that blonde hair looks ridiculous, let it grow out.'

'But it'll look terrible while it's growing out! It'll take ages!'

'Ask the hairdresser if she can dye it back to its original colour. I don't care what yer do, but get rid of the blonde, it makes yer look like a tart.'

'All right, Wally, I'll have a word with the hairdresser. And I can go full-time where I work, they've asked me to a few times. Anything you say is all right with me, yer know that. I only want to make yer happy.'

I speak and she jumps, Wally thought. I'd never get another woman as obliging as her. He held out a hand. 'Give us one of those bags to carry, they must be heavy.'

Nellie Carson opened her door to find herself facing a woman of about her own age, with her hair combed back into a bun, a black shawl draped around her shoulders and wearing a big grin. 'I know who you are,' she said instantly. 'Ye're Mrs Aggie.'

'And you are Mrs Nellie.'

Both women laughed and Nellie held the door wide open. 'Come in, ye're very welcome. I've been dying to meet yer 'cos I've heard so much about yer.'

'All good, I hope.' Aggie's eyes were taking in the spotlessly clean and comfortable living room. Here was a woman after her own heart.

'Well, from what Bob and Lucy have told me, yer've got the heart of a saint and are the funniest woman on two legs.'

'Only when I'm standing on me two legs, queen? I thought I was just as bleedin' funny standing on me head.'

Nellie chuckled. 'If yer wear fleecy bloomers like I do, then ye're probably a damn sight more funny standing on yer head.' She waved Aggie to a chair. 'Sit yerself down and I'll put the kettle on.' Her hand on the kitchen door, she turned. 'Did Bob know yer were coming?'

Aggie shook her head. 'There was bleedin' murder at Bob's house last night, that's why I'm here. But you put the kettle on first, then while we're waiting for it to boil I'll tell yer what went on.' She followed Nellie into the kitchen and when the gas plopped under the kettle, she leaned back against the sink. 'I wasn't there to see all this, more's the pity. But Irene repeated it word for word, so I'll give it to you as she gave it to me.'

Her arms folded across her tummy, Aggie soon got into her stride. And before long there were gasps of horror and tuts of disgust coming from Nellie. 'I'd have strangled the buggers with me bare hands.'

'Yeah, me too, Nellie. They want stringing up. But you haven't met Irene yet, or her husband, George. They're a match for anyone, believe me. And they think the world of Lucy. I believe they did right not sending for the police because it would have only filled neighbours' mouths. As it is, George and Irene put the fear of god into this Wally feller, so he'll never show his face again. And Irene, God love her, had the sense to send Ruby packing with him. Lucy was very upset, she was as white as a sheet going to work this morning. It must have given her an awful fright having this man come into her bedroom. But she'll soon get over it when her dad's back home. They dote on each other.'

'Yeah, Aggie, I know. Bob will be over the moon at being able to go back to his house, but he'll be blazing about how it came about. I've got to know him really well, and I know he'll blame himself for leaving Lucy there. Still, once they're settled down they'll soon put all the trouble and heartbreak behind them.' Nellie poured boiling water into the brown teapot. 'Now we'll sit and have a nice cuppa. Are yer waiting for Bob to come home, to tell him?'

'No, I'll leave that pleasure to you. I left Irene cleaning the house so it's nice for him to come home to, and I'm buying a bit of shopping for their larder on me way back. But I will have that cuppa with yer, Nellie, 'cos me throat's parched. And yer can tell Bob we're all looking forward to seeing him later on today.'

'Would yer think it was cheeky if I came with him?' Nellie asked. 'I've heard so much about all of yer, I feel as though I know yer.'

'We'd love yer to come.' Aggie knew if Titch could hear what she was about to say, he'd shake his head and tell her not to be so nosy. 'Why don't yer bring Kate along with yer? I'd like to see if she's all Bob said she is.'

Nellie finished pouring the tea and set the pot down. There was a twinkle in her eyes when she asked, 'Yer wouldn't be matchmaking by any chance, would yer, Mrs Aggie?'

'I certainly am, Mrs Nellie. I most certainly am.'

'Good! That makes two of us! I can see you and me are going to get along like a house on fire. We're both as devious as each other.' She handed a cup to Aggie. 'I've grown very fond of Bob, and I want to keep him in the family. I know he's a married man, but me son-in-law, Howard, said there'll be no problem with a divorce. And after what happened last night, and Ruby going to live with another man – well, that should make it easier.'

Nellie sipped her tea, then rested the cup and saucer on her lap. 'The trouble is, Aggie, both our Kate and Bob are so shy, they'll never make a move. I think you and me are going to have to give them a nudge in the right direction.'

'You have my full support, Nellie. Even if I say it meself, I'm pretty good at giving nudges. So let's drink to our partnership.' Aggie had the cup to her lips when she said, 'D'yer know, I haven't used a swearword since I came in?'

'Oh yes, yer have. Yer halo slipped when yer were telling me how bleedin' funny yer are standing on yer head.'

Both women laughed so much the tea spilled over on to their skirts. But they didn't care. It wasn't every day you found a friend and ally.

'Ay, I wish yer'd slow down a bit,' Rhoda said, red in the face and puffing. 'I know ye're dying to see yer dad, but there's no need to kill me in the process.'

Lucy's face was aglow. She'd told her friend what Mrs Pollard had said they would tell all the neighbours – that Ruby had left home and gone to live with another man. Nobody knew the man or where he lived. There'd be gossip for a few days then it would be forgotten. 'I can't wait to see me dad, Rhoda, so I'm going to run on. You can take yer time, then.'

'Will I see yer tonight?'

'Not tonight, Rhoda, 'cos me and me dad will have loads to talk about. I'll call for yer as usual in the morning. Ta-ra.' With a wave of her hand, Lucy took to her heels and didn't slacken her pace until she came to her front door. With her heart beating like mad, and her tummy churning with excitement, she delved in her pocket for the key. Holding it in the palm of her hand, she gazed at it for a while. Then, with a grin on her face, she put it back in her pocket and lifted the knocker.

When Bob opened the door he had to swallow hard to keep the tears back. Never, even in his dreams, did he think he'd be back in this house and opening the door to his daughter. He stepped down to the pavement and picked Lucy up to spin her around. 'I feel drunk, pet,' he said, laughing up into her face. 'Drunk with happiness.'

'I don't half love yer, Dad.' Lucy's arms were tight around his neck. 'More than anything in the whole world.'

'And I love you, pet.' Bob set her down. 'Let's go in and see what a nice surprise I've got for the working girl.'

'Have yer made me a dinner, Dad? Is that the surprise?'

Bob tapped his nose. 'Wait and see.' With a secret smile on his face, he pushed her ahead of him and closed the door. Then, filled with emotion, he watched as his daughter stood on the threshold of the living room, her eyes and mouth wide open.

There wasn't a sound in the room that was full of people with happy, smiling faces. Mrs Aggie and Mrs Nellie were sitting in the fireside chairs either side of the hearth, Titch and Olive were seated at the table opposite Irene and George, and Mrs Kate occupied a corner of the couch. And standing in the kitchen doorway, still in their working clothes, were Jack and Greg Pollard, with Steve.

Lucy took her hand from her mouth. 'I don't know what to say. I think I'm going to cry.'

'Don't you dare cry, sunshine,' Irene said, not far from tears herself. 'We've all come to welcome yer dad back to where he belongs.'

Titch scraped his chair back and held out his arms. 'Come here, sweetheart.' And holding her close, he said, 'How can I tell yer the plans me and Olive have made for the wedding if ye're crying yer eyes out?'

Lucy sniffed up. 'I won't cry, I promise. Tell me what the plans are, I'm dying to know.'

'Hadn't yer better say hello to yer visitors first?'

'Never mind saying hello, I'm so happy to see them I could kiss them all to death.' Her eyes swept the room, taking in Mrs Nellie and Kate. 'Me old friends and me new ones.'

'Yer can kiss them as much as yer like when I've told yer what the arrangements are.'

Lucy grinned up at him. 'I'm all ears, Mr Titch.'

'Well, before I begin, can I ask Bob to sit down on the couch with Kate? She's all on her lonesome, there. Anyone would think she had an infectious disease.'

When Bob did as he was told with alacrity, Kate smiled that gentle smile that had already made her a favourite with Bob's neighbours. They'd taken to her right away.

Titch chuckled. 'That's better. I don't like having me thunder stolen by someone else sharing the stage.' He pulled on one of Lucy's curls. 'Now to the big day. Me and Olive are tying the knot five weeks on Friday. We couldn't get a Saturday because the priest said they're booked solid for three months ahead. It's at two o'clock and I want to see yer there with a big smile on that pretty face of yours.'

'I'll have a smile on me face every day, now me dad's home. But I'll have an extra special one on the day you and Mrs Fletcher get married.' Lucy's infectious giggle filled the room. 'I'll cry me eyes out all morning and get it over with. Then I'll put a cold flannel over me face to take the red blotches away. How about that, then?'

Titch gave her a hug. 'Me and Olive will have to go now, we've got a lot of sorting out to do. I've to be away by six in the morning.'

'If there's anything I can do while ye're away, just shout out,' Bob said, feeling he was at last the master in his own house. 'And remember, everyone is welcome here now. My front door is always open to yer.'

Jack piped up, 'Does that mean we can come here and play cards, Mr Mellor?'

Bob thought his heart would burst. He owed so much to these people he'd never be able to pay them back. When he got home it was to find Irene had cleaned right through the house and it was warm and welcoming. Aggie had stocked their larder and made a steak and kidney pie which was now in the oven on a low light and smelling delicious. 'Of course yer can! At last I can repay the hospitality yer've always shown me and Lucy.'

George chuckled. 'I think yer might have reason to regret saying that, mate. My two will never be away.' He rapped his fingers on the table and for a few seconds considered whether anyone would be upset if he said what was on his mind. Having decided, he turned to Aggie, who had been unusually quiet. 'Ay, Aggie, haven't yer always said the day would come when Bob would be back home?'

Looking very superior, Aggie nodded. 'I did predict it, George, yes. Yer all thought I was crazy, but I've been proved right.'

Olive smiled across at the woman who would soon be her mother-in-law. 'Aggie, in all the years I've known yer, yer've never been wrong.'

'I've been thinking about that,' Bob said, from his seat next to Kate. 'I'll sit up and take notice next time yer make a prediction.'

'I'll make another prediction for yer lad, so take notice. The happiness yer feel right now is nothing to the happiness that's going to come your way.'

Nellie leaned forward in her chair. 'I agree with yer, Aggie. I have the same feeling.'

Titch roared with laughter. 'Nellie, don't get too carried away by what me ma says, she'll get yer into trouble.' Then he glanced at his mother, and the face he held so dear caused him to shake his head. 'I didn't mean that, Nellie. Yer won't go far wrong with me ma, she only does what's right. The best mother a son could have, she is, and I love and adore her.'

Olive punched his arm. 'Ay, it's me ye're marrying, Titch McBride.'

Irene followed suit, giving George a hefty punch. 'How come yer never say nice things like that to me? Yer've no romance in yer, George Pollard.'

Bob turned to smile at Kate. Neither would say it, but both were wondering whether the time would ever come when they'd be close enough to act daft with each other.

Aggie and Nellie didn't miss the wordless exchange. They smiled across at each other and winked, as if to say Bob and Kate might be slow, but they were on the right tram lines.

Bob had his arm across Lucy's shoulder as they were seeing Titch and Olive off. 'Only a few weeks before the big day, eh, mate?'

'Yeah, it'll fly over.' Titch tucked Olive's arm in his. There was a twinkle in his eye when he said, 'Kate is everything yer said she was, Bob. If ye're daft enough to let her get away, yer want yer head testing.'

Lucy's wide green eyes rolled from her father to Titch. What did he mean about Mrs Kate? Then, before she had time to put her foot in it, the penny dropped. She felt a thrill of excitement travel down her spine and a smile played around the corners of her mouth. Oh, that would be the best thing ever! 'I'll go back to our visitors, Dad, while you talk to Mr Titch and Mrs Fletcher.' After a quick hug and kiss, she made her way back inside.

'Where's Iris, Mrs Kate?'

'She'll be at home now, love. I left her a note explaining I was coming here, and wouldn't be late. She could see to her own dinner, it only needed warming up.'

'Will yer come down again one night soon, and bring Iris with yer? She could have a game of cards with us young ones and you can keep me dad company.'

'Yes,' Kate smiled. 'I'm sure Iris would love that.'

Aggie and Nellie looked at each other. 'Another partner, d'yer think, Nellie?'

Nellie grinned. 'Most definitely, Aggie. One on the spot, too!'

'Me and George are going now, sunshine, so you and yer dad can have yer meal in peace,' Irene said. 'Will yer see to the boys, they're talking about a game of cards tomorrow.'

Lucy went into the kitchen. 'Yer can't come tomorrow night because I've promised to do Rhoda's hair. But yer can come the next night.'

'Rhoda won't mind us seeing her with curlers in,' Steve said. 'I bet if yer ask her in the morning she'll tell yer she couldn't care less.'

Jack nodded. 'Tell her we promise not to laugh at her.'

'I'm not promising anything of the sort,' Greg said. 'If she looks funny, I'll laugh.'

Lucy giggled when Jack went for his brother's throat. What a wonderful day this was.

Chapter Twenty-Seven

'So, yer mate's getting hitched tomorrow, eh, Bob?' Peg Butterworth's elbows were resting on the table as she held an enormous sandwich between her two hands. 'Yer should have introduced me to this Titch feller, he sounds right up my street. He wouldn't be getting married if he'd seen me, I'd have put him off anyone else.'

'How's that, queen?' Elsie asked. 'D'yer mean that because ye're a woman, yer'd have put him off all women? Oh, I don't think so, queen. I mean, ye're no oil painting but ye're not exactly ugly.'

'You cheeky sod!' Peg huffed with indignation. 'Have yer looked in the mirror lately? If yer had yer'd know what ugly means. It would be staring yer in the face.'

'Oh, I don't ever look in no mirror, queen. Me sense of humour wouldn't run to that. I can't understand why you do, it must be very disheartening for yer.' Elsie narrowed her eyes to look at her friend. 'Is that why ye're a bit miserable some days? Down in the mouth, like?'

'Elsie Burgess, what would yer say if I parted yer from yer two front teeth?'

'I wouldn't say nothing, queen, 'cos I'd be too busy knocking the stuffing out of yer. I'm very proud of me teeth, I am. My feller says they're me best feature.'

'They're yer only feature, girl.' Peg was gloating inside. She'd been dying to use this big word on Elsie, but there'd never been the right occasion to fit it into a sentence. 'Apart from them, there's nothing. Ye're just nondescript.'

Elsie's jaws stopped chewing and her eyes slid sideways. Putting on a posh voice, she asked, 'Would yer kindly explain the meaning of that word?'

'It means ye're very ordinary.' Little Ada Smithson's thin face was twitching. 'It means yer wouldn't be noticed in a crowd.'

Elsie pondered for a while, then slowly put her sandwich down. Lifting her bosom to rest on the table, she glared at the little woman. 'Is that so, now? Well, listen to me, smart arse, and take heed. Me and me mate are having a private fight, and we don't like anyone poking their noses in. So just mind yer own bleedin' business.' She turned to Peg. 'It's coming to something when yer can't have a fight in peace, isn't it, queen?'

'Yeah, I don't know what the world's coming to, girl. Years ago, folk would go out and pick their own fight, they wouldn't muscle in on someone else's.' Peg winked at Ada to let her see this was all in fun. She felt sorry for the little woman 'cos, God knows, she didn't have much of a life with that bully she had for a husband. 'It makes yer think, though, girl, doesn't it?'

'What makes yer think, queen?'

'Well, us fighting so much. Perhaps that's why we're both ugly. I mean, you with yer cauliflower ear and me with me broken nose, that's bound to detract from our attractions.'

'I haven't got no cauliflower ear, queen! But if yer don't stop using those big words, so I don't know whether I'm coming or going, I'll break yer bleedin' nose for yer with pleasure.'

Bob was shaking with laughter. He laughed easily these days. In work, having a pint with George and when the neighbours or Lucy's friends called. His house was a real home now, not a place where he and his daughter knew nothing but misery. They were happy and contented, and as free as birds. And he felt no guilt over Ruby, because Peg and

Elsie made it their business to find out how she was. From all accounts she'd settled in well with Wally Brown and Bob was pleased about that. For all the heartache she'd caused him, he bore her no ill-will.

'Ay, Bob?' Peg interrupted his thoughts. 'Is Titch having a party tomorrow night? I'm only asking because me and Elsie would come along and entertain.'

'Sorry, Peg, but it's only a quiet wedding. Just a few friends for a drink, that's all.'

Peg jerked her head. 'Just our luck. But when you get married, Bob, me and me mate will expect an invitation.'

Elsie slapped an open hand on her chest. 'Ooh, er! Is Bob getting married, queen?'

'Well, he's bound to, isn't he? I mean, it stands to sense, a man as good-looking as him won't be on the shelf for long.'

'You and Elsie will be top of the list if I ever get married.' Bob was grinning like a Cheshire cat. 'Mind you, yer'll have to wait a long time.'

Billy Gleeson, nursing a toothache, had his chin cradled in his hand. 'Are yer taking a full day off tomorrow, mate?'

Bob nodded. 'Yeah, me and Kate.'

Peg turned to face Elsie, and without a tape measure anyone would be hard put to say whose mouth was opened the widest. 'Yer mean Kate's going to the wedding?' Peg croaked. 'How come she can go and we can't?'

Kate spoke for the first time. 'I've been kindly invited by the bride. And I've got to say I'm really looking forward to it.'

'And yer never said a dickie-bird!' Peg pursed her lips. 'Ye're a dark horse, Kate Brown.'

The bell rang to signal the end of their break, and tops were put back on carry-out boxes and chairs scraped back. 'Enjoy yerselves tomorrow, both of yer,' Peg said. 'And don't forget to have a drink for me.'

'Yeah, have a really nice time.' Elsie smiled as she linked

her friend's arm and they made their way out of the canteen.

'We'll have to buy a new dress for the wedding, girl,' Peg said.

'What wedding, queen?'

'Bob's, of course!'

'Bob's not getting married, is he, queen?'

Peg squeezed her arm. 'My money's on him marrying Kate as soon as his divorce comes through.'

'Ooh, er! Ye're right, queen, we will have to buy a new dress.'

Lucy was up bright and early on the Friday morning, and the first thing she did was draw the curtains. The sky was clear blue and the sun was doing its best to shine. 'Oh, it's going to be a beautiful day.' She was hugging herself when she heard a noise from the living room and knew her dad was already up and about. The cardigan she'd worn the night before was lying on the bed and she slipped it on before tripping lightly down the stairs.

'Good morning, Dad. It's going to be a beautiful day for the wedding.'

'It looks like it, pet.' Bob plumped the cushions on the couch and picked up last night's *Echo* ready to take to the bin. 'Have yer got yer day planned out?'

Lucy stood with her hands on her hips. 'What are yer doing, Dad? I'll tidy up in here, I've got loads of time. Rhoda's coming over at eleven so I can curl her hair with the curling tongs, then I'm going next door at twelve so Mrs Pollard can dress me up like a dog's dinner. I've got plenty of time to tidy this place.'

'I'm only doing it to occupy meself, pet.' Bob grinned and spread his hands. 'Anyone would think it was me getting married, not Titch. I'm a bundle of nerves and God knows what me tummy's up to, it's fluttering like mad.'

'Today will be good practice for yer, Dad, for when you get married.'

'Yer mean *if* I ever get married, pet! Nothing is certain in this life.'

'Oh, that is, Dad. If yer don't believe me, ask Mrs Aggie or Mrs Nellie. We all think yer'll get married and we can't all be wrong.'

Bob lowered his head and pretended to straighten the chenille tablecloth. 'And have the three of yer decided who I'm going to wed?'

There was no hesitation. 'Mrs Kate, of course.'

'Lucy, me and Kate have never discussed the future. She probably doesn't think of me in that way.'

'Yer'll never know if yer don't ask her! Don't tell me ye're not taken with Mrs Kate, 'cos I wouldn't believe yer.'

Bob pulled out a chair and sat down. 'Of course I'm taken with her, she's everything any man could wish for. But I'm still a married man, pet, and likely to be for another year or so. I'm not in any position to ask Kate to marry me.'

'Yer could ask her to wait for yer and see what she says. Then at least she'd know how yer felt about her and could decide for herself. But she does like yer, Dad, anyone can see that. And there's nothing to stop yer taking her out and courting her. There's no law against that.'

Bob couldn't keep the smile back. 'Who was it told yer that?'

Lucy giggled. 'Me two partners, Mrs Aggie and Mrs Nellie. And Mrs Nellie's son-in-law who's helping yer with the divorce. He said that me mam is the guilty party and there's nothing to stop you courting. Yer can't get married, though, not until the divorce is through.'

'I didn't realise my life was of such interest to people.'

'They want what's best for yer, Dad. They all love yer and want yer to be happy.' Her head tilted to one side, and her hands on her hips, Lucy said, 'Mrs Kate's only waiting for yer to say something, so don't keep her waiting.'

'This is all supposing Kate would have me, but would you be happy if I married her?'

'Oh yes, Dad! She's kind and caring and I couldn't ask for anyone better for a step-mother. And Iris said she'd be made up to have you for a dad and me for a sister.'

Bob puckered his lips and let out a whistle. 'So, Iris is in this too!'

Lucy dropped her head back and her laughter filled the room. 'Dad, you and Mrs Kate are the only ones *not* in it! So yer'd better pull yer socks up unless yer want to be the only one not at yer own wedding.' She wrapped her arms around his neck and kissed him. 'I'm going to get washed now, but you sit and think about it. If yer don't put a move on, Mrs Aggie and Mrs Nellie will get fed up waiting and propose for yer.'

Irene stepped back for a better look at Lucy. 'Yer look beautiful, sunshine, a real treat. What do you say, George?'

'Yer look good enough to eat, love.' George wasn't a person for showing his feelings but he had to fight hard to keep them hidden when he looked at the young girl from next door. She made a beautiful picture in her pale blue dress which fitted her to perfection. And Irene had made her a bandeau for her hair with pale blue flowers sewn on. But it was the smiling face that would capture anyone's heart. And for the umpteenth time, George asked himself how any mother could walk away and leave her. 'In fact, love,' he told her, 'I think yer'll steal the show today.'

Lucy shook her head. 'No, I won't, Mr Pollard. Mrs Fletcher will do that.'

'Well, I think yer look lovely, Lucy,' Jack said. 'Like a film star.'

'Yeah, I think I will marry yer after all, Lucy.' Greg was leaning against the sideboard. 'Yer are pretty, and on top of that yer've got stacks of buttons.'

Jack glared at him. 'She'd have to be hard up to marry *you*.'

'It's only me buttons he's after, Jack,' Lucy said. 'I'll give him half of what I've got and that should shut him up.'

'The only thing that will shut my youngest son up, is a gobstopper.' Irene looked down at herself. 'I'd better get a move on, I'm the only one not ready. And don't forget, Lucy, you won't be leaving with me and the boys. You are going in the wedding car with Olive and Steve.'

Lucy rolled her eyes. 'Aren't I going to be the posh one!'

'Is there any chance of a cuppa, Ma?' Titch stood at the kitchen door moving from one foot to the other. 'Me mouth's not half dry.'

'Listen, son, will yer go and sit down. Me and Nellie are up to our eyes in it and we can't work with you under our feet.'

'I've tried that, Ma, and it won't work. I can't sit 'cos me nerves are shattered.' Titch held his hands out and started shaking them. 'See, I'm a wreck.'

Aggie grinned as she smoothed the front of her wrap-around pinny. 'Don't try and soft soap me, son, 'cos it won't work. I bet if I held a pint of bitter out to yer, yer hands would soon stop shaking in case yer spilled a drop.' Then she took pity on him. After all, it was his wedding day and he was bound to be nervous. She wouldn't let herself dwell on the thought that this was the last day this house would be his home. If she did, she'd end up bawling her eyes out and the sandwiches would never get done. 'Go and sit down and I'll put the kettle on. Me and Nellie could do with a drink, we're gasping.'

'That's the spirit, queen, it's no good flogging ourselves to death.' Nellie had been there since nine o'clock and had baked enough fairy cakes to stock one of Sayer's shops. She'd also made jellies in little white pleated paper cases and these were standing on a tray in the yard to set. When they were ready she would finish them off with a blob of cream on top.

'I don't know what I'd have done without yer, Nellie,'

Aggie said, filling the kettle. 'I'd have had to buy the cakes from a shop, I couldn't have managed all this if I'd been on me own.'

'Olive did offer to help yer, Ma,' Titch said. 'And Irene.'

'What! Olive making sarnies on her wedding day! Not bleedin' likely, son. She needs the time to make herself look nice for yer. And Irene's got her two boys to see to, and George. Not to mention helping Lucy. Besides, this kitchen is only big enough for two. Me and Nellie fit in fine, don't we, queen?'

'I like being busy and I've enjoyed meself.' Nellie's hands moved like clockwork as she buttered slices of bread and piled them high ready for the fillings to go on. 'Another half-hour should see the end of it. Then you and me can start to titivate ourselves up. Me best dress and shoes are in the bag I've left in the hall. And I've even borrowed one of our Kate's lipsticks.'

'Go 'way!' Aggie poured the water into the teapot. 'Yer haven't, have yer?'

'I certainly have! It's not often I go to a wedding so I thought I'd go the whole hog. It's a pale lipstick, mind yer, not a bright red colour.'

'I think I'll have a bash at that meself, Nellie. Can I borrow some?'

'Of course yer can, queen! We'll both look like mutton dressed as lamb, but I couldn't give a sod, so there!'

'What time is Kate coming?'

'She's going straight to the church with Iris. She said yer'd have enough to do without an extra two.'

Titch had been listening to the conversation with a smile on his face. He was glad his mother had found a friend her own age. And they got along so well, there was no doubt that it would be a firm and lasting friendship. He walked to the kitchen and leaned against the door. 'Ma, just out of curiosity, how can yer borrow lipstick? Once it's on yer lips yer can't give it back, can yer?'

'Only if yer kiss them, clever clogs. So I'll make it me business to kiss Kate first, then she'll get the bulk of it back. And if that answer satisfies yer, will yer pour this tea out and then go and get yerself ready?'

'Anything yer say, Ma. Anything yer say.'

Steve paced the floor as he waited for his mother to come down. She was cutting it fine for time because the car was due in ten minutes. Then he heard the creaking of the stairs and his eyes were on the door when Olive walked through. She looked so lovely his heart burst with pride. Her pale beige dress had a pleated cross-over top, long tapering sleeves and a full flared skirt. And perched on the top of her head was a pill-box hat in the same colour, with a veil that came down to her eyes. 'Oh Mam, yer look beautiful. Mr Titch will be knocked out when he sees yer.'

'And you look very handsome, love. I'm really proud of yer.'

Steve pointed to two posies on the sideboard. 'Is the biggest one for you, Mam?'

Olive nodded and picked up her posy. It was made up of small white and blue flowers with sprigs of fern, and there were strands of ribbons in the same colours hanging from it. 'We'll give Lucy hers in the car. She'll be delighted with it.'

'We just made it in time, the car's pulled up now.'

The street was deserted and Olive breathed a sigh of relief. But Steve was puzzled. He thought some of the neighbours would be out to see his mam off. It only took the car a minute to get to the Mellors' and Lucy had been watching for it. She had the door open before the chauffeur had time to knock.

'Doesn't she look lovely, Mam?'

'Lucy always looks lovely, Steve. And she's got a lovely nature to go with it.'

The chauffeur opened the passenger door and Lucy, careful of her dress, climbed in. Her smile was as wide as her face. 'Yer look a picture, Mrs Fletcher. Very beautiful.'

'So do you, sweetheart. I'm well blessed with me handsome son and a pretty bridesmaid.' Olive passed the posy over and Lucy's eyes nearly popped out of her head. 'Is this for me? Oh, it's absolutely gorgeous.' She was still staring at it when the car pulled up outside the church.

Steve had rehearsed his role over and over again, and he carried it out to the letter. He tucked his mother's arm in his and covered her hand. Then he looked back and asked, 'All right, Lucy?' When she answered with a wide grin, he straightened his shoulders and led his mother into the church. He only faltered when he saw the church was packed. They were only expecting their close friends to be there, but it seemed every neighbour in the street had turned out to see his mother and Mr Titch get married. And it filled his heart with joy.

When the guests arrived back at Aggie's house, they found Olive and Titch waiting for them. Titch had his arm around Olive's waist and they looked as happy as any lovebirds could look. There was much hugging, kissing and shaking of hands as congratulations were given and Olive, no longer nervous, looked radiant.

Aggie stood back and watched with tears in her eyes. She'd waited a long time for this day and couldn't have been happier about the woman he'd married. But the happiness was tinged with sadness. Well, that's only natural, she told herself. Every mother cries when one of her children leave home. And he'll be living in the same street, for heaven's sake, it wasn't as though he was moving to the other end of the world. So giving herself a pep talk about not crying, she approached the newlyweds.

Olive moved forward to meet her and took her in her arms. 'Is it all right if I still call yer Aggie?'

'Of course it is, Mrs McBride!' This brought laughter from their friends as it was the first time Olive had been addressed by her married name. 'You just look after him, that's all, or yer'll have Mrs McBride Senior to answer to.'

Titch nearly squeezed the breath out of her. 'I've got two lovely women in me life, now, Ma. I must be the luckiest bloke alive.' He set her down and his arm went back around his new wife's waist. 'I'm glad I let her talk me into marrying her. I did say no at first, then she taught me the error of me ways.'

There were loud hoots from all the women present. 'Get a load of him!' Irene said. 'Anyone would think he was God's gift to women!'

'Put yer foot down with him, queen,' Nellie advised. 'Start as yer mean to go on.'

'Don't put it down too hard, Olive, or he might come back home.' Aggie took a sip of sherry from the glass Steve handed to her and tried not to pull a face. She didn't like the stuff, but Titch said she wasn't allowed to toast his marriage with milk stout. 'And he can't come home because his bed will be occupied.'

Titch looked puzzled. 'How's that, Ma?'

'I've asked Steve to sleep here. He can keep me company and it'll give you and Olive some time on yer own to get to know each other.'

Olive blushed to the roots of her hair, but Titch was delighted. 'Ma, yer think of everything.'

'Yes, I do, son. And right now I'm thinking it's time folks found themselves a seat and we can start giving the eats out. I'll leave the men to see to the drinks.'

'I'll help, Mrs Aggie,' Lucy said.

'What – in that dress? Not ruddy likely!'

'I'll help,' Rhoda said, and looked to where Iris was sitting next to her mother on the couch. 'How about it, Iris? It'll give yer a chance to get to know everyone.'

Iris was on her feet like a shot. She wanted to be near the young ones and this was a good chance. 'Yeah, I'd like that.'

'This thing's killing me,' George said, running a finger around the inside of his collar which had been starched and was rubbing his skin. 'I can hardly breathe.'

'Here, let me undo that top button before yer choke yerself.' Irene smiled into his face as she relaxed the pressure on his neck. 'Yer made a really handsome best man, love.'

'I told yer yer were getting a bargain when yer got me, didn't I?' George ran a finger gently down her cheek. 'But I got first prize when I got you.'

When Iris had left her seat, Bob didn't hesitate to slide along to sit next to Kate. 'Are yer all right, Kate?'

'Yes, I'm fine. Everything went off very well, didn't it?'

Bob nodded. In his mind he was telling himself to get on with it and ask her. In the end what he felt in his heart gave him the courage. 'Kate, would yer come out with me one night?' He put a hand on her arm before she could answer. 'No, let me get it all out while I've got the nerve. Can I court yer with a view to marriage when I'm a free man?'

The slow, gentle smile made his heart flip. 'It's taken yer long enough, Bob Mellor. If yer hadn't asked me by the end of the night, I'd made up me mind to ask you.'

Bob closed his eyes and took a deep breath. Her words were music to his ears. 'We'll talk about it tomorrow, eh? All I'll say now is that I'm a very happy man.'

When everyone had a full plate in their hand and a glass either on the arm of a chair or on the floor, the six youngsters congregated in the kitchen. 'Yer don't half look nice, Lucy,' Rhoda said. 'Very pretty.'

'So do you, that new dress really suits yer. And Iris looks lovely, as well.' Lucy's infectious giggle rang out. 'Make the most of it, 'cos tomorrow we'll be back in our scruff.'

Jack was munching a sandwich, his face thoughtful. Then he took the plunge. 'Lucy, will yer come to the pictures with me one night?'

'Oh yeah, I'd love to!' Lucy had made her mind up a long time ago that Jack was the boy for her. She thought he was very handsome, but that wasn't the reason. He was kind and caring, and on the bad days, when she'd suffered from her mother's hand, he always had the power to put a smile back on her face. 'I'd better go and ask me Dad, though, eh?'

Jack looked as though he'd lost sixpence and found a pound. Reaching for her hand, he said, 'I'll come with yer.'

'Hang on a minute,' Steve said. 'We agreed to do this together.'

Jack huffed. 'Well, go on, ask her.'

Steve's face was red as beetroot. 'Rhoda, will yer come out with me one night?'

'I certainly will, Steve Fletcher, I'd be delighted.'

Jack didn't wait to hear any more before leading Lucy through to the living room. And without bothering to lower his voice, he asked, 'Mr Mellor, is it all right for Lucy to come to the pictures with me one night?'

There were smiles all around, and the widest was Irene's. Was the wish she'd harboured all these years going to come true?

'If that's what Lucy wants,' Bob said, 'then I've no objection.'

Nellie pulled her chair nearer to Aggie. 'That lad's got more gumption than Bob.'

'Don't speak too soon, queen, 'cos Bob and your Kate are looking very pleased with themselves.'

Steve strode from the kitchen to the door leading to the hall. 'I'm going out for a minute, Jack, I won't be long.'

'Where are yer going?'

'To ask Mrs Fleming about taking Rhoda out.'

'Yer've no need to ask me mam.' Rhoda appeared with her face aglow. 'I've already asked her.'

Amid roars of laughter, Steve asked, 'How could yer have asked her? I've only just mentioned it!'

'Well, it's like this, yer see, Steve. I think it's best to be prepared for any eventuality. So I hinted to me mam that yer might ask me, and would it be all right with her. And of course she said it would be okay because ye're a fine, upstanding man.'

'Oh, I'm enjoying this.' Aggie wiped a laughter tear away. 'It's better than going to the bleedin' pictures any day.'

'Listen, queen,' Nellie said. 'If a house comes empty round here, give us the wire, will yer? You've got some lovely neighbours.'

'The secret of keeping yerself feeling young, Nellie, is to mix with youngsters. This lot have taken years off me.'

'I wondered why yer only looked about twenty,' Nellie chuckled. 'I thought yer were on some special miracle pills.'

'Ay out,' Aggie said when Greg and Iris came through from the kitchen. 'All we need now is for these two to say they're putting the banns up.'

Iris was looking very shy, but not Greg. He looked his brother straight in the eye and said, 'Me and Iris would like to go to the pictures, but they won't let me in at the door. Even though I'm working, they say I'm too young. So will you take us in?'

'Will I heckerslike! I'm not having you tagging along on me first date.'

'Don't be so miserable, Jack,' Irene said. 'Once yer got in, yer wouldn't have to sit near each other.'

'Oh, all right.' Jack relented. 'But yer'll owe me a favour.'

Bob coughed before saying, 'Can I get a word in, please? Would you all let me know what night ye're going out, and which picturehouse ye're going to? Just so me and Kate can go to a different one.' He waited until his words had sunk in and all the faces around him were lit up with pleasure. Then he said, 'To Aggie, Nellie and Lucy, who, for those who don't know, are the members of the committee, I'd just like to say their work is finished. I've asked Kate to be me intended and she's agreed.'

'Yer forgot to say I was very happy to agree,' Kate said. 'And very honoured.'

Titch jumped to his feet. 'That's the best news I've had in a long time. Except for Olive saying she'd marry me, of course. So I think we should get all the glasses filled up for a toast.'

'Me and Jack will do that, mate,' George said, lumbering to his feet. 'Seeing as it's your wedding day.'

When everyone was holding a full glass, Titch held out his hand to Olive. 'Come and join me, sweetheart.'

'I'm no good with words, Titch. You're much better at it than me.'

'Mrs McBride Junior,' Aggie said, 'are yer saying my son talks too much?'

'Okay, Aggie, I give in.' Olive joined her husband, who put his arm around her waist and held her tight. 'The first toast from me and my wife, is to all of you. To thank you for all the help yer've given us, and the presents we have yet to open. But most of all to thank you for being such good friends. We think we are well blessed.' The couple raised their glasses before sipping the wine. 'Now I'd like yer all to toast the best mother a man could have. This is for you, Ma.'

'Don't start me off crying, son, for God's sake.'

'Okay, Ma, we'll move on to the next one. To Bob and Kate. And I don't think there's a person in this room who isn't happy for them. Two nice people, with two lovely children, they'll make a perfect family when the time comes. And it's what they deserve.'

Not a word passed between them, but Lucy and Iris moved together. Lucy to sit on Kate's knee, and Iris on Bob's.

Aggie pulled on Jack's jacket. 'Ay, lad, run and get the bucket out of the yard, will yer? The way things are going I'll be shedding enough tears to fill the bleedin' thing.'

'Don't cry, Mrs Aggie,' Lucy said. 'Today I've been a bridesmaid, I've learned I'm going to have a new mam and sister, and I've got meself a boyfriend. This is the happiest day of me life.'

Sweet Rosie O'Grady

Joan Jonker

Neighbours Molly Bennett and Nellie McDonough are thrilled to see their children settling down. Doreen waits patiently at home for Phil's next leave, accosting the postman every day in the hope of another letter, and Jill and Steve are saving up the pennies for their wedding. But the horrors of the Second World War threaten to separate loved ones forever and, with rationing and air raids on everyone's minds, the future looks bleak . . .

Then Rosie O'Grady arrives in Liverpool from Ireland to stay with Molly's parents, Bridie and Bob. With her sparkling blue eyes, childlike honesty and heart of gold, sweet Rosie O'Grady is like a breath of fresh air. A smile forever lights up her face and a joke is never far from her lips and Rosie soon has everyone crying with laughter – particularly when she makes no bones about setting her cap at Molly's unsuspecting son Tommy. Tommy Bennett thinks girls are nothing but a nuisance but he's in for a big surprise!

0 7472 5374 9

HEADLINE

Last Tram to Lime Street

Joan Jonker

Molly Bennett and Nellie McDonough were newly-weds when they became neighbours in a Liverpool street of two-up two-down terraced houses. Over the years their friendship has helped them through lean times when their kids were little and money was scarce. They've shared tears, heartache and laughter – and often their last ha'penny.

When Nellie's son, Steve, proposes to Molly's daughter, Jill, their happiness knows no bounds. The pair soon have their heads together planning a knees-up, jars-out party to celebrate.

But a cloud hangs over their plans when unsettling events in the community are brought to their notice. A new family, the Bradleys, have moved in up the street and they're a bad lot. Things start to go missing – toys, milk money, washing off the line – then an elderly widow is robbed of her purse, and Molly and Nellie decide enough is enough . . .

0 7472 5131 2

If you enjoyed this book here is a selection of other bestselling titles from Headline

ANGELS OF MERCY	Lyn Andrews	£5.99	☐
A LIVERPOOL LULLABY	Anne Baker	£5.99	☐
THE RIVER FLOWS ON	Maggie Craig	£5.99	☐
THE CHINESE LANTERN	Harry Bowling	£5.99	☐
RICHES OF THE HEART	June Tate	£5.99	☐
TOMORROW THE WORLD	Josephine Cox	£5.99	☐
WHEN DAY IS DONE	Elizabeth Murphy	£5.99	☐
THE WAY THINGS WERE	Hilda McKenzie	£5.99	☐
SWEET ROSIE O'GRADY	Joan Jonker	£5.99	☐
NELLIE'S WAR	Victor Pemberton	£5.99	☐
A THIRSTING LAND	Wendy Robertson	£5.99	☐
KATIE'S KITCHEN	Dee Williams	£5.99	☐

Headline books are available at your local bookshop or newsagent. Alternatively, books can be ordered direct from the publisher. Just tick the titles you want and fill in the form below. Prices and availability subject to change without notice.

Buy four books from the selection above and get free postage and packaging and delivery within 48 hours. Just send a cheque or postal order made payable to Bookpoint Ltd to the value of the total cover price of the four books. Alternatively, if you wish to buy fewer than four books the following postage and packaging applies:

UK and BFPO £4.30 for one book; £6.30 for two books; £8.30 for three books.

Overseas and Eire: £4.80 for one book; £7.10 for 2 or 3 books (surface mail).

Please enclose a cheque or postal order made payable to *Bookpoint Limited*, and send to: Headline Publishing Ltd, 39 Milton Park, Abingdon, OXON OX14 4TD, UK.
Email Address: orders@bookpoint.co.uk

If you would prefer to pay by credit card, our call team would be delighted to take your order by telephone. Our direct line is 01235 400 414 (lines open 9.00 am–6.00 pm Monday to Saturday 24 hour message answering service). Alternatively you can send a fax on 01235 400 454.

Name ....
Address ....
....